MY FRIEND IS
MY ENEMY
Part I

MY FRIEND IS MY ENEMY

PART I

MICHAEL J. COUCH

Although this novel is set in an historical context, the characters are entirely fictitious and any likeness in name or personality, to persons alive or deceased, is co-incidental.

MY FRIEND IS MY ENEMY
Part I

Copyright © Michael J. Couch

Published in Great Britain 1991 by Michael J. Couch
68 Chesil Street, Winchester, Hampshire SO23 8HX

First printed (2,000) May, 1991
Reprinted (3,000) September, 1992

Typeset in 10/11pt Baskerville

ISBN 0 9517531 0 X

Made and printed in Great Britain by
The Guernsey Press Co. Ltd., Guernsey, Channel Islands.

Further copies may be purchased by sending cheques/postal orders made out to M. J. Couch, 68, Chesil Street, Winchester, Hants. SO23 8HX.
Part I £4.99 plus 60p postage and packing.
Part II £5.50 plus 70p postage and packing.
Part III £4.75 plus 50p postage and packing.

I wish to thank the following people who have been of assistance with research and advice.

Deputy Raymond Falla, O.B.E. — Occupation Essential Supplies and Commodities Committee.

Deputy Bill Green

Mr. R. Heaume — Occupation Museum

Mr. A. Benjafield and the Workers' Education Association

Mr. and Mrs. E. C. Robins

Mrs. D. Lawrence

Mr. A. Buckingham

Mr. J. A. McCormack

Mr. D. C. Maguire

Guille-Allès Library

This novel is dedicated to
my mother
WINIFRED LUCRETIA

Chapter One

Almost home now, he was relaxed. At times like these he always considered his car an extension of his own limbs. No more thought was needed to guide the vehicle than a walker gives to his walking. He and his car were at one.

John, the driver, would soon be leaving his faithful servant. Just eight miles more. He absent-mindedly fiddled to tune the radio.

The appliance, unlike his car, was not subjugated to his will and resented the intrusion into its peace.

It was a September evening, just dark now, the air was cool and still, autumn not far off. The sky ahead, which had lit his journey with a brilliant red, and was now the deepest purple, indulged a whim and permitted itself to wear its first evening star, as John absently toyed his receiver, while the cool air allowed the first mists to rise and set above the ground.

The stations were myriad on a night like this, the words of the many foreign commentators, and sounds of international music, galumping into each other jerkily as the tired hand grew impatient with his set's disobedience.

What was that? That voice, what was it? Whose was it? That voice picked up then so quickly missed and lost, that voice come back through the dark, through almost a lifetime.

Who was that, who had spoken? Who was he?

The fumbling, now involuntary, persevered. The car continued to drive itself – as the legs walk – independent of the master it carried.

There it was again. That gentle, clear, smooth, youthful sound, its timbre laden with laughter and enquiry. The words were German, the voice was that of an old friend, his lost friend.

The car drove on. John would talk to the long lost enemy returned from yesteryear. At last he had found his friend.

1

The car sped on, oblivious of the green light which had turned amber then red, as it had been oblivious of the sky changing from red to purple, whilst its master had been its decision maker. The master was listening to his brother long since lost who had once been his enemy, but also his friend.

Neither the car, nor John, nor the German friend saw or heard the other traveller at the cross roads, until they felt the impact which turned them all, in an instant, from immortal dreams to vulnerable metals, glass, and flesh, and bone.

*   *   *

Where the steep grey stone prison walls meet the footpaths of the Rue Marguerite and St. James' Street, John in his desire to get into the shade, away from the now sinking but still stifling sun, almost fell round the corner. Cool at last! He rubbed his hand along the smooth granite of the wall, as he had done when a little boy. He even dragged his feet along the granite pavement worn shiny by centuries of walkers. The pungent odours, left by dogs at the corner and on the prison wall-wedded lamp post, wafted through the air, seemingly all to seek out his dry and sensitive nostrils. John didn't mind, however. In fact, in some strange way he liked it for the smells now were those familiar to him. He was all but home.

A few steps more, that was all this tired and sweaty youth needed to take. Just down the dip past the prison door, round the corner, those tedious few paces uphill again and then he would turn into the gate, set in its wooden railings, and he would be home!

First he had to pass the German sentry outside the prison. 'Jerries', Dad called them. Only the evening before he had asked his dad why he referred to the Germans as 'Jerries', to which his mother had anxiously intervened, 'Don't let the boy pick up such ideas, he'll get into trouble.'

Why was his mother always such a fuss pot? As Dad would say, 'Always looking for trouble where there's none.' She seemed frightened of the Germans, he couldn't think why. They seemed all right to him, in fact he rather liked them. They were always smart and clean and, if they spoke, were always polite. One German in fact had given him a cigarette only the other day and let him stroke his horse, telling him the animal's name was Elsa and she was 'A fine big mare'. Not that he would tell his dad he'd been speaking to Germans. He would not understand and go off into one of his lectures about being a collaborator and a traitor, and mum would get upset again.

These grown-ups really were a problem. How could he be a traitor if the German was being friendly and saying, 'Not long now and you English will be with us, fighting alongside us as brothers, against the Marxist tyranny.' How could he be a traitor if they were both on the same side? And there was that Mr. Bichard at work saying that the British could take a leaf from Germany's book at any time. What had he meant? Was he a collaborator? And what about Mrs. Renier? She knew of a crippled neighbour who had been given a lift in the car of a German. She thought that was kind.

"Say what you like," she had said, "those Germans aren't as black as they're painted."

Was she a collaborator?

Mrs. Brouard, whose son had caught the last ship to England and joined the British Army, had told Mr. Bichard and Mrs. Renier off and had said, "You'll eat your words. You wait and see!"

'Funny, these grown-ups,' thought John, 'These grown-ups?' He was always being told that he was a grown-up now that he was fifteen. That was, when it suited. His father had said only last week, "We should have gone to England so the lad could have joined up." To which his mother had replied, "Let's not go into all that again. He might be fifteen but he's only a boy still." 'Who is right?' thought John, 'I'm fifteen and I'm a man, for I have to work, and yet Mum calls me a boy and even makes me come in an hour before curfew. What's the point of having a late summer curfew and have to get in early?' He wished he was still at school.

Thirteen months before, John had been at school still. Both his parents were proud of him for, at fifteen, most boys would have been out at work for a year or so already, but John had gained a scholarship at the age of eleven and gone to the Intermediate School. It had been hoped he would have stayed at school until eighteen and then gone to a

University in England. His father had said it would have been a struggle but well worthwhile in order to give the boy the chances he had not had.

John had overheard his aunt talking to his mother. It was always on the same theme.

"Why University? What's wrong with leaving now and getting a good job here in Guernsey, in the States, or a bank or the Police? You don't want him to go to University. He'll go to England and won't want to come back." His mother repeated it all to his father but his father had insisted on John's future being better than his life had been. John sometimes used to wonder if he would ever have a say in things. Probably not.

'When you pay the piper then you can call the tune,' seemed vaguely appropriate.

He hadn't felt too keen on the idea of going to England anyway, for he had never been further abroad than the nearby islands of Alderney, Sark or Herm and he was quite satisfied with his own island. Very proud in fact, as he used to boast to the English visitors he met each summer. It had been his great delight, when asked directions, to offer to take the enquirers to the place they had wanted. This had not been for reward, for he took a pride in refusing money, but to impress his audience with the magnificence of his homeland. Perhaps this was what he was missing? Perhaps this was why he would really like to get talking with the Germans?

Anyway, his problem, about deciding to leave Guernsey, had been solved for him in June 1940 when the Germans had arrived and taken over the Island.

It is true, the family could have evacuated, as half the population had, along with most of John's chums. They had, however, or rather his mother had, decided not to go.

"We will stay and take our chances."

John's father had been persuaded that he was happy to stay and 'take his chances' and his mother had been inwardly relieved that she was not to lose her 'little boy' to the British army or some University in England.

"How silly," his aunt had said. "You can't keep the boy tied to your apron strings."

However, 'tied' he was, at least for the present.

The gate outside clanged shut behind him, as he stepped

from the light into the cavernous dark passage which was the entrance way to No. 12, Rue Marguerite. Two floors up was their flat, their home.

The light coming from behind him formed a sharp but rapidly narrowing shaft of silver, brought alive with a universe of dust particles, as he pulled the door shut.

Now he saw the black-stained umbrella stand, the dark wallpaper, the shadowy stairs, the drab carpet, the yellowed ceilings, the greasy paintwork. All dulled through the contrast with outside, and years of neglect, a depressing patina what must surely have originally been smart Victorian decor. The only living thing in sight was a spiny plant which he supposed to be a cactus and for which he had always felt sorry, thinking that it would have been far happier in the sun.

The smells of meals being prepared in the large old house assaulted and titilated his nostrils by turn. That from the ground floor was the odour from their old landlord, Gaudion, preparing one of his inevitable stews. Tomato stew! From above wafted the smell of his own meal. Fish, he thought. Yes it must be, for Mum had been going to the market today, her ration number having been announced in the paper last night. Fish, potato and perhaps some beans? Maybe even some raspberries or loganberries for afters? No cream and sugar these days, not even milk to spare but perhaps, with luck, some dried milk, mixed with water, which might at least look like rather lumpy cream. Dried milk which had 'fallen off the back of a German lorry' as his father had said, with his mother's anxious caveat. "Don't say such things for the boy to repeat."

By the time he reached his kitchen John was completely oblivious of everything except his own anticipation. He burst into the room and was met by a delicious smell and a smoky atmosphere. Mum was saving the fat ration again and frying with milk.

John's mother was a wiry, rather anxious woman with jet black hair which had a tendancy to wave when permitted to grow from its fashionable pre-war short crop. She wore bangles on both her sinewy arms. Her face had a constant look of anguish held in place by years of practice.

"Hello, love," she said, addressing the stationary John while she darted over to administer her statutory kiss. He didn't mind this, when there was no one to notice, but nonetheless did not reciprocate, on principle. He had, after all, now that he was fifteen, earned the well sought concession not to be kissed by his mother in public. His aunt still tried it on and occasionally got through his defences but more often than not retreated to a safe distance, firing off comments to the effect that the boy was getting very surly, or,

"I'm not important enough for him now that he's been to the Intermediate School."

"Where's Dad?" John asked casually.

"I don't know, dear. He's very late. Go and ring him up, there's a good boy."

"OK."

"And be careful what you say over the 'phone."

"Yes, yes!" John's voice was edged with irritation. What was he likely to say over the 'phone? What could be subversive about having burnt mackerel?

*   *   *

"Well son, hot in the greenhouses today, I'll bet, eh?" asked John's father.

"You're right, Dad. We had all the top lights open, and both doors, but there was no breeze. It reached 105 this afternoon."

John looked at his stewed gooseberries, a green jellyfish covered in yellow spots. How he longed to go for a swim down at the pool. Little more than a year ago he would have been down there every day after school, diving in at high tide and jumping at low. Oh to clamber over the seaweed or to dive for 'spiders'! What joy to be able to float on the water affecting sleep, showing off to the visitors.

"Come on, John, eat your gooseberries. Stop day-dreaming, love," said his mother.

"They're too sharp."

"Sharper where there's none," she had retaliated.

"There is 'none'," suggested his father.

"None what, Dad?"

" 'None' sugar," he replied, with a chuckle. At this they all laughed. They always laughed at Dad's jokes. His family was renowned for its wit.

Right through the meal John tried to pick his moment to break the bad news. But the moment didn't come. All the way home he had thought about how he would tell Mum and Dad.

'I'll just tell them straight,' he had thought, 'then go off to my bedroom while they make their fuss. It's not my fault I've been told to finish work there today. It's not my fault the Germans are here and we can't sell our tomatoes to England anymore. I can't be blamed that people are fed up with tomato stew, and roast tomato and tomato jam. I didn't ask them to take over the greenhouses to grow vegetables for their armed forces. I could have been kept on but they only want women as they're cheaper. I suppose mum will worry at less money coming in but then, as Dad says, this German money is not worth the paper it's printed on. Anyway, it's not my fault.'

"Mum I'm leaving Brouards next Friday. . ."

No, that won't do, it's too direct. How about, "Would you mind if I changed jobs, if you thought I'd be happier?. . ." or

"Dad, how would I set about getting another job if I were to hand in my notice?" or . . .

"Come on dear," complained his mother. "You are in a bad way this evening, the heat's really got to you. You're letting your tea go cold now."

She looked irritated.

John sensed she was working up to a 'scene'.

The next thing would be 'You had better have an early night.'

'Shall I say now?' he wondered. 'Shall I say now and run out of the house before the shouting and weeping starts?'

"Son, come on now, let's not upset your mother. Either eat your meal and talk to us a bit or leave the table and go out."

"Go out Dad? Up to the park to listen to the Band?"

"Certainly not!" exploded his mother, "It's a German band!"

"So?" asked John petulantly.

"That's enough!" said his father. "You won't be so bloody fond of the Jerries when they take your job away."

"What do you mean, take his job away?" asked his mother

with a frightened look on her face, a look that would go well with wringing hands. "Why should they take his job away?"

"They haven't!"

"You just said. . . ."

"Oh don't be so stupid, woman!. . . ."

"You wouldn't call me stupid if you'd seen how I queued for two hours in the market for fish and just as I was about to be served. . . ." Her voice was rising.

'Oh no!' thought John 'Oh no, not now!'

Here she was, building up into a scene. Here was Dad raising his voice, an action for which he would suffer for days while mum would weep round the house and his sister-in-law would take great Christian delight in being civil to him despite he was not at all the sort to be husband to her little sister. And all over a conjecture, something that was not true. Yet it was. Oh hell! Dad, in inventing an example, had exposed the truth of the matter.

"Stop! Stop it, both of you!" shouted the youth stamping his foot under the table, as when he had been a little boy thwarted of some childish want. They stopped, everyone stopped, everything stopped. The clock stopped, the colour drained from the walls, the hot evening sky froze, the heat through the open window no longer belonged to this time. John knew he was dreaming. He had only to will himself awake, as when he was chased while his leaden legs refused to move, like when he was falling off cliffs, or when he was taken off to Gestapo headquarters for terrible interrogation. But no, the dream went on.

"You what?" gasped his father and mother in one voice encapsulating their deep horror, shock and lost faith in the sanctity of family life occasioned by John's irreverence and immaturity. How could he, who had been the recipient of all their sacrifices, in order to give him a decent upbringing and education, have turned into such an ingrate?

Chapter Two

The noise and smell and sound and sight had all welded into one, frozen grotesquely into the minds of all those involved, as the screech of six great sets of tyres and the burning of their rubber, with the desperate cacophony of a hellish horn accompanied the great lorry's entanglement with the cowering car which had disobeyed the lights.

The driver of the lorry had screamed for the car. He had screamed out the greatest concern he had ever felt in his life. He had screamed but the power of his yell had not held back his victim. His vehicle had shuddered as the ripping of metal and the smashing of all the glass for miles around had overcome his voice.

He had viewed the disaster, as it had come, with all the abject misery his body had been able to muster, focused on that miniscule car far distant below. Nothing his reflexes could have done would have saved that pathetic little car with its lonely and fated driver.

"Why? Why?" cried the lorry driver, hopelessly as if he had all the time in the world, while this tangle proceeded to knot itself like a ball of wool played with by a kitten. While he allowed the great steering wheel of his to be wrestled with and the pedals of his brakes to be forced at still he mouthed the helpless "Why?". The tears ran down his cheeks, as the horror of his own conjecture was forced upon him, and still his great load pushed them on, and still the shudders and sounds and smells of entanglement and destruction continued interminably.

He was enveloped with smoke as he lept from the cab. All seemed dark around, the light of the sky could not bear to look even, to see what had to be his alone.

The shaking lorry driver crunched over broken glass and small objects under his feet. Gone now were the shrill screams of metal in torment. Only his fast heavy breathing, enveloped in the loneliness of absolute silence was there as he stood waiting for proof that he was not the only person in this alien place.

The smoke of burning rubber cleared, the sky ventured a little of its evening beneficience and gradually the world returned to this spot. He took a cautious footstep forward, accompanied by the sounds of grinding underfoot and the raucous scraping and jangling of debris as it scattered. The fraught driver could hear once more.

Where was the car? Had it really been a car which had pulled across his path, seemingly completely oblivious, those eons ago? There was a sound, lots of sounds. What were they all?

Could that possibly be a voice? Yes, it was a voice, faint but clear. A voice calm and excited. Strange but unharmed.

The voice, however, that first sound of life and hope in this hellish place, was soon denied him. It was smothered by the sounds of approaching vehicles. The whole world, the real world, was coming to their aid.

*   *   *

Mr. Le Prevost was decidedly irritated. It was already mid-morning and his day had taken a definite turn for the worse. Breakfast had been the first thing to upset him. He had resigned himself two months ago to drinking coffee once their supply of tea had run out, the last quarter being reserved for weekends, Christmas, Easter and the King's birthday. He would not entertain the idea of his wife buying tea on the black market 'on principle'. Besides he 'couldn't run to it. Not black market tea, as well as black market sugar.'

"A man in my position must set an example in such things. People look to us for a lead in these times of difficulty".

So coffee it was, at least until this morning.

"What is the matter, dear?" his wife had asked, knowing full well what had been the matter, as she had watched her husband grimace theatrically while his waxed moustache had twitched with the habit of complimenting his facial expression of horror and disgust, of disbelief and wonderment at what the world could possibly have been coming to.

"That!" said Mr. Le Prevost, as he had mustered his full strength of awful sarcasm, the sort of sarcasm that had been rumoured to have had his office ladies reduced to tears for hours on end. "That was the most enjoyable cup of coffee I have tasted since the Germans graced us with their presence. Thank you, my sweetheart, for such a delightful start to the day!" Mrs. Le Prevost had taken it in good part, suggesting that if he could have done better he had been welcome to try and that the import of French roasted barley 'coffee' had been preferable to roasted acorn 'coffee', which offer she had declined on Saturday's shopping spree, adding sweetly that on second thoughts he might have preferred the acorns seeing that he had certain characteristics in common with the pig albeit not as considerate!

His second upset had been occasioned by having to bicycle to the office. Not that there was anything 'infradig' about that. It happened to the best these days since the Germans had requisitioned all private motor cars. He had been fortunate indeed to be permitted to keep his vehicle, for the time being at least, on condition that it was kept on blocks to preserve the tyres. Yes it was good to be a person of influence and to have contacts who were on social terms with the enemy.

Why had Doctor Morris not picked him up in the car as usual this morning? Life really was unfair! The man could have 'phoned. Had he not been grateful enough to come by ten pounds of wheat at only five times the official price, with no ration coupons required?

He dared not be late at the office, not after only recently having admonished Miss Le Huray, in front of all the ladies, for being 20 minutes late owing to a puncture. At least he had the luxury of inflatable tyres whereas, he understood, Miss Le Huray was now reduced to a rear tyre comprising a hay-filled length of hose pipe.

Mr. Le Prevost, the senior clerk in the States' Employment Bureau and Department of Agriculture and Fisheries, had a position to keep up and, as a Senior Civil Servant, endeavoured to keep it up. Most people knew who he was and of the important work he did. Those who made the mistake of not knowing were very soon put right and it was hardly likely that they would make such a ghastly error of judgement the second time. In his office, consisting of two male clerks and four ladies, including a shorthand typist, his word was law. He drew respect as a magnet draws pins. Mr. Le Prevost was not unused to streets full of raised hats, or offices full of scraped chairlegs, with occupants struggling to their feet out of respect and due deference.

This important gentleman was much surprised, upon arriving two minutes late, to find an officer of the Wehrmacht waiting for him at the office steps. He was even more put out by this foreigner's complete ignorance in insisting on referring to Mr. Le Prevost as 'Monsieur.' How dare anyone imply that he was anything other than British!

However, the Major, on urgent Feldkommandantur business, did not concern himself with the niceties of protocol. No, the fellow even had the impertinence to question Monsieur Le Prevost's late arrival, as he clicked his tongue, stating that all people in authority should be setting a good example and helping Europe's liberators with the war effort.

Perhaps it was as well for Monsieur that the emissary from the master race had not noticed the senior clerk's brave stand as he allowed his moustache almost a full and defiant twitch?

The green Major led the way to Mr Le Prevost's own office and there, without further ado, having seated himself in the senior clerk's own chair behind the desk, produced his papers.

He had come with a requisition; to order, not to request.

"This is the first requisition of labour. The Feld-kommandantur requires thirty men, aged between fifteen and twenty five years, to work forty-eight hours a week until further notice."

Mr. Le Prevost was given until four o'clock the next day to comply. No amount of protesting would have prevailed. The fact that he had no such young men was not considered an impediment.

"Then unemploy some," he was told.

How could the Nazi be so unreasonable? There were few youngsters left in the island after last year's evacuation. How was Mr. Le Prevost to find those few remaining young men, and how was he to persuade them to work as forced labourers? Like him, they would have observed the plight of the pitiful wretches from Poland and France; dirty, dressed in rags and with string-tied sacking for boots. They would have seen them roughly rounded up each day by the O.T. They would have heard of their billets in Vauvert, with ten to a room, of their meals of cabbage soup and sour black bread. How could Mr. Le Prevost, as British as Winston Churchill himself, persuade people of this glorious opportunity to work for a better Germany?

However the Teuton was a master of persuasion. He had only to mention Mr. Le Prevost's own two nephews of military age, but no doubt too cowardly to have gone to England, and other youngsters who just happened to live near him, for that selfless clerk to realise that it would be selfish for him to reserve the glory of working with the master race for his family and neighbours. No, Monsieur Le Prevost would be the last to indulge in such nepotism.

*　　　*　　　*

It was a cool morning. The violent thunderstorm during the night had freshened the air.

As John stepped out of his house, his feeling of guilt, at being so late, was heightened by the three quarter chimes of the old Town Church clock, seemingly clearer and sweeter after the rain. Chimes which were brought to his consciousness now distinct, now muted, as the brisk easterly wind played with and carried them his way. By this time he would normally have long since been at work but today was different, he was on holiday. He was unemployed. He was free.

As he left the wooden gate and turned towards the town his feet scuffled through a broken dam of saturated dead leaves and twig debris washed from the drains during the last night's deluge.

He remembered how that night he had snuggled deep into his large warm bed, cosily, as the lightning and thunder had flashed and boomed together, while the rain had beaten frantically at his window and the wind had howled and pleaded to be let in. He had loved that storm. It had been big and wonderful, full of power and strength and had made him feel like the child of destiny that he had imagined he

13

was immune from material concerns and caught up in the driving force of the universe.

This morning he was not so sure of himself. He had to seek employment. How would he set about it? He had not done-this before. When he had left school last year, the job he had worked at until recently had already been arranged for him. He had no such comfort now.

John's mother, despite her resolve to sulk, after having had words at the table the day before, had managed to speak to his father this morning, the need for comfort during the storm having proved stronger than belligerance. "You must go with the boy. He will need someone to give him support at the Employment Bureau."

John's father had demurred, saying that the boy was old enough to stand on his own feet and that if he were late for work there would be two out of work instead of one.

His mother had not liked it but her stomach still being 'in knots', as she had said, from the night before, had been in no position to argue.

The journey from his house in the Rue Marguerite could have been measured in minutes, but he made it last a quarter of an hour so that he arrived at the doors of the States' Employment Bureau and Department of Agriculture and Fisheries as the hour struck. He had extended his journey by various deviations, such as walking the paving stones, carefully avoiding the mortar lines, (a game which took him up some side streets), and standing to watch for a full five minutes, as a nest of frenzied black ants recovered their eggs, washed out by the storm.

*　　　*　　　*

Miss Dawn Le Huray, a sweet Sunday school teacher, a Methodist from that part of Guernsey where to be non-Methodist was almost akin to being of a heathen faith, got off her bicycle to walk for a while.

She knew this would make her late at the office, and that she would have to face Mr. Le Prevost's ire once more, but she had little choice in the matter.

Dawn's own selflessness had led her to this particular impasse, therefore she was prepared to turn the other cheek and suffer for righteousness' sake.

Turning the other cheek was in fact very apt, for Dawn now suffered incredibly in that part of her anatomy. Selfless to the end, and resolute to do the Lord's work, she had given her inflatable bicycle tyre to her fiancé who had greater distances to cycle, being their chapel's very own Local Preacher. In its place she now had hose pipe packed with hay, hence she walked where normally she would have ridden.

This was Dawn's mistake for, whereas usually she would have sped past the sentry post, today she was invited to stop. In all the thirteen months of occupation, this was her first close encounter with a German. She did not even know if there were any Methodists in Germany.

Dawn blushed to the roots of her hair as she was addressed.

"Halt! Why for you walk?" assaulted her ears.

She remained silent with shock.

"Fraulein, speak!"

She could not utter a word.

Dawn was pushed roughly so that she almost lost her poise.

This ghastly oaf then proceeded to inspect the contents of her wicker basket, ripping open the well-used paper bag to expose the good lady's meagre tomato sandwich.

Dawn watched, horror struck, as first, he sniffed her repast and then decided to sample the same with an enormous bite, while green slimy pips oozed from his chomping lips.

"Gut!" he grunted, as he returned the remains to Dawn's basket.

Her final degradation was when this Aryan knight placed his tomato-stained fingers on Dawn's cheeks, allowing them to stray towards her neck, as their pressure made white trails on her scarlet visage.

"Go now!" he shouted.

Dawn raced away so fast that her plaintive;

"Jesus loves you," hardly registered. Why should that not be so? He was German after all.

*　　　*　　　*

So distressed was Dawn, that the prospect of an admonition from Mr. Le Prevost held no fear for her.

Predictably, her senior wished to see her in his office when she arrived. She entered meekly, savouring the fact that he was not a German, therefore could not be too awful to her.

It took a few moments before she realised that, contrary to her resigned expectations, the formidable gentleman was not at all irritated with her and seemed quite oblivious of her misdemeanour. He was in one of his rare considerate moods.

"Do come in, Miss Le Huray. Please take a seat, won't you?"

Dawn was puzzled, but not for long, not when he began his uncomfortable preamble;

"Miss Le Huray, we have worked together now for years . . ."

"As you know, I have always looked upon you . . ."

Oh yes, she knew the signs. Mr. Le Prevost was after something. He had a very tricky assignment in mind for her. Yes, she anticipated being manipulated, yet at the same time flattered at the prospect of the trust he was summoning up the courage to bestow.

When he gave Dawn the assignment of finding the thirty young men, to work for those un-Christian beasts, she was aghast but quickly managed to control her feelings of nausea and inner disgust. She was, after all, very flattered that it was she who had been chosen. Well, who else better? She had already learned to communicate with her errant brethren.

"Oh, and by the way, my dear." added Mr. Le Prevost, as if to set the seal of authority and responsibility on to his chosen deputy, "the Police are at our disposal to help expedite this order."

*   *   *

John stood there at Miss Le Huray's desk, his new cloth cap held rather too tightly in his nervous grasp.

He wore his new grown-up suit which had been bought for him for his confirmation just before the Occupation began. Fortunately his mother had allowed for growth, so his wide double turn-ups had first been made single and now were reduced in depth. John wondered, if the war went on for another year, if he might end up without turn-ups altogether.

He stood there, legs stiff and straight, back straight, chin up, tie straight, parting straight. A blond-haired, blue-eyed, five foot seven navy-blue pin-striped tailor's dummy.

He felt very tall and manly as he seemed to tower over the petite, seated Dawn.

He was smart and presentable with suit just pressed and boots freshly polished by his mother. He even managed a convincing smile but kept forgetting to sustain it so that it switched on and off like a faulty electric light bulb, lighting his polished white teeth and sparkling his eyes, then as quickly leaving them dark and worried. He wanted the lavatory.

"Sit down, dear," said Dawn. Her kind reassuring tone let John become himself again. He was, after all, just a boy. He forgot his grown-up clothes, his grown-up cleanliness and grown-up polishedness and relaxed, confident that he had found a 'friend' in these unfamiliar, austere surroundings. He was quite happy to let Dawn take charge while he remained himself.

Dawn Le Huray conducted the interview in her usual efficient and caring manner, skilfully putting John completely at his ease and getting from him all the details of his fifteen years which she needed to know.

The inevitable word 'Germans' came into the conversation. Dawn surpressed the urge to shudder visibly, showing her predeliction. Instead she turned her thoughts towards the plans so recently and hurriedly formulated between herself and Mr. Le Prevost. However distasteful, she resolved that she must carry out her task efficiently. She could continue to detest the conquerors secretly but, in the manner of a good Christian, must put on a bold face.

John, on the other hand, inwardly thrilled at the word 'Germans'. Although he was not consciously aware of his own feelings in the matter, the mention of the master race filled him with a variety of feelings. He thought of their smartness, their colourfulness, manliness, the loud powerful hammer of their jackboots on the cobbled streets, the heavy square helmets which filled him with an almost primitive fear as though in the presence of some totem.

He was fascinated by their ceremony and their symbolism. The swastika flags with their stark black growths, contrasted by white and blood-red hung everywhere. The bright direction signs were painted on walls and trees at all road junctions, their gothic symbols lending both mystery and a sense of permanence. The music and their singing, as they marched about the Island, filled him with a secret joy. Their happy singing faces delighted him. He loved to attend their concerts in Candie Gardens. He enjoyed watching their films at the Gaumont, showing how they were winning the war for Europe.

All these pleasures, however, were tinged with feelings of guilt, for he was torn. All his friends and cousins had evacuated to England and were now fighting in the British forces. His own dear friends, whom he missed so much, were fighting a war against these Germans whom he secretly, almost unknowingly adulated.

His father disliked the Germans and his mother seemed to have a constant fear of what they might do next. Yet, as John saw it, they did nothing wrong to the people of Guernsey. There was a war on and all countries suffer privations in wars. This must be so, he had read it in the *Star* only last week.

> 'Your hardships and rationing are as a result of the war, they are not the result of the German people who at all times endeavour to protect and sustain you, as our brothers, so that we may be the stronger united in our vigil against international Marxism. . .'

John was not quite sure what international Marxism was but felt it must be bad if it united the Germans and, by implication, British forces, against it. He had not been too clear either about the dastardly rôle of the Jews, which was one of the main contributory causes to their present shortages of all commodities. He had tried to ask his father who had promptly dismissed the subject as a 'load of Jerry propaganda'.

Right since the beginning of the Occupation he had lived in a different world, one in which his parents seemed less open with him, less inclined to discuss things that he was not old enough to understand. Over the period, the feeling that anything German was unclean had been imbued in him. Somehow even to look at or to think about them was a disloyalty to one's family and friends. To touch the handle of a shop door just held by a German was akin to the feeling he would have from not washing his hands after using the lavatory. His whole island seemed tainted by their collective filth and yet, this was not true. His senses told him it was not true; these Germans looked and sounded like, and behaved as real people, in his conception.

There were young lads of his own age in Herr Hitler's army. How he wished to be with his friends again. His parents would not have understood, of course. When they did suspect he had been to the concerts and the cinema there was always a bad atmosphere at home, often heightened by his own feeling of guilt.

Having learned from John all she needed to know, Dawn Le Huray grasped the nettle, telling him the bad news.

"John, I'm afraid we have no ordinary work for you. There are no vacancies for young men of your age either in commerce or on the land." She took a slight pause. She was finding this more difficult than she had imagined. She had planned to give him the news that he was about to be conscripted compulsorily into the German labour force, coldly and briefly, and then comfort him in his devastation. And now she was ready to continue, to tell this young lad of his awful fate but to sugar the pill with reassurances that his hours would be regular, his pay the same as for any other job in Guernsey, and that he would go home at night, have Thursday afternoons and Sundays off, as in any other job, and would keep his ration book. She gulped, looked down at her feet, took a breath and began.

"I . . ."

"Oh . . ." said John simultaneously.

"Sorry!" apologised both together, and both laughed. It was the sort of laugh of relief experienced at the end of an ordeal. They both laughed a little too loud and a little too long. Dawn took the opportunity.

"We ourselves cannot supply you with work but there is work to be done. We have to give your name to the Germans as part of their compulsory labour requisition." She rushed out the last few words as though fearful they might change their minds, rebel and refuse to come.

She waited, words of explanation, words of compulsion, words of comfort at the ready, but John gave no response. She thought he must be shocked or stunned by the news.

The wait seemed interminable. Not a sound, not a movement. The silence interpreted as a hiatus by Miss Le Huray was suddenly dismissed by John, who, rising to his feet and changing his cap from right to left hand, announced.

"Thank you, when can I start?"

Dawn was taken aback at his smiling countenance, his eager expression, his look almost of excitement, of gratitude and confidence.

Chapter Three

Where was he? Who was he? What was he? Why was he?

The man raised his head. This was not right. He knew nothing any more. This was his world, his lot but he did not know it. He knew this was his to endure, that he must have experienced it always and must suffer it for eternity yet he did not know it, did not understand nor ever would. Yet he was all acceptance for he knew nothing else.

John groaned as he focused on his surroundings. Encumbrances so strange and yet his only reality. The pain lifted him, whirling him round. His whole left side was a misery of distress, but surely it had always been so?

What was this entanglement around him? It was dark and cold, so cold. Black clouds loomed down towards him, bent trees of metal were all around him and he had been showered by rains of glass. He was still wet, he could feel the trickling across his freezing skin, its warmth as it streamed, contrasting with the stiffness of his cold, pain-bared body.

All around him was the tight knot of bent and twisted metal which had so recently been his car, the extension of his limbs. His only limbs now were racked with pain and dampened with the sticky warmth of his own blood as it seeped away his consciousness.

John wanted to scream with the agony inside him but he could not move to effect such energy. All around him was the evil transformation of what had once been his normal and peaceful existence. He felt that this ghastly mutation, which trapped and stifled him, was his encasement for ever. It was to be his hell. Not only was he buckled and bent like his prison, clamped by the round ebony of his steering wheel and held down by the uneven and paint-flaking sky, so cold and foreign, but he felt that its very awfulness was inside him bursting him apart so that he could not endure more.

21

John vomited, the retching scouring his internal wreckage with wire brushes and molten lead while slivers of glass penetrated his belly. He gasped to scream away the pain but his voice was not heard. Only to be heard was the voice of his erstwhile friend laughing at him. John passed into unconsciousness.

*   *   *

Larry got up from the kitchen table, stubbed out his last cigarette in his saucer and walked slowly towards the window.

Frances, her eyes red-ringed with sleeplessness and tears, followed his movement with her expressionless eyes, seeming almost too exhausted to move her head. She was so tired, so demoralised, that she let the cigarette-stubbing pass without comment. She had even lost her handwringing, anxious look. She wanted to be able to go back to bed and sleep. Sleep away the anxiety, the fear. Sleep away her husband and son. Sleep away the pain and misery, the Occupation, the war. She wanted to sleep, to let sleep take over and obliterate her fears of the unknown which seemed like a moving black creature consuming her mind. A creature like a living vibrant swastika destroying her reason, devouring her will to go on.

There was a muffled boom in the distance, the windows rattled, and across the road the birds on the walls of the prison chattered loudly, the more frightened of them flying up into the air.

"What was that?" Frances screamed out. "What is it?" She jumped up, knocking over her chair, and clutched the kitchen table.

Larry rushed to her, took hold of her firmly by the shoulders, holding her tightly to him, while her body was racked with sobs.

"Oh, what are they doing, what is happening to us?"

"Love," soothed Larry, "calm down love, don't fret yourself. That was only the twelve o'clock gun. Your nerves are bad. Look at me. Now calm down. Please. Please. There."

He held her in his arms, she looked up into his strong weatherworn face with its thinning blonde hair, now turning golden with the approach of middle age. She wilted like the tiny flower she was, confident that all was well. Somehow, despite the impossible state they were in, all would be well, for Larry always managed difficulties.

Larry too was not feeling his best. The worries of the past twenty-four hours had definitely taken their toll. He must hold himself together, for if he cracked who would look after Frances? Who would look after his 'business' contacts? More importantly, who would look after his son and make sure he came to no harm as a forced labourer for the Germans?

More muffled distant explosions. Frances bit into Larry's shirt and clutched frantically at the nape of his neck.

"Hell!" exclaimed Larry. "Bloody hell, it's a raid! They must be bombing the harbour". As he spoke, the house began to shudder and the windows to rattle violently while the sound of guns was heard rattling faintly in the distance.

John burst into the room.

"Dad! Dad, they're bombing the castle! They're bombing the castle, it's the R.A.F!"

Today was the first time in all his working years, since he had left school, that Larry had gone 'sick'. Despite his principles of hard work, loyalty and honesty in such matters, he could not and would not, go to work that morning. He had been unable to let John leave the house by himself, to walk the half mile into the unknown, to the Feldkommandantur headquarters at the top of St. Jacques.

Strange, he thought, how they had always warned John not to go near St. Jacques for fear of bombing raids. Now, on this very day, when the minimal chance of extermination, by their own side's bombs, paled into insignificance against the magnitude of the unknown dangers of forced labouring for the enemy, the R.A.F. had decided to salute his family in their hour of dark despair. Larry was heartened and only hoped the R.A.F. had killed a lot of the bastards.

Larry and John had set out from home at ten minutes to the appointed time that morning, Larry having estimated that ten minutes would get them at the German headquarters exactly on time.

"Don't give the buggers a minute more than you have to, not a minute more," he had instructed.

John had got a reasonable job all right, despite what had been seen as Larry's unwanted interference, an interference which, if it had not stopped, and if Larry had not left, might otherwise have resulted in a far more unpleasant employment for his offspring.

Herr Tropp, the civilian administrator at the Feldkommandantur, for all his beguiling smile and twinkly blue eyes, had been very much in control.

"If we feel your son is worthy, he will be given Messenger responsibilities. If, however, he is not satisfactory, or if we feel his family is antagonistic to the German forces . . ." He left his statement inconclusive, but Larry had got the message and had left.

So now John was to be an official Messenger for the Reich, he was even to have a uniform! Well, an armband, but it was inscribed in illegible gothic. He was not aware that his parents did not share his euphoria at this great honour.

*　　*　　*

Franz thought he was going to be sick again. He tried to remember what they had taught him at youth camp when they watched those terrible films.

'Take deep breaths,' they had said. 'Take deep breaths and think of something else. The Führer has no use for weaklings.'

Franz supposed now he was a weakling. This was why he now stood chained to a guard, outside the door of the Feldkommandant's office.

He stood there nervously, taking his weight, first on his right foot then on his left. Now leaning forward, now hunched against the wall. At each move the guard would pull at the chain as though annoyed at having to associate with this mere boy, this child almost.

Each time the guard showed signs of animation Franz would look up towards him, perhaps seeking some sign of recognition, some faint chance of comfort. Maybe a smile or a friendly word? Each time the guard would turn away as though in disgust and nauseated by the odour of vomit still wafting from Franz's soiled uniform.

Franz supposed his guard was right to treat him with disdain. He was, after all, a coward and a traitor. He knew about such things. He had been taught well at school and in the Hitler Youth. 'Always obey orders,' they had said. 'Orders come from the Führer and are passed down to you by your superiors. It is your duty to obey without question at all times!

He had always obeyed orders without question. Sometimes he had not understood or liked what he had had to do but he was a good German and knew that what he did was to enable his country to master and free the world of its diseases, to free the world from the evils of Marxism, of capitalistic democracy and of Judaism. He had not enjoyed it when, at their last summer camp, before the annexation of Czechoslovakia, their Youth Officer had suggested they go and teach a few Jews a lesson. He had gone along, for the others were all so keen. Once they had found a bearer of the Star of David he had even joined in the punching and kicking and had been quite invigorated. He had felt ashamed afterwards but had been unable to tell anyone of his feelings for they would not have understood.

Now he was realising he was different, for this morning he had run away. He had run away and refused to stop when challenged. He had been lucky not to have been shot in the back as he had run. He could count himself lucky that all those who might have fired at him were too busy tending their injured comrades or sheltering from the bombs.

Franz had not known where he had been running or why he had been doing so. Perhaps it had been something to do with his friend, Corporal Schmidt, who had been sitting next to him in the open launch bringing them the three miles from Herm. Maybe it had been to do with the bomb that had exploded on the breakwater above them, the bomb which had blown a shower of dust and granite blocks into the air, the bomb which had turned his friend into a faceless man. Had he run so blindly because of Corporal Schmidt's screams which had changed from burning, piercing sirens into gasping, choking gurgles as he had drowned in his own blood?

They had taken him to some barracks, Military Police he supposed. But why was he now at the Feldkommandantur? He was not sure, it was all too confusing. Much easier not to have to think. It was probably all to do with his uncle, but was not that august person Gestapo, not Feldkommandantur? Well it didn't matter anyway. All Franz knew was that he was in deep trouble with his own people, be they Gestapo, Feldkommandantur or just plain Wehrmacht. He was in trouble and he felt ill. The fact that, in his moment of trauma he had bandied around his uncle's name and position was, for the moment, irrelevant. Wherever he was, he was in dire straits.

He remembered the horror of that moment. The gaping hole where the face had been. The gushing blood, the blonde hair turned pink and the pieces of flesh hanging by strips of skin like some grotesque and hellish decoration. The screams, those haunting screams which seemed to have gone on and on. Those screams which seemed to have followed him as he had jumped ashore at the jetty, as he had run on and on and on. Those screams which had filled his head, his whole mind, which filled him now as he stood there tottering.

From deep inside him Franz heard the screams. They grew stronger and louder. He no longer felt like vomiting. The scream welled up in him like some vast cacophony from Lucifer's orchestra tuning its instruments for a mighty performance. The power and sound forced up through his own body, through the hell that was his body and mind as he joined with it. His own anguished scream filled the whole of the Feldkommandantur headquarters until he was mercifully silenced by a philanthropic blow to the side of his head.

*   *   *

John walked through the main doors of La Porte to be confronted by a seething activity. His attention focused on the centre of this turbulance, on a young soldier lying in a semi-conscious stupor on the floor. His short dark hair was dishevelled, his green eyes staring vacantly ahead. His uniform was soiled with blood and vomit. The guard, who was still attached to this creature, was kneeling by his side in a ridiculous, self-conscious manner while Herr Tropp, the Feldkommandantur Administrator, stood behind giving him a very thorough verbal dressing down. A medical orderly had been summoned and was busying himself about the victim.

John stood bemused, as he watched. It was as though he were watching a film, as though he were not party to what he saw. He felt he was invisible. Yet he knew he was seen, for those green, stupified eyes appeared to be fixed on him so that he could not look away.

Herr Tropp, having, for the time being, completed his bawling abuse of the guard, took several large steps to the open door of his office, clapped his hands in a petulant manner and snapped out incomprehensible instructions to the unseen occupant.

Within seconds a middle-aged civilian lady whom John assumed to be a secretary or clerk, rushed from Herr Tropp's office, out of the building and minutes later returned close on the heels of a Military Policeman.

Herr Tropp snapped at this new arrival who appearing completely unmoved, and retaining his blank almost innocent facial expression, knelt down, taking a bunch of keys from his waist, and unlocked the chain about the young soldier's wrist.

The guard, by now so used to his kneeling pose, remained where he was, like some comical garden gnome, until jerked from his temporary trance by a torrent of abuse from the policeman. He jumped to his feet, stood stiffly to attention, eyes protruding, chin set firm, shoulders quivering with enforced smartness. So smart was he, so at full alert attention that he seemed hardly cognisant of the forceful blow he received to the side of the jaw, apart from perhaps the flexing of the spine to an even more straight stance, an increased protrusion of the eyes and an extra blink. This all, followed by a sharp heel click, a precise and respectful, "Heil Hitler", and a stiff march out of the building, followed by the donor of the assault, whilst continuing his tirade.

John shook himself from his invisibility, as a person does when trying to wake from a bad dream, and became part of the group.

"Ah yes," said Herr Tropp seeing him for the first time. "Come, you have your first assignment." He bent over Franz, gently cradling his head in his hands.

"You take his feet," indicating John. He spoke to his secretary in words incomprehensible to John but in the stern tone one might associate with speaking to a dog which had not yet been naughty but was likely to be so at any moment.

Between them they half lifted and half dragged their limp and odorous load into a nearby room, where the lady had hastily pushed together two chairs and cushions to make a bed.

John was not quite sure what was expected of him but he supposed he had been put in the room, with this young soldier, in order to look after him. Herr Tropp had not in fact given any instructions other than a swift hand movement, reiterating the dart of his eyes towards the unfortunate young Franz. Remembering Herr Tropp's petulant behaviour, and his display of anger, John was quite content to accept this as the Administrator's wish.

Franz appeared to have fallen asleep on his makeshift bed. 'He looks about my own age,' thought John.

John did not really know what he should do. Should he stand at the far side of the room ready to warn Herr Tropp of any dramatic changes in his charge's condition? Should he stand near him or sit by him and in some way try to comfort his distress?

His distress? What was the matter with this German? Had he been injured? Was he sick? Why was he so dirty, so smelly? His uniform was soiled with what John supposed to be blood and he smelled terribly of vomit.

Why had he been chained to that oafish looking soldier and why did Herr Tropp seem to be so interested in him? Why had the Military Policeman hit the oafish soldier? So many questions but no one to answer them.

He was still undecided what to do, how to pass the time, when his patient opened his eyes. John looked at him, not knowing quite what to do or say. Those green eyes just stared, transfixed on his face.

"Hello," said John tentatively. "Hello, how are you?" He heard himself saying these words while thinking what a stupid thing it was to say.

The dark green lights closed and the pale face whitened against the almost black hair. Again the lights opened and looked at John.

John moved closer as two tears, two jewels of sorrow and

bitter anguish, left the soldier's eyes and ran down his cheeks.

The soldier murmured something in incomprehensible German. John raised his eyes, contorting his face into a mask of pity. He knew not what the trouble was but he guessed it was bad and he felt empathy with its victim.

Again the soldier uttered the German words, this time with more urgency as though he were on the brink of some terror, seemingly in John's face seeing a picture which only he could perceive.

John bent over him.

"What is it? What is the matter?"

Franz looked up into Corporal Schmidt's face. He could not speak.

'So you have come,' he thought. 'You have come to see me, my friend. You have come to see me.'

'But this is not right, you cannot come to see me. Something has happened. Why am I lying here? You should be lying here. Why should you be here, not me, and me visiting you? What has happened?'

'What is wrong? You cannot see me here. Why?'

"Was ist los? Warum bist du hier?" he murmured to Corporal Schmidt. Why was Corporal Schmidt speaking in English?

Corporal Schmidt lent over him now.

'Why am I crying? My eyes are clouded by my tears,' Franz thought, 'I cannot see your face. Your face?'

He could not see the face of his visitor. His visitor could be anyone. It had to be Corporal Schmidt, but why?

"Was ist los? Warum bist du hier?"

"What is it? What's the matter?" asked John concerned.

'That is not Corporal Schmidt's voice,' thought Franz. 'It is him but not his voice.'

'It is not his face. It is not a face! I can't see a face!'

'No face? Should that be so? Are there people without faces?'

The soldier lifted his arm, moving his hand in the air searching for what he could not see. His quivering hand touched John's cheek. He sat upright. His other hand joined the search. So very gently he held John's face and let his fingers trace his nose, his eyes, his lips. The tears rolled down his own visage.

John did not know why but he seemed to understand.

He sat there quite still while the helpless hands searched and the young German sobbed silently.

The tears quickly subsided. Franz's eyes lost their vacant look. As though suddenly awakened from a nightmare, he contorted his face with a questioning look, a mixture of suspicion and fear. He wiped his wet cheeks with the cuff of his tunic.

Hesitantly, Franz spoke in his mother tongue words which in normal circumstances should have been meaningless to John but this time John sensed he was being asked about himself.

"I don't understand German".

"English?" quavered Franz's emotion-loaded voice. "You are English not German?" He seemed to find this hard to understand for he had assumed this person to be a fellow soldier.

"Yes," replied John, deciding against going into the intricacies of Guernsey's relationship with Great Britain which should, strictly speaking, have rendered his answer 'no'. "Yes, I am British. Are you German?"

"I am German," replied Franz. "I am German and we will win this war for Germans are superior!"

John did not like to argue about this for he did not particularly know whether it was true or not, having never really thought about it. He presumed that this soldier must believe it whether or not it was so.

"Sprechen sie Deutch?" asked Franz, suddenly speaking the only phrase of German which John knew.

"Nein," replied John, by now having depleted five of his six word vocabulary.

"Nein?" queried Franz with a weak laugh. "Nein is a German word for 'no' and yet you are speaking German when you say it!"

John saw the joke and joined in the amusement with Franz. He thought how his father always so forcibly maintained that Germans did not have a sense of humour but here he was proved wrong for this one had just made a joke.

"I see. You English are too proud in your schools to learn German," stated Franz. "In Germany we are every day learn English. We learn English have so that we can tell you what to do when we this war have won."

"Oh," commented John, "but you may not win the war."

"We will! It is half won now. Already we have these islands and they Britain itself are part. All Europe is ours! We this war will win, the Führer has said so!"

"What is your name?" asked John.

"My name is Franz Müller. We will win this war!"

"We'll see," was John's reply.

"I tell you we will win!"

"Maybe," replied John. "My name is John Collins by the way."

Franz put out a stiff polite hand. John took hold of it and they both shook.

"We will win you know," said Franz, but this time with a smile, as he sought only to tease his new acquaintance.

The moment of tranquillity was rudely broken, as the door rattled open, while Franz appeared to try to shrink into insignificance.

It was however, only the Doctor. John was permitted to remain while that gentleman carried out his thorough examination. Franz groaned miserably when the man reached his neck, causing the Doctor to click his tongue in annoyance as he fired an incomprehensible order at the newly appointed Messenger.

"You are for me to bring an ambulance," explained Franz.

When John returned, he found an extremely anxious young German who, nevertheless, collapsed back onto his bed with relief that it was only the Guernsey person.

"Oh it is you. That is good."

"Who did you think it was?" asked John.

"I am not know but I think they will come, me to take away."

"Take you away? Who will take you away and where?" replied John.

"Oh I do not know who they are or where they taking me are but I will have to be punish. They may shoot me!" Franz sat up suddenly as he said these last words. He appeared petrified at the enormity of his own statement.

31

The pain hit him and he cried out as he sank back in misery.

"Oh John I am frightened. I so frightened am! I don't want to die. Please don't let them me shoot". He tugged frantically at John's sleeve and pulled him near. The doctor had moved the chair so that John had the choice either of falling down on to the floor or of sitting on Franz's makeshift bed. He sat on the bed.

Franz was shaking now in his terror. John felt the fearful vibrations passing through the bed and into his own body.

"I am not really a traitor or a coward. I am a good German. Please don't let them me take. Please do not let them me shoot, please!"

"It is all right," comforted John, as he self-consciously moved Franz's arms which imploringly clasped round him. "They are not going to take you away. You are going to hospital."

'How changed he is,' thought John. 'When first I arrived he was so brave and sure of himself, so proud and arrogant. But now he is terrified and weak.'

"Ah yes, hospital! But what then? Where do they me take from there? When they are coming for me? You stop them must!"

"Who are these people you are afraid of? Are you in trouble with your police, with the Gestapo?"

"I do not know," groaned Franz. "I do not know what will happening. All I know is I this morning away ran and the Führer has no use for cowards."

"But you're not a coward," insisted John. "Just because you ran away doesn't make you a coward. You couldn't run far in Guernsey could you? Why did you run away anyway?"

"Oh, it was terrible," moaned Franz. "What your people did to us this morning was terrible, terrible!" He looked at John angrily, almost accusingly, as he spurted these words. His eyes flashed with anger and he seemed to shrink away from him.

"Your killer planes this morning came and dropped their wicked bombs. Murderers are the R.A.F.! They killed my best friend!"

As he said these words he hated John. He hated the British and all they stood for. Was it not the British who started this evil war? Oh yes, he remembered now, he remembered it all. The Modern Political History he learned at the Academy. The British with their insidious Democracy, sheltering the Jews and all other kinds of perverts. The arrogant British who had attacked his peace-loving country, trying to prevent the Führer from liberating Poland, just as he had liberated Czechoslovakia and Austria. Britain the aggressor! He was glad that he was a German. He was proud that he fought on the right side. He revelled in their motto 'God with us!' God must certainly be on Germany's side for, despite the evil cowardly ways used by the British forces, the Führer continued with his struggle to free Europe and rid it of its poisons.

It was working too. Almost the whole of Europe had been freed. Even this part of the British Isles which was temporarily their home before their march onto England itself.

He looked at John, now seeming to have forgotten his pain. His mouth tightened, his lips narrowing into a thin cold line. A sneer grew across his ashen face.

"You English murderers! You fools! My friend you killed today!"

John did not know what to do or say. He recognised that here was his new friend changing so rapidly in mood from fear to fury, from insecurity to extreme confidence. He realised that Franz was not well and, although he had no great experiences of life upon which to draw, he accepted that this present was not the real Franz. He knew in his heart that the real Franz was his friend present and friend to be.

John said nothing and did nothing. He sat. He waited, waited for Franz to change once more as surely he must.

Down Franz plummeted from the exhalted heights of his master race, with Hitler in all his glory, to the depths of fear and despondency with him a tiny creature, ready to be ground in under the heel of the Gestapo and the shadowy, sinister, ever-aspected, just behind the scenes, S.S.

"My friend was Corporal Schmidt. He died next to me in the boat. He died and I ran away! It was very bad, and I ran away because I could not bear it." He clutched at John again.

"He was so good to me you know? They took his lovely face away. He no face has!" He groaned in his misery at the

memory which he once more relived. He began to relive the
scene he had called up only a while before as he had stood
in the hall of the Feldkommandantur. His body shook, his
face contorted and he turned towards John. The skin of
Franz's face was stretched so tightly over his cheek bones
now, as his mouth opened wide and his eyes expanded, that
it looked like waxed paper. His whole facial misery seemed
fixed like that of some hideous gargoyle. He began to cry.
He cried but not a tear wet his eyes or his deathly cheeks.

John put his arms around his shoulders and said,

"I am very sorry. Please tell me all about it."

*　　　*　　　*

Franz had been born in a small village seventy kilometres
from Hamburg. His father had been a farm labourer while
his mother had worked as a maid. They had married in
1918, just after the Great War. Franz's sister Inga had been
born soon after this and Franz came along seven years later
in 1925.

"You are a gift from God," they had told him, for, as he
had often been reminded, all were surprised at the second
child. Surprised but delighted.

Franz had been brought up in the village and had wanted,
like his father, to work on the land. However, this was not
to be, for Germany had to rid itself of all its ills and be led
by its new saviour, who set about putting the world to
rights.

Franz had an uncle Pieter, a former policeman and now
an officer in the Gestapo, who had persuaded his brother to
put the boy into the Hitler Youth.

It seems that Uncle Pieter had been a strong, if not
necessarily good influence in the youth's upbringing, for in
1939, when Franz's father had gone missing in Poland,
Uncle Pieter had arranged for his education to continue at
boarding school and for his elder sister Inga to train to
become a school teacher to help spread the gospel of National
Socialism.

In 1940 Major Pieter Müller had been seconded to the
Guernsey Feldpolizei, ironically referred to by the locals as

Gestapo. He had made behind-the-scenes arrangements to have the youth posted there also.

This was simply for family reasons and soon after the youngster's arrival, the uncle had written to make it absolutely clear that he did not wish his nephew to communicate with him in any way.

As Franz unfolded his story to John, the patient and interested listener, he seemed to gain visibly in confidence and some trace of colour began to vanquish the pallor from his cheeks.

Franz went on to explain that he was not particularly bothered that his uncle had forbidden contact, or reference to their kinship, for he had never felt particularly close to his father's elder brother.

However, the day came quite recently when, despite the coolness of Uncle Pieter Müller's instruction to the contrary, Franz had felt he had to contact that man. There are times, surely, when family considerations should be permitted to take precedence over military aloofness?

Franz showed John the letter which brought him to this conclusion. It was an official document with embossed swastika and eagle, confirming the family's long held fears:

'Paul Müller, son of Germany, died in glory for his Fatherland and for his Führer about the month of September, 1939. Heil Hitler.'

So Franz had made his way to his uncle's Headquarters and had tried to see him. If he had been successful he had held no ideas of what he would have said to the man but nevertheless, felt he might have been treated to some sympathy, to some words of comfort.

"Do you know what they do to me, John?" asked Franz rhetorically.

"They lock me in a room, my uncle not to see!"

John just nodded. What was there to say?

"Then, they take me back to my barracks and I do not even see my uncle."

Yes, the young German was beginning to sound assertive again, angry almost.

Franz continued:

"But it is not all bad, my friend. My commanding officer,

35

he ask to speak with me. He tell me he is sorry and I am to have compassionate leave."

Franz's face gave a slight hint of a smile which he quickly extinguished as he prepared for the next stage of his saga.

"So I think I am go to Germany to see my mother. Yes, that is good, yes?"

John agreed, only then to be equally included in his new friend's dashed hopes.

"But what is they do? No Germany? They send me to that little island Herms!"

"Herm," corrected John.

"I want to cry when I know this. But it is all right to cry for my best friend Corporal Schmidt he say he has the iron cross and he cry when his brother die."

Franz recounted to John, despite his initial disappointment, what a marvellous time he had had in the tiny island of Herm, which lies less than three miles to the east of Guernsey.

They used to snare rabbits and would make lovely stews which they ate out under the stars, round driftwood fires. Oh yes, it had been like the Hitler Youth camps, with all the men singing patriotic songs and drinking schnapps.

One evening, his best friend the Corporal had announced that he was going to open some bottles of real German beer, for they were all to celebrate that he had noticed Franz smile for the first time that day. Oh yes, it was fun and the other men had carried Franz round on their shoulders and had included him in their ribaldry.

In the daytimes, when it was not Franz's turn to burn the rabbit stew, sometimes he would join in the football on the beach. At other times he would help one of the older soldiers who had discovered a whole beach which was made up entirely of shells, instead of sand. Yes, this man had taught Franz how to turn these shells into little dolls with beautiful shell dresses and limbs. Franz had one ready to take to his mother once Germany had won this war.

But by far the best part for Franz had been when his Corporal friend had taken him to inspect the mine fields. Well that was what he had said it was but really they had used the excuse to sit high up on the peaceful cliffs and observe the gulls and wildlife with the Corporal's field glasses.

"Do you know, this young Corporal is a university

lecturer?" asked Franz, then correcting himself to "was" as his face clouded at the stark reality.

"Oh yes, he has a wife and three children, Anna, Clara and Bern. He say he write to his wife and tell her to get the extra bed ready for me. He say I be an uncle to his dear children after this war."

"And now this will never be!"

Franz flailed his arms in his despair.

"Never will I meet them as you murderous British have kill my friend!"

John did not have opportunity to respond, for the door was unexpectedly and roughly opened as the two stretcher bearers, accompanied by Herr Tropp, came to collect their patient.

Franz's angry bravado receded as his face became gripped by fear once more. Oh yes, they had come, ostensibly to take him to hospital, but to where in reality?

As the young Aryan was taken towards the door, he knew he had something more to say to John, but time was fast closing and the words would not out. He had to say it. There was nothing for it but to speak out his plaintive request, yet still the words would not come.

At the end of his journey through consciousness and terror he allowed his instinct to take control, as he begged;

"John, you must tell my uncle!"

*   *   *

'Bugger!' thought Keith, 'the bastards are going to search.'

Keith de la Haye, fisherman, had just returned from Sark. He watched fearfully as the jackbooted oafs gently began to rip his small boat apart.

"Up!" he was ordered, as the way up the slippery granite steps was indicated.

"Papers!"

Keith took his identity card and fisherman's permit from his pocket.

"Where have you been fishing today?"

"I haven't been fishing," Keith deliberated through clenched teeth, sorely tempted to suggest they read his papers.

"Ah yes, you work for us?"

"I have a contract with the occupation forces to take supplies to Sark from time to time." Keith's effected boredom ill hid his irritation.

"So you for us like working?"

"No," was his stark reply.

"If you do not like for us to work, then perhaps against us you work?"

"Perhaps," shrugged Keith, for which gesture he earned himself a hefty push, as he bent forward to retrieve his papers.

As Keith looked round on the top of the jetty he could now see why the Jerries were so bad-tempered today. There was a mangled crane like some wounded animal lying on its side. Several sheds were gutted, there were bomb craters in the road, and one of their invincible new concrete bunkers was cracked right round like a cheese cut through by wire.

'Bloody good shots our lot,' thought Keith. It was only a pity the R.A.F. had to pick a day when he was carrying.

The boarding party had almost reached the bilges, where Keith had hidden the purloined whisky, when, by an enormous stroke of good fortune, a fleet of small fishing boats entered the boom and attention was switched from his craft.

*   *   *

So, it was a slightly unnerved and rather late Keith who, having moored his boat in the Old Harbour, made his way to the Golden Lion, aching from the blow he had received from his 'Brothers All.'

He had not bothered to unload his illicit cargo. No, that would keep. First, he had to find out if he had a contact and where and when to meet.

Therefore, although the pint of Breton cider seemed more welcome than usual this evening, despite its specific gravity having been watered down, he carefully paid over his sixpence note, scrutinising the change to discover if it was over or under.

Well, at least he had a contact. Now to find out when and where.

The landlord good-naturedly gave him a whole packet of

French matches in which, by a carefully arranged code of numbers, which could easily have been his wife's dressmaking measurements, Keith knew where and when to make his contact.

Ten minutes later Keith de la Haye and Larry Collins met in the shadowy twilight of lower Rue Berthelot.

*　　*　　*

John was rather proud of the new armband he wore. He could not understand the words embossed on the crepe background. Even if he'd had command of the German language he might have had difficulty in interpretation, for the letters were gothic.

He had asked Herr Tropp what the words meant but the Administrator had completely disregarded his question.

John could only assume that this armband designated him as an official messenger for this was what he now was.

He was proud of the smart official appearance the band gave him and only hoped it would not be too long before he received a full uniform.

As he walked home, after his first day as Civilian Messenger for the Feldkommandantur, John felt six feet tall. He had decided to keep his uniform on so that all he passed might see how smart he was.

His thoughts were full of this exciting day. It had, he thought, been the most exciting day in his life. There had been this morning's visit to the Feldkommandantur. Also he had received his medical and academic examination at which he must have been considered outstanding to have been given such a responsible job.

He recalled the excitement of the R.A.F. bombing raid, then his mind switched to the misery it had caused and to what they had done to his new friend. He remembered the scene of violent despair he had witnessed with poor Franz the innocent victim.

John thought of his new friend and how his mood had changed from one of arrogant self assuredness to despair and fear. He began to think of some of the things his friend had said. Was he really his friend or was he just another so-called enemy?

Had John been excited to see the R.A.F. planes bombing the enemy this morning or was he annoyed at what they had done? He loved his new job and his new armband and had been excited at taking messages to the strong and camouflaged fortresses that afternoon.

John hated the *Gestapo* for the way they had treated Franz and kept him locked up for four hours when he had tried to find uncle Pieter. Yet it was not uncle Pieter who had given orders to bomb the harbour and kill Franz's friend. Uncle Pieter had sent Franz on the best holiday of his life.

John himself had ordered the R.A.F. to spoil his friend's holiday. Now he could not bear the guilt of it. He wanted to be with Franz. He wanted to sing the stirring songs and sit round the camp fire drinking the schnapps and beer saved by Corporal Schmidt. But Corporal Schmidt was dead and Franz was in hospital. All this because of his aggression, British aggression.

Why did his own people have to be so aggressive? Why could they not leave Germany alone to spread its system to unite the whole of Europe so that glorious peace and brotherhood could extend to all men, to free them? John could be part of this creative glory.

*   *   *

The tourniquet round de Carteret's head was tightened another turn. The Sarkee thought he was going to scream but managed instead to dig his nails into the arms of the chair to which he was strapped.

*   *   *

John was nearly home now. He had been told he need not wear a helmet any more for there were no more air raids now that peace had come. He looked down at his polished jackboots and could literally see his face in them.

As he passed a British sailor he impressed him by doing the goose step.

It was a British soldier who stopped him at the sentry post in the Grange. When John showed him his papers and turned, so that the other would notice his Iron Cross, the tommy saluted smartly and shouted,

"Heil Hitler!"

'Not as smart as me,' thought John as he clicked his heels together.

*　　　*　　　*

De Carteret was now screaming. One continuous sound came out in gulps like water from his pump at home. Now fast, now slow. His eyes bulged, his ears sang and his throat was dry and rasping. From beyond the swimming haze of the bright lamp shining in his eyes, he could make out two, or was it three, human outlines. He could not be sure how many there were for they kept moving sideways into one another so that sometimes there were two and sometimes just one.

Another turn. De Carteret hiccoughed and was sick across his clothes and the table in front of him.

"Now you pig, tell us where you hid the whisky!"

*　　　*　　　*

'We have won the war!' thought John. 'Europe is free, the British have surrendered and Germany has graciously forgiven them. Now I will be able to help them build a better place for us all to live in. Now we can turn against the Russians.'

'I had better get home quickly as Frau Schmidt is arriving tonight. I must get the spare bed ready. Franz is coming out of hospital tomorrow and we will have leave together. We can go to Herm taking our nephew Bern and our little nieces Anna and Clara. We will play with them on Shell Beach.'

*　　　*　　　*

"All right! All right!" screeched de Carteret. "I'll speak, I'll speak. I'll tell you what I know but for Christ's sake stop! Stop!"

"Where is it? Where is the Whisky?"

"It is not here, it has gone to Guernsey."

"Gone to Guernsey? How so?"

"By boat, the fishing boat which brought your supplies this morning."

"So. Thank you pig! And now. . .," the tourniquet was tightened one twist more. . . ., "this is just a little thank you from your countryman, the one you have betrayed."

The feldpolizist signalled to his assistant to release the cloth and untie the straps. De Carteret passed out, and fell, face down on to the table in his own vomit. To bring him round the German gently ground his face into it.

De Carteret, now free from the unbearable torture, and weakened by the ordeal, wept plaintively imploring,

"Don't say I gave him away, for God's sake don't tell."

"We tell no more than we need. We like to help our friends," said the German with a beguiling smile. "Oh and of course, needless to say, you do not know us do you? I think you fell and bruised your head, no?"

With a chuckle the feldpolizist added, "Too much Whisky perhaps?"

*   *   *

John, soldier of the victorious Reich, entered his gate. He hesitated at the front door removing his armband, placing it in his pocket.

The German band stopped playing, the sound of his marching comrades died away, his smart uniform became his best clothes once more and he became plain John Collins, forced worker for the German Occupation forces.

The acid smell of stewed tomatoes burned his nostrils as he stepped out of the light and into his dark hallway.

*   *   *

In Sark the German wound the handle of his telephone.

"Guernsey. . ., Feldpolizei!" he barked.

*   *   *

De Carteret groaned as he lay in the bushes.

Chapter Four

"My man, are you all right? My God, this is a mighty fine mess!"

The lorry driver was brought back from his momentary trap of inactivity and indecision, as he turned away from that almost unrecognisable human person inside the wreckage, to face the first of the advancing army of the human race come to take away a little of his hell.

"Quick," said another. "Don't just stand there. Turn off his ignition or we'll all go up!"

"Has anyone called an ambulance?" a voice asked.

"I'll go for help," shouted a young man, as the question was answered.

There were lights now. Many cars had stopped. Some were curious, some imbued with horror at what they saw. Some offered to help, most felt helpless. Many turned about and went on their way slowly but guiltily.

"We mustn't move him," came a decisive voice. "It's quite safe now. The ignition is off and there's no smell of petrol, thank goodness."

"We can't move him anyway. He's well and truly trapped. Has anyone gone for an ambulance yet?"

"Yes," panted a young man, "that bloke just now went off to find a 'phone."

"It's such a lonely spot," trembled a woman, "Oh, I wish they'd hurry up."

"What about you, old son?" asked a kindly helper, speaking to the lorry driver, "Won't you come and sit down in my car?"

John was unconscious now. The shattered side windows had been penetrated and the ignition switched off. With that manipulation Franz too had wandered off. His voice no longer filled the air of that nightmare forest.

In no time a police patrol car happened on the scene. The

drivers took a quick glance as they flashed colour on to John's lonely prison. One confirmed that help was on the way.

Sirens were heard and the sparks of blue grew larger and closer. Once the experienced eyes had requested the attendance of a fire engine with releasing gear, the police set about their business of organising the helpers. They released those who could no longer be of assistance, and directed the great queue of traffic which had built up at this lonely crossing on Winchester's By Pass.

*　　*　　*

It was a fine morning. John was up promptly and decided to get to work early. He wanted, if possible, to speak to Herr Tropp, in his own time, in order to make enquiries about Franz and find out where he was and when he could visit him.

John could not have been more surprised at the response of the Administrator. He had, after all, expected the German gentleman would be more than pleased that here was a person of occupied territory taking to heart their daily newspaper exhortations to brotherhood. John knew that, by asking courteously, his request to contact his new friend would be granted.

"Good morning Herr Tropp. May I please ask you something?"

"Ask," said Herr Tropp, a grandfatherly smile working his lips.

"Sir, I would like to know about Franz Müller."

"Who? Who is this man?" Herr Tropp asked.

"Franz Müller. My friend, the soldier I looked after yesterday. The one you sent to hospital."

No, Herr Tropp no longer smiled, his face lost its benevolence. He did not respond, nor did he accede to John's simple request.

Instead, this Messenger, this subjugated person, was left in no doubt that he had ideas far above his station and that to presume to be a friend of one of the occupying forces was not only socially unacceptable, it was akin to treason!

Oh yes, 'Brothers all', in the newspapers, but in real life, not so!

There was nothing for it but for him to accept that he,

and he alone, would have to seek out and find his new illegal friend and that the meeting would have to be blessed with malevolent furtiveness.

After considering all the possibilities, John decided that Franz was most likely to be at Victoria Hospital. He made up good time on one of his Messenger errands, and by a great stroke of fortune, his idea proved correct.

He brazened his way into the military hospital to seek his friend, running the gauntlet of a ward of Germans so recently mutilated by the evil and feared R.A.F.

No, Franz was not in bed, he was not even wearing bed attire. He was, in fact, to John's surprise, working in the kitchen, peeling vegetables for the meals of those less fortunate of his compatriots.

"You cannot come here!" exploded Franz. He seemed both angry and embarrassed.

"Why?" asked John, surprise and shock reducing his question to little more than a whisper.

With a mixture of emotions of fear and guilt, the young German explained to John that he had already caused him a great deal of discomfort, possibly even danger. It seemed that Herr Tropp had wasted no time and had seen to it that Franz was in no doubt that he was being un-Germanic, almost unpatriotic, to be dabbling in so called friendship with a member of an inferior conquered race.

"That's so bloody ridiculous!" protested John, who resented having to feel defensive over this whole affair. Franz let him go on for there was nothing more he could say. He was, after all, a German and to be a good German he had to be an obedient one.

"But the papers tell us you Germans are doing good things for us," tried John, "and that we are friends and brothers."

"Oh yes," agreed Franz, "but those are your papers, they are English newspapers. In our papers, in Germany, they tell us the truth about you Britishers. Our papers are very different."

"Are you saying our papers tell lies?" John asked, "for if so you're wrong! Oh, you're so wrong! Your people control our papers!"

"No," contradicted Franz, "they tell the truth. There are two truths, one for you, one for us."

"That doesn't make sense!" exclaimed John. "How can there be one truth for you and one for us, eh?"

"I do not know," replied Franz, with arrogance, "but it is so. Let us finish this silly talk please!"

John felt put down. It was the second time in the same day that he had been made to feel inferior, inferior to those he had almost adulated in all their mastery.

He did not intend his words to cut so deep and yet his hurt pride spurred him on, against his better nature.

He informed Franz that, if he was so sure of the truth and right of his superior Germany then he had better sort out himself the matter of communicating with his uncle, in the Gestapo.

This quickly reduced Franz to the low and terror stricken state in which John has first known his enemy friend. John was sorry, but it was too late. Yes, hurt pride was now satisfied, but was replaced by guilt that he had been so thoughtless and ungenerous.

At least they parted as friends, as equals once more, the master petitioning the help of the subjugated and the vanquished with the power to promise help.

*   *   *

Oh yes, it had been easy enough to promise his help to Franz but how, in practice, was it to be achieved?

At the meal table that evening John so wished he could enlist his Dad's advice but how dare he bring up the word German with his father, let alone imply friendship with one? Besides, Dad left the table early.

"A little business," he had said, to his anxious wife.

John racked his brain. His aunt had had dealings with Germans but that was only when they had been billeted on her. Besides, she hated them too.

What about their next door neighbour Betty? No, she would not do. Hadn't old Gaudion referred to her as a 'Jerry Bag', whatever that was?

Then John was inspired. Of course, Father Peters from St. Luke's! Why hadn't he thought of him before? He was bound to know. He held services, so had to get gathering permits, and his sermons were regularly scrutinised. Yes, that was the answer!

*　　*　　*

"Hello, St. Luke's Vicarage, Father Peters speaking."

"Hello Father, this is John here."

"John? John who?"

"John Collins."

With recognition, the priest launched into small talk, including John's recent absence from Mass and the possible re-opening of Boys' Club.

John was impatient.

"Father I've got a problem."

"How can I help?"

"Well Father, its about the Germans . . ."

"What about them?" barked the priest.

"I need some help Father. I have a very difficult problem concerning them . . ."

"Get off the line! Get off! Do not 'phone me about such things!"

Father Peters replaced his receiver.

That was it. John knew he had caused trouble now! Predictably, within minutes, old Gaudion was calling up the stairs to announce the priest, who despite the fast approaching curfew, had pedalled hurriedly to his errant sheep.

John accepted the Vicar's admonition about using the telephone to discuss such matters. Didn't the thoughtless youth realise that the Nazis controlled the telephone exchange as surely as they controlled the press?

When John eventually got his words in, and his confessor had calmed himself sufficiently to be able to listen, he was able to offer some degree of sympathy but did temper his advice with the words:

"Well he is only German you know?"

John could not accept this sentiment from his own priest and, for the first time in that demoralising day, found himself on the offensive.

Father Peters was forced to concur that even a German

could be a friend. Yes, even a German was one of God's children.

So, this priest, detester of the Nazis yet man of peace, had to bury his prejudices and accede to John's more worthy cause.

Already Father Peters had become a legend with his anti-German remarks and sermons so skilled that the masters could never quite fault him. Oh yes, the man was anti-German but he was honest too. He would no more accept any benefits of the black market, even when it was purloined German goods, than would he give credence to the acts of defiance, such as the resistance groups daubing 'V' signs on walls, or cutting military telephone lines.

Yes, the priest could think of a way of getting a message safely to Major Müller in the Feldpolizei. It would mean that he would have to enlist the help of one of his parishioners, and that would mean in turn, that Father Peters would have to fight his own conscience and allow himself to sink to his level. However, the alternative was to deny John and then have to justify that to turn the other cheek and help one's enemy was wrong.

By strange co-incidence, that very afternoon the priest had become party, during confessional, to a means of communication with the enemy. He had granted absolution to one of his black sheep named Philippe de Bourgonnière.

De Bourgonnière was a despicable creature who not only dabbled in the black market, to the disadvantage of the sick and the elderly, but also had dealings with the Germans themselves. Yes, he was made to feel very important with cups of coffee and cigarettes when at the Feldpolizei he was shown lists. De Bourgonnière was a collaborator and an informer. He picked out people whom he suspected had illegal wireless sets and he marked out those whom he believed to be Red.

"Red?"

"Yes, like the Labour party in England."

But what had brought de Bourgonnière to confession that very afternoon had been a cruel blackmail which had gone badly wrong, resulting in an imprisonment, a suicide and a family of children placed in the Children's Home.

Oh yes, the priest could make de Bourgonnière help, even

though the prelate's own conscience would have to pass through contortions of guilt to achieve this end.

When Father Peters left 12, Rue Marguerite, it was with the simple message in his pocket ready to type at home at the vicarage.

> 'Uncle Pieter,
>   I am in trouble. I am in Victoria
> Hospital, Mont Arrivée. Please help me.
>   Franz.'

Unfortunately his meeting with John, had made Thomas Peters late, he cycled back after curfew.

The priest was stopped, papers demanded and the draft letter observed.

It was a fortunate thing for the priest that the sentry patrol did not understand English, for his papers, including the letter, were returned to him.

They might not have understood the English draft but were sufficiently discerning to know that, to detain a man of the cloth, might cause more trouble than it was worth. The errant priest was sent on his way.

Chapter Five

As the doctor and ambulance men set about their work the fire engine arrived.

It was decided to administer morphine, for the bloodied wretch, his dark red rivulets shining and reflecting the strong lights of the rescue tender, was stirring again and his whispered grunts were becoming more of an incessant groan.

"All right," said the doctor after quick consultation with the helmeted brigade leader, "I don't think I can wait that long. If I can't get to the fellow to help alleviate his pain, we'll have a screaming wretch on our hands before you've got a hole big enough to manoeuvre him."

"Excuse me, Sir," interjected a policeman, "but the passenger window's shattered. Do you think if we cleared a bit more of the glass you might. . ."

"Exactly so," interrupted the doctor, as he picked up his bag and moved to where the fireman was already effecting this course of action.

"That's it," muttered the doctor with some satisfaction, as he smoothed down his coat and shook off jewels of broken glass. He surveyed the sagging, pallid victim, now oblivious to pain.

"Our next task is to fix up a saline drip. The fellow must be in deep shock. How long did you say it will be before we can take him?"

The question was rendered rhetorical as the doctor did not wait for an answer but turned towards his assistants. They had begun to set up the necessary equipment.

"What about his limbs?" asked the younger of the two ambulance men.

"Well, that's out of our control at present. Besides we can't get to the side which took the impact."

"Most of his bleeding looks superficial but I'll lay a dollar he's in a bad way internally. It's just damned lucky that steering wheel didn't break," added the driver.

They set about their work efficiently. The doctor wriggled repeating contorted entries through the passenger window while the cutting continued above.

From time to time John was aware of the noises as he floated with them but he did not object. It was quite pleasant really. He enjoyed looking at himself and he felt no pain. He had no more fear. At other moments he drifted away.

It was quite in order to go away and leave them to it. They knew what they were doing, and, besides, Franz had drifted away so why couldn't he take a break too?

*   *   *

Father Peters anxiously paced the aisle of the Lady Chapel. He looked at his watch, 2.30 p.m. and no sign of de Bourgonnière. He had conducted a funeral at one o'clock and had rushed back from the interment at the Foulon to be here for two. Where could he have got to? It really was too bad!

The priest had found himself guilty of rushing from the mourners with undue haste. Worse still, he had found the thoughts of this meeting with a reprehensible sinner intruding into the prayers he had made for the departed.

Father Peters was nervous about the task he had to commit to de Bourgonnière. Also he felt conscience-stricken that he was about to sell absolution to this wretch just as an unscrupulous shopkeeper would sell his last item of food to the starving, willing to pay any price.

However, he had gone through that most of the night with prayer. Prayers which had been taken over by his dreams in the turmoil of his nightmare.

For the sixth or seventh time he thrust his hand into his cassock. Yes, the crisp envelope containing the letter for Gestapo Major Pieter Müller was still there.

*   *   *

Pieter Müller slowly and deliberately undid the wrapper of his cigar. He walked purposefully across the carpeted floor of his office and stood looking out onto the Grange.

The road outside was very quiet, the mid-day rush of bicycles having subsided now.

The only persons he observed were a lady, wearing a long coat, pushing a pram with a toddler trailing behind. As he watched, one of his own sentries, smart in green with polished helmet, seen from above looking rather like a Roman gladiator, crossed the road to this little trio. Pieter had no idea what passed between them but the lady smiled and the toddler pulled at the sentry's trouser leg for attention

'Idiot,' thought the Major, 'The fool really thinks we mean it when we tell them to put on a friendly face.'

He mused on the state of discipline within the mighty German war machine and wondered where it would all end. How could that fool know a member of the occupied race well enough to evince a smile, and provoke recognition from her offspring? Major Müller had heard that some of the weaker soldiers went with these inferior women. Well, at least the infant was too old to be his.

Pieter dare not think who had fathered the mite in the pram.

'Oh well,' he thought, 'It could just be that the scum is billeted on her.'

He dismissed the idea of looking into it, for he had more important matters. Besides, he was here for a quiet time was he not? After all, he had done his part.

Pieter Müller took a very old lighter from his trouser pocket and proceeded to cup his hands to light his cigar, a rather unnecessary habit as there was no breeze, but the ways of the trenches were hard to lose.

* * *

De Bourgonnière dashed into the church. Father Peters stepped anxiously towards him.

"Sorry I am late, Sir I was called in by the Gestapo."

* * *

"Enter," sighed Müller in a bored tone. The visitor was already half way in.

"Ah yes, you have the information. Good. Sit down please."
The young Lieutenant clicked his heels, bowed slightly

then, bending his knees like an immaculately tailored piece of meccano, lowered himself on to the seat.

"Yes, Sir. Here is the information you requested on Theft Ring 15 and also on Anti-German Person 21. Which would you like first?"

*   *   *

"Called in by the Gestapo? Whatever for?" questioned Father Peters.

"Well, you're not going to believe this Sir, but you were on one of the lists. They wanted information about you!"

Father Peters heard these words as though he were far off. He had the sensation he was invisible or the words were somehow in his past. He was detached from what was taking place. In those few seconds he felt he had discovered what he had known all along but had never dared to commit to thought. He knew the worst and yet he did not dare to face up to the truth and come to terms with it. He wanted to ask de Bourgonnière what he meant, but if he did so he wanted him to say that everything was well, that he, Father Peters, was not wanted by the Gestapo, that he would not be systematically called in, that he would not have his mission to these poor helpless lost Guernsey people cut short.

"Oh," said the priest, "that does not surprise me. They seem to keep lists of most things."

He hoped Philippe would agree that this was probably the reason. Philippe, however, did not comply with Father Peters' impossible dream. With childlike innocence he divulged all he knew.

"They 'phoned me up this morning and asked if I would be so kind as to give them some assistance. The buggers are always so polite, it's a job to say no. I am sorry it made me late but I couldn't really get out of going."

"Yes, yes. Please go on, get to the point."

"Well it was just lists really, they gave me two lists. I noticed your name on one of them because it said 'Peters, Minister'. I didn't let on that I knew you."

"What was the list for? Who else was on it?" demanded Father Peters.

"Good question. I wasn't really sure. It was quite short. When I saw your name I thought I would find out so I joked and said, 'What's this lot then? Reds?' They don't laugh much, those shit! Oh sorry Father! They just said, 'Do you know anyone on this⁻list? Do any of these people speak against the German forces?' "

"So what did you say?" asked the Vicar.

"I said I don't know any of them," replied de Bourgonnière.

"Then what?"

"They just shrugged and showed me the other list."

"What was that?" demanded Father Peters, his voice beginning to sound nervous and agitated.

"Oh well, that one, they said, was a theft list and they asked me if any of the people had tried to sell me anything. I said 'no' because I'm always afraid they're after me really. They said, 'Come on Philippe, we know you are in the black market. Tell us what we want to know and we will not see you.' Well they seem quite good to me really and it is true they could shop me at any time but seem quite happy to let me go on if they can, so long as I keep them informed.

There was one man on the list, in fact they asked me about him. His name is de la Haye. I knew he was in the trade but I didn't give him away. It didn't seem right with me coming up here, to confession and all, to give him away, did it?"

"Quite so," agreed Father Peters suppressing a grimace.

"They asked me if I thought anyone on your list knew anyone on de la Haye's list but I said 'no' because, honest to God, I didn't know."

Father Peters felt almost relieved. So that was all it was. They just had him on a list because they suspected he was anti-German. Anyway, he knew that was all it could be really for he had never been involved in anything subversive. He wondered who this de la Haye could be. Probably all a mistake. The Germans had just gone off on the wrong tack in their investigation. After all, they were rather thick-headed and tied up by their own pig-headedness.

'Good, he thought, 'while they investigate me they are not spending time on others!'

*   *   *

54

"What have you got on No. 21?" drawled Pieter Müller.

"Oh yes, he is the minister," said the Lieutenant. "Nothing much really."

"Why in God's name are we wasting time on him then?" shouted Müller, thumping the table.

The young Lieutenant looked momentarily surprised but his mask quickly returned to its unquestioning nothingness.

"Well, we were watching him in the usual way, you know. He is anti-German, Sir. He has been known to ridicule our forces. These arrogant ministers think they are above the law. They think because they are next to God that they are superior to us Germans. It is good to watch because they are the sort of scum who would try to undo all the good we are doing. One has only to remember how those idiots tried to help the Jews in Austria, if you remember?"

Pieter was bored. He agreed. He was just about ready to agree to anything to get this enthusiastic fanatic out of his office. He was due to play tennis at four.

"Yes, so what is special about the pig?"

"Well it is just a little thing, but last night he had a telephone call. . ."

"Interesting. What was it, a confession from the parish virgin?"

"No, someone 'phoned and said he must talk to him about the Germans."

"Oh. Good, good! And what did he say?"

"Nothing, he hung up."

"Shit! What a waste of time!"

"No, not exactly, Sir. It was last evening at the quiet time, we got the caller's number!"

*   *   *

Father Peters handed the letter over to Philippe and gave him absolution. The priest sank into the pit of guilt and anxiety.

*   *   *

"Thank you. Please continue your investigations. I am most interested to know as much as you can find out about this priest," said Pieter. "Now, if you will excuse me, I must go."

"Before you go, would you please spare a thought to No. 15?"

"Surely it can wait? I have important business."

"Well yes, it could wait," hesitated Lieutenant Hansel, "it is just that we have him in the building now."

"Where?"

"In interrogation, Sir."

"Right, five minutes only!"

*   *   *

De la Haye had been picked up the evening before. He had been quite prepared to be roughed up immediately, feeling he could brazen it out. Better to get a few bruises then than to spend a few years in France.

He had not been touched at all that night. Nor had he slept, the bright cell light having remained on all night.

When he had dozed off at all it had been to dream of his wife. Each dream had been the same. Each dream had her biting her bottom lip so hard that it bled, the terror in her eyes making her look like her aged mother. He had left her like that.

Well, at least Collins knew they had got him, for Larry had not yet got round the corner when the door hammering had begun. At least that would give him time to get rid of the stuff before Keith cracked.

He had been questioned all morning. The same questions and statements over and over again.

"Where have you hidden it?"

"Who is your contact?"

"We know who is working with you. Why not tell us everything and accept our mercy?"

"Come Mr. de la Haye you don't want to go to France do you? You don't want to be in France when the war is over do you? You in France and your wife here?"

He had been given breakfast. The first time he had ever had cabbage soup for breakfast. He had also been given coffee, real coffee.

A cigarette had been offered, an English Players, but he

had refused saying he did not handle stolen property and did not intend to start.

That was the moment he had thought he was for it but they had just thrown him back in his windowless cell.

And now he was seated in The Chair. He had heard about it from others but had always believed it was built of imagination and exaggeration. However, here he was, feet, hands and chest securely strapped to this solid wooden armchair. He was not really quite sure what was happening to him as the door opened and Gestapo Major Müller floated in, seeming to swirl like a green mist around the bare electric light bulb.

The pain in his nose was like nothing he had ever experienced. It kept coming at him, then receding like the winter waves which crash on the rocks then drag back their captured pebbles. Back and forth came the searing pain as the pebbles were scoured across his face, a face which was all nose. A nose with pain that screamed at him as he tried not to breath. He kept passing from consciousness. The prisoner had bitten his lip too.

'You silly girl,' he told himself. 'You damn silly girl, you don't need to fret. Look at you! You've bitten your lip! Don't fret, my darling, they won't keep me. They won't send me to France. I'll be home tonight, you'll see. Your lip! Your poor lip.'

His wife bent over him, that same anguish as last night, in her eyes.

"You have broken his nose," she sobbed.

"You have broken his nose!" growled Pieter Müller in anger.

'I'm sick and tired of all this beating up,' he thought, 'I came here to Guernsey for a quiet time. Why do these stupid animals have to resist and disobey us all the time? They must know we will get our information. We have methods, they have information. It is our job to get it, we always get it. And these pigs here, little better than the English! They enjoy doing this to the scum. They should have been in the S.S., not despoiling the Feldpolizei with their perversion! And I have my tennis match at four. I am to beat the club champion!'

"How long has it been now?" asked Major Müller.

"Twenty minutes," replied the interrogator. "This one is slow."

"Will he talk by 15.30?" snapped Müller, thinking his staff car would be waiting for him.

"No, he is a long job."

"Let me speak to him. What is the shit's name?"

"De la Haye. He is a fisherman."

"Ah yes, he is the one our man 'phoned about from Sark. Let me speak to him." He signalled to the interrogation assistant to release Keith.

"De la Haye?"

"I am all right," mumbled Keith. "I'll be home tonight, you'll see."

"De la Haye, listen to me you swine. You are being spoken to by an officer of the Gestapo!"

De la Haye, finding his free arms suddenly weightless, gave a drunken salute to Pieter Müller.

"Yes, Sir," he slurred, "Yes Sir indeed!"

"Right de la Haye, you scum, you are going home to your wife now. We will come for you when we are ready. Maybe your wife would be a little more cooperative than you? You will talk! Your friend de Carteret cracked!"

He waited for de la Haye's reaction to this but there was none. De la Haye was asleep.

*   *   *

De Bourgonnière made a half salute towards the guard who shifted his boots slightly and almost smiled.

He walked straight in, up the stairs and right past Major Müller's door. He was delighted to note the door was ajar, signifying the absence of the incumbent.

Within seconds he whistled his way out of the front door, his assignment, a white rectangle left behind, propped up against the telephone.

*   *   *

Franz sat in the Feldpolizei staff car next to the chauffeur. He had not really been surprised when the nurse had told him to be ready. He had been told a car would be collecting him at 16.15 hours.

At first he had a feeling of impending doom. He felt this car could be from uncle Pieter. Worse though, it could be the S.S. coming to take him away for punishment. However, having relaxed and been tranquillised for two days at Victoria Hospital, he had rationalised that the S.S. would not have bothered to have forewarned him. They would just have burst in upon him. No, this definitely seemed more like uncle Pieter. He was always a stickler for time and could never bear to be kept waiting.

The car sped its way to St. Martin's Lawn Tennis Club. Franz enjoyed his ride as the car sped round corners and as cyclists, who found themselves in its path, hastened to dodge on to pavements.

He enjoyed the salutes, towards the Nazi flag, made by sentries.

An English policeman even saluted them and Franz realised he was in London speeding to the King's palace to receive his Iron Cross.

At the palace gates the Führer himself stepped forward to greet him.

"Franz Müller, we have no use for weaklings!"

At these harsh words the King pushed the Führer to one side.

"Do not be hard on the boy," he demanded, "it is all right for men to cry when there is good reason."

Then the Queen came and kissed him on the cheek.

"Hello, Franz," she greeted, "we have your spare bed ready for you."

"Come on uncle Franz," beseeched little Bern, "come and help me to catch some rabbits for our dinner."

"Do you want some beer Franz?" asked the King.

"Yes please," replied Franz, smiling.

The beer bottle exploded and the King became faceless.

Franz screamed.

"Come on son," said the chauffeur, "we are here!"

*　　*　　*

Major Müller was already at the St. Martin's Lawn Tennis Club when Franz arrived. He felt he belonged here. After all he was a German, therefore could not be refused. Yet he preferred to think he would have been welcome there anyway, because of his expertise and prowess at the sport. He had only to trounce Lilly Brown, the Club Secretary, to become Club Champion.

Lilly had agreed to leave the Clubroom so that Pieter could interview Franz in private. Not that she felt ordered to leave, oh no, she wouldn't countenance that sort of nonsense in her club! She had chosen, of her own free will, and told the Major so.

"Well, boy, what is all this nonsense?" demanded Pieter, indicating Father Peters' typed letter.

"Sir, I am in trouble."

"I know that, you young fool! I know all about your goings on. Do you think I'm stupid?"

Franz remained impassive as his uncle's tirade fell about him. That stern man did not wish to concern himself with his nephew's fears.

Not out of any sense of consideration to the pathetic kinship before him did Pieter announce that Franz was not to be charged with cowardice, but that his behaviour was listed as a medical condition. No, he used it to degrade the youth.

He blamed Franz's father for bringing up such a namby-pamby of a lad.

"It is obvious the man was a fool or he would not be rotting in Godforsaken Poland right now!" shouted Pieter.

That did it, it was too much for Franz. Gone now were his lethargy and apathy. How dare that man accuse his own dear father of being a fool! His father had been no coward either, if that was what uncle Pieter implied!

"How dare you speak like that about my father!" he raged. "Why are you in the Gestapo, when you could be fighting in this war?"

Pieter would not hear this, not from Franz, not from anyone! It would not be tolerated. With one mighty swing of his arm he hit Franz across the face, flooring him.

There was an unnatural silence which followed. Both

protagonists were temporarily spent. Only the sound of balls on racquets broke the deathly silence.

"I shouldn't have done that," offered Pieter, as he attempted apology. His words were rebuffed by silence as Franz picked himself up to retrieve his dignity.

Pieter realized he looked on Franz as his substitute son. It was only this creature left now to further the Müller name.

"I said I'm sorry," he coughed with embarrassment, "I should not have hit you, Franz. You are like a son to me."

Franz did not wish to be 'like a son' to this person. Ungraciously he remained silent.

Uncle Pieter further tried to explain his feelings to his silent and captive audience. He spoke of his extreme concern at Franz's illicit liaison with one of 'those inferior scum.' Oh yes, Herr Tropp was a fast worker when it came to passing news.

Major Müller was very concerned at the breach of security, perpetrated to get the letter to him, and could only think to lay the blame at the door of that 'sly Guernsey person', who felt he could, despite Herr Tropp's direct order, visit in hospital and plot with his nephew.

"Perhaps we should question him at the Feldpolizei?" queried Pieter.

"No," cried an anxious Franz, at last breaking his silence. "No, that is not necessary. He likes Germans."

"Likes Germans? Don't be ridiculous! These people can no more be trusted than the French!"

The interview ended with Major Müller adding his voice to those proscribing the friendship.

"If you get into trouble any more, I will disown you!"

Chapter Six

"You're the lorry driver, then, are you, my friend?" asked the patrol car policeman, his nervousness making him sound more stern than he knew was really necessary.

"Yes he is, poor chap," interrupted the kind old gentleman who had sat the driver in his car and given him a drink of tea from his flask.

"Don't you think, officer, you could leave the questions for now and get someone to take him up to the hospital? He must be very shocked."

The policeman acknowledged the logic of what was said but by comparison with that poor human wreck just a few yards away, the driver deserved no special treatment. He had, after all, been the weapon to cause the wound.

*   *   *

John was excited. It was the end of his first week working for the Germans and he had with him his first pay packet. He had not opened it but had saved it for Mum.

Well, his excitement was not exactly reciprocated by Frances Collins. There was no food ready. Instead, Frances was lying down with one of her sick neurotic headaches.

"What's the good of money?" she asked, as she went into a long tirade about queuing for food, and the tightening of the already meagre rations.

"Oh, come on, Mum. The Germans have at least put me on heavy workers' rations," he attempted. However, Frances was not to be that easily brought out of her depression;

"Yes, I suppose you think that's fine! Well you'll smile on the other side of your face, my lad, when you see that your precious heavy workers' bread ration has been cut too!"

"Well, what about Dad? He can usually manage a few extras, so why are you in such a state?" asked John, genuinely trying to be helpful.

"That's another thing," she retorted. "That's got to stop too! Out 'til all hours, past curfew even. No, it's all just too much. Your Auntie Rita's right!"

"Eh?" John forgot to correct himself to a more polite query.

"Auntie Rita says the St. Julian's soup kitchen is starting up again."

"So?" interrupted John, but fearing he knew what was coming next. He was right.

"Well, you can jolly well eat there at dinner time. It will save some of our coupons, that's for sure."

"Oh yes," retorted John, petulantly, "very nice too! I'm expected to eat cat and dog to save our coupons."

"Don't be so stupid!" admonished his mother. "At least you can give it a try on Monday."

*   *   *

"Welcome to St. Peter Port holiday camp," bellowed the chubby Captain, as Franz dropped his kit bag at the top of the steps leading up to his new billet.

"I am Weiss, your officer in charge while you are here," said the portly young man.

Franz saluted smartly.

"Yours to obey, Sir."

"Good, good. Now I understand you have not been well. Food poisoned in that tiny island eh? Too much eating and drinking no doubt?" He laughed at his own humour.

"Well, you won't suffer from too much of that here, my lad, and that's a fact! Will he Fritz?" The Captain shouted over his shoulder through the open door. From inside a voice, presumably Fritz's, retaliated.

"What are you complaining about now, Captain?"

"I was saying to young Franz here, he won't be suffering from overeating," then aside to Franz,

"Listen to this. He is the cook."

A good natured bawl was heard from Fritz, followed by a shower of abuse.

"Well, come in, lad, don't stand around letting the flies in. Come in and make yourself at home."

Franz stepped into what had most certainly been a large private home before the war. Large enough, he thought, to

63

house a family with servants. It was very comfortably furnished and made him feel he was going to enjoy his stay here.

"Come into my office please."

Once seated, Weiss, still beaming, and obviously enjoying the task in hand, set about inducting his new member.

"You will enjoy your stay here, my lad. There are twenty of us. Although our job is relatively pleasant, it is very responsible. It is not arduous. Now, I know you have been ill so, during this first week, at least, your duties will be with the 06.00-12.00 hours patrol. You are to understand that this is a special privilege, for it is the most popular watch. Should you be bothered by other soldiers referring to the unfairness of this arrangement, you are to say you understand you will be moving to a later patrol soon. As most of your present companions will be moving on to other duties in a week or so, they will not be any the wiser. Do you understand that?"

"Yes, Sir."

"Quite so. We would not want anyone to know we had someone in our midst who had been ill, would we?"

"No, Sir."

"Have you any questions?"

"Yes, Sir, please, Sir."

"Ask then."

"What will my duties be, Sir?"

"Ah yes. Obviously a thinking German here. We are hand-picked you know. We have a very special task. Oh yes, we are quite important here. Some of us have friends in high places. Yes, it is our duty, our honour, to guard all important places which are used by our soldiers during their leisure times. We guard the cinemas and the theatres and, although we do not make it too obvious to upset the natives, we keep an eye on the Inns where our men relax from time to time. Does that answer your question? Pleasant but responsible work. Anyway your Patrol Leader will tell you more when you go out."

"Thank you, Sir."

"Oh, and one thing more."

A grin escaped from Weiss' lips, spreading across and dimpling his greasy face.

"There is one other place we guard, which is probably of little interest to you."

He paused, hoping Franz would be curious, but there was no response.

"I said it may interest you."

Still no response.

'What a child,' thought Weiss.

"We guard the House of Pleasure."

"Oh," said Franz, "What is that, Sir?"

Weiss sniggered, thinking how he would enjoy reporting this to Fritz later on.

"Oh nothing of interest to you, boy, just the prostitutes!"

"And on the subject of prostitutes, you have probably worked out why the 06.00-12.00 patrol is so popular, eh? It gives you free time to avail yourself of the local pleasures, if you see what I mean?" He winked.

Franz did not see what he meant but gave what he considered to be a non-commital, neutral "Sir".

"My boy, it is good here. We do not spoil it by being reported associating with the riff raff, do we? If we do associate with the peasant girls we do not get seen. Do you follow me? Besides, my boy, there is no need for it, you will have lots of good friends here."

Another wink.

"Now please report to your Patrol Leader in room 7."

Chapter Seven

John was aware, once more, as they finally prized him from his prison. He heard the groan of crowbar on metal, just as he had enjoyed the cutting and pulling above. But he was detached and felt no pain at present. It was all vaguely amusing.

He should have felt guilty that he was not alongside them helping to pull and push, to lever and lift, but he did not feel this emotion. He was glad of the rest. Let them do it. he would will them to manage. He was going away for a while.

*   *   *

Mid-day break. John left the front door of La Porte, collected his bicycle from the side wall and, using the crank as a foot rest, put on his cycle clips. Then, almost as an afterthought he stopped. He put his hand on his armband, fingers under, ready to remove it, but hesitated. John changed his mind. Why should he take off his badge just because he was going to the Communal Kitchen? Why should he not be proud of his important job, working for the Germans? There would be many who would be envious of him. Besides, going to the Kitchen was not like going home. He would not meet anyone he knew.

In less than four minutes the aspiring young Hermes was in St. Julian's Avenue.

He found the Kitchen without bother. Outside was a horse and cart and at the side were several bicycles.

Wafting through the open door was a smell which was almost like food.

On the open door was pinned the menu of the day:
'Vegetable Stew with real pork fat
Price 4d. (O.A.P.s and children's portions 2½d.)
Registered Members only.
One portion only!'

As John entered the hall his ears were filled with the clatter of dishes and cutlery.

The far end of the hall was set up with benches where several Guernsey people were eating. At a table stood a little old lady ladling out steaming, watery, lumpy, soup called stew.

John joined the end of the short queue.

While waiting, he eyed the benches to decide where to sit. He half hoped he might spy someone he knew. All the trestle tables were occupied and all the occupants sat spaced well apart from the others as though jealously guarding their own portions.

John watched as some sipped the thin juice slowly. Others prodded and broke up the potatoes, carrots and turnips while others mashed the vegetables. Some seemed to be stirring and searching, listlessly possibly looking for 'the real pork fat'.

As he watched, John noticed one old man pull a small piece of bread from his jacket pocket. He slowly and deliberately wiped his bowl clean. Another picked up his bowl and licked at it.

There was an air of slowness and deliberateness in their actions. Not a soul spoke or smiled.

"Come on, sonny. Let's have your card," said the lady serving. "Oh, just a minute. I'll get my husband."

John was pulled back from his musings.

'Get my husband', he thought. 'What has he got to do with it?'

A little old country man, complete with cap, shuffled up to John. He was followed by his tiny wife, as though prompted from behind.

The old man hesitated and then said slowly, in his broken accent, "I am very sorry, Sir, for to tell you this but we don't serve members of the German forces here, Sir. Like as I says, Sir, it's not my rules. It's from your own people, from them that's at the top there."

John was not sure what was happening. He could not believe he was being addressed. This was too ridiculous to be true.

He turned to face the diners in the hall in order to elicit a response that they too thought this was ridiculous. As he turned to face his supporters the many blank stares which were focused upon him, silently turned back to their studious eating.

It was a very red-faced John, who, arm band removed, sat himself down next to a local lady.

As she got up and moved further away John heard her mutter.

"Can't understand it, how we are not allowed to wear the uniform and yet you want to wear theirs!" She was a lifelong member of the Salvation Army.

John tried to will himself to become unnoticeable. His gruel was now more tasteless than he had imagined it to be. He tasted only the bitterness of being misunderstood.

As he ate, so he thought, John was surrounded by his own people yet he ate alone. They all ate alone.

This loneliness took over his thoughts so that he felt he had always been alone and always would be. He had no friends, no companions, no interests. A nothingness and a loneliness stretched before him for an eternity. He was lonely and bored.

His mood was one of self pity. He felt he was misunderstood by his own people who were patently misguided. This following a rejection by those very Germans whom he admired.

This mood of introspection was soon broken by the appearance of a young foot soldier, smart in green, with leather straps. He walked proudly and with confidence.

John reclaimed himself from his apathy as he observed this kindred spirit.

He heard the sharp, fast, German words as food was demanded. This was followed by a replay of his own experience, with the little old country man and his wife refusing to serve.

The German said not a word but turned on his heel and marched out. Within seconds he was accompanied by four grinning comrades who followed him to the couple. All were smart, all had rifles. Two wore helmets, two pointed hats. One was older, appearing rather serious or dull. Two, in their mid-twenties, seemed of a giggly disposition rather like two silly schoolgirls who had quickly run up to join in someone else's sport. The other was young and quiet. He had a pale anxious face and dark hair. Yes, it was Franz!

The old lady removed her ladle.

The old gentleman left the room.

The soldiers set their jaws like square rat traps and faced the old lady.

The hall of customers seemed all to finish their soup at once.

All got up.

John stood up.

All the men and women started to leave.

Franz looked at John.

John looked at Franz.

Franz looked away.

The shouting began.

The old lady held on to the table.

Franz looked at John.

John smiled.

Franz looked away.

The foot soldier shook the table.

John moved towards Franz.

Two other soldiers shook the old lady.

The last of the customers left.

John stood by Franz.

Franz signified the door and left.

The old lady shouted in anger and fear.

John followed Franz.

The older German spat in the stew.

Outside, Franz stood looking at the ground.

John was aware of the dull, silent hate looks from the last of the men and women as they slowly retrieved their bicycles.

'Go away, go away all of you,' he thought, 'Why don't you hurry up and go? I want to talk with my friend. I do not want to share him with any of you. You do not understand. You hate us.'

The last man left. He looked at John. John thought he was almost smiling at him, as he wheeled past.

He spat at John's feet!

"Franz, are you well?"

"Yes. How are you?"

"I'm fine, me."

There was a long awkward pause.

"Oh Franz, I'm so glad to see you. Is everything all right? Did it work?"

"Yes." He paused, "Thank you very much." From behind John came an echo,

"Yes. Thank you very much." Then it was repeated by the second giggly German.

They went up to Franz giggling and chattering.

"Oh Franz, I'm so glad to see you." They were derisory and degenerated into fits of laughter and German chatter.

Franz looked embarrassed. He shrugged his shoulders and tried to laugh too.

John was unable to speak. Two more Germans joined the group with loud talk and guffaws. The older German went up to Franz and theatrically put his arm around him.

"My little Englander," he said. They all laughed. Franz laughed. John had to laugh.

The taller giggly one's face set hard. He did not like John to laugh with them. He put a hand on John's shoulder and, scowling into his face, pushed him away.

With that they all moved off, except Franz.

"Meet me this evening," said Franz hurriedly. "Meet me here at 19.00 hours." John had no chance to protest or agree for Franz was dragged away. All were laughing and shouting like excited schoolchildren.

*　　　*　　　*

Father Peters was waiting in the Feldkommandantur foyer when John walked in.

John's heart was in his mouth, when he saw him, thinking there must be trouble to do with the letter.

"Hello John, I'm glad you're here, I wanted to see you," said the priest. "I'm here about Boys' Club. Do you remember I told you the other night?"

"Oh yes," sighed John in relief. "When is it starting?"

"Well, that's why I'm here actually. Apparently we no longer need a permit to meet but just have to give eight days notice. So, all being well, we can meet tomorrow week. I hope you'll be along with some friends. You must all bring a friend you know. I'm going to put an advertisement in the papers too."

*　　　*　　　*

Anne de la Haye was busily fitting her mother for a costume, when the 'phone rang.

"Who could that be?" she asked.

"I don't know, my girl. There's only one way to find out, eh?" Anne had always been timid of the 'phone but was more so now that Keith had impressed on her never to make calls unless really necessary.

"Oh let's leave it, eh, Mum? They'll stop ringing eh?"

"Ah, but that's silly!" scolded her mother, taking the receiver.

"Yes, who is it?"

"Mrs de la Haye?" asked the soft, almost sugary, male voice at the other end.

"No, this is her mother. Wait, I'll get her. What do you want?"

"No. You will do," said the voice. "Just pass on a message to Mr. de la Haye please. Tell him on Friday evening to be ready, the 18th. We will call for him."

"Who's 'we'?"

"Why the Feldpolizei of course."

*　　　*　　　*

John had managed to extricate himself from the meal and had achieved his objective of leaving the house before seven. It had not been easy, especially as it was not in his nature to show such disregard for food. However, he had managed. He had had to endure self-pitying comments such as;

"Another evening alone, with you and your father both out enjoying yourselves, I suppose!" but he had tried not to rise to them.

He had been irritated at the quizzing as to where he was going and with whom. Wasn't he a fifteen year old working man now? Surely he deserved some privacy?

Frances also felt hurt that John couldn't have invited his friend round there for they could have stretched what they had. But no, Larry would have been funny about it.

"Oh you wouldn't know him, Mum," John said. "He hasn't been here before. Besides, he's a bit shy."

"Well you just see you don't get up to mischief! Don't you

go getting into trouble with any of those Germans. One's enough!" She had answered.

*   *   *

Franz was waiting, anxiously looking in all directions. When he saw John he almost ran towards him.

"Hello friend," said Franz, holding out his hand.

"Hello, friend," replied John laughing as he slapped the outstretched hand.

"This is really good," said Franz, "this is the first time we have meet since last week when we meet. What shall we do?"

"I don't really mind," answered John, having no ideas on the matter and not really caring. He was just happy to be with Franz.

"Well, you say. It is your island. You must know what there is to do."

"Let's go for a walk," suggested John.

"Yes, go for a walk, good," replied Franz. "Where?"

"I know," said John, anxious to get off the main road. "Let's go up through Candie Gardens."

They walked up through the Gardens. As soon as John got off the road and into the secluded privacy he relaxed. Franz too relaxed and removed his hat, placing it in his tunic pocket.

John asked if he was allowed to remove parts of his uniform like this and Franz laughed and slapped him saying that he was off duty. Besides, he was now in the St Peter Port holiday camp, not the S.S. punishment camp.

By the statue of Victor Hugo they rested on the grass. Franz asked questions about Victor Hugo and John was ashamed to confess he knew very little about that famous son of France.

He did however try to make his joke about Victor Hugo with his "Victor, Hugo! No you go!" but this evinced only a blank stare from Franz so that he had laboriously to explain the humour bit by bit.

"Oh yes," Franz said at last, "I see the joke. Yes, very funny, very amusing."

Not a smile passed his lips as he politely produced the sounds of laughter.

John pushed him over declaring, "You Germans have no sense of humour!"

Before he knew it Franz was on top of him and they rolled over and over in their mock fight.

"I'm hot," declared Franz as the two lay side by side perspiring and temporarily exhausted.

Franz removed his tunic top and once more they began to antagonise each other. They flicked bits of grass and daisies at each other, and let fly more friendly light punches.

This was how they passed a whole hour, an hour which to them was diminished to but minutes. The hour passed through their consciousness as night passes from the sleeper. They were aware of the sounds of time, of the chimings of clocks. They were aware of the sights of time, of the lengthening and darkening of the shadows. They were aware of the feel of time as cool grass grew cooler. Both were aware of the smells of time, as the perfumes of the grass and plantations grew stronger. But they were not aware of the length of time for their pleasure was condensed into the shortness of extremity. Both experienced the pleasure of a new-found friend, their confidence in each other then and in time to come. Both were one in the strength of their friendship.

Franz rolled to face his friend and injected seriousness into their meeting.

"My uncle says you are scum. I should not be your friend," he said.

John's face portrayed his hurt and his fear. It told Franz how he feared that this then portended the break up of that which, although so recent, was a friendship which had been signed in time to continue in perpetuity, truth its witness. Franz, cognisant of John's unspoken feelings, laid his hand on his hair and, gently smoothing added,

"But I don't care, for you are my best friend. He is an old fool. He does not understand younger people."

John took Franz by the wrists, gently preventing the combing.

"I know," he said, "My father hates Germans too and my mother is frightened of you, but we are brothers."

Time was John's currency, precious and scarce, for he was subjected to the curfew while Franz was not.

They walked from the Gardens, through the high-walled lanes of the Vauxlaurens, until they came to Les Côtils, where John proudly showed his friend the lovely view of the whole harbour and Castle Cornet, with the islands of Herm and Jethou in the near distance.

The sea was so calm that whole patches of it seemed like dark blue glass set in silver shimmering frost.

The island of Sark, further in the distance, seemed to have lifted itself up onto a plinth of white marble as it sat veiled in a smoky mist, secretive and alluring.

The fast-setting sun, which had left the friends in the cool evening shadow of the east coast, now shone on the islands of Alderney and Jersey in the far distance so that their steep cliffs, reduced by their remoteness to the thickness of carpets, glowed gold, their many indentations appearing as pencilled lines on a sketch.

"That is beautiful," whispered Franz. "So very beautiful." He replaced his hat out of respect for the scene.

"You know, John, when this war is over, I will live here and we can go to visit all those islands. We will get a boat and go first to Herm there and then to her little sister. Then we will visit that big island over there. What is it called?"

"Sark," replied John. "You will love it in Sark. It has cliffs all around and lots of pretty lanes. There are no cars there, not even before the war. The Dame won't allow them, or bitches, or doves."

"What is this bitches?" asked Franz.

"That's what we call lady dogs," answered John.

"Sometimes it's used as a swear word too. If you call someone a bitch it's very insulting."

"Oh, I see," said Franz slowly with deliberation as a smile pursed his lips.

"I see. So I could call you an English bitch then, yes?"

"No you can't!" shouted John in mock annoyance. "If you do I'll call you a Jerry Bastard. Besides you can't call men bitches, that's for women."

"So?" asked Franz with a laugh. John laughed and hit his friend once more, the short interlude ending with both boys arms across the other's shoulders as they stared out to sea.

It was like this they stood, unselfconsciously, unaware that each had a friend who was his enemy. Unaware that there was a war taking place, unaware that they, in the form of their countrymen, were killing each other at this very time.

At a slight sound from behind, Franz turned. Slowly he raised his arm from John's shoulder and gradually allowed it to take its correct vertical, soldierly position next to his leg. His whole body seemed to pull itself in from the various parts of his uniform where it had been relaxing. Without wishing to appear under duress of any sort, he almost imperceptibly changed from a uniformed civilian to a correct German soldier. He was facing his Patrol Leader, now off duty but still immaculately uniformed. The Patrol Leader was accompanied by a soldier dressed in the smart black of the S.S.

They exchanged polite brief words. Franz felt at a disadvantage.

John was unable to assist in any way but remained a witness to the uncomfortable etiquette played out before him.

The Patrol Leader looked at his watch, opened his mouth into a broad, teeth-closed, smile, then looked at his companion. A final smile was exchanged then a few words later Franz was saluted casually, this action emulated, but more smartly so, by the ebony companion.

As the two dark figures slid into the shadows and the approaching twilight, it was as though they had never been, except for the hiatus they left behind them.

Neither John nor Franz could broach the subject, as they hastened their ambulation towards John's home, with the fast approach of curfew, yet each was aware that things had been said. Franz was puzzled at what had passed and John was curious to know.

With urgency and desperation John eventually broke the silence.

"What did they say to you?"

"Who?"

"That soldier and the SS?"

"Oh them," said Franz, as though no one had been further from his thoughts. "They just say I should get my friend home quickly before curfew."

"Is that all?" asked John. "Didn't they get funny or anything?"

"Get funny? What is this, 'get funny'?"

"You know, didn't they ask about me?"

"Oh yes, they ask who you are."

"What did you say?"

"Why you ask all these questions, John?" asked Franz angrily. "You are worse than my uncle!"

"Sorry about that!" retorted John, in a hurt tone. "But I would like to know what they said, especially as they spoke about me!" Then adding as an afterthought, " and you."

Anticipating the awkward silence, which would follow, John added:

"If they spoke about me I've a right to know."

"Right to know?" emitted Franz. "Rights? You are English. You have no rights!"

It was too late, the words were out. Franz bitterly regretted their creation but the harm was done.

John too, wished he could unhear their hatefulness.

Soon they would part company but what a way to end that which had started as a good evening. Despite feeling wronged, John knew it would be he who would have to apologise. Better that than to lose his new friend.

His attempt at apology was grasped eagerly by the German and he too was contrite.

Franz told how the Patrol Leader had, instead of making predictably unpleasant remarks, on the contrary had said it was good to see some of the German army trying to make friends with the locals. He had hoped to meet them both again, before too long, perhaps in more comfortable surroundings. The S.S. had said that he also looked forward to that.

"What do you think he meant?" John asked.

"I'm not really sure. I think maybe they meant that I might be able to bring you to one of the Relaxation evenings."

"Oh. What is that?" asked John.

"Well I'm not sure, as I haven't been to one yet," replied Franz, "but I think it is a sort of club where all the men of our house meet. I think they play gramophone records. Maybe there's dancing but I not know. Perhaps they bring their girlfriends if they have any?"

"Girlfriends? How would your soldiers have girlfriends? You don't have any women in your army do you?"

"No I know but there are your girls aren't there?"

"No, no! Our girls don't go out with Germans. They get called bad names if they do."

"Ah but you are wrong! They do go out with our soldiers because I was told so by the Captain," countered Franz. "He said if we go out with them we must not be seen."

"There you are then!" retorted John.

"There I am what?" queried Franz.

"They do."

"Do what?" replied Franz.

"Oh I don't know! Let's talk about something else."

"But what better to talk about than girls?" mused Franz, preening himself.

"Have you a girlfriend got, John?"

"No," said John, while feeling that some explanation was needed, adding, "There are no girls my age left in Guernsey. Besides, we did not know any when I was at school because it was an all boys school you see."

"Yes, that was like me." said Franz. "We had no girls at my school but I will make up for that now."

"Oh yes and how will you do that if there are no girls here now?"

"You will see. Maybe we can find some older women? Perhaps we can go to the House of Pleasure? But of course you would not know about that, would you?"

John did not know and Franz, this so recently educated theoretician, took great delight in sharing his knowledge with his friend.

John still declared himself somewhat mystified by the whole concept.

"Never mind," said Franz, "we will learn as we go along, yes?"

"Yes," said John. Anything for a change of subject.

"So you will come with me to one of our Relaxations if that is what the Patrol Leader meant?"

"Maybe," was John's reply. He suddenly had an idea, it

was a good idea. Why had he not thought of it before? It was also a way of changing the conversation back on to familiar subjects.

"Franz?" he asked, "Can you come out on Tuesday evening next week? You could come to our Church Boys' Club with me."

As they approached Rue Marguerite, they were accompanied by, and passed by, increasing numbers of islanders who seemed to accelerate perceptibly by the second, as curfew's guillotine approached. John had not been out this late before. The strangeness of the normally quiet streets, now busied by increasing numbers of fast walkers, filled him with an excitement akin to walking through Town on Christmas Eve. This excitement seemed tinged with forboding so that to John he was passed by myriads of black faceless spirits all travelling together and yet all alone.

At the top of Le Febvre Street they paused. They had passed the main door of the prison and were now within sight of home. Secluded from the view of the sentry, they paused to make arrangements for their next meeting.

"I am free every evening this week," said Franz. "Shall we go out tomorrow?"

He was excited and, without waiting for John's answer, confident that it would be affirmative, added.

"You know, John, this really is like a holiday camp. Just think, a whole week and we can be free together."

"Not so free," said John. "Remember we must be careful. We don't want your uncle to know, do we?"

"Oh him! He will not see us. We do not go the places where he go. Besides, I doubt if he ever goes out to himself enjoy. He probably just works all the time. He is a party member you know? He has met the Führer."

"Well, he might see us," insisted John. "You never known, he might just be out in his car."

"Well then, you must take me the way that cars do not go, like tonight."

"OK, but what if someone like that Patrol Leader or the S.S. say anything?"

"They won't. You worry too much!"

"I'm only thinking of you," said John.

"Thank you," said Franz, "and I too am thinking of you

for if we together are seen they might stop our friendship. You are right to worry, but only just a little bit, yes? Not all the time."

"All right," replied John, with a broad smile of relief, "I'll only worry a little bit, just for you."

"Good, then what for shall we worry about tomorrow evening?"

"Well there is a good film on at the Regal tomorrow," suggested John. "It's a comedy film with James Cagney in it. It should be a real laugh. And there won't be many Germans there either as it's in English."

Franz pulled a face at this and John realised what he had said.

"Oh I didn't mean it like that, I was forgetting. . ."

"Forgetting I was German?" asked Franz with mock severity.

"Yes," replied John, "you seem so sensible!"

They both laughed.

"Well Englishman, I might forget what you are if you are not careful."

"Anyway," continued John, "I don't think the Regal is such a good idea after all because I think we'd have to book."

"Book? What is this 'book'?"

John explained.

"Ah yes, and maybe uncle Pieter would be there as it is an English film." said Franz sarcastically. "He so admires the English!"

"Well, that is where you're wrong," explained John, "It's an American film, stupid! How do you think we could get it here if it was English?"

Franz laughed. The hour chimed. "Quick," he urged, "you are out late. What shall we do tomorrow?" He then answered his own question with sudden inspiration.

"I know John. Let us go to that cinema near the Kitchen where I saw you today. What is its name? You know the one with our Führer's portrait outside."

"Oh, the Gaumont."

"Yes, that is it. There are some really good war films showing there."

"Yes I know that", replied John. "I have been, you know? But there is one problem."

"Oh yes, I know, you poor ill-educated little English boy can't understand German but we of everything think. We subtitles have for you put!"

"No, it's not that," said John, "but if we go to the Gaumont we will not be able to sit by each other. You know there is that barrier down the centre with Jerries, sorry Germans, one side and civilians the other."

"Oh yes," said Franz quite dejectedly, "I had quite forgotten that."

"Can't you come in civvies?" asked John.

"In what?"

"You know, ordinary clothes. Out of uniform. You'd be quite all right. You wouldn't have a speak. I could buy the tickets."

"Oh no, we do not ever wear anything but uniform. It is an offence. And that is your fault!"

"Why?" asked John in genuine puzzlement.

"Because, if your Commandoes capture us out of uniform they will have us shot as spies."

"Oh that is ridiculous!" shouted John. "That is a lot of nonsense!"

Franz looked hurt.

"You may think so but that is what they tell us. Those British Commandoes are animals, they do not keep to the Geneva Convention. They tie up their prisoners and cut off their heads with cheese wires. They are cowards and murderers. That is why we even wear our uniform in bed."

"You what?" asked John with a laugh of incredulity.

Franz too saw the humour of what he had just said and explained, with fits of uncontrollable mirth.

"Not all our uniform! Just parts of it. Sometimes our regulation socks or sometimes our shirts, or other things."

John too was siezed by an uncontrollable fit of mirth. Both the boys clasped each other as they gave way to their laughter. John said how he imagined Franz in bed with his pyjamas over his full uniform, his boots on in bed and hat on his pillow. Franz laughed so much that his hat fell off and he collapsed on to the pavement doubled up almost unable to breathe.

Their laughter was set like a jewel in the now silent night. Curfew was five minutes old and apart from the two of them, the streets were now deserted. Well, almost so.

As they forgot the time, indulging in their fun, a man, who all this while had been watching them from the shadows of the Royal Court plantation, stirred himself and walked slowly and silently towards them.

That he moved slowly was not surprising, that he walked silently was. That he walked at all was very surprising. It took a great effort of willpower for this stranger to approach them at all, for he was very, very drunk.

As the two humorists agreed to meet outside the Gaumont early next evening, in order to try to get seats next to each other either side of the barrier, so they both felt and then heard the intruder's presence.

It was Franz who froze first for it was he who noticed the man standing not more than three yards away in the middle of the road. He stood there swaying slightly, legs open, arms at his side. He moved fitfully backwards and forwards seemingly to no pattern or rhythm.

John turned.

"Dad!" he gasped, as Larry lurched forward trying to steady himself on Franz but ending on the cobbles, still staring at the young enemy's face.

"Dad, what . . .?" John did not get a chance to continue.

He heard the prison sentry calling out through the curfew, as his drunken father addressed Franz;

"Ple -as - ed to meet you. I'm Larry Coll - in - s," he slurred. "I'm a Guer - ns - ey don-key, me. My s-on w-as a Guer - ns - ey don-key but n-ow he's a G -er -ma -n, him. My s-on's a G -er -ma - n! A bloo - dy G - er - man!"

Already a curfew patrol was on its way, alerted by the sentry's cry. They all heard approaching jackboots on cobbles.

Before he realised what was happening John was separated from his friend, with torch flashed in his eyes, as he was roughly stood against the cold granite of the prison wall, while all around was the noise of confusion.

Not only were there Germans milling, authorative ones and those ordered, but at the call, a civilian police constable had also run out from the station. It was Bert Bisson, Uncle Bert!

As Larry was raised to his feet, Bert tried to take the heat out of the scene by offering most forcefully to deal with the wretch and take him into police cells for the night, rather than hinder the patrol in its work. John felt immense gratitude towards his uncle for this, for it spared his father from the imagined fate, the like of which he had heard on some poor drunkards in the street below his bedroom window as the night-time brutes had made their sport on them.

Bert's offer was accepted but not before those, denied their fun, tried to lift Larry in order to administer some punishment.

It was a pain-racked John who, having placed himself between Larry and the stomach aimed punch, was helped to his feet by Franz.

"Come my friend," he said, "I will take you home."

Chapter Eight

Now the victim was strapped into his stretcher. He was bobbing and rocking in long gentle sweeps as the ambulance sped him to hospital.

John was almost conscious. He could almost hear the distant siren as doctor and ambulance man worked to save him.

Not far now. Soon the craft would take its upward tilt and the engine sounds would change to greater intensity as the hill was climbed.

The police forerunner was not really necessary for few people came out at this hour to see this man. He passed by almost unnoticed.

The driver radioed. The lights kept their icy flashing glare. The doctor bit his lip as he watched the ambulance man attend the drip while dancing like a puppet. John whimpered. More morphine was needed. Would he last it out?

No screech of tyres. No skids. No crowds. No panic teams of nurses. The urgent load pulled in quietly at its bay and the alerted team efficiently and smoothly effected its work.

*   *   *

Larry awoke with a searing, flashing pain which passed through the network of nerves from his eyes and ears to his consciousness. He tried to shelter from the shaft of early morning sunlight, now forcing into his cell, where the smell of his own vomit and urine nauseated him. He just wanted to die, undisturbed.

This was not to be, however, for in marched Bert Bisson, as the door bolts expostulated, the handle groaned and yelled and the hinges screeched, while Larry tried desperately to take refuge in his cranial shelter.

It seemed that P.C. Bisson did everything twice as loud as necessary, just to torment his captive further, as he crashed down a pail and a tray of utensils as close to Larry's closed eyes as possible.

"Well now, look at you, young Collins. What sort of bloody sight do you look like?"

Larry's conversation only extended to "Bugger off!" He could not stomach Bert's witty repartee. "Just bugger off and go to hell!"

But Bert knew Larry well. He knew offence was not intended. Hadn't they both been friends when Larry, a much sought-after new boy from England, at the age of eight, had chosen Bert to be his best friend?

"I suppose you bloody well know where you are, you drunken oaf, do you?" laughed Bert.

"St. James Palace?" came the weak attempt at humour.

'He'll live,' thought P.C. Bisson. 'If he can make a corny crack like that, there's hope for him yet.'

Yes, the two had been the closest of friends. They had even walked out their first girls together. Frances had been Bert's first girl.

Well each had gone his own way. Larry had become a mechanic and Bert a policeman. Bert would probably have been a sergeant by now except that the Jerries only permitted promotion to those favourable to them. Still, Bert felt he was serving a useful role. He was able to turn a blind eye when need be and he informed his friends in lots of helpful little ways such as when searches for undeclared food were pending. By using his facilitity to be out during curfew hours he collected and passed on stolen Jerry supplies. This latter habit had been dropped of late owing to pressure from his superiors whom Bert suspected of dabbling in a similar trade, the difference being that the goods in which they traded were stolen from the civilian population's essential commodities store.

His link with Larry had not ended with the coming of the Valkyries. He knew of Larry's 'business interests', in fact he had been actively involved during the early days. He had done so partly out of frustration. Being a policeman, he had been pressured into staying at the time of evacuation so had not been able to enlist to fight the Hun. By joining with Larry he had been able, in some small way, to get back at them. Besides, it had kept alive his link with Frances. It was only in the last six months that he had withdrawn his active support, for he had sensed a big clean up was on the way. He had tried to caution Larry but he knew it was wasted effort. Larry was more stubborn than a born Guernseyman. He had trained him well.

"Right, my lad. First things first. You may not realise it, but the rules of this house state that you have to clean up your own cell before you leave."

P.C. Bert indicated the mop and pail he had so noisily clattered down near Larry's head.

Larry groaned again.

"And think yourself bloody lucky. I've brought you a cup of tea to help you come round. Well at least it's almost tea."

He handed Larry the cup of carrot tea and watched as he sipped and winced, then retched and sank back on the bare bench bed.

"What's happening?" asked Larry beginning to recover a little of his zest for life, a little of his constant fear creeping into his consciousness once more.

"To tell you the truth mate, I don't really know," was Bert's reply. "You'll probably go off to court later and just get a fine. At best ten marks, at worst a week in jug. But then there's a waiting list for the prison so you wouldn't get taken in straight away."

"Thanks very much," replied Larry, "that's all I need!"

"I should think a fine or a week inside is the least of your worries," added Bert.

"What do you mean by that?" Larry's face contorted itself into a mask of fear.

Bert, realising he must have hit a nerve, that Larry, although uncertain, must at least suspect what was coming, suddenly felt terribly sorry for his friend. His friend who seemed to have changed from a happy-go-lucky, carefree, confident fellow the last time he had seen him, to the rather care-worn, broken creature he now was. The whole impression was heightened by a mighty hangover.

"Come on, Larry, let's face it, you must know you're a wanted man. It's only a question of time."

"What do you mean?" asked Larry, playing through his act to the point of insulting the very last person he need try to deceive. "Come on, tell me what you know!" His voice was almost a desperate plea.

"Don't worry, old son. It's nothing to worry about. Forget it." ...

"Forget it? Forget it? How can I forget it when you come out with half a story like that? Come on, tell me what you know. What's happening?"

Bert wished he had kept his mouth shut but it was too late now. He had said sufficient to get Larry really worried. He had better tell him all he knew, for to leave him in only half a state of conjecture, where he would fill in the missing parts with hysterical imaginings, was probably far worse than to tell him what he knew. At least if he told him Larry would be prepared and better able to cope with eventualities.

"Look, all I know is you're on one of their lists. You know what they are for their damn lists. It might not mean anything."

Larry let out a long steady breath, almost a sigh of relief. It was not the relief of being spared, but more the relief of, at last, being discovered, for now he could be himself again. At least, while they let him.

Quite calmly Larry asked, "Come on Bert, you don't believe that for a minute do you?"

"No," admitted P.C. Bisson. "The only thing that surprises me is that you'd be mixed up in subversion. Black market yes, but in with that lot, no. You're a dark horse, that's for sure."

"Subversion! What do you mean subversion?"

"Come on, you don't need to put on an act with me," was Biss's reply. "This isn't a blasted interrogation you know!"

"I know, I know, but what the hell do you mean by subversion? Trading yes, but mixed up in that other, no. That's a mug's game."

"Well all I know," explained Bert, "is that we've been asked to check our records and make investigations about you and any connections you might have with Father Peters . . ."

"Father Peters! Father Peters! I haven't had any dealings with him. He's so straight I doubt he'd buy a tomato without surrendering a ration coupon!" shouted Larry.

"O.K., O.K.," replied Bert. "It's not the trading they're interested in with him. They're just after all contacts made with the priest. I think they're gunning for him."

"Well I hardly know the man. I haven't been to church for months," said Larry. "So they're wrong. They can't tar me with anything there."

"They can do what they like and you know it. They'll say black is white if it suits them. There must be something in it for them to go to all this trouble."

Larry was temporarily relieved to feel the Germans must have made a mistake, for he had never had dealings with Father Peters. Despite what Bert said, he felt the Germans were tolerably fair. They liked to stick to the rules and rubber stamp their decisions in legally constituted courts. He felt, if they took him to court on some error, it would come out and he would be acquitted. He had known of guilty people who had bluffed their way with the Gestapo and had actually got acquitted in court. Besides, he felt it would not even get that far if they were working on a misconception. They did not like to be made to look stupid, especially by a court operated by the occupied.

"No, this is too ridiculous for words!" exclaimed Larry. "What sort of reasons do they have for assuming such a thing?"

Bert was clearly uneasy. "Look, Larry, I shouldn't be telling all this so damn well keep it under your hat. They picked up a telephone call from your house to Father Peters. Last week I think."

"Well it certainly wasn't me," insisted Larry. "It was probably the wife or the boy. They're the church-goers."

"Whoever it was," continued P.C. Bisson, "said he had some information about the Germans."

"No, they've got it all wrong. We don't talk about those pigs in our house, let alone think about them."

"Well, your boy obviously doesn't mind them does he?" asked Bert.

"What do you mean by that?" said Larry defensively.

"Oh come on now! You saw him last night with that young Jerry."

"Oh yes," replied Larry rather vaguely for his memory of last night was also somewhat vague.

"Anyway," said Biss, trying to bring the conversation to a close. "You just watch that young John. He's playing with fire mixing with them. And you watch yourself too, my lad. I'd cut my activities right down if I were you."

As Bert left the cell he called, "I'll try to find out what's happening and let you know later. Do you want me to tell Frances you're O.K.? You never know, I might be just in time for some bacon and eggs." They both laughed at the ridiculous fantasy.

*   *   *

When old Mr. Gaudion called up the stairs, Frances' heart missed a beat. She knew he must be announcing a visitor. He really was a nosey old man, he never missed a soul.

Ever since last night, when John and Franz had told her Larry's fate, she had waited this announcement.

Over and over in her mind, had turned her thoughts. Larry was in prison, he had been sent to France, he was held incommunicado. They were beating him and mocking him. He had fallen, hit his head, and was no more.

In the early hours' fantasy of Frances' troubled night, the S.S. had come and battered down Gaudion's front door and, holding her at revolver point, had ripped their home apart. And all for what? Because Larry had been out after curfew? Or were there more sinister motives?

All these thoughts had been on her mind as she had waited for the knocking or the hammering and kicking on the door. All this had been on her mind when she had watched John leave for work only minutes before. She had wondered if she would ever see him or Larry again. And now the knock had come and she had missed it.

Bert came into the room forcing his mask into a reassuring smile.

"Oh Bert!" she gasped. "Oh Bert I thought you were . . ."

"I know, Frances," said Bert cutting her short. "I know, but he's all right, honestly. I have just come round to tell you he's fine."

As Bert spoke, Frances stepped hesitantly towards him not knowing whether to remain apart and be the formal friend with this friend of Larry's, or to let him take over and gentle her down a bit as she remembered so well he could.

"I didn't think you were Larry," she whispered. "I thought you were them."

She did not know whether to laugh or cry. She did not know if she should laugh at Bert's mistake or cry at her own misery, now that she had an understanding soul who would comfort her. She did both. As she bit her finger-nails the tears welled into her eyes so that they became big and clear, holding the tears, preventing them from running. She cried in anguish while her face smiled, filling her pools of salt water with light.

She stood like this and waited for Bert to bring her back into time.

"Frances, Frances, my darling," said Bert as he took her to him, "it's not that bad. Nothing is ever so bad that you should have to cry." He was filled with tenderness as she pressed against him.

Frances had been his first love. He could feel her naked body now, as she pressed against him, as she became part of him. They were both transported back over the years to their youth when the world was theirs and they had been each other's. They both now thought the same thoughts, allowing their senses to detach from the present and spread open the pages of the book of nostalgia. A book which, once opened, can take for itself a tiny particle of time and expand it into eternity. Time present has a strange characteristic of taking this book and re-writing its pages to recall and exaggerate only those events which are pleasing to it, forgetting and diminishing those which are not.

So with Frances and Bert they now forgot, in time present, all that was hurting them, and in time past, all that had caused them pain. They no longer thought of Larry present or Larry past, Larry in prison, Larry the Sir Galahad who had captivated and captured Lady Guinevere. Bert no longer missed his Maggie evacuated far off in England.

They both remembered those heady afternoons spent on the cliffs. Both felt the soft cool of the green springy grass underneath. They breathed the perfumes of the gorse and the heather. Both heard the plaintive cry of the gulls and the chirping of the grasshoppers. As they stood there, locked in each other's arms, they felt the warmth of the sun, with the breeze on their cheeks. Bert and Frances felt that powerful burning ache of their youth.

It was that ache which Bert now suppressed. This self-denial transported him through time and space from youth to his present course which was inevitably to become worthless, lonely and utterly divested of pleasure. He forced himself back to the present to be the loyal friend of Larry now in the cells, needing his help.

Frances had also returned from her journey, refreshed by her emotions. Her confidence was restored in human nature. She trusted Bert's wisdom, explicitly breathing her words of relief.

As they sat either side of the kitchen table, celebrating their new-found faith in the future, indulging themselves in past memories and revelling that they still had feeling for each other but proud that they had both remained faithful, they celebrated with a pot of real tea.

"Larry got this quarter for only a pound," she explained.

"Very nice too," acknowledged Bert. "Half a week's wages for half a year inside."

"Oh!" said Frances. "I forgot you're a policeman."

They both laughed.

They all three laughed as Larry joined them.

"Wotcher!" said Larry, as Frances, flying to him, almost dropped the pot of precious brew. "You nearly spilt two weeks of my freedom."

They all laughed with enforced gaiety.

Bert felt frustrated that his friend had arrived then, yet this emotion was mixed with concern for Larry. It was not like the Germans to arrange the release, so unconditionally, of any fish who happened to swim into their net.

However, Bert kept his forebodings to himself. Far better to tell the re-united couple of his other concern:

Before leaving the station that morning, Bert had read the report of the incident at St. Julian's Communal Kitchen. John had been implicated, along with five soldiers of the Reich. It was recommended that the Germans should deal with their recalcitrants, whereas the offending local should be severely reprimanded.

Bert had taken it upon himself to carry out the instruction

so that John's name should not be linked with his father, who was currently under investigation.

"I don't think the Chief will have any reason to associate the two names," explained Bert. "Besides, I think he's OK, he's one of us at heart. That's probably why the Gestapo don't involve him too much."

The main thing was to keep John within the law. It would be far too dangerous, at present, for him to get taken to court.

Larry admonished Frances for being too lax with the boy and for encouraging his liaison with the enemy.

Frances felt that was unfair and expressed that it was a father's place to see that his son behaved himself. Only recently Mrs. Philips had reported seeing John proudly strutting along, displaying his German arm band. Surely it was Larry's place to put a stop to that?

"Anyway," retorted Frances, "they're not all bad, these Jerries, you know?"

"What d'you mean?" asked Larry.

"Well, that young friend of his did see him safely home last night after he'd been hit trying to protect you."

"What?" declared Larry, incredulously. "You mean that German came to our door, with Gaudion and all?"

*   *   *

The gaffawing Rudolph no longer laughed, nor did his friend Helmut. Each was silent as they packed their kit bags. Neither dare speak a word in case the emotion should sound in their voices.

They could still hear the stinging tones of Captain Weiss reverberating in their ears from just minutes before.

They were well and truly punished for their episode in St. Julian's Kitchen. They were posted to either end of Guernsey's south-facing cliffs. Fifteen kilometres apart might as well have been fifteen thousand. Packing their kit bags now was probably the last thing they would ever do together. Oh it was beastly!

Then it was Franz's turn. He was dealt with separately, after all the other recalcitrants had received their justice.

"No doubt you are anxiously awaiting a holiday on the

cliffs, with some excitement from the British naval bombard-
ment and Commando raids?" asked the convivial Captain,
as Patrol Leader Morten leered. Franz remained silent. The
Captain scowled.

"Müller, you do not like it here? Am I correct?"

"Sir?" asked Franz, puzzled. He liked this place well
enough.

"I said you do not like being in the Town Patrol," explained
the Captain, glancing at Patrol Leader Morten.

"You prefer to keep the company of civilians rather than
your fellow countrymen, so I hear."

Franz did not have a chance to reply, not that he felt he
could have framed a suitable answer.

"Well, young man, as you so detest it here then your
punishment in this affair will be to stay here. . ."

Franz was not sure if he heard correctly. Did this mean
that he was not to be banished to some outpost? Was he to
be able to continue to meet his new friend?

The Patrol Leader, of last night's shadowy encounter,
grinned his whitest, as the Captain continued.

"You like it so much, Müller, that when you are not on
duty you are to be confined to the discipline of this house,
unless your Patrol Leader decides otherwise."

So, Franz was to be spared his posting but had no possible
way of meeting John this evening, as arranged.

"Perhaps," said Patrol Leader Morten, once the two had
left their senior's office, "your friend might like to join us at
our Relaxation this evening? Then he would not feel you
had let him down."

*   *   *

It was the second evening in succession that John had
upset his mother and left without his meal. However, whereas
last night she had not known of his plans, now she was fired
with anxiety that he was going to meet 'that German.'

"He's not 'that German'!" John stormed. "He is Franz."

"John, you'll be the death of us!"

"Don't be so silly, Mum," he had patronised, as he made
his way out, despite her protestations.

"They'll say you're a collaborator and it will put your poor father in prison."

*　　*　　*

John waited outside the Gaumont. There was no sign of Franz in the military queue.

The programme looked quite good.

'The Battle of the Atlantic (Heroism of Germany's Navy). In German-English subtitles. Also full supporting programme. Mickey Mouse and Berlin Newsreel.'

As both the military queue and the much shorter civilian line moved towards the entrance, John was anxiously scrutinising all the German faces and looking up and down the Avenue.

Local girls were enjoying the whistles and remarks made by Germany's heroes, while some of the older generation, with no sense of fun, were muttering and clicking their tongues at such a disgraceful display, especially when one young girl accepted a proffered cigarette, repaying its donor with a friendly smile.

Officers arrived by staff car. No queuing for them, no smiles either, just stiff and starchy dummy-like salutes.

Still no Franz. The civilian queue had gone now. John was confronted by the Commissionaire.

"Are you going in, sir? Door closes in five minutes." John said he'd only be a moment. Why was Franz so late? Could he possibly have got the wrong day? Maybe he was already inside, sitting on the German side of the cinema? Perhaps John had missed him? Surely not?

Then, just as John decided to go in anyway, a familiar figure hurried into sight. It was not Franz though, it was his father, striding with anger.

Well at least, Larry was relieved his son was going in alone.

"If you must go and watch that Jerry rubbish," he conceded in annoyance, "at least make sure you're straight home after, as all three of us need to have a serious talk."

John's reply, as he extricated himself from his father's

company, was unintentionally, more stinging than he intended;

"OK, Dad. That's if you're back from the pub."

* * *

He got into the main hall just as the German Anthem played to announce the start of the performance. There was a mighty clatter of seats as the loyal officers and men of the Führer's victorious forces raised themselves to attention as one man.

John stood there straight and smart, as he listened to the joyful voices, from the packed side of the auditorium, singing the glory of their Fatherland.

On his side John noticed the sparsely-filled seats with Guernsey people here and there slouched over the seats in front. Some had heads bent, others legs apart. A few nonchalantly looked at the ceiling or turned to regard the walls. Anywhere but at the vibrant swastika and marching smartness distorted onto the curtains like a colourful waterfall. Some even spoke during the anthem while others raised themselves with exaggerated slowness in the hope that the ordeal would be over before they had to compromise themselves.

There was a group of young men near the front, who had remained seated but were now struggling upwards as a guard approached them rifle butt held forward.

'It's a jolly good thing they have the anthem at the beginning,' thought John. 'If it was at the end, half this ignorant lot would walk out. I bet they'd soon enough stand smartly to attention if it was God Save the King. Why can't they have a bit of respect? If they don't like the Germans, well at least they should be grateful to them for providing exciting and educational films.'

John enjoyed the Mickey Mouse film. The whole cinema was in uproar, both Germans and civilians forgetting their differences and indulging in amusement. It was so much appreciated that it was shown for a second time.

The Berlin newsreel film was completely in German. It showed the full glory and might of Herr Hitler's victorious forces. At every scene showing the devastation of British cities, and the advances made against the Bolsheviks, there would be sporadic clapping from the German side of the cinema.

One shot showed a British warship. At this there was a jubilant shout from the civilian side of the rail, followed by some half-hearted cheering and clapping. The locals were damned seconds later when the same warship was shown in all its devastation. It was the Germans' turn to stamp their feet. John sensed, in the darkness, the Germans all directed their gaze towards the small group of misguided patriots who had so prematurely made a laughing stock of themselves.

Someone near the front of the cinema stood up and started waving his arms in the air, shouting. John could see his silhouette against the black and white background of the Luftwaffe. There were German bombers accompanied by their insect-like fighter planes as they purged England's cities of all that was evil. He could hear the fellow shouting above the roar of the aircraft engines and the hisses and profanities directed his way from the occupiers. He could not make out his words.

The film sound died as strings of bombs were seeded above Manchester, above Liverpool, on to Rochdale. There was a deadly silence all the better to set off the sound of explosion as they hit the cities below, as surely they must. During the pause the whole of the German audience settled themselves as though listening to the poor deluded man in his tirade against his masters.

His voice could be heard as the first bombs targeted; "Bastards, bastards. . ." erased by the sound of explosions. The screen changed to silent cartoon with comic figures of English people flying through the air.

". . .our children, our little ones. . ."
In bold print, 'MANCHESTER,' superimposed on the screen.

". . . .murderous bullies. . ."
Another explosion. Green and yellow people thrown into the air with arms and legs and decapitated bodies raining comically down.

". . .Hitler, I say. . ."
An explosion of colour on the screen with comic multicoloured points. This followed by,
'ROCHDALE,' accompanied by a huge rumble of explosion

as though to hammer on the already demoralised civilians. The firework display was over.

'Rochdale,' thought John. 'Hell, that's where the Intermediate School is. That's where my friends were evacuated. How could they do that to Rochdale? What have we done to be treated like this? We're not hurting them, we give no trouble!'

As the interval lights came up he watched the two guards rushing down the aisle and trampling across feet, as they made their way, like determined tortoises, towards the man who had allowed his feelings to take over.

John's mind was in utter confusion as he watched helplessly while they kicked and punched the man. He saw his father, blood streaming from his nose, hands held across his face, head bent forward, staggering, now pulled, now pushed. He watched smiling Franz, as he punished his poor father. He heard the cries of protest from his fellow Guernseymen. He heard his mother sobbing and pleading for the brutality to stop.

He heard his aunt weeping. Even old Mr. Gaudion was imploring them to stop as the poor man was hustled away.

John became aware of the white sea of smiling Aryan faces who had enjoyed the spectacle. They all looked like Franz. All had terrible hate in their smiles!

John closed his eyes as this crowd of abusive men was jostled past his row. This crowd became his poor father again, as his poor father became the unknown stranger with the bloodied nose. The stranger who had tried to stop the bombing of his loved ones.

Where was Franz? He should have seen the bad things done in the name of his war. Where was he? He should have been here to help his friend who now felt so sick.

*   *   *

Franz, confined to barracks and feeling rather miserable, having finished his meagre meal, was ordered to do the company's washing up. He did not mind too much for he felt he might as well do this as get to the Relaxation Evening too early, for he was not particularly looking forward to it. By now he would have been with John and he felt very bad at having let his friend down. However, he knew John would understand if only he could know the reason.

That Patrol Leader seemed quite a decent fellow really. He had given Franz some helpful advice that if he appeared more friendly to his fellow compatriots, the Captain would soon permit him to go out into the town again.

"Do you remember last night, Franz," asked the Patrol Leader, "when I met you out with your friend?"

Franz nodded.

"Do you remember my friend was with me?"

"You mean the S.S.?" Franz replied.

"Well yes, but I don't normally think of him as such. He is really a nice fellow, you know? His name is David of all things!" The Patrol Leader laughed at the irony, "But of course he is not a Jew!"

"Of course," Franz replied.

"Well, what I was saying was that David, who is on leave from Alderney, rather took to your friend and said how good it would be if you two came along to one of our Relaxations."

"Yes, you said," replied Franz.

"Well, why not make the best of a bad job? This evening, you come along to the Relaxation with me. You have to anyway, Weiss has as good as ordered it. Besides, once he sees you really mixing in well I think I can persuade the Captain to take you off confinement."

"Oh, could you really?" Franz gave way to his excitement.

"Yes, I think so, but of course it all depends how friendly you are into the bargain, if you know what I mean?"

Franz did not know, but to be friendly was to be friendly so there seemed to be no problem.

It took little persuasion for Franz to agree that S.S. David Huffmeier should get the message of invitation to John.

*   *   *

During the interval, when the Aryan side of the auditorium was addressed by one of their officers, the civilians sat quite still, subdued by the recent incident.

John waited for the main picture to start, hoping it would be soon.

He was startled when a girl from further along his row touched his arm and said;

"Here mate, your friend over there wants to speak to you." She could hardly contain her mirth, as she imparted this message, covering her mouth to prevent her splutterings of hilarity, while pointing in the general direction of the German side.

John, who had been completely taken by surprise, reacted with puzzlement.

"Eh? What did you say?"

"Your friend, 'im over there, 'im with the black uniform." Again she giggled and laughed.

John looked in the direction to which she pointed. Just the other side of the rail he saw a smart soldier in dark uniform isolated from the rest of his crowded compatriots by a sea of vacant seats.

The man was looking John's way. He had a broad smile which was the same colour as his water flattened hair. Realising John had at last received the message, he slowly, almost hesitantly, raised his hand in greeting.

John was aware of a second girl looking his way. She was also laughing. He did not know this man but the man seemed to know him. The girl who had passed on the message started her clumsy return towards the dividing rail, casually asking as she went, "You funny or something, mate?"

John blushed to the roots of his blonde hair. He felt the whole of the civilian side must be penetrating him with their eyes and thoughts. He heard their thoughts. 'Is he funny or something?'

The man stood up. There was something familiar about his slim smart stance. 'I know him,' thought John, 'but how? Where have I seen him before?'

The man signalled to John to go to the foyer now, to meet him. The wave of his hand was familiar. Where had he seen that wave before?'

The lights began to fade. John was glad of this twilight to hide his blushing. Then he remembered! It had been twilight last night when, out with Franz, they had met the Patrol Leader and the S.S. soldier. Of course, it was that S.S. who had spoken to Franz last night!

The recall of Franz suddenly filled him with consternation.

He felt disappointment and betrayal. Franz had let him down this evening. He felt anger that Franz's people had attacked his loved ones who had evacuated to Lancashire. He felt degraded that they had forced the islanders to watch their own destruction.

At the same time John wanted Franz to be with him. He needed him to look after him, to tell him it was all right, that he, Franz, was not like that. He needed Franz to explain that the German people were basically good, that it was just a few who did these evil things and that the rest were all right really. The German people were still the friends of the British and still needed them as cousins to help build that better world. Better world? With bombs and broken bodies? With punching and kicking?

John had to know Franz was still his friend, unchanged. He wanted to talk with him. He needed to walk with him. He wanted to be with him. Franz seemed to be the only real German left at this moment. Franz had taken him home and looked after him last night. Franz had not punched him. Franz had not taken his father to the police station, or just now beaten that poor man who had shouted in anger, at the destruction of his children.

"If you're going, sonny, then go. If not, sit down, the picture's starting", came a voice from behind.

John stumbled his way to the foyer.

* * *

Franz opened the panelled door of what must once have been the family drawing room.

He had to take two steps down into this Aladdin's cave. Melodious sounds of singing came to him from a gramophone somewhere in the room. There was the sweet smell of cigar smoke in his nostrils, momentarily transporting him back to those happy Christmas days of his childhood, when his poor father would unwrap such luxuries and pour out glasses of Yuletide brandy.

The room was spacious. The large carpet was rich and colourful like that at the farmhouse where his parents had worked. The furniture was old and dark and still showed signs of the polishing received from the now long-absent parlour maids.

Through the haze of perfumed smoke and nostalgia he heard the contented voices of several of his countrymen. Looking around the room he saw several men engaged in activities. Some he knew, such as Captain Weiss, Fritz the cook, and the Patrol Leader. Others he had seen before but knew not their names as they were on different patrols.

Two men sat playing chess. A small group played cards, looking very serious. One man sat by himself reading. Two were by the gramophone sorting through a pile of records.

Captain Weiss sat on a sofa with a civilian while the Patrol Leader stood speaking to them. Fritz was busy pouring out drinks at an open cabinet.

No one showed any interest in Franz's entry. One or two looked up, then continued with their preoccupations.

Franz who, not long before, had eaten his elegant sufficiency of bean soup, a slice of mutton and a ladle full of turnip and carrot, found his whole consciousness drawn to the large table set in the centre of the room. On it were all manner of delights. There were salads with lettuce, radishes and eggs. He had not had an egg since his fifteenth birthday. A plate was piled high with sausage rolls, another with portions of roast chicken. There were white bread rolls with pats of real butter, bowls of coleslaw and potato salad. Several dishes of plums and peaches were displayed there. There was also a large fruit cake!

Franz could not believe his poor hungry eyes.

*   *   *

Keith de la Haye picked up his bowl and licked the last remains of his cabbage soup before starting on his main course. As he slowly cut into the yellow lump of woody swede, weeping on his large plate, he looked up at Anne and gave her a reassuring smile.

"Here's to your mum," he said. "It's thanks to her we're eating at all tonight."

Anne's mother had given them the cabbage and swede from her own stock as Keith was now without income. His boat had been impounded by the Germans and his licence withdrawn.

When he thought of all the goods that had passed through his hands in recent months it bothered Keith to feel too frightened to go out to collect some now.

"I'd never have dreamed that we'd be too poor to even afford our bread ration," he said.

"That's all right, my love" replied Anne gently.

"It won't always be like this. Dad gets paid tomorrow and he's promised to help out."

Keith did not like to be 'helped out'. It hurt his pride. But then his pride was not as painful as his poor nose. He still had to pay the doctor, and the hospital, for treating his injuries. Heaven knew what he would need them for after next Friday's session with the Gestapo. He was almost out of aspirin too.

*   *   *

"You are John Collins, yes?" enquired the S.S., his lisp filtering through the clamp smile.

"Yes," replied John neither feeling the need, nor the inclination, to elaborate his answer.

"We meet last night, no?"

"Yes," came John's rather surly affirmation.

"You are to come with me please. You are to come to meet your friend Müller, Franz Müller."

John had not only been embarrassed by the method of this S.S.'s communication minutes before, but he was also still feeling confused and angry at the way the Germans had deliberately made him watch the destruction of Great Britain. Especially he who had admired them so and was ready to put himself at their service in the quest for the freedom of the world. He did not feel inclined to be ordered by this person of the master race.

"I'm watching a film," he replied firmly.

David did not quite understand the logic of that statement. To him it was quite obvious that John had been watching a film but now it was equally apparent that he was going to stop watching it and accompany him for he, David Hüffmeier, was a member of the S.S. To request someone to do something was to order it. His request was the velvet glove hiding the iron fist.

"You are to come with me. It has to be!"

"I am not. I've paid for my seat here and intend to use it."

David Hüffmeier was taken aback. He would have frowned if it had been possible. It is very difficult however for one with an angelic baby face to frown to any effect.

He thought how wilful this boy was, how stubborn. What a challenge! He had come across his like before. In Germany one look, one word, and the young boys obeyed him, for he was the S.S. He was Hitler's chosen man, was he not? He had never felt his power to be ineffective. This was a new experience, coming across one so young who had such a mind and will of his own.

He wondered how to handle this predicament. He knew he could use force, for such action would be thought quite legitimate owing to his uniform. He did not want to alienate this beautiful John though.

It would have been different if he had been a mere Jew. David had a particularly good reputation where Jews were concerned. He had to have with a name like his. He had to prove, contrary to his Hebrew label, he hated them as much as the next man or even more. He felt he had established his point with his comrades and was no longer teased by them in that regard.

"Your friend wishes with you to speak."

"Then why didn't he come like we arranged?"

"Ah yes, why?" Hüffmeier hesitated. "I think he had something more important."

"More important? I like that! We had an arrangement. He could have told me!"

"My dear boy, he is telling you! That is why I am here."

There seemed some logic in this quick-witted, or perhaps accidentally apt reply of Hüffmeier's. John in his very confused state seemed almost ready to concur.

"Well where is he? If I come, what is happening?"

*   *   *

"Come in. Come in boy!" ordered Weiss, with a laugh, as he saw Franz standing there mesmerised by the sight of the feast. The Patrol Leader straightened himself up and, stepping towards Franz, said.

"Come over here, Franz. I have someone for you to meet."

Franz moved forward and the Patrol Leader put his arm across his shoulder, guiding him towards the civilian seated with the Captain.

"Jules, I would like you to meet Franz. He is our youngest, but quite a little man really."

He affectionately tousled Franz's hair.

"Franz, this is Jules. He is a Parisian."

Franz looked down at Jules while extending his hand. Jules remained seated as he condescendingly put out his limp soft fingers with long, carefully manicured nails. He seemed aged about twenty but it was difficult to tell really, for his face appeared smooth like a woman's. He had long eye-lashes curtaining very sleepy, pale eyes. His hair was quite long and almost girlish with its curls. Jules wore a mauve silk shirt open at the neck, showing his lily-white chest. He wore tight slacks and delicate kid leather shoes. On his right wrist he wore a gold bangle.

Franz neither liked the look of him, nor the cool clammy smoothness of his hand as it allowed itself a limp shake. There was a most unusual smell emitting from this pretty creature. Franz thought it to be some type of perfume but felt sure he must be mistaken for these days, with all the war effort, Germany's matrons rarely indulged themselves, let alone men. Men? This creature was not a German so possibly it accounted for it. But then, of course, John and his father were not German either, but at least they looked and smelled and behaved like men.

Jules, his sleepy eyes still fixed on Franz, took his cigarette in its long black holder. He placed it between his lips, took in a long draw, then casually and deliberately exhaled a cloud of smoke into Franz's face.

Jules permitted a delicate smile to break open his china facade while observing Franz's annoyance.

"Sit down my dear," he implored in his musical voice, heavy with French accent. He took Franz's wrist and pulled him down between himself and Captain Weiss. "I have been much looking forward to meeting you."

"I'll get us some drinks," said Weiss, raising himself.

"Morten, you sit here with our two young friends while I'm gone," he instructed, addressing the Patrol Leader.

So there sat Franz, or rather froze Franz in all his affronted innocence, a pretty flower on his right and a clinging vine on his left.

Franz did not know what was expected of him, so with an aim of righteous indignation and of being the world's most hard-done-by citizen, resolved to do nothing at all.

He decided that, as he was required to be there, so he would be. Join in and enjoy himself, however, he would not.

So there he sat counting the minutes until he could excuse himself and go to bed.

Weiss returned with the Schnapps. Franz refused on principle. He was then all but ordered to drink. As a lever to his resolve it was suggested that he would not enjoy his food later on in the evening if he did not first lubricate his throat. And the food did look very good!

The second glass of Schnapps went down far more easily than the first. Jules was no bother really. All seemed more tolerable once Franz got used to the perfume and the arm resting lightly across his shoulders.

After the third drink, even Morten the Patrol Leader seemed less of a nuisance. Franz found he was quite comfortable, wedged in between the two. The music from the gramophone records was invigorating while the laughter from various parts of the room became quite infectious. He caught himself laughing at jokes he did not understand but for some reason everything began to seem very hilarious and enjoyable. He did not much like the way Morten kept rubbing his thigh and he picked up the rough vice-like hand to remove it a few times. But after several Schnapps it seemed very heavy and hardly worth the effort.

So there he sat. The two on either side decided to play cards, managing to do so quite well with Franz as a screen. From time to time Morten would nudge Franz to show him a particularly good hand and Franz would dutifully show his pleasure.

Those dreaded long minutes of an evening which had

earlier stretched before him portending to be an ordeal, now began to slip away faster and faster. Schnapps followed Schnapps to lubricate his throat. Each drink made the prospect of the next seem more desirable.

To young Franz the room became a sphere with him at the centre and all the activities revolving round him. There were Jules and Morten still playing cards, Morten with his hand still rubbing his thigh and Jules caressing his shoulders. They seemed by turns to sip their Schnapps while Jules took frequent puffs of his inexhaustible supply of French cigarettes.

Franz felt it was not he they were fussing over. He could no longer feel their touch or the sense of annoyance at their familiarity for he felt outside it all, as an observer.

The next circle of consciousness was Weiss, who seemed continuously to drift in and out of view, always smoking his cigar, always laughing contagiously. He regularly topped up Franz's drink from the cut-glass decanter which appeared to be part of his uniform.

The further circles of consciousness were those of the noises. There was the music and the laughter and the stamping of feet with the bawdy singing.

Then, in the far reaches of Franz's consciousness, so far away it seemed that they bordered on the edges of the universe itself, on the merger from consciousness to unconsciousness, were the shady and blurred creatures and objects of the outer circle. From time to time Franz could make out these hazy figures. He thought he could see people standing, or were they sitting? He imagined he could see people walking, or perhaps running? He believed he could see men fighting together, or were they dancing? He was not sure. They came in and out of focus like the view through a camera lens. The only thing which seemed real to him, in his inebriated state, was the way all the concentric circles of his consciousness were revolving, each moving in the opposite direction to the other, yet strangely, as though braked by external forces, jerkily pulled back to their correct relationships. Everything was moving and Franz looked on immobile, his own body now as heavy as lead.

He sat there, held the prisoner of a thousand gravities, everything unreal. The food they brought him was unreal. As he greedily bit into the sausage rolls they disappeared.

As he swallowed the salad he felt its coolness but tasted nothing. When his face became wet with the juice of peaches and plums he tasted nothing. As the stollen mutilated his countenance and broke into fresh crumbs there was no aroma. As he ate, his hunger did not abate. All the time he wanted more. Always, it seemed, there was a hand extended holding out yet more food. More food, more food! He had never eaten such a feast and yet he was only the observer, for the Franz eating was not him.

He looked down at the Franz seated between his two unlikely friends and observed his battle-soiled uniform with its marshes of coleslaw, its bunkers of chicken bones, its trenches of peach skins and its mine-fields of stollen crumbs.

*   *   *

It was this sight which greeted John as he followed S.S. Hüffmeier down the steps into the noisy, hot and smoky drawing room.

John immediately located Franz. He saw him with his food-soiled uniform and his leaden arms weighted on to the adjoining knees of Morten and Jules. He saw Franz with his vacant, drunken stare and inane open mouth. He observed him being cuddled by the bangled arm of the sparkling Jules. Franz was lying back, his thigh being caressed by the jubilant Morten.

Morten saw David and John as they came across the room towards them. He shook Franz and informed him that his friend was there. Without seeing him properly, Franz was sufficiently temporarily revived, by the sound of his friend's name, to struggle to his feet to greet him. As he raised himself from his comfortable prison, so Jules prevented his freedom, pulling him back. Franz fell back lying half on the sofa and partly across Jules. He lost his resolve, he forgot his mission. John was lost to him. Jules allowed him to settle where he had landed, sprawled across his bosom, an unloving lover in a lover's pose. Jules cupped Franz's head between his two delicate hands and like one used to performing, took this Communion Chalice raising it to his lips. He took Franz's face and kissed his lips. Franz was asleep.

John, unaware that Franz was now asleep, and an unwilling party to all this action, was cut through by what he observed. He saw the room filled with cigar smoke, its sounds and alcohol, as alien. He saw the food and heard the music and laughter and singing as foreign. He heard the voices and saw the uniforms as abhorrent. Above all, he saw Franz as alien, as an enemy. He now understood what his parents had been trying to tell him. He realised his friend was his enemy, that everything about him was wrong.

It was true, his father hated them with good cause, for they were brutal and careless of people's feelings. His mother was right to fear them, for they were unpredictable.

All evening John had been trying to make excuses for Franz and his race. He had told himself that Franz had probably let him down in the cause of duty. Yet here he was, all the time, eating and drinking like some very rich person from before the war.

When he had watched the bombs fall on Rochdale John had been able to tell himself that it was all wrong, 'Just propaganda', as dad would say. He had reassured himself that Franz was not like that, that Franz was a good and pure German who lived up to the true ideals of his Fatherland. Now here he was wasting his time and letting his friend down by behaving like this!

Why was be behaving so? Why was he so dirty, so drunken and debauched? Who were those men? Why was that sickly-looking Patrol Leader fussing over him so? Why was he so familiar with Franz. Franz was nothing to him, just one of his soldiers. He was too young to be the Patrol Leader's friend and too subordinate for him to be so familiar. Why then did he allow this person to be touching his leg? What was the reason for such behaviour? And why was Franz lying sprawled across that other person, that fellow dressed like a young girl, with his silky blouse and tight slacks? What was going on? Why was the creature kissing him?

With all these angry, unanswered questions racing in his mind he turned upon his heel and, before S.S. David Hüffmeier realised what was happening, had left the party.

He rushed from the room and was outside the house before he heard David's voice as insignificant background to his crude nightmare. As he rushed up past the police station, neither sure whether he was walking or running, awake or asleep, he heard the plaintive voice of the S.S. as background only.

"Wait John! Wait I tell you. . . . Wait!. . . . please!"

The cry was not part of him, it was all unreal. He was in a dream or nightmare. He knew he had only to will himself awake to find it was not true, that his innermost fears and realisations were only figments of his troubled imagination. He could not wake however.

The journey home, although several minutes, was insignificant to the trauma in his mind.

He crashed through the front door and up the stairs.

Chapter Nine

"Yes that's right," said the policeman, "thank you for that. I'll take the lorry driver up to the hospital now, shall I? We can take his statement later."

Operation control affirmed while the duty clerk set about the routine registration enquiry with Swansea.

*   *   *

John was awake now, at least he thought he was, but perhaps he was just dreaming he was awake? Where was he? This must be the hospital. Perhaps it was the mortuary? Perhaps he was dead? Well, there was a fine thought! It made him smile.

Well, he could be dead, couldn't he? He could feel nothing. He was not even sure if he could hear properly or see properly either. He thought he could but he was not sure.

What sounds should he put to his surroundings? Should he allow the crashing and smashing and grinding and groaning that he had somewhere in his dead mind? Should he replace all those jerky persons, ghosted in white, for the moving and churning, buckling and tearing, shattering and cascading of strong yet fallible materials?

Could he smell anything? Did he smell the unmistakable hospital smell or was it hot rubber, oil, steaming anti-freeze or violated tarmacadam? Could he smell and feel and taste his own blood and vomit?

Shouldn't Franz be there somewhere? Hadn't they found him? John should have been concerned and anxious, frightened at his own plight and the conjectured demise of his friend, found after so long a search and so cruelly removed. Yet he felt none of these emotions. It was all too much effort. Far better to lie back and enjoy all the attention and to smile at the world.

As he left them all, John was smiling at them. Well, he thought he smiled but he was not too sure. They didn't smile back that was for sure, but what did that matter?

He was off now to find Franz.

*   *   *

When Franz awoke it was already daylight. He knew he was in his own bed, and that the room was his, but he could not think why he was there or how long he had been in it. What day was it? What was the time? He seemed temporarily to have no memory. No memory, or projections into the future, apart from a nagging foreboding that things were not right.

The other beds in the small room were empty. They appeared to have been made up but unused. Could it be the middle of the day?

He was in his nightshirt. He still had on his socks. How strange! His nightshirt was on back to front.

'Where are my clothes?' he thought. He looked around the room. The sunlight was penetrating the window. It must be mid-morning for the sun was never through when he left on 06.00 patrol. 06.00 Patrol? 'Should I be on patrol?' he thought. 'The others must have gone. That's it, they must have gone off and left me. Why have they left me? Am I ill again?' He considered the hypothesis. Was he ill? He was not sure. He did not feel too good. His stomach ached as though he had been retching but, except for a slight headache, he felt fine, apart from the light hurting his eyes a bit.

He sat up. The square rectangle of light which was the window, turned black. Franz became dizzy and began to feel sick. As he lay back down in his bed the whole room began to spin round him. He closed his eyes. Then he felt his bed tilting vertically. He clung on for fear of crashing to his death.

His memory now flooded through the temporary dykes of amnesia. The spinning of the room brought back the previous evening. As he clung to his horse-hair mattress he remembered Jules.

'They must have put me to bed,' he thought.

Franz wanted to vomit. His whole body became hot and clammy. As he threw off all the covers, to lie back on the bed, he heard hissing in his ears. Everything was very clear now. The beds were empty because his comrades had been banished to the cliffs. He, Franz, was the only one spared. He had been the only one to be subjected to last evening's ordeal.

Besides the physical discomfort, Franz was aware that he was worried. He could not decide exactly what was disturbing him but he felt there was something left undone, still needing his attention. Something was causing him anxiety but he could not remember what.

Lying there, his attention focused on a crushed concentration of blue on his pillow. It had once been a hydrangea. It must have been put there by that obnoxious, perfumed Frenchman. Franz felt the sickness welling up in his throat. He picked up the flower and, crushing it still more, fumbled his way to the open window from which he hurled it, to be followed by his own vomit as he disgorged himself of all that was vile from the previous evening.

It was, as Franz purged himself of this depravity, that he remembered his friend John. His floods of guilt took over. He could now picture his friend standing there in the drawing room, mouth open, aghast at the sight of him, disgusting Franz. John had stood shocked, Franz clearly remembered that.

From that moment Franz recalled nothing but falling back to his captors and then the deep oblivious sleep.

Where was John now? What had happened to him? What must he have thought? What must he now be thinking of him, Franz?

*   *   *

When John got to the office he was not in the best of moods. He had not slept at all well last night, his sleep having been disturbed by nightmares in which he and Franz had been chased by the effeminate civilian and the leering Patrol Leader. His parents had been in his night escapades also, with his father thumping the table in the petulant manner of Herr Tropp. His mother had implored them not to get involved with such people.

He had watched the bombs dropping on England and, as the cartoon bodies had been hurled into the air, had seen on them the faces of his school friends long since gone. Strangely

also, Franz's face had been there. As he had stood on the
Côtils watching the cinema screen, which was stretched out
between the islands, he had been joined by David Hüffmeier
who had sidled up to him and put his arm across his
shoulder. He had been unable to move as the iron like
fingers had walked over his body with spidery deliberation.
In his dream he had become Franz squeezed in there between
the two obnoxious men. He had watched John Collins rush
out of the room and up the deserted cobbled streets. D :⁴
Hüffmeier had followed john and had hammered on the
door which had been shut in his face. He had watched as
the door opened and old Mr. Gaudion had looked out to
enquire about the noise. Old Gaudion had been shouting in
protest about the bombing of his family in Rochdale. Two
sentries had stepped out from the shadows of the prison
walls and punched and kicked the old man and dragged him
away bruised and bleeding. All the while S.S. David Hüffmeier
had been laughing. His laughter had echoed horribly backwards and forwards between the walls of the prison and the
tall old houses on the other side of the Rue Margeurite.
There had been a devilish, evil persistence about that laugh
as it had disturbed John's whole night.

Last night it had been apparent to both his parents that
John was distressed. As his father had sat talking with him,
while the youth had drunk a hot drink in bed, it had all
come out. Larry had been sympathetic and concerned. He
had feared for Franz and had warned his own son not to get
involved in these 'men's things.'

Yes, such things were awful. How could Franz allow
himself to become involved in it? No, John was determined
not to get involved. But what if poor Franz was unhappy
though? He had no father to warn him. Besides, if John did
not have Franz as a friend, who was there? Franz was his
only friend. No, John could not be the friend of such a
depraved person. Yet, he so hoped Franz would be safe.

* * *

And now this morning at Larry's insistence, John applied
for a new back tyre.

"You use up your tyre working for the buggers, so let

them sort it out," he had said. Larry was not prepared to 'find' one for his son to do Jerries' work!

To his surprise, once John had sorted out his day's deliveries, Herr Tropp, the Administrator, issued him with a requisition for a new tyre. As easy as that!

He was admonished for his aparent lack of gratitude, told how, as a mere civilian, he should be grateful to the military government in France, and reminded,

"Remember you British have lost the war!"

"May I go please?" John controlled himself to reply.

"May I go!" echoed Herr Tropp, in his irritating manner of repeating every statement of John's which he felt to be controversial.

"You may not! When I am ready for you to go I will inform you! Young man, you have a lot to learn. You seem to be lacking in discipline. What you should have had was a good German education. One thing you must learn in life is to respect your betters. You do not ask. You are told. Do you understand?"

John was quite bemused and really did not know to what Herr Tropp was referring. In his manner he stood there looking and feeling rather blank. His mind was miles from the office as he cycled in the leafy, grass-banked, lanes of St. Andrew's and St. Saviour's. He dreamed of the sun shining on the hedgerows, of the birds singing in the trees, the delicate sparkling streams chattering over stones at the sides of the lanes. He could see little granite cottages nestled into high earth banks, cottages with old ladies weeding the flower gardens. He was passing old farms with their sweet and pungent smells and their churned up yards, bent old barn roofs of heavy red tiles and rusted corrugated iron. He could see ducks and chickens in the yards and could hear the pigs snuffling in their cool grey sties of granite with little openings like castle windows. He could see the orange and white quilted cows all staked out neatly in the fields, all turning to watch him curiously as he cycled by. Up on the hills were rows and rows of greenhouses of the vineries, now and then catching the sun, as he rode by, trying with all their concentrated power to dazzle him. He was passing cheerful whistling men and smiling singing women as they managed their daily labours. All were happy. There was not a German in sight, not even a sentry post. There was no war, no Occupation, in John's fantasy.

"I ask you if you understand?" reiterated Herr Tropp.

"Yes," answered John, having forgotten what Herr Tropp was talking about.

"Then if you understand, why do you not act accordingly?"

"Eh?" asked John, quickly correcting himself. "Pardon?"

"Are you attending to me, boy? I find your manner quite deplorable! I am seriously thinking of having you moved. This morning you arrive nine minutes and forty-three seconds late. I am watch you. To make matters worse you did not seem at all worried. You just take your time with in coming. Then, when Frau Bormann told you about it, I understand you are very rude. . ."

"Very rude?" exclaimed John. "How was I rude?"

"Frau Bormann tells me everything. She said you just your shoulders shrug!"

"What did she need to tell you that for?" interrupted John. "Surely a fellow can shrug his shoulders. What's rude about that may I ask?"

"There you go again. Rude again!" ejaculated Herr Tropp, beginning to get very petulant, waving his arms around like a rebellious windmill.

"That's two times you have interrupt me now! What Frau Bormann does is nothing with you to do but what you do is everything to do with her. Just remember, Collins, that while you have the honour for the Reich to work, you will be closely scrutinised all the time. There is nothing that you do that my attention will miss. I will not. . . ."

"What do you. . . ." John started, his sense of indignation getting the better of his puzzlement. John's outburst was in turn cut short by the near hysterical Herr Tropp.
The German stamped both feet in turn.

"There you go again! Get out! Get out of this office!"

He looked so comical stamping his feet like a thwarted angry infant. John was confused and frightened by this outburst so that he could not prevent a nervous smile as he made his way to the door, only too glad to leave.

"Where do you think you are going?" boomed Herr Tropp.

"You told me to leave," said John, by now very nervous and wishing himself elsewhere.

"Go? Nobody told you to go! Wait here until I have finished! Stand straight when I am speaking to you!"

John stood his straightest.

"This other form," continued the Administrator, indicating a piece of printed grey paper. "This will stop your laziness."

"Laziness?"

The paper was thrust at John.

"Yes that is what I said. You are very lazy, very slack. You are to complete this form every day."

John looked at the form. It had columns titled in German. There were total lines at the bottom.

"What is it?" asked John in amazement.

"That, young man, is your time sheet. You are to complete the time of leaving whenever you go with a message."

He stubbed his finger at the place.

"And here is where you write out your time of return. I personally will look at this sheet to ensure you are not slacking like you were this morning."

"But that is ridiculous," said John. "What is it supposed to show?"

"It will show me that you are fully employed."

"But what if I am delayed anywhere?" asked John, feeling panic that somehow Herr Tropp had learned of his devious visit to the hospital.

"If you are delayed you must the time make up. I think that way you soon ensure that you are not delayed."

He looked at John. He could tell from the youth's shocked expression that the message had sunk home. He decided to follow up with a definitive admonition.

"If you do not take notice of this, my friend, you will yourself find extreme trouble. No more for you the pleasant rides into the countryside wasting our tyre resources. Oh no! For you it will be the concrete mixing for the Atlantic Wall and staying overnight in the camps with the Russians and the Poles."

He sneered as he mentioned the foreign nationals adding as a final warning.

"We know how to deal with those who lie and deceive and refuse to obey orders!"

John was now sure he knew about Franz and himself. He was too frightened to say anything but stood there at school once more just hoping the bell would ring, signifying the end of the French lesson, before Mr. Le Pelley could pounce on him.

*   *   *

Franz had spent almost half an hour trying to get up out of bed, but every attempt had been thwarted by bouts of dizziness with swarms of black dots coming up over his vision like a vast army of disturbed ants. He had desperately wanted to relieve himself but knew that if he had reached the door he could neither have attained the lavatory nor have got back to his bed before passing out, or vomiting, or both.

He was now making his sixth or seventh attempt. He reached the door, turned the knob, took a deep breath and felt reasonably steady. He knew that he had reached the point of no return. From now on he was going to be all right. Today was a new day, the past was gone and forgotten.

Cautiously he stepped from his large plain bedroom, with its unused beds like waiting coffins. On now to the wide, carpeted landing with its polished ebony banisters, affording a view of the entrance parlour through the low hung chandelier. He walked straight into Morten, the Patrol Leader.

Franz's reflex action was to step backwards almost in the pose of a cringe. Morten was solemn. He looked Franz up and down and pulled a face, sour with disgust, at the sight of this weakling of a boy still in his nightshirt at eight o'clock in the morning.

"I was just coming to get you, Müller," he said. "Why weren't you on Patrol line up at 06.00 this morning, eh?"

Franz could not think of an excuse. The day, which at last looked as though it might start living once more, was now taking a decided turn for the worst. If he could only have made it to the lavatory without being asked irrelevant questions.

"Excuse me Sir, I must get to the lavatory please. . . ."

He went to lurch forward. Morten stepped in his way. Franz looked up into the creased face, its solemn expression now contorted by a smile. It was a cruel smile, a smile which said.

'Suffer. I want you to suffer a bit!'

Although Franz had never suffered at the hands of another who deliberately enjoyed the prospect, he felt that now was to be his first experience. His mind, already opened up and scoured by the events of the past twelve hours, not least by the surfeit of alcohol, accepted the unknown which he felt was about to come. His acceptance was expressed by the questioning expression on his face as he fought the army of black dots devouring Morten's lower half. He saw Morten's torso slide over the miriad aliens. He lunged forward into the gap afforded by Morten's movement, at the same time pushing his hands forwards and sideways to brush aside the black fog. All the while he thought.

'The lavatory, I must make the lavatory. I must not be sick here. Not here!'

With a harsh chuckle the Patrol Leader grabbed the tottering Franz's outstretched arms. The lad's forward momentum, and the clasped hands, pivotted him round giddily like a large pair of compasses so that he collided with the banister. He looked once more into Morten's cold smile. The Patrol Leader's teeth appeared as flashing knives seeking a victim.

The only question Franz could manage was a whispered. "Why?" as he thought. 'This man seemed so much to want me as his friend last night and now he wants only to hurt me. Why? Why?'

"Why what, Franz?" came Morten's cold reply. Franz was incapable of answering but waited for release with the patience of one who expects nothing.

"Well, my little Franz, you are in a bad way this morning, aren't you?" said Morten with a chuckle. "I think maybe you should go to the lavatory. Then, when you return, you and I will have a little chat, yes?"

Franz moved once more, only to be prevented by Morten again. He resigned himself deciding if this was how it had to be then so be it. The cat, however was only playing with its mouse and let it go again. There would be plenty of time for playing.

*   *   *

Larry was a car mechanic by trade but with the advent of the Occupation, and all its stringent war-time measures imposed by the master race, he had found himself without the wherewithal to ply his skills. There was very little call for car mechanics in a community whose cars had all been requisitioned by the military authorities for one pound each, or where the fortunate influential few had been able to keep their vehicles on condition they were placed on blocks to preserve their tyres against such times as they might be graciously accepted by the Teutons.

When his job had looked likely to cease to exist, Larry had had to make a rapid decision. He had been faced with staying where he was and then becoming unemployed, or of finding different employment before this happened. He had reasoned that it was better to look for a new job before becoming unemployed, feeling there was a stigma attached to seeking work once one became unemployed. Unemployment was an experience he had never sampled and which he felt he never would. He considered himself to be a worker. To be a non-worker was anathema.

Larry's resolve had been strengthened by a rumour that the Germans would be looking for skilled men to work for them. Logic had suggested that they, efficient as they appeared to be in every regard, would like water, take the easiest course and would first fill their vacancies from the unemployment list. He had determined not to become a name on any such register.

That was why he was now a bicycle mechanic, working in the very shop, where he had learnt that same trade, upon leaving school aged thirteen.

It was a wise choice of employment. He was good at his job. With bicycles being the only means of transport for the islanders, he was unlikely to find himself out of work. Not only did he have more than enough work, to keep him fully employed, but also, he was virtually his own boss. The old man who had taught him his trade all those years before was quite contented to sit confidently back and leave Larry in charge. The owner's son was not mechanically minded, so, apart from doing some of the clerical work and accounts which Larry was pleased to lose, interfered little in the running of the shop.

There were certain restrictions on him, outside his control, such as being compelled by law to attend to the bicycle of a

German before that of a civilian. The letter of the law was that Germans must not be kept waiting in any shop or at any place of service. The law had been brought about in the early weeks of the Occupation because, like Larry, many shopkeepers, had taken great delight in keeping the Germans waiting while the locals were served. Larry was amused when he thought of what an admission of defeat for the policy of brotherhood between the two nations, this passing of the law had been.

Even now he was able to use the law to his advantage. He would make subtle hints to the Germans that he would need additional payments, in cigarettes or sweets, if he was to do their work, not only quickly, but satisfactorily. The law made no mention of the quality of work or service.

Another restriction was the almost complete dearth of replacement parts. Not only that tyres were almost non-existent but all the other things from wheels and frames to spokes and ball bearings. It was true, the States, Guernsey's government, was able to send trade deputations to France from time to time to try to purchase essential supplies, but the upheaval of the evacuation, when half the population had disappeared virtually overnight, had had a devastating effect on the economy with no Mother Britain to help out. The French authorities were often reluctant to trade with a tiny country whose currency was based on vague promises of British backing at the end of the war. The French authorities were rather dubious about the eventual outcome of that war, too. Not only these considerations but they were also very much depleted of supplies for their own consumption. It was mainly through the kindly intervention of the conquerors that the French were persuaded to part with anything at all.

So it was, in this atmosphere of goodwill all round, that the French were able to speed the machinery of trade, as appropriate to their enjoyment of the relationship, and at the rate of their bureaucratic machine.

The States of Guernsey Essential Supplies and Commodities Committee had to draw up lists of priorities. They had to weigh up the relative importance between luxury foods such as flour and potatoes, and extravagances such as shoes and warm clothes for the winter. Between coal used for the winter fires and the production of meagre gas supplies and oil for the generators to provide light and to pump and purify the water and dispose of the sewage. Between sugar for making jams for the winter and seed for the land for the coming spring. Between the occasional rations of meat, chocolate and medical supplies, and parts for bicycles. How did these men make their impossible decisions? How could they decide it was better to have bread and vegetables to keep the population sustained than to replace the worn-out shoes and to clothe the hunger-sapped bodies from the cold easterly winds of the winter? How could they cut off the gas supplies, as the only means of cooking the meagre rations, in order to purify the water and dispose of sewage to prevent epidemics? How did they decide whether people should have coal for their winter fires or sugar to keep them healthy? How did they decide whether bicycle parts should be purchased so that the men could get to work, or meat and medical supplies to keep the population alive?

Their task wasn't helped by the recalcitrance of the French Authorities who understandably, while wishing to comply with German orders, resented losing their commodities.

In consequence, and using the expensive and elaborate French black market, a little of everything was purchased so that no one was over-fed and few had warm clothes. Gas, electricity and water had to be severely rationed to the point almost of non-existence. Instances of neighbours sharing ovens to save gas were now quite commonplace. A coal fire was a luxury saved for the weekends, with resort to early bed being the alternative. Sugar and chocolate rations were very rare, while meatless weeks were becoming the norm.

In addition to scarcity at source, there were the taxes made by French pilferers in the Docks, where the supply ships were often delayed for several weeks. There was also the Royal Air Force and Royal Navy sport on these pathetic cargoes. The Germans would make great propaganda from supplies lost owing to British attack. It hurt too to learn of whole cargoes having to be condemned as unfit for human consumption owing to delays by French bureaucracy.

Understandably, therefore, Larry received few spare bicycle parts. Necessity became the mother of invention while the black market thrived. Larry knew the best way to stuff hosepipe for the most comfortable ride, just as he had friends who knew how to fashion boots out of German lorry tyres or clogs from logs. Each to his own trade.

Right from the start Larry could see the potential for black market trade at his place of work. Not only did be have the opportunity for contact with large numbers of islanders, and for fleecing the German forces, but, probably far more important, a place of work which afforded privacy for his discussions, business transactions, and the temporary storage of supplies.

Like most Guernsey people of the time, he had started in a very modest way, using barter as a means of getting the extras which were not afforded by official rations. In the early days his 'business' was quite legal for it was permitted to sell one's services, or even parts, in exchange for the odd few eggs or a skein of wool. In those days Larry found that, not only was he able to help out the family rations by taking home part of his wages as food, but that people began to use him as a go-between. Old Mr. de Garis would come in and say, "Try to exchange this bag of wheat for some white linen! My wife needs white linen."

Larry would effect the transactions and either have a pound of wheat or a yard of material for his trouble and all parties would be satisfied. Or Mrs. Deveaux would say, "I have killed a pig. Can you get rid of some pork in exchange for some dried fruit or some tea for me?"

"Leave it with me," would be Larry's reply. A few days later he would be on the telephone to her, "I have sold your red material for you."

Things had gone well for several months. It was surprising to see, during the first winter, how much tinned and dried food, hastily hoarded away the previous summer before the invasion, suddenly began to emerge as its owners decided that as nice as it might be to have two dozen tins of corned beef or five pounds of tea, wouldn't it be nice to have a bar of soap or a new gas mantel or a drop of Scotch? So Larry had provided an essential service.

As the first months passed, the Germans worked rapidly through their priority lists. They proscribed non-existent Jewish activities. Performances of music, by composers from countries allied to Great Britain, were banned. The Boy

Scouts, Salvation Army and Free Masons became illegal societies. The communication systems and news media were controlled. Supplies were requisitioned from civilian shops and warehouses, the goods being paid for in good German paper money. When the civilian legislature had protested against the requisition of the whole butter supply the Germans had generously promised to replace the same with pork fat should the need ever arise. They were to be the arbiters of when it should be deemed necessary.

As the German Bureaucratic Machinery became established, so grew their pressure on the States of Guernsey, for the listing of all hoarded supplies plus restrictions on their sale. In their wisdom the masters used the puppet government to call in all non-perishable supplies. The whole procedure was a modern day Domesday list but on a smaller scale.

The restrictions came in piecemeal, with maximum and minimum prices for most commodities. Then the inspectors and boards were set up. There were the milk yield inspectors, the potato board and the various other controlling bodies. All crops grown in private gardens had to be handed to the authorities, just a small percentage being retained by the gardener with the right to purchase seed the following spring, should any be available.

It became illegal for farmers to slaughter animals. Frequent armed searches of private residences became the order of the day. Many examples were made of black marketeers. The prison began to fill and the birch was taken down from the wall.

Along with the privations of the depressed community came the inevitable petty jealousies. Mrs. Davey would learn that Mrs. Brehaut had held back part of her potato crop. She would telephone the board. Mr. Bougourd, unable to persuade Mr. McCormack to part with some of his hoarded tea, would write an anonymous letter to the Gestapo Headquarters. There were some vigilant postmen who would, when possible, steam open hand addressed letters to the Germans in order to warn people. However, letters and information still got through, and raids and searches were made. When they did not act immediately the Germans would open files and add to lists. They had no rush, for time was theirs to manipulate. Even the anonymous informers and collaborators were not immune, for the masters would often ask the accused if they recognised the anonymous handwriting. They liked to keep lists of their friends as well as their enemies.

It was in this atmosphere of bitterness and distrust that Larry continued to operate and provide his service while his legality was rapidly eroded as is a sand fortress at high tide.

By the end of the first year of European Unity the inhabitants of Guernsey had almost stopped visiting each other's homes. People who continued to socialise gave such prior notice that the host could adequately hide anything controversial from sight.

The few remaining children were constantly told not to talk to anyone about their families and they were discouraged from bringing anyone home.

Women no longer 'phoned each other for a chat or gossip. Men no longer discussed the B.B.C. news they had heard on their sometimes legal, sometimes illegal, wirelesses. The innocent question, 'Have you heard the latest on the Eastern Front?' would be greeted by a cool rebuff of incredulity.

People no longer dared be observed talking to the Germans and only replied to them with curt answers. Even people who had Germans compulsorily billeted on them with the choice: 'Take in this man or leave your house completely', had to resist the attempts at friendly advances, for fears of neighbours denouncing them. Young girls, whose only crime was to have fallen in love with the young foe, were ostracized and their parents became social outcasts, the prey of the malicious letters. Such is hunger and distrust, such is the result of a deliberate policy of divide and rule. A policy with the respectable motto of 'Brothers all'.

Larry had seen the writing on the wall some months earlier and had begun to curtail his activities accordingly. He had decided that his family might not get so many luxuries such as soap and tea and wool for knitting or tins of pilchards or corned beef. Better that than lose the bread-winner.

It had hurt Larry to have to suggest to John that he resort to the Germans to replace his tyre. He could easily have manipulated his stocks to help out his own son but he was only too aware that someone would have noticed and might have denounced him. Far better for his son to get a tyre legally. How he wished be could have explained to John but he had dared not. The fewer who were aware of the consortium the better.

Consortium? Last March Larry had been seriously considering curtailing his barter trade, which was rapidly becoming illegal black market 'Crimes against the Community'. He received an anonymous letter.

The letter invited him to join a group of like minded enthusiasts to distribute and sell goods taken from the Germans. It explained and coerced by suggesting that, not only were there good rewards of material supplies in such activities, but also they had the added advantage of helping the civilian population and weakening the resources of the Occupation forces.

Larry had needed little persuasion and had written off by return, using the somewhat devious and theatrical method of communication at his disposal. He had, in fact, been severely reprimanded by the group's organiser for appearing so willing.

"What if I had been from German Intelligence when I first wrote to you? You must always use extreme caution in all your dealings," he had been told.

It was true, the consortium was cloaked in secrecy and, even to this day Larry did not know who the organiser was. For all he knew, the organiser could actually be from German Intelligence.

Larry considered a lot of the cloak and dagger secrecy in communication and contacts, with codes and changing meeting places, contingency and dissolution plans, to be unnecessary. In a small community, despite the best organisation possible, he knew most of the contacts he had dealt with, by sight at least, if not by name.

Larry knew Keith de la Haye from his school days. Keith, a younger boy, had always been the hardy, sporty, outdoor type. He was popular with everyone and well known. Larry had been extremely worried since last week, when Keith had been arrested. He had felt it was just a matter of time before he too would hear the night time banging on the door. These were the worries which had driven him to drink and made him so unbearably irritable with his family. He did not really think his nerves could take much more of it. He had felt so bad, at one stage, that he had almost contemplated giving himself up to get it over with. He had reasoned, however, that it would not be as simple as that, for the Germans would want information out of him and he would be forced to provide names.

'Poor Keith must have gone though it,' he thought. He wondered how Keith could give names of people he did not know. Then he supposed that he, Larry Collins, was one of the names he could divulge when the going got too bad. His anxiety started all over again.

Last night, when he had just nipped into the *Golden Lion* for a quick pint of cider, Larry had heard that Keith was out again and that his face looked an awful sight. No one had really wanted to talk about it much and Larry had really had to drag out the information. In his nervous state he had wondered if they were holding back their information because they were talking to him, Larry Collins. Maybe they all knew something he did not? Perhaps they felt Keith had been arrested because of him? Maybe they felt he was really a collaborator because his son was friendly with the Germans?

He learned that the bastard Jerries had impounded Keith's boat.

Not that he would have been fit to go to sea yet, by the description of his battered face. What with all that, and his wife expecting too, it was all terrible for Keith.

Larry decided he must take Keith some food. But that had been last night after the second cider. Now, in the cold sober light of day, he was too frightened to even take some meagre supplies to his friend, in case the house was being watched, in case he was caught.

'What is up with me?' he thought. 'Hell, I'm more interested in my own skin than helping out an old friend! What have they done to me to make me like this?'

Larry was agonising his jumbled, anxious thoughts, round and round in his exhausted mind. Always they brought him to that one point; the banging and kicking on the front door, in the dead of night.

As he worked there on an old bike in the back room workshop, Larry heard the door bell. The sticking door opened jerkily, then slammed shut behind the incomer.

He went out into the shop to be confronted by a huge shabbily-dressed man silhouetted against a frame of bright morning light from the shop door.

"Can I help you, Sir?" asked Larry, moving his way towards the counter.

"I reckon you might be able to," came the dry response. Larry knew the husky voice. He moved so that the speaker's face came into clear vision, realising who it was. He took in a momentary gasp at the sight then steadied himself against the counter, trying desperately not to let his horror transmit itself to his visitor. As he steadied himself mentally and physically, Larry took in the face. The swollen nose, the two black eyes with bruises of changing shades of black, blue and red spreading across both cheeks like some ghastly blight. A blight which has devoured and destroyed that which was once pleasant. The swollen split lips painfully curled in a greeting smile.

"Keith! Bloody hell, man!"

Keith shrugged his shoulders in the fashion of one who is resigned to everything. he was sensitive of Larry's reaction.

"C'est la guerre," he said with a false chuckle.

"Why have you come?" asked Larry with urgency coloured by fear. "You needn't have come, I was coming round to you and Anne with something to help you through."

"Thanks," said Keith in a tone which signified he neither believed nor disbelieved. He did not really care.

"Thanks, but you mustn't. Get rid of it all, Larry for Christ's sake! I've come in to warn you, mate. They're taking me in again on Friday and, honest to God, I can't hold out much more. They want names and contacts and I know I'll crack. I can't take much more of this."

Larry's face paled. He could tell Keith was at breaking point. Hell, he was at breaking point anticipating collection by the Gestapo. How much worse it must be for Keith waiting for his second session.

Larry was embarrassed. Although he had heard Keith had been badly beaten he had not been able to imagine the sight. He was conscious that he should not stare, but just as one feels compelled to look at any forbidden sight the urge becomes all the stronger once it is proscribed. He could not enter into normal conversation for he was not existing in normal circumstances. He heard himself speaking, as one distant, as he made a brave attempt at joviality.

"Well you never were very good looking, were you?"

He was completely nonplussed by Keith's reaction. The tall bronzed fisherman just stood there, his body racked by sobs, as the tears streamed down his swollen and mutilated cheeks.

Larry was filled with tenderness and shame. He momentarily forgot his fear and embarrassment.

"Come in the back, mate. We'll have a brew up."

Keith followed meekly, watching as Larry busied himself with his paraffin stove and bag of ersatz coffee.

During the operation, Larry made several attempts at conversation but could get no response from Keith who just sat staring ahead.

There were some interruptions as customers entered the shop. Larry had to leave Keith from time to time to attend to them. He was glad of the opportunity to get away for he felt he might be able to steady his nerves. Larry found his hands were shaking so much that he spilled his drink as he lifted it to his lips.

Keith had stopped crying when at last he spoke. The salty tear trails shiny like the paths of snails.

"I'd have gone off to England in the boat but the blighters have impounded it, haven't they?"

Larry ignored the rhetorical question.

"I tell you, Larry, I can't go through last week's interrogation all over again. It was bad enough last time but, if they touch my face again, I don't think I can take it." He shuddered and terror flashed across his eyes.

"The bastards!" mouthed Larry slowly, suddenly forgetting his fear as he watched Keith, the idol of all the girls of yesteryear. Keith of the school swimming team, Keith of the school football team, Keith who had played for Centrals. That hero now reduced to a quaking, broken bundle of fear. He became angry that they should have done this to one who was an esteemed plinth of his society. As Larry's anger grew, so his fear subsided and he felt the old fight returning. At last he became released from all tensions of the past week. He became, once more, Larry the champion of the weak, Larry the hater of injustice, Larry the politically aware.

"But they can't treat you like that!" exclaimed Larry, angry and defiant. "They're not allowed to beat you. There's the Geneva Convention to protect you!"

"The Geneva what?" sneered Keith. "The Jerries don't need any conventions to tell them how to behave. They've won this bloody war, haven't they? They can write their own damn rules!"

"Don't say that!" shouted Larry, "they haven't anywhere near won. You talk like a defeatist!"

"Wouldn't you?" demanded Keith, dramatically pointing to his face.

Larry, forced to look Keith straight in the eye once more, felt the temporary return of the chill of fear, which had gripped his stomach for so many recent days and nights. He pushed it away, using to sustain him, his new found enthusiasm in his just cause.

"No I wouldn't! If I get taken in, heaven prevent it, I'll take it like a man. You won't find me complaining and crying. You knew what you were taking on when you started. You just can't complain and back out when the going gets a bit rough!"

*　　　*　　　*

"Right then Müller, I take it you have finished fouling the lavatory with your excesses from last night," snarled the Patrol Leader. "Now maybe you can explain why you have broken the military code?"

"Sir?" came Franz's querying reply.

"God in heaven, lad! I'm asking you why you missed 06.00 Patrol line up this morning!" stormed the Patrol Leader.

"You know why," answered Franz plaintively, pricked into animation by the forcefulness of his N.C.O.'s tone.

"I know nothing, lad! Nothing that is, except that you are in serious trouble. Do you know what happened to the last soldier who missed Patrol line out? Do you?"

Franz just stared.

"I'll tell you. He was confined to house for a month and had double patrol for six weeks. Just think of that, my little Franz. No more outings for six weeks, no more meetings with your boyfriend! What would you do then, eh? Just think of all those lovely Relaxations you could come to then, eh?"

The Patrol Leader gave a cruel chuckle as he watched Franz's face whiten with the realisation. He decided to twist the knife a further turn.

"Just imagine, Franz, getting up at 05.30 every day ready for 06.00 patrol and not finishing 'till midnight. How much sleep would you get Franz, eh? Tell me that?"

Franz considered it pointless to reply. If he answered, he felt whatever he said would be turned against him. Besides, he felt too ill.

"You pretty little boys need a lot of sleep don't you?"

A further twist of the knife.

"And just think, if I were a good friend to you, I could get you off some duties and you could come to another Relaxation and have lots of delicious food. You could have cream cakes and Schnapps and ham and fruit. . . ."

Franz felt decidedly ill. He saw the black spots reappearing. Morten enjoyed watching his colour change.

". . . and there would be Jules to look after you . . ."

'Strange,' Morten thought, 'how people always refer to someone turning green when they're about to be sick!'

Franz looked more yellow than green.

"You like Jules, don't you, Franz? Do you know Jules is a good friend to you? Oh yes, he is very fond of you. He put you to bed last night, you know? What's the matter, boy? You look ill, are you about to be sick or something?"

As much as he was enjoying the sport the Patrol Leader did not want Franz to be sick here in Weiss' office, on his carpet.

'No,' he thought, 'I must be careful. I mustn't push him too far. It was good of Weiss to let me take charge of Franz's punishment but to make him actually sick here would be stretching Weiss' good nature too far.'

"You dare to be sick! Smarten up, lad. If you are sick I'll have you beaten! What are you, a German or a weak pig?"

"Now listen, enough of this fooling around. Captain Weiss has left your punishment to me. You have a choice. Either you go on double patrol for four weeks or you allow my friend S.S. Hüffmeier and myself to beat you. What is it to be?"

"Beat me, Sir?" asked Franz in a moment of fear and panic. "What do you mean, Sir, beat me? How?"

As Franz spoke he noticed a glint in Morten's eye. His face seemed imperceptibly to transform to a shadowy smile as he contemplated the fantasy of beating this pretty young boy.

With delight, Patrol Leader Morten explained the whole ritual, but his anticipation of pleasure was not reciprocated.

"Then I will have to take the double patrol Sir," decided the pathetic weakling who stood before him.

"God in Heaven, I despise you!" seethed the frustrated bully.

How could all that kindness from last evening have turned to such hatefulness in the light of day?

"It was all in jest!" conceded Morten to the coward before him. "Captain Weiss is no longer punishing you but has put you on 18.00 Patrol!"

Morten would be incapable of understanding such things. He was never to know that Franz, despite his reprieve, just as the prisoner, receiving sentence of death, forever bears the scars of his imaginings, even though subsequently commuted.

* * *

Franz knew the way to the Feldkommandantur. The painful memories of the raid, with all its trauma, invaded his consciousness, as he rushed up the Rue des Freres, with its ancient and grey tombs.

He vaguely remembered having seen John last night, while he had been too incapacitated through drink to be able to greet his friend. Oh yes, Patrol Leader Morten had really enjoyed telling him that his English friend had been too proud to stay and that he despised Germans, especially Franz Müller.

Franz could not bear the thought of losing his new friend, his only true friend. Nor could he just so easily dispel all his dreams that their new, if brief and tumultuous friendship had formed. How could he let John think so badly of him that he would no longer feel welcome in the presence of Mrs. Collins? Was he now condemned to face a lonely winter without any companions of his own age? Not another meagre and unhappy Christmas like the last, his first away from Germany! No, he just had to meet up with his Guernsey friend to reassure himself that everything was still all right, or at least could be repaired.

As Franz approached the building, through Elm Grove, looking towards the large black windows, like dark, all-seeing eyes, he did not know what to do. Well, he knew he needed to meet his friend and this was the place of his employment, but how he was to accomplish the reunion was another matter.

He certainly couldn't just loiter outside. That became quite apparent when he observed, not only the door sentry, but the military police sentry, on duty at the barracks across the road.

His heart pounded into his throat as he walked on past, just hoping he would not be recognised or look conspicuous.

What should he do? Could he just walk on round the block? Well, on inspection of the left fork of La Gibauderie, it seemed most unlikely that any such return route was at all possible. Nor could he return to the other fork, to the top of St. Jacques, for fear of the two watchers.

John's bicycle was there, outside the garden wall. That, at least, gave Franz courage.

Then he saw the solution to his problem. Opposite where the bicycle was parked, was a hole in the wall, an unbarred doorway, obviously leading to a back way, presumably to garages or back gardens of local residents. Franz would be able to wait there, hidden from the view of his own country-men, while at the same time able to keep watch of his friend's machine.

Each time he heard approaching footsteps, as he carried out his seemingly endless wait, Franz hoped it was John, yet also cringed a little as though fearing discovery by others. However, the civilians who passed him by, seemed to ignore him with almost disdain. All except one middle aged lady, smartly dressed. This person, tending a bundle of letters she carried, seemed vaguely familiar to the young German, as she scrutinised him quickly in the manner of an all-seeing schoolmistress.

Eventually, John appeared although he did not notice his

observer at first. As he bent to put on his cycle clips, he was not aware that Franz approached, until he was startled by his tap on the shoulder.

"Hello, John," quavered Franz, with broken voice. He held the expression which anticipated the response of either friend or enemy.

John's response was to stare. His face was solemn, his mouth angry. John's voice barely whispered yet the words spat out;

"I can't talk to you! I have to go!"

"John I've come. I must tell you. . ." Franz's words were cut short as John, in his haste to remove himself from this presence, roughly brushed past him.

"John!"

John did not respond but placed his foot on the pedal and, quickly scooting, mounted his machine, moving into full view of the Feldkommandantur.

Franz, desperate at seeing his friend leave in such a state, and angry at the dashing of all his organisation with the risks he had taken to engineer this meeting, ran forward and grabbed John's handlebars.

"John stop. . ."

John, already moving, tried to wrench free the unwelcome hand.

"John, wait . . . please."

The words reminded John of another call plaintively pleaded by the reprehensible Hüffmeier only last evening. He became extremely angry and the little boy in him allowed his face to contort with annoyance.

"Bugger off can't you. Bugger off!" Franz did not understand the words but was cognizant that he was being sworn at. He retaliated in anger, using a German expletive of his own. He was not to be thwarted. He gripped the handlebars securely so that John was forced to dismount.

"How dare you speak to me like this? Me who has waited here to speak to you! What have I done that you must be so rude?"

The struggle had attracted the attention of the Feldkommandantur sentry and the Military Police guard. Both were staring in their direction. Franz was the first to observe their stares. The sentry called to him in German, to which he replied with a shrugging of his shoulders. John was now aware of their presence and looked at the two men grinning at each other, obviously sharing some joke at his and Franz's expense. Through gritted teeth he hissed.

"Let me go, Franz. We'll be reported!"

"No!" was Franz's adamant reply. "No, come with me, quick, you fool!"

He moved towards the alley where he had waited for that interminable age. He felt confident John would follow. John followed.

Once out of sight, they both stopped. John was panting through temper and the recent struggle. He took time to regain his poise while Franz was left to initiate the next belligerence.

"Why won't you let me speak?" came Franz's plaintive question. "What have I done that you are treating me like this, less than a friend?"

"If you don't know, then there's no point in our talking about it," came John's sarcasm tinged reply.

"I don't know!" objected Franz. "John you'll make me angry again if you are not answer me!"

"So," said the little boy again, "I'm frightened."

The scorn was lost on Franz who was more concerned to prevent his friend moving on, for John was again handling his bicycle with deliberation.

Franz had one last attempt.

"What is it, John? Why are you not my friend anymore? What has happen?"

"Look," answered John, "I can't stop now, and that's the truth. If I stop now I'll be in trouble. If you're really wanting to talk we'd better meet this evening."

"I can't do that. . ."

"Oh I see," sneered John. "I suppose you're going to another of those disgusting orgies?"

"What?" asked Franz in bemusement. "What do you mean orgies? What is this orgies?"

"Oh come off it!" replied John. "You know what was going on!" He went to move off but Franz stepped in his path once more.

John really was worried at the thought of being late back

from his message, for being just a short distance he could not account for any lost time.

"I don't know what you are say," said Franz. "I can't talk to you tonight because I will be on patrol for the rest of the week. I was drunk last night and I am sorry for it, but it was not my fault. They got me drunked. I was order in the house to staying."

"And what about those men?" persisted John.

Franz coloured as the realisation hit him. "What men?"

"Oh come on Franz, I've got to go. You know which men I'm talking about."

"No I don't! You just can't go saying things like that and not backing what you say."

"Saying things like what?" asked John, as he brushed past.

"Like 'those men'," replied Franz, now in extreme discomfort. "Why do you saying, 'those men'?"

"Well they are your friends aren't they?" asked John, his voice, to Franz, seeming charged with hate.

"No John! They are not my friends. I hate them! You are my friend."

"Well you looked friendly enough with them last night when I came in. Do you know what I mean?"

"Yes, I think so, John, but, please believe me, it is because they get me drinked. I don't want any more to do with them. Will you please believe me? Please!"

John had heard what he wished to hear. He had to believe Franz for he wanted to. He too needed to talk more about it but his message was urgent and he was very much afraid of Herr Tropp with his implied threats.

"Franz I've got to go. Yes, I think I believe you but I want to talk to you about it some other time. My father had a chat with me last night about what you were doing. There are lots of things I want to know before I can feel sure."

Franz felt a sense of relief that John had been capable of softening. This relief was accompanied by frustration that they had no way of meeting and completing their discussion. It would be at least next week before he was on a different watch.

"Now I'm off, Cherrie," were John's parting words, as he slipped past Franz and 'cycled on up the alley.

"I come at your house on Sunday!" shouted Franz.

John froze. Despite his hurry he stopped, and with great urgency said.

- "No, you can't do that. You must never come to my house, you are a German!"

*   *   *

As Franz returned to Town House, his footsteps were leaden. At least he had made contact, but it was the first time he had ever had to entertain the concept that to be German was inferior.

How then could he contact John, if he could no longer call at his home? Writing or telephoning would be out of the question. He dare not wait outside the Feldkommandantur again, not with the way those two sentries had noticed their behaviour.

If only he were not on 18.00 Patrol, at least they could meet in the evenings, but that possibility of change was most unlikely.

Then Franz had his inspiration! Of course, all he needed was a bicycle, then he could accompany his friend as he went about his Messenger work! Franz's footsteps lightened and he began to whistle, as he made his way back towards the commercial centre of St. Peter Port.

*   *   *

Larry Collins was concluding a business transaction in the back workshop of the bicycle shop.

He left his customer, to peruse some of his other goods, while he went to find the scissors in order to relieve the visitor of some of his ration coupons.

The man viewed excitedly; German socks complete with insignia, to keep his feet warm next winter. A bar of soap would not go amiss, or a tin of meat or some pipe tobacco.

So lost was the man, in this Christmas stocking, that he was hardly aware of the ringing of the shop door bell, presumably just the return of the vendor, and continued to examine greedily the display of the Reich's treasures.

"Excuse me, please," announced the young Teuton, walking into this Aladdin's Cave, "I wish to do business with you."

So shocked was the civilian that, in his attempt to cover up his disadvantage, he only drew more attention to himself. He scooped up all the traces of illegal trade, trying, unobserved, to place them in hiding. Unfortunately the bucket he selected for this purpose already contained black and oily cleaning paraffin.

As the young German stepped forward to assist, the anxious civilian added further to his problem by knocking over his liquid immersed cache.

Larry returned, to observe with horror as the two tried to clean up the damage.

The young soldier did not appear at all angered by what he had seen. On the contrary, he was much amused, yet this sentiment quickly changed to embarrassment when Franz Müller realised that, quite by coincidence, he had come to do business with his friend's own father!

Larry was more anxious than angry. He had not recognised Franz from their encounter two dark, and drunken, evenings previously.

Occasionally young Germans would try to trade with Larry, but he was always cautious, fearing traps, and most often sent them away unsatisfied.

Today, however, Larry Collins, ostensibly a bicycle mechanic, yet clandestinely a blackmarketier and underminer of the occupying forces, dearly wished this young soldier, who had seen the damning evidence of his trade, would offer him some illegal goods thereby implicating himself in such a way that he could not denounce him.

"What do you want?" asked Larry.

Franz, by now recovering from his amusement, and feeling less embarrassment, realising that Mr. Collins had not recognised him, came straight to the point.

"I wish a bicycle to buy."

"A what!" mouthed Larry incredulously, as bicycles were currently said to be 'worth their weight in gold'.

"A bicycle. I wish to buy a bicycle. This is a bicycle shop, no?"

"No . . . I mean yes. You can't buy a bicycle, mate. We haven't got any bikes for sale."

"But this is a bicycle shop. I have money. I can pay."

"That's not the point, my son. We have none for sale."

"This is very stupid," replied Franz, in frustration. "How then do you make a living with no bicycles in a bicycle shop?"

Franz's futile, petulant response was mistakenly taken by Larry, as a veiled threat. He was however, not to be intimidated by it, for his earlier talk with Keith de la Haye had strengthened his resolve to be firm and face adversity like a man.

"Look, young lad. We've got no bikes for sale because there's a bloody war on and we can't get any supplies. Do you understand?"

"Yes," replied Franz, subdued at the realisation of his own silliness.

Larry was now fully wound up and decided to follow with another statement.

"We still have to repair those we've got though, haven't we? British bikes do wear out, we're not perfect like Germans, you know."

"I know," replied Franz, "but even our bicycles wear out."

Larry could not suppress his amusement at this.

Franz could not understand why Larry smiled to himself, but took it as a good sign, making himself laugh too.

"Well, Sir, I understand you but have you just a bicycle I could use for one day, for tomorrow?"

"Look, I'm not in the hire trade, lad," said Larry with a shrug. "Even if I wanted to help you, I've nothing to help you with. I've only got my own bike and that's too precious to part with."

"I pay you well."

"What's pay? You couldn't get me another bike if anything happened to mine could you?"

"But nothing happen. Please trust me, Mr. Collins," pleaded Franz.

Momentarily the words 'Mr. Collins' seemed odd to Larry, out of context, but as such were relegated to his subconscious, only later to be drawn to full realisation.

As the familiarity employed was so hastily filed away in the far reaches of his mind, Larry involuntarily found that he was touched by this young lad's pleading. Here stood a

German, one of the enemy and yet he could be little older than his own boy. He, in his way, was as much in need as his own family were.

Larry was curious and his feelings went out to the lad. He thought back to last night's long and embarrassing chat with John, about that young German friend of his who seemed to be getting into bad company.

'Just supposing,' he mused, 'this German here was that same young boy. Would I then want to help him?' He decided that he would, for in his heart he knew that any friend of John's would be a friend of his despite the rigours of war.

"I can pay you with things if you like," pressed Franz. "I can get you cigarettes. I maybe get you soap or socks like the ones out there," indicating Larry's back room.

Larry felt rather guilty. The association of ideas of this young lad and of his son, and his son's friend, suddenly made him realise what was happening to his morals. Here he was putting this young German who might so easily under other circumstances have been his own boy or John's friend, in a position where he would have to steal and risk frightful penalties, just in order to fulfil what seemed such an urgent and yet innocent, or boyish wish. Normally it seemed fine to Larry to allow these creatures to put themselves at risk but the distinction seemed less clear when he associated these enemies with his son's own friend.

He thought of the things John had divulged about his friend last night, and remembered how the lad had no father.

'Just supposing this boy had no father,' he thought, 'no one to care for him, no one to get him a bike? How would I feel if John had to beg and plead of some stranger for one?'

"I'm not sure," pronounced Larry, in such a way that Franz felt sure he was about to soften. "Why don't they supply you with one if you need it so badly? They could steal one for you. They're good at that."

Franz did not understand.

"What is this steal please?"

"Oh forget it," said Larry, "I was just being funny."

"Oh?"

"What do you need it for then?"

"Pardon me?"

"The bike, why do you need the bike?"

"Oh just for tomorrow. I would looks after it, really!"

"Yes, but why do you want it? It's not to do with your work is it?"

"Oh no," said Franz, "I'm not on duty until the evening."

"Then why do you need it?"

"I want to go for a riding," was Franz's reply.

"Yes, well that's obvious isn't it?" Larry exclaimed. "But what do you want to ride for? What's the point?"

"Oh I see," said Franz, with induced innocence. "Well, I want to see a bit of this island, I hear it is very beautiful."

"It was until last year," was Larry's droll reply.

"What is you mean please?"

"I mean this place was fine until you lot arrived."

"Oh," said Franz rather puzzled. "What have we done to spoil it?" He asked out of innocence.

Larry was about to answer but suddenly became tired of the trivia and, remembering that he still had another customer, turned his attention from Franz.

"Wait there, son, I'll see to you in a minute." He was gone for less than a minute and emerged from the workshop with his other customer now clutching a newspaper bundle. He quickly dismissed the man.

"Right, young man, let's see what we can do?"

Franz's spirits took a decided leap.

"Do you smoke?"

"No thank you, Sir."

"No, no!" snapped Larry, "I wasn't offering you one, I just want to know. What do you do with your cigarette ration?"

"Oh," replied Franz, "I usually give them away or exchange them."

"Good, then maybe we can do a deal. I'm not promising, mind!"

"Yes, yes," said Franz, taking Larry's tone as a sure promise, despite his protestation to the contrary.

"When do you need it, you say?"

"Oh, tomorrow morning, please. For the whole day."

"Hmm," murmured Larry, "yes, I might be able to help you. Come in when I open, O.K.?"

"Oh yes, thank you very much," said Franz, the delight at the prospect shining in his eyes.

"It's not a promise, mind."

"Can you tell me, please, what I am pay?"

Larry was taken aback at this. Usually he could strike a hard bargain but this time he did not feel at all inclined to make gain out of this particular enemy. He felt he must be getting soft, or old, or maybe just like his son, and many others in the community, getting used to them, or to like them. He felt he would like the lad to have the opportunity to fulfil his wish at no cost to himself.

'Hell,' thought Larry, 'it's a poor thing if one has to charge a mere scrap of a lad just to use my bike for the day.'

"I'll have to think about that," he replied. "Maybe a few of your cigarettes would do." Then, as an after thought adding. "And of course you'd need to keep your mouth shut about this place."

"Mouth shut?" asked Franz, confused.

"Yes, you know what I mean. You don't tell your friends you came here and borrowed my bike, understood?"

"Understood!"

Franz made to go.

"There's one other thing," said Larry.

Franz turned back, attentiveness itself.

"You didn't see anything in the workshop this morning." He winked at Franz.

Franz tried to wink back but succeeded only in blinking both eyes.

"The workshop?" said he, "I've never been in the workshop."

Chapter Ten

"Good-evening Madam. Do you mind if I come in? I'm a police officer."

The latter part of the statement was more than obvious, but Gerda did not indulge in its nonsense for she knew then, as surely as the cold gripped her heart, what he was going to tell her.

* * *

His clothes were cut off, as deftly as a butcher skins a rabbit. Cut off and removed. Nurses bathed the superficial wounds, every now and again holding back to allow the doctor passage for his examination.

The doctor's face was grave and stern as he muttered and frowned, from time to time signifying with a nod or an inclination, where the assistants could resume and from where they must absent themselves.

John was unconscious now. Concussed most likely but there was little time to confirm the unalterable circumstance.

The blood pressure was predictably low and his pulse was racing. The signs, with the areas of intense bruising, confirmed the undoubted internal injuries. Well, at least he had a strong heart, despite the deepening shock.

Good, the team was working efficiently. Already the patient's blood group was known. His nurses were ready for the doctor to start transfusion.

And now the senior Doctor was here and the anaesthetist was making his assessment.

* * *

"Would you like me to drive you to the hospital, Mrs. Collins?" the policeman asked kindly. He was concerned for this woman. This was only the second time in his career that he had had to break such serious news.

She had not taken it the way he would have expected. It had almost been as if she had known, had been waiting for

141

it to happen. She had just stood there, once he had told her
and impassively asked:

"Where? When? Will he live?"

"No," she replied pausing, changing her direction of stare
as she searched for words, while trying to chase her thoughts.

"No, thank you, I have my mother-in-law."

The answer did not make sense but such nonsense seemed
appropriate.

"You quite sure, Mrs. Collins?"

"Yes, quite sure, thank you."

*   *   *

John woke early on that bright Thursday morning, even
before the sounds of his father busying about upstairs.

As he lay there reflecting on the past ten days, the most
exciting of the whole Occupation to date, and yet most
mind-devastating, he knew that he could not face going into
work. He could not contemplate working for the Germans,
for the enemy.

Yes, they were now the enemy. Even Franz could no more
be thought of as a friend and brother, not after all that
strange business that he had got himself mixed up with.

'Got me drunk,' he had said. Well, he hadn't needed to
let himself get drunk, had he? He could have said no,
surely? What sort of friend was he who could allow such disgusting things to happen?

Yet John was still concerned. What if he dropped Franz
now? What then, if he turned to that reprehensible S.S. or
the leering Patrol Leader for friendship. No, that could not
be tolerated!

Had John been wise to ban his friend from the house?
Well yes, probably, as old Gaudion was ever watchful.
Besides, he wouldn't want the nosey old landlord thinking
that he was in any way mixed up in anything like that. But
still John agonized.

What was there for him now? Just working for them. How
would he fill his spare moments, now that he no longer had
a friend, just an enemy he had hoped better of?

John could not contemplate going to Billy Shepherd's
dance band, and especially not to the German military
bands on his own. What pleasure would there be in going
out walking without a companion? Sunday was to have been

good. Hadn't he hoped to have made some arrangements with that German? There had been the prospect too, of letting his companion come along to the new session of Boys' Club. But how could John now permit himself to be seen associated with a person in Nazi uniform, especially if people might think even worse things?

No, there was no point to getting up, or going to work, or even thinking of any sort of future. There was nothing good any more. Even that which had appeared wholesome to the youth, was now tainted.

And yet, he missed Franz, his only friend. If only Franz could be normal. If only Franz were safe and not in danger.

John's lethargy however, was not to be. His father, bringing what purported to be a cup of tea to his son's bed to shake that lazy youth, was not prepared to listen to puerile argument.

"I don't think I'll go in today," bleated John.

"You what, son?" asked Larry, half in mock surprise, partly in concern. "Why's that, then, eh? You sick or something?"

"Dad, I just don't want to work for them today. I just can't face Herr Tropp and his moods. Can't you just leave me here, please? Couldn't you 'phone them up?"

Larry was incredulous. Did John really expect daddy to write a note to teacher?

"Now, come on, son, shake yourself out of it!"

He asked his son to imagine how he must feel, day after day, having to drop everything and do Jerry bikes as soon as they brought them in. How would he feel with their lack of 'please' and 'thank you', and even giving instructions how to do his own bloody job?

It was no good. John had to bow to superior argument. Yes, he did want to live at home. No, he did not want to be sent to one of their forced labour camps. Yes, he realised, if he went sick, they would probably send one of their medics to examine him. Yes, he was aware it was against the law to refuse to work. Besides, Larry was bigger than his son and even more of a Guernsey donkey in having his way than was his offspring.

"Anyway, son," sympathized Larry, "It's not all bad, you know. Its Thursday, after all, and its bloody half day."

*   *   *

"O.K. then, young man, here's the beautiful machine you've ordered," said Larry with a chuckle. "Make sure you look after it, now I want it back in one piece."

Franz took hold of the bicycle, a smile spreading across his pale thin face. He held the handlebars and saddle at arms' length while he admired the bike. Oh, it was lovely. It had large wheels with sturdy tyres, the frame felt solid and heavy and was painted dark green, almost the same shade as his uniform. The pedals were solid rubber and the chain was encased to protect his trousers from grease.

"I will look after it as though it were my own," promised the lad, his sentiment of extreme gratitude coming through his excited voice.

"You'd better, my lad, or I'll be round to see your officer!" said Larry in fun.

"My officer?" asked Franz in surprise as his face clouded, his smile evaporating.

"No, no lad, I'm pulling your leg. Forget it."

"Pulling my leg?"

"Oh nothing, nothing. You Germans have no sense of humour, have you?"

"Yes, I have," replied Franz with a chuckle. "John . . ." He had been going to give the instance of when he and Larry's son had laughed and laughed until they had nearly dropped, outside the prison on Monday evening, but he just stopped himself in time, thereby preventing Larry from learning his identity.

"What was that?" asked Larry, his attention having been pricked but not really vitalised, by the word 'John'.

"Oh I'm not sure," came Franz's faltering reply. "How much must I pay you, please?"

With his evasive answer Franz had employed one of Larry's pet hates. He was always telling John off for saying 'I don't know' or 'I'm not sure'.

"You youngsters are all the same, you know. You're just

like my son. He never gives me a straight answer to questions. I reckon you Germans must be as bad as us!"

"We are not bad!" voiced Franz partly in arrogance and partly in anger. "You must not say we are bad. We are destined to be the rulers of the world!"

"We'll see," said Larry, not wishing to be drawn on that subject. He neither wished to antagonise the lad, for fear he might mention what he had seen on the previous day, nor did he wish to appear in awe of him in case he decided he could make a habit of this favour.

"OK, then I want this bike back here by closing time. All right?"

"All right. When is this closing time please?"

"Five o'clock," replied Larry, his face suddenly twisting with the realisation that there was a monumental error in his plans. Of course, damn it, today was early closing day. He had completely forgotten that. Oh hell! What was he to do now?

"Yes, five o'clock will be very convenient," agreed Franz, politely clicking his heels and extending his hand in order to seal the deal. "And what payment do you require, please?"

"Payment?" Larry's train of thought had been completely derailed. "Eh? What do you mean, lad?"

"How many must I pay you?"

"Oh that," said Larry, still wondering how he was going to deflate Franz and break his dream. "Some of those cigarettes you don't smoke would do."

"Yes indeed," agreed Franz, having anticipated this fee, taking a whole fifty from his pocket and placing them on the bench.

Larry was about to protest at this excessive payment, when he had only required a token to satisfy honour on both sides. However, Franz, having completed his business transaction, exercised his prerogative and started wheeling the machine from the workshop.

"Wait!" said Larry. He rummaged round for words but, on seeing Franz's surprised, and at the same time, elated face, could only manage, "We'd better check the saddle height, eh?"

As he helped the pale young soldier on to the bike Larry realised how incredibly thin and light he was.

145

'Poor bastard,' he thought, 'they probably don't feed him either.'

Larry had never really thought of them as fellow humans before but here he was now, feeling sorry for this one.

He fixed the saddle height and then Franz was ready to leave. But Larry had a problem. It had been with him from the moment he had tried to cheer his son with the prospect of having to suffer only a half day.

How was he to get his machine back? He was not going back to open up the shop especially at five, that was for sure! No, his planned walk out with Frances this afternoon, was to be sacrosanct. But could he risk the lad returning the bike to Rue Marguerite? What about old Gaudion?

He decided to let the old man go hang. Why should he disappoint this pathetic enemy now? Wouldn't he want the same for his own son if roles were reversed?

Larry explained the dilemma but, from the German's reaction to his final deliberation, he was thankful he had been able to say and do the right things.

"Thank you Sir for keeping to your side of the bargain. I too will keep my part and your bicycle will return at five o'clock to the placing of your choice."

"The placing of my choice, eh?" echoed Larry with a smile. "Well I don't know about that, but let's say I'll settle for my house."

"Your house," repeated Franz hesitating, wondering quite how he would manage that if he were with John. Life was so full of problems. He had not really considered what John would think, once he recognised his father's bike. In fact, the thought had not entered his mind until that moment. Well, at least he would have all day in which to explain to his friend. John might not even recognise the machine. If that were the case he could always leave John and then go back with the bicycle once John had gone inside. And if he did find out that he had got the bike from his father would that not be a good thing? Would it not show John that he, Franz, was a good person, good enough to be trusted by his friend's own father? The only trouble being that he had not told John's father who he really was. Would he be angry once he found out? (if he found out). Should he tell him now? Maybe not, for he might change his mind about lending the bicycle.

"Yes, thank you, Sir. I will at your house leave your bicycle at five. Now thank you I must go please. Already my day I am waste."

"Good," concluded Larry, "just pop it through the front door and leave it in the passage way."

"Yes, I will do that," agreed Franz, his business executive manner, of assumed confidence, having returned. "Good day to you."

He wheeled his pride through the shop and opened the door.

He was half way through the door, its bell tinkling above, when he was stopped by the question.

"Don't you think I'd better tell you where I live?"

"No, I know. . . ." He realised what he had begun to say and froze, his back towards his benefactor, his whole face livid with embarrassment. Trying to make the best of the error he enquired as he turned.

"Where must I returning your bicycle please?"

While asking he could tell from Larry's expression that the ambiguity had registered, albeit quickly banished, as Larry's face cleared itself of any doubts.

Larry replied, "Twelve, Rue Marguerite. It's up by the prison."

"Yes, I know the prison." Franz turned away again.

Larry realised now that, by some contrivance of coincidence, this young lad, this first German he had ever considered human, was in fact his son's friend. What the hell was the boy's name, Hans or something?

"Have a good time then." And as an after thought, "What's your name, by the way?"

"Müller, Sir."

"Müller, eh? I suppose your first name is Hans?"

"Hans? No my name is Franz."

'That's it!' thought Larry, 'Franz Müller.'

"Off you go then!"

*　　　*　　　*

Having been persuaded by the strength of his father's argument, John had rushed around and got to work on time. His father had awakened dormant fears in him that he was heading for trouble, with possible transfer to a labour camp, if he did not cooperate with his masters. He was now prepared to believe his father's advice whereas two weeks previously he would have dismissed such conjectures as fantastic. He now knew too well, by experience of Herr Tropp's irrational doggedness, that the Administrator was all too capable of turning on him and issuing dramatic threats which he would all too readily activate. No longer, for John, was there the protection of knowing that right was on his side, for such armour is defenceless in a regime in which the norm for expedience is injustice.

On reaching the Feldkommandantur, John was pleased to find no evidence of Herr Tropp.

Frau Bormann was actually friendly, as she presented him with his new tyre, explaining that the Germans would require the worn one in exchange. John was taken aback that this was expected immediately, even to the extent that, if the whole exercise delayed his daily deliveries, he would just have to work on late. This seemed most unfair, as the Germans offered no tools and, as he did not carry any, it would necessitate a visit to his father's shop in Town.

"That's most unfair!" exclaimed John. "I'm going to complain!"

"And just who do you think you can complain to?" admonished the Secretary. "You would be very unwise to complain to anyone about anything. You're in enough trouble as it is!"

"Trouble?" asked John, incredulous. "What trouble?"

Frau Bormann, realising she had almost divulged information which should have been kept from John, attempted to change the subject by continuing.

"You're all in trouble, you British! You're losing this war. Even the Ukrainians have turned against the Marxists and are helping us to crush you now. Now, come along, be a good boy and thank me for saving you from all that extra work."

John, a little slow to take the point, enquired "Extra work?"

"Yes, you foolish boy! I persuaded Herr Tropp to let you return the worn tyre tomorrow."

"Oh that," said John casually. "Oh yes, thank you. How did you persuade him by the way?"

"I told him it would be better for your father to do the job, for he was more qualified and would not damage the old tyre. . . ."

"It's only changing a tyre, anyone could do that. Besides, what do you mean, my father is more qualified than me?"

Frau Bormann realised she was being very silly today and letting out far too many snippets of information.

'That's the trouble,' she thought, 'as soon as I start to get friendly with anyone I say too much. It really is much better to be unfriendly and just do my job. I just can't understand why this sudden change in Herr Tropp, asking me to get friendly with the boy.'

"Anyway, enough of all this silly talk. There is work to be done!"

John had a number of communications to fold and seal into envelopes. He then had to consult the large map of the Island in order to plan his journey. The task was the largest that had yet been entrusted to him, involving delivering to all the gun emplacements of the south coast from Pleinmont to Jerbourg. This would mean an initial ride of about six miles, to Pleinmont and then working his way along the coast to Jerbourg, a distance of about six miles as the crow flies, but which would inevitably be much longer owing to detours around the many valleys which indented the cliffs. The road was frequently set well back from the military zone, involving much retracing of lanes to and from the headlands and bays.

"Whew!" expressed John to Frau Bormann, when he realised the enormity of the assignment. "I doubt if I'll get that lot delivered by one o'clock."

"Well then, you'll just have to work on until you are finish," she replied acidly.

"But it's my half day. I finish at one."

"You finish when you finish! Now a little less talk and you could be on your way before tea," she said. Then, as an after thought, remembering how she had been instructed to ingratiate herself with this native, "If you are late finishing you can go straight home from your final delivery. You need not come back to the office."

John was quite thankful for this small concession. Not that it would save him very much in time but at least it would mean one less attendance at this nauseous place. He felt, somewhat cynically, that Frau Bormann was more concerned to get away early from the office herself than to consider his feelings.

*   *   *

It was half past nine when John finally let the front door of the Feldkommandantur slam shut behind him while he struggled his way to his bicycle with his heavily loaded dispatch bag fastened to his back in the manner of a school satchel, his coiled new tyre across his arm. He was feeling pleased that he had finished his clerical work so quickly and had managed to sketch out his route for the journey without too much difficulty. These Germans really were clever with their method of numbering and lettering all roads on their maps with corresponding road signs at all junctions.

He had been so absorbed in his task, and so pleased with his progress towards an early start, the incentive being an early finish, that he had forgotten all his previous unhappiness.

When John saw Franz standing there by his bicycle, holding a bicycle of his own, he had the surprise of his life. His immediate and natural response was one of pleasure which, if he had tried to, he would have found difficulty in disguising.

"Franz!"

"Yes, it is I," announced Franz, beaming. "What do you think, John? I have a bicycle for the day. Now I can ride with you, yes?"

"This is super," John replied. "Yes, let's get going quickly, away from this place. I've a lot of deliveries so we can ride together and talk as we go."

He clipped his trousers and both set off.

The German regulation was that all cyclists should ride in single file at all times. Normally John would have followed this rule, partly out of respect for the authority of the conquerors but, mainly because, on most occasions, he cycled by himself anyway. Today was different. He had a friend with him, his very own friend, a friend who belonged to no one else, and it felt good. Today John suddenly felt cheerful, carefree and full of bravado. The office, the haunt of Herr Tropp, was to be left far behind. He and Franz were to escape into the countryside, it was a lovely hot day and, hell, he just felt like rebelling!

So they went. Down the Gibauderie, down the Rohais and into the Foulon. On the main Rohais road John was sensible enough to ride single file, for he did not wish to risk a large, on the spot, fine or into having to go to the police court. Worse still, he did not wish the embarrassment of having to be charged jointly with one of the enemy. It might have been awkward for Franz too. Recently he had read much controversy in the *Press* on the subject of such crimes. In the Letter Box section some people maintained that it was unjust for both' cyclists to be fined where it was only the one on the outside who was committing the offence. That was how the German law was being interpreted in Jersey. Well, John wondered, if Franz were to take the outside position, would he, as a German, be excused?

Once they reached the quiet Foulon, dropping down into its rural valley, and the network of lanes which was to lead them out into the peaceful countryside, John threw caution to the wind. What is the point of being a rebel if you don't do something wrong? So light and happy did John feel, as they both laughed and chatted, that, in his bravado, he reverted from riding on the right to the left hand side of the road as had been custom before the conquerors had arrived. Franz remained on the right, which was not at all foreign to him. He looked at John in confusion.

"What you are doing, John? You are on the wrong side of the road!"

"Hell I'm not!" came his hearty reply. "This is the right side for Guernsey people!"

"No, John that is the left. This is the right."
John realised the unintentional pun and laughed into his friend's aghast face.

"Oh Franz, wake up my friend. In Guernsey the left is right and the right is wrong?"

Franz did not understand but he felt John was making one of his English jokes so joined in the laughter.

Between them, as they wended their way down the narrow road they effected a compromise using neither right nor left but settling for the centre.

Both dismounted on the steep hills and there was much back-slapping and pushing. They seemed to have the whole island to themselves.

What fun it was, trying to force each other's bicycle into the hedge. How hilarious, when they splashed through the puddles of a bankside spring which had trespassed onto the roadway.

How they laughed and screamed when coming suddenly upon some old and rustic farm yard which seemed to become part of the road itself, they were taken by surprise and forced to ride through a mire of cow dung. All over John's trousers it splashed. Franz was laughing so much his front wheel skidded and he had to save himself with his foot which sank beneath the sludge. To make matters worse he dismounted and then, clown like, plodded his way to the side of the road. John could not go on. He lay prostrate against the grassy bank and howled in mirth at his friend's discomfort. Franz, at first concerned at the state of his boots, looked terribly worried but then he reasoned the day was too special to hold anxiety. And 18.00 patrol line-up was years away. He too joined in the hilarity and threw himself down next to his friend.

John had been brushing his trousers then, without thinking, wiped the tears from his eyes. His face now looked like that of a commando. Franz pointed to it unable to speak for his guffaws.

"Eh?" asked John in the familiar diction he reserved only for family and close friends.

"Your face, John, look at your face!"

"What about it?" asked John, rubbing it and making it worse, much to Franz's amusement.

"Schizer! Shit face!"

"Eh?" said John, looking down at his hands and at last realising the reason for Franz's reaction.

"Oh hell! Have I got that bloody boozette all over my face?"

"Yes, John. Oh she won't kiss you tonight!" and with that Franz once more lost control of his sanity.

John too was laughing at himself.

"We'll see," he said. "And what about you Franz? Will she kiss you?" As he so asked he deftly slipped his finger onto Franz's bespoiled boot and transferred the deposit on to the tip of his Aryan nose.

"You swine!" shouted Franz still laughing as he hit out at the fast receeding John. "You wait till I get hold of you!

"You've got to catch me first, eh?"

John ran off, pursued hotly by Franz. Through the farmyard they ran, scattering the ducks and chickens. Past the sleepy old dog on its long chain, into the orchard, out again into the field, where the placid tethered cows looked up in temporary curiosity then, disdainfully, set about their business. Past the beehives they ran, through the barn and along by the pig sties.

Finally, out of breath, John stopped. Franz, similarly exhausted, and having forgotten that his mission was to punish John, collapsed against him.

"Oh John, what a lovely day this is! Where else could we find such a farm? Where else could we find for our shoes such polish?"

"It's better than being at work," said John soberly, suddenly remembering that was where he was. Hell, what about his time sheets? But of course, no, it didn't matter today for he could go straight home once he'd finished. So, what if he finished late! It didn't matter. Today was his half day off. His holiday had started already!

He remembered other summer Thursdays, which now seemed a lifetime ago, when he was still at school. He remembered how all the schools used to close on July Thursday afternoons so that the various Sunday Schools could plan their annual outings. What fun they always were with all the kids crowded into the tomato lorries and hundreds of paper streamers flying from behind. The raucous singing with prospects of jelly, blancmange and chocolate biscuits for tea. He remembered how on those Thursday mornings no one worked very hard at school, not even the teachers. He felt the same today, he had a holiday feeling. But suddenly too, he missed his freedom, he missed his friends. How were they all in England? Were they thinking of him? Were they too remembering those heady days of endless summer with swimming and dancing and picnics? Did they recall all this as the Nazi bombs rained down on them at night? What would they think if they could see him now with a German as a friend? He loved them all and he missed them so. When would this bloody war end? He wanted them back but even so he would not give them this day. No-one would take away this day with his friend Franz. His face became solemn as these thoughts raced through his mind.

"About what are you thinking, John?" asked Franz, turning to his friend.

"Who, me?" asked John, reluctant to release his dreams. "Oh, I was thinking of the days when we were free, when I had friends." He spoke the last words casually, almost unwittingly, as his old friends were transported in his mind away from his island back to their misery and the blitz in England. He did not realise the hurt he had caused Franz.

"Et tu, mon vieux? Penny for your thoughts," asked John.

Franz had not reacted to John's unintentional but hurtful statement, sensing that his friend's mind had been far away, for his too had been transported back to his home momentarily.

"Penny? What penny?"

"What were you thinking of?"

"Me? This place, this farm. It makes me feel so happy and so sad at the same time. Can you understanding what I mean?"

"Yes," replied John, knowing exactly how such a feeling could be engendered. "Tell me how."

"Well, you see John I am a farm boy and this farm so reminds me of my home. I wishing I am home with Mama and Papa and Ilsa. It is so stupid, John, I am happy to be here with you today but I wishing I am home and Papa is alive. Do you understand me?"

"Yes, of course," said John. "I was also thinking of before the war and my friends and all the good times we used to have. I wish this damn war would come to an end!"

"So do I," agreed Franz, "but what end will it be?"

"Well, that's funny, coming from you!" exclaimed John in surprise. "I thought you Germans expect to win this war before the end of this year."

"This is true, John. But what then?"

"I just don't know," said John. "I really dread to think."

"Tell me one thing, John, whoever wins this war, will we still be friends?"

"I don't see why not, do you? If we can manage to be friends while we're really enemies, why shouldn't we manage it in peace time, eh?"

"Thank you, and I am sorry about the other evening."

"Oh, forget it. It's in the past."

"No, it's not in the past, John. I want to talk about it." John sighed.

"OK, what do you want to say? You've already told me they got you drunk and you couldn't help it. What more is there to say?"

"You are angry?" asked Franz with a concerned look.

"No," answered John, "But why spoil a good day by bringing it all up again?"

"Why, Why? Because I must!"

"OK then, tell me."

"John, those men, that Patrol Leader and that Frenchman. They are . . . they are . . ."

"Go on, they're what?"

"They're strange, they're different . . ." Franz was finding this very difficult to say for he was embarrassed. John too was uncomfortable as his face turned red. He looked at his spotted trousers and slowly and deliberately made himself say.

"You mean they are funny."

He remembered how those two girls had laughed at him in the pictures and asked him if he was 'funny or something'.

"They're queer, or if you want the proper word for it, they're homosexuals," said John, feeling a great relief at having finally given birth to this concept.

"Er . . . yes. Yes that is it, exactly so," agreed Franz. "How did you know?"

"I don't," said John, correcting himself. "That is, I didn't 'till I told Dad."

"You tell your father?"

"Yes."

"Why?"

"Because, oh I don't know, can't we just drop it?"

"No. Why do you tell your father? What did you say?"

"Oh, I don't know. Let's just say I didn't like what they were doing to you."

"What were they?"

"Oh come on, you know."

"No John, believe me I don't. I think I know but please tell me,"

"Well, if you must know, they had their arms round you as if you were a girl."

"Oh?" said Franz, by now quite scarlet. "And?"

"Well they . . ." John paused.

"Please go on, John. I want to know."

"Well, that womanish looking one was stroking your hair and kissing you."

"Oh no! Oh, please believe me, I did not know. I think something like this but I do not know."

"And the Patrol Leader was rubbing your leg."

"Rubbing my leg?" asked Franz involuntarily touching his calf. "You mean like this?" rubbing his own leg.

"No, you fool. Higher up!"

"What there?" enquired Franz, touching his own knee.

"No, up there," explained John rubbing his own thigh, at the same time laughing to hide his discomfort.

"I see," acknowledged Franz, too laughing to hide his feelings. "Well now I know, thank you. Do you believe me when I tell you it is not my wish . . ."

"Yes!" interrupted John. "Yes, yes, yes! I believe you. Now can you please shut up or I'll start rubbing you and it won't be your leg. I'll rub your nose with my fist!"

Franz laughed and the tension subsided.

"I'd like to see you try," he suggested, laughing.

They retraced their steps towards the bicycles, both now relieved that they had cleared the air.

'Franz is more like a brother than a friend,' thought John. 'We argue so much, he's just like family.'

John now felt confident that, as when he had arguments with his family, so it was with Franz; no permanent damage could be caused and that the confidence of reconciliation was always there. There would be no need for apologies now for with complete acceptance and understanding faults and difficulties would always be swept away by the ministrations of time.

They paused at the pig sty and delighted in the snuffles of the big sow as she placed her clean pink perforated disc of a nose through the granite feeding hole.

"Doesn't she smell!" complained John. "I'd hate to live by that pong all the time."

"That is a good farm smell," replied Franz. "It's good for you. It keeps your head clear and your body fit and healthy."

"I doubt that very much," said John.

"It's true, this is the life!" was Franz's reply.

"Well, OK, I'll believe you, if it makes you happy," said John, "but I think maybe I'd rather have the cows. They don't stink quite so much!"

"John, we'll never make a farmer of you, will we?" teased Franz. "You said you like this place just now but you're complaining about little things like smells."

"Little things! They might be little to you. Maybe you're used to living like a pig," replied John, quickly stepping back to avoid Franz's fist.

Franz was laughing.

"Who are you calling a pig?" he exploded in mock severity. "Pigs always find pigs for company!"

"You mean," retorted John, "birds of a feather always flock together," remembering the old adage which had stuck with him from his English teacher of primary school days.

"Birds? What is this birds, please? John, I think you are funny. First we talk about pigs then you change to birds."

"It's just an expression," said John.

"What is this expression?"

"That is."

"What is?"

"Oh nothing."

"Don't say 'Oh nothing' to me, English pig," ordered Franz, pinning John's arms to his side and giving him a good shake in jest.

"Why not?" asked John, freeing himself and, without premeditation, grabbing his friend around the waist and picking him up in the air. He discovered Franz was surprisingly light so his task was easy. Once he had his friend airborne he did not really know what to do with him, so deposited his load on the wall of the pig sty.

"Put me down!" stormed Franz at this indignity.

"Put you down. What in the pig sty?" enquired John with a broad grin.

"No, no!" squealed Franz, relieved that John had smiled, so must be joking, but nonetheless anxious that he might yet deposit him in the sty.

John forced him back until he reached the point of imbalance. As he held Franz, struggling but secure, he turned his friend with ease so that he was forced to face the filth inside the sty, while the old, pink eyed porker snuffled up into his face.

"Stop John! Please stop, I fall in! Think of my uniform!"

"I thought you liked the smell of pigs."

"No, not that much! Please stop!"

"I won't stop 'till you tell me who's a pig."

"Who's a pig? What do you mean?"

"Say 'I'm a pig' and I'll let you go."

"No!"

"Right then!" John tipped Franz further towards the mire. The old sow squealed and shuffled backwards, fully expecting company at any moment.

"Yes, yes!" shouted Franz, "I'll say it. I'll say it! but stop. Please!"

"Go on then, say, 'I'm a pig'."

"You're a pig!" shouted Franz. "No. no! I didn't mean it. I'm a pig! I'm a pig!"

John let go and Franz jumped down smoothing his ruffled uniform with both hands.

"Come," he said, "you English bully. Thank goodness you are not going to win the war."

With that he walked on ahead of John.

"Come, John. What is the time do you think?"

"I don't know, but it must be getting on. Let's go. We've got a lot to do."

Passing the cows Franz suddenly left the path and made his way to the nearest herbivore.

"Come, town boy. Let's have something to drink."

"Eh?" asked John.

"I suppose you town boys don't know that milk comes from cows?"

"Of course I do," proclaimed John.

"Have you ever milked a cow?" asked Franz.

"No."

"Then you must have your first lesson."

"What do you mean?" asked John, thinking he knew what Franz had in mind, but hoping he was wrong.

"Well, we'll milk this cow."

"No," said John. "You can't."

"Why not?"

"Because. . . .," replied John.

"Because, what?"

"Well, the farmer," said John, feeling decidedly uncomfortable at the prospect of the transgression. "Besides, you've nothing to put it in and it is a terrible waste."

"We don't need anything to put the milk in," explained Franz. "We can squirt it straight into our mouths."

"Ugh, No!"

"Why? You silly town boy."

"Well, it's unhygenic."

"What it this 'unhygenic'?"

"It's not clean, it's dirty!"

Franz laughed. "It is not dirty. All the milk you drink comes this way, doesn't it?"

"I know," said John still wishing himself anywhere but there, "but. . . ."

"Come, John, quick, come here please," interrupted Franz, as he knelt by the placid animal who seemed quite unperturbed by all the attention being paid to her. John reluctantly stepped forward whilst pondering how best to protest.

Franz touched the cow's udder so that she turned her neck and looked towards him, licking her lips as though with pleasure. As he took one of her teets deftly in his fingers, she let out a lazy moo. John was looking around guiltily, seeking the appearance of an angry farmer who would surely come running at the sound of the lowing.

"There!" exclaimed Franz with satisfaction. As Franz let out the word John felt the noise, rather than heard it, as he looked down to see his friend skilfully directing a tiny but powerful white jet on to his mud splattered boots. "There

John, that your boots will polish for you. That will pay you back for trying to put me in with your sister!"

Franz was up and away before John realised the enormity of his action.

"Hey, you! Wait here you dirty little bugger!"

His words came to a halt as he focused on the fast retreating Franz with his head turned back and laughing as he ran full force into the little old farmer.

Despite feelings of annoyance, coupled with guilt, at what he had watched Franz do, and fear of the consequences, John could do nothing but laugh at the spectacle before his eyes. There on the grass lay the little old country farmer struggling as though trying to disassociate himself from his large wellington boots, his baggy tweed trousers, thick Guernsey topped with a tweed waistcoat and jacket sporting a gold chain, presumably attached to a gold pocket watch. The only item of clothing which had managed to escape seemed to be his black beret which had so easily slipped from his bald pate.

As the old man struggled, shocked, on the field, so did Franz struggle on top of him. The sight was both grotesque and hilarious and of only a few seconds duration. But being so out of the ordinary, they seemed to take on to themselves a greater part of time in John's consciousness than they had actually been granted. Like remote puppets, the two partners performed their humorous copulation and, as suddenly, both were up, looking first at each other and then down at their disarrayed clothing.

As John joined the two, the old gentleman let out a rather breathless protest.

"Hyer! What the devil d'you think you're doing?"

Franz, trying to extricate himself from his embarrassment and his ridiculous position, took comfort from his uniform and the authority it gave him over this local peasant.

"Good morning, Farmer, I trust you are not injured after your careless accident. In future please to look where you are going."

The old gentleman was taken aback and scratched his bald head. He was rather confused having had his part of protagonist changed to that of antagonist.

John, trying to alleviate the situation, added.

160

"Good morning, Sir. I'm sorry if we disturbed you, we were just admiring your animals."

"Admiring my animals, is it?" exclaimed the old man, with a dry cackle. In the manner of a country farmer, more at home in his native patois than English, the man added;

"And why for is it that admiring them you are?"

"Well," attempted John, "my friend here was. . . ."

"Your friend!" interrupted the old man. "Is it that you are all right in the head? This hyer is a German. How then is it that he is your friend, him?"

John's first reaction was to feel belittled by the old man's comment, his second was to feel incensed at his insult, an insult partly directed at him but mainly directed towards Franz. Why should this old man spoil his day for him? Why should he, in a few thoughtless words, spoil something that he could not ever expect to understand in his narrow surroundings. Friendship is stronger than the man-made imposed strictures of politics, religion and prejudices. No, he would not have this day taken from him by anyone! As he thought, and as his angry words grouped themselves ready to attack this assailant, John realised that the old man's tone of voice was not one of criticism or offence, it was more of genuine enquiry, one of bewilderment. He was not sitting in judgement on the two.

Before John could reply, Franz intervened.

"Come, my friend. Let us leave this place."

"No wait," John urged, "let me explain. . . ."

"No, that's all right, mon vieux," interrupted the old man. "You two are friends, that's all right. When this war it is finished, you two boys remember it, eh?"

"Yes," said John, not really understanding what the old man was getting at, or being able to decipher his thick accent. "Yes, thank you, we must go now, cheerie."

"Cheerie," replied the old man, "a la prochein!"

They made their way to their bicycles. Franz stooped down for a handful of grass to wipe his boots and John did likewise. Having completed these running renovations, they were ready to set off. Curious to know the time, John called to the old man.

"Have you got the time, please?"

"Eh?"

"The time?"

"Ah oui. It is ten hours and en qua."

"What did he say?" asked Franz.

"It's a quarter past ten, I think. Hell, we'd better get a move on!" And to the old man, "Thank you!"

"Wait a moment!" called the farmer as he hobbled his way toward them. "Wait, I have something for to give you."

"Oh no," muttered John to Franz, as the farmer entered the low arch of his granite farmhouse. "We're late already."

"Let us go, then," urged Franz.

"No, we must wait," insisted John.

The old man re-emerged.

"Hyer you are!" he called with delight, as he made his way towards them, "Try this, mes vieux!"

He held high a stone flagon which swayed from his outstretched hand as, with great pleasure, he beamed at them.

"What is that, Sir?" asked John.

"This, my son, is for you to drink, eh? This hyer is the very best St. Pierre du Bois cider, it. This hyer cider, it was made from last year's apples. Last year's apples which them grew before it was that you came." He pointed to Franz, his smile belying the insult which, in any case, had not been fully comprehended.

"Thank you very much," said John. "Look, Franz, some real Guernsey cider!"

"Oh that is very kind," enthused Franz, looking at the old farmer who was obviously taking great pleasure from their anticipation.

"Well then, get on, you two, you must be drinking my health it, eh? cor demme!"

John took the flagon, unstopping it.

"Have you any glasses please?"

"Eh?"

Franz grabbed the flagon from John and put it to his mouth, taking a long swig while John just gaped at him.

At this sight the old man shook up and down with mirth. Franz eventually stopped to draw breath and thrust the now much lighter vessel at his friend, while wiping his mouth with the cuff of his tunic.

"That was good!" he said. "Go on, John, you try."

John hesitated. He was not in the habit of drinking or eating from another's utensils.

"Come on, mon vieux," cajoled the old man. "It won't hurt you, it. Your friend hyer won't give you any diseases, him."

Trying not to think of Franz's saliva and germs, which must by now have invaded the flagon, he raised it to his lips to take a slight sip.

"Go on, up higher," encouraged Franz.

John raised the vessel to his lips and tasted the cool sweet liquid. He had not realised he was hot and thirsty until that moment. He opened his lips fully to allow the full tide to flow. No longer was he bothered at sharing the same vessel and instead he felt strangely in communion with Franz by so breaking a lifetime's phobia.

"Right, enough!" exclaimed Franz. "Save some for me!" He snatched at the jar but John having now tasted blood, was reluctant to release his prize.

"Come, John, it's my turn," ordered Franz as he snatched the handle. The seal between lips and stone was broken and the sweet elixir exploded on to John's face. He was left wet and choking as his friend stole the prize.

The old man, evidently having one of the best days he had had for a long time, left them and, turning his back disappeared into his house once more.

The two boys did not notice his disappearance, so busy were they bantering and snatching the flagon from each other. By the time the old man reappeared they had between them consumed half the contents of the vessel and Franz was hiccoughing loudly while John was wheezing with laughter and, in his enjoyment, dancing on the spot.

"Right!" observed the man. "Now is it that you are no more thirsty, eh? Good. Then look hyer." He held out a plate on which were two large slices of what appeared to be freshly-baked cake.

"This hyer gâche melai has just been baked by my wife her. She's put in it some early fallers them. It's for you, it."

John sobered himself.

"Thank you very much Sir. You are very kind." Both John and Franz took the apple filled yeast cake and began to bite into it, greedily.

Chapter Eleven

"I advise immediate X-Ray," suggested the Casualty Surgeon. "That bruising and those contusions there can, I feel, only signify one thing."

It was true, the Doctor too had come to the same conclusion. Despite the transfusion the pulse rate had not improved quickly enough and shock was accelerating.

The fractures to arm and leg were only secondary to the confirmation that John's pelvis was badly shattered. The Orthopaedic Surgeon would have his work to do later but first the prime need was for internal explorations to repair, if possible, the mutilated organs.

Well, the heart and lungs were sound enough and the anaesthetist was sufficiently satisfied to start applying his expertise.

The trolley was on the move now, the team fitted exactly into the lift while John continued his search.

* * *

Major Pieter Müller slouched in his chair in a relaxed manner, his feet stretched out under his desk, while trying desperately not to have his day-dreams interrupted by that fool of a lieutenant who sat opposite him.

It was Thursday, after all, and this afternoon he would be playing lawn tennis with Lilly Brown at the club. He had ordered her to play him for she was the club champion and he wished to beat her. He felt he had ordered her to play for he knew that she did not like Germans and would not wish to be thought friendly towards them. Had he really ordered her? Had she responded to his implied threats that the club might be closed down if she were thought to be uncooperative with a high ranking party member? He liked to think that she had submitted out of respect for his rank, or fear of his potential even, but in his heart he felt she had only decided to play him because it was her choice and she wanted to beat him. Fool! Did she not realise she was taking on one of Germany's amateur champions?

"Hmm hmm hmm," delicately coughed his Lieutenant. "Don't you agree, Sir?"

"Eh? What?" said Major Müller, so rudely drawn back from the future. "Yes, go on, man. I'm listening!"

"Well, Sir, should we move in on him or not?"

Pieter Müller was temporarily disorientated by the question as he sighed deeply, drew in his outstretched feet and used a time-making, face-saving, ploy by answering the question with another.

"Well, you tell me, man. You're in charge of these operations. Tell me what you think. Go over it again."

"Very well, Major, if you insist," said his Lieutenant, with a slight shrug of his shoulders, almost indicating a concealed contempt he might be harbouring against his senior.

The atmosphere was received by the Major who retaliated. "Yes, I do insist! Please do not waste my valuable time. Get on with it!"

He stood up, scornfully pushing the open files across his desk, as he strode towards his window.

Outside, the early morning rush was in full motion. There was an almost continuous stream of bicycles, nose to tail, free wheeling down the hill outside. The occasional gaps in this line would open and close as the whole forward movement would grind to a halt and then, by fits and starts, move on again. He could quite understand why the peasants resented having to ride single file under such circumstances. It must be very frustrating for them to see most of the road surface unused, just in case military or police vehicles should, by chance, require it. Still, it did not really matter what they thought, for their feelings and opinions did not count for anything. They were just a conquered people who had yet to have their spirits broken so that their energies could be used for the furtherance of the aims of the Reich.

Thinking of spirits he noticed one or two young men overtaking the rest and some even daring to ride two abreast. The courts were far too lenient on them, imposing mere fines on recalcitrants If he had his way they would be deported for breaking any rule imposed by his glorious

Germany. Maybe, once the whole of Britain had been subdued, things would be better and they could tighten up.

He noticed there were fewer hold ups on the right hand side of the road nearest to him, for the riders could not cope with the hill and many walked. How weak these people were! Barely twelve months with reduced rations and they went thin and weak and became listless and lethargic. So much for the British! He would not find stalwart Germans reacting to a little starvation in such an immature manner.

The Lieutenant excitedly reiterated the evidence in front of him.

"On the 9th he received that 'phone call, Sir . . ."

"What 'phone call? God in hell! Explain yourself!"

The Lieutenant proceeded unperturbed.

"He received a 'phone call from a certain person with some information about Germans . . ."

"Who did? Who the hell are you talking about?"

"Sir!" protested the Lieutenant, almost raising his voice but quickly repressing the urge. "Surely you are with me. I am giving you the evidence against that Minister, that one called Peters, the one who thinks he's so much better than the German people? Why, only the other day he said . . ."

"Oh, him. Yes, of course. What are you telling me about him? I thought we had this discussion the other day."

"We did, but now I have more evidence against him. We can have him arrested, if you give the word, Sir."

"Have him arrested? Why? What has he done? What can a minister do, in this God-forsaken place, that can be so serious that he needs to be arrested?"

"He hates the Germans, he keeps saying . . ."

"I don't want to know what he says!" stormed Pieter Müller, returning to his desk, "I want facts! Don't waste my time with silly tittle-tattle and what people say and what they don't say . . ."

It was the Lieutenant's turn to interrupt.

"Sir, I must protest! To speak against us is to speak against the Führer himself!"

"Look, man, don't lecture me about what is right and what is wrong. Just remember I have been a party member far longer than you. And let us just get something clear, I do not arrest people because you, Hansel, have a personal animosity towards men of the cloth. I work within the law, understood?"

"Understood," replied Hansel, dutifully reprimanded. "May I continue, please?"

"Continue," said Pieter Müller. "You have fifteen minutes before my visitor arrives."

"On Wednesday 9th he had a 'phone call from a certain person, then he went out on his bicycle. The thing is that . . ."

"Wait a minute," interrupted Pieter. "Who is this certain person you refer to?"

"Ah, yes indeed, well you might ask," explained Hansel. "I am coming to that. Well, later that same evening he was caught out after curfew . . ."

"Hold on. Who was?"

"The minister was, Sir."

"How do you know? Do you keep lists of all our petty criminals now? Surely you don't waste your time looking at the lists of petty offenders when you have a far more important brief."

"You are quite right, Sir," said Lieutenant Hansel, delighted at this chance to prove his efficiency. "I do not interest myself in the trivia, but each Security Post has the names of watched people. Thus I knew of this minister's offence."

"Ah. So you arrested him, then?"

"No, Sir, I was more subtle than that. I did not."

"But surely he was taken in for the night?"

"No, sir."

"Why not?"

Hansel looked at his boots.

"I am afraid the Patrol Post let him go. Do you see what we are up against? Even our own men give these ministers too much respect. Our man let him go with a warning!"

"What!" stormed Müller, quite incensed by this. "I take your point. We can't have these sort of exceptions made! I wish to see this Sentry man personally. Have him sent to me later this morning!"

"Yes, sir, but, as I was saying, I have been investigating this Peters . . ."

"And?"

"I sent for our man de Bourgonnière . . ."

"What, that little worm! How I hate the creature! He'd sell his own parents to make a mark!"

"Agreed, Sir, but he is very useful to us."

"Haven't you contacted the police about this man?"

"Yes, Sir, I did but they have nothing on him."

"Bah!" grunted Pieter Müller. " I sometimes wonder if the police themselves are on their side. Do you know, it would not surprise me if some of their men were actually working against us and informing the enemies of the Reich of our movements."

"Agreed, Sir, and we are carefully watching one or two suspects on that very suspicion. Believe me it is all under control."

"So it should be," was Major Müller's grudging response.

"Well, Sir, the amazing thing about this de Bourgonnière, that you so despise, is . . ."

Again Müller interrupted.

"What the hell are you on about, Hansel? Can't you get to the point? First you're talking about this Peters person then you change to that shit de Bourgonnière. Would you please go back to the beginning and keep to the facts. You're wandering around like an old woman!"

"Very well, Sir," said the Lieutenant with a half stifled sigh. "There are two facts about this Peters' case. One: his 'phone contact and two: de Bourgonnière. Which do you want first?"

Was this a hint of sarcasm, or just dumb insolence? Pieter Müller was not sure. He was getting very bored with Hansel. He wished the interview were over but even if it were he had only that boorish visitor to look forward to.

"Tell me your great discovery about de Bourgonnière so we can get that little rat out of the way."

"As you wish. Well, you see, the interesting fact about him is that when I showed him the list with this minister's name on it he told me he doesn't know the fellow."

"Well that's possible surely? What is the population of this hole, twenty thousand or so?"

"Ah yes, I take your point Sir but, don't you see, I keep very detailed checks on all my informers. Each one is investigated thoroughly. One can't be too careful . . ."

"Go on, surprise me, tell me how astute you have been,"

said Major Müller ungraciously, feeling somewhat that he had been trapped into a 'build up of Hansel'.

"De Bourgonnière is one of Peters' parishioners! He and his family attend his church! Why then would he pretend he does not know the man? Tell me that, Sir. Why is he protecting him?"

"Oh, that's very weak, Hansel. I've told you before, you've a lot to learn. You can only use facts, not stupid conjecture which can't be substantiated."

"But, Sir, he probably knows something about the minister, so is covering up for him."

"Nonsense! He probably thinks the man is in trouble, just because you've got him on one of your damned lists, so he's purposely pretending he doesn't know him. It doesn't mean he knows anything about him."

"But, Sir, I didn't tell him the list was about anything wrong. It could be about anything."

"Yes, of course," replied Pieter Müller, giving vent to his deepest sarcasm, "I had forgotten, you keep lists of the friends of the Reich too. Maybe our worm thought it was a list recommending civilians for the Iron Cross."

"No, Sir, as you know, civilians in occupied territories are not entitled to the Iron Cross . . ."

"God in hell!"

"Sir?"

"Oh nothing, Hansel," sighed the Major. "What is your other piece of irrefutable evidence, please?"

A smile broke across Lieutenant Hansel's lips. He would yet have the last laugh.

"Yes, Sir, yes indeed. We have the name of the man who telephoned the minister."

"And?" asked Pieter Müller quite grudgingly, obviously unaware of the importance of this revelation.

"His name is Collins, Laurence Collins and he lives in the Rue Marguerite."

"Good, so you have the priest's contact for his embezzled bread and wine. So what are you doing about it? Tell me how you are going to shorten this war by six months because of your great discovery?"

Unperturbed, Hansel revealed all.

"We have a great deal on the man, Sir. In fact I have

169

taken a personal interest in the investigations and I am delighted to say his little escapades seem to have some far-reaching. . . ."

"Yes, yes. To the point, man. You only have ten minutes."

"Do you remember, by any chance, the smelly little fisherman whose interrogation you attended last week, Sir?"

God, the audacity of this Lieutenant Hansel! Did he honestly believe that Gestapo Major Pieter Müller would forget something that he had attended only one week before? Did he really think that witnessing the torture of another being was so commonplace to him that he could have forgotten it already? Was he implying that the Major was some sort of cretin? Hell, how could Pieter ever forget that creature there, strapped to the chair, both his eyes blackened, his lips split and blood pouring from his broken nose? Not that he hadn't attended some pretty gruesome sessions in his time, especially on the occasion when he had been seconded to the S.S. camps for six months, but physical violence of this sort always sickened him. It did not seem fitting, somehow, for the master race to resort to basic, almost primitive, methods of dealing with the unenlightened. In a way, to see the enemies of the Reich bleeding, or to hear them screaming, or to smell their vomit and urine of fear, made these enemies, through their very mortality and misery, human. It disturbed Pieter Müller to think of Germany's foes as human beings. He was quite content to think of non-human Jews and non-human criminals, such as Communists, resistance fighters and British Commandoes, going off to extermination camps, as long as they were not given human attributes. He was all for speedy and efficient solutions.

"Yes, I vaguely remember the person," answered Müller, staring Hansel straight in the eye. "Name of Keith de la Haye, born July 10th 1908, resident No. 7 Rue Le Febvré, fisherman, frequenter of Public House the Golden Lion, married, no children, one on the way. Ready for collection 1900 hours tomorrow. Yes, I vaguely recall him!"

Hansel stared at his superior, mouth agape as the Major displayed his extraordinarily able memory.

"Well, Sir," continued Hansel, having regained his poise, "this de la Haye seems to have links with Collins which makes it very interesting as we already suspect de la Haye of being in a theft ring."

"Yes, I see" conceded Pieter Müller, letting out a long slow breath and indeed sounding somewhat interested in this information. "Go on, tell me more. You might actually be on to something, Hansel."

"Thank you, Sir. You are right, of course."

"Oh Hansel, just one thing; we don't suspect de la Haye of being in the theft ring, we know he's in it, don't we? Remember the confessions of de Carteret in Sark? What more do we need?"

Now who was confusing facts and circumstantial evidence, Hansel thought. But he bit his tongue and did not say it. Major Müller was, after all, his superior and as such had to be afforded respect even when he was inconsistent.

"May I just run over the extensive file I have on Collins, please? I think he might be a key man in the organisation of this crime ring and the distribution of the spoils."

"Go on."

"We asked the police to investigate him."

"And?"

"They have produced some interesting facts," said Hansel. "For instance, they suspect he has been involved with black market and, in particular, with one of their own policemen."

"I see." Pieter Müller sounded impressed. "Yes, Hansel, go on. This is interesting, very interesting."

"Thank you, Sir. They have suspected for some time that he operates from a small bicycle shop where he works in the town."

"Are you saying that he uses this shop just as a cover for his illegal activities.?"

"Well, not exactly" answered Hansel. "He does seem to carry out quite an extensive repair trade."

"Have the police any proof of his activities?"

"Well, no, not yet."

"Why not?"

"They think he might have been tipped off by one of their own men when the investigations started."

"Good. I suppose they know who the informer is?"

"Informer?"

"Yes, man, the police swine who has been warning Collins off!"

"Oh yes, Sir, he is. . . ."

"Right! And how is he involved with our fisherman? We know how he is involved with the fisher of men." Pieter Müller was obviously interested, for he was making a dry pun.

"I beg your pardon, Sir, I do not understand?" came Hansel's puzzled reply.

"No, Hansel, I wouldn't expect you to. Forget it."

"Do you want to know about his police contact, Sir?"

"No, I mean yes. No, sorry, damn it! Come back to him in a minute. Tell me first about the link with de la Haye."

"Very well, Major," said Hansel smiling, thinking to himself that at last he had a chance to prove how excellent he was. "When I learned that the police suspected Collins of crime, I put into action a very detailed plan. You see, Sir, I. . . ."

"Yes, yes. Go on. Go on," interrupted Pieter Müller impatiently, "You have only a few minutes."

"Thank you, Sir. As I was saying, I put into action my very detailed plan. . ." Müller sighed.

". . . . I had the shop, where Collins works, watched and I introduced plants".

"You introduced what?"

"Plants, Sir. You know, people who go in and try to trick people into breaking the law. The French call them Agents Provocateurs."

"All right Hansel, it's just for a minute I thought you were going to tell me you strangled the man with tomato plants." Pieter Müller grinned at the confused looking blockhead in front of him. What a fool he was!

"Yes, I sent some soldiers in with German items for sale and I sent one of our civilian informers in to try to purchase some goods."

"And? Tell me what happened."

"Unfortunately nothing, Sir, but I was informed he looked very worried."

"Do you mean to tell me he didn't buy or sell any goods to your people?" exploded the Gestapo Major.

"Exactly, Sir."

"Well, what do you make of that, then? Surely it makes you look rather stupid, doesn't it?"

"Oh no, Sir, on the contrary, with respect, it confirms my suspicions that he is involved in something big."

"How do you mean?"

"Well, I think he is the organisation for something much bigger and all his genuine contacts use a code. That is why he didn't respond to my plants."

"Well, maybe," conceded Major Müller grudgingly. "Tell me how de la Haye comes into it?"

"After our police report we have had Collins followed. It seems he goes to the Beer House known as the Golden Lion near the Market, and as you so rightly observed, Sir, that is where the fisherman drinks also."

"Good, go on, please."

"We put one of our agents in there in the evenings."

"And?"

"This Collins went in there on Monday and Tuesday evenings. Incidentally he got very drunk on Monday evening, there was a bit of a scuffle and his friends attacked him and turned him out."

"Why?"

"Our man is not too sure, but it seems he was shouting out something about being a father to a German."

"He what?"

"I don't know any more than that, Sir. Apparently there was so much noise going on. . . ."

"You having his 'phone tapped?" snapped Müller, abruptly changing the subject.

"Of course, Sir!"

"And?"

"Nothing, they don't seem to use the 'phone much at all," replied Hansel, barely concealing his irritation at this deviation.

"Nothing? Are you telling me they don't use the telephone at all?"

"They have only telephoned relatives since the call to the minister."

"You have checked the persons called?"

"Yes, Sir."

"Good, Hansel. Good. Let me have transcripts of all the conversations."

"May I continue, Sir?"

"Yes, go on."

The telephone on Pieter Müller's desk rang. He snatched at it like a tormented dog.

"Yes?. . . . Right. Tell him to wait. I'll be three minutes!" He slammed down the receiver.

"Time is up, Hansel. Quickly finish what you were saying about de la Haye and Collins."

Hansel put all his effort into being brief, for when Major Müller said three minutes, he knew he meant exactly that.

"In the Golden Lion on Tuesday, Collins was asking questions about de la Haye. My informer got the impression that Collins was not too popular with the other civilians and he did not stay long. . ."

"Yes yes. Proceed."

"Yesterday, de la Haye was seen going into Collins' shop. He was in there for twenty five minutes. He neither took in a bicycle nor came out with one".

"So!" exclaimed Müller. "Anything else? Quick!"

"Yes Sir, a young foot soldier was observed going in to see Collins both yesterday and this morning."

"What is wrong with that. Many of our men have bicycles."

"Yes, Sir, but very few of our men have bicycles with Guernsey tax numbers on them, do they?"

It was Major Müller's turn to feel belittled. He was not prepared to accept defeat at the hands of his Lieutenant.

"Who was this soldier? Don't tell me you haven't got a track on him?"

"Not yet, Sir, but we are investigating."

"Anything else?" asked Müller, as he raised himself towards the door.

Hansel hesitated. He desperately wanted to bring his investigations to their culmination so that he could reap the full glory of his success. He knew, however, that Major Müller had to say yes or no to his coming request. Tactfully he put his question to his superior in a way which would make him feel he was making the decision.

"Sir, in your vast experience of these cases, would you recommend that I should have Collins arrested so that we can crack this whole ring and you will know that the enemies of the Reich have been eradicated?"

Hansel's fear was realised in the answer he received.

"Indeed not, you fool! Arrest him now and all the rest will go into hiding. No, no, just keep watching him, Hansel. Watch and build up your evidence. That way we'll get the lot. Look into that police traitor and that foot soldier, keep up your good work with those informers of yours and keep me in the picture. I must say, Hansel, this is not bad. Not bad at all." Pieter Müller paused adding the two words, "for you," as his sting in the tail.

"Thank you, Sir. That was the advice I hoped you would give," replied Hansel, biting his tongue at his very hypocrisy.

"Right. Now you must go. Come back to see me at noon and submit your plans to me for my scrutiny. Oh, yes, and bring that soldier with you. I'm going to make an example of him."

"Soldier, Sir?" queried Hansel thinking he meant the one who had been seen entering Collins' shop. How the hell was he going to have him tracked down by noon?

"The one who let the priest go after curfew!" snapped Müller, as he opened the door for Hansel and all but pushed him out.

"Oh, and Hansel. . . ."

"Yes, Sir?"

"You'll find a civilian downstairs waiting to see me. Please don't use any rough tactics on him. He might look like a peasant but he is in fact a Government Administrator. Please be good enough to escort Herr Tropp up to my office.

"Yes Sir. Heil Hitler!"

*   *   *

And so the two friends, by now with hardly a care in the world, and having consumed a gallon of cider between them, left the old farmer with much handshaking and smiling and promises that they would return. Yes indeed, they would be back nearer Christmas for some more cider. Yes, they wanted to try the good lady's special Christmas cake, in which she was to use some of the old gentleman's own grapes, which he would soon be drying to make raisins.

"So we'll see you again, boys, is it?" asked the old man with a chuckle.

"But of course," replied John, as he struggled to mount his bicycle. It just would not stay still enough for him. Franz was having the same problem. He had already scooted on the muddy road but had given up that method when he had fallen into the hedge. What hilarity that had caused! John had laughed so loud and for so long he had forgotten why he was laughing. The tears had streamed down his face and he had had to disappear behind the hedge yet again.

Franz eventually mounted his machine, lady's fashion, and John did likewise. John seemed a little more the worse for wear than his friend and pulled alongside him, leaning on his shoulder for support.

"We must go now," he called. "We're very late. We'll see you again."

As he spoke his words slurred and Franz hiccoughed loudly, causing John to have another fit of the giggles.

"OK, cheerie!" called the old man, suddenly realising that he was about to lose two sons of peace temporarily loaned to him by Sister Time. Two sons from an age when there was no war and no bitterness or sadness to disturb his idylls. He smiled at them. It was a sad smile. His lips curled back revealing his gums and his few yellowed and mellowed teeth. His wrinkled old face grew tight with the effort of smiling as all his emotions instructed his muscles he should be crying, not smiling.

Would they ever come back these two, them? Would mother Britain win the war before Christmas her? Would the young German be sent off to a prison in England, him? Would the Jerries win the war, them, and send all Guernsey's young men to camps, them, on the continent, it? It did not bear thinking about.

As the two wended their tortuous way, up the narrow grass banked lane, they kept looking back to wave at their old friend. There he stood, waving. Waving as he got smaller and smaller. John kept waving back even when, through distance and probably more so, through excess of cider, he could no longer distinguish the old man from the hawthorn bushes, or his cows from the trees, or his little granite cottage from the weary roofed barn, sagging under the weight of its ancient tiles. He was thankful when, once at the top of the steep lane, they turned the corner and the necessity for formalities was over.

"Wait for me, Franz!"

"No, you're too slow," came his friend's reply. "You catch me up!"

Franz raced ahead, his light lithe body responding well to the liquid stimulant so recently imbibed.

Poor John, the cider had had an opposite effect on him. Maybe it was that he had not had Franz's recent training with Schnapps, in Herm and at the Relaxation. Possibly it was that he had drunk more than his half of the flagon, or perhaps he had just eaten his gâche too fast and too eagerly, but he did feel strange. He had never felt like this before.

As he rode after Franz, first his feet and then his calves and, by gradual creeping degrees his knees then thighs became numb and heavy. As he pedalled, he had the sensation of walking through thick deep mud. It was like those nightmares when he tried so desperately to move from the path of a charging bull or out of the way of a crashing, burning aeroplane but became paralysed.

His whole being was slowing down, yet things external to him were moving erratically. The bank on his right kept moving away from him slowly, then, quite unexpectedly, that on the left would come rushing towards him. What was happening to his world? He would wrench his handlebars out of the path of the stupid hedge, then the other bank would rush towards him. Why could not the sides of the road stay still? He was steering a straight course but they were taking no notice of him.

Where was Franz? John looked ahead but could see no sign of him.

Ahead of him John saw a blue sky which changed imperceptibly to white as he lowered his vision. In the distance his land horizon ended abruptly, contrasting its dark greens with the white haze which must be the sea. As he looked, John felt that same thrill that he always did when, as a little boy, the family would suddenly sight the sea in the far distance.

Now he could see the breakers on Vazon Bay, he could taste the salt. He watched all the pale visitors from England, grownups, some in their swimming costumes, some with rolled up trousers and skirts held high, while they paddled and shrieked in delight as the ripples assaulted their sensitive legs. He heard the seagulls and saw the little boys and girls with their buckets and spades. In front of him he had his dinky cars with a maze of sand-carved roads and tunnels.

There, for all to see, were his dams across the freshwater streams, as the tide receded from Moulin Huet. There, on show, were his dykes at Grandes Rocques keeping the rising tide at bay.

'Oh what a good fortress this one is.'

'Yes, you can help but you must do what I tell you!'

'OK, quick! Build up that wall!'

'Quick, that wave there has burst our outer defences!'

'No don't do that, it will cave in!'

'Quick, you lot. Inside and start baling.'

What was that there? A queue for ice-cream at Cobo. Oh, it was so hot! Lovely cool ice-cream and a bottle of pop. John crossed the road to join the queue. He was so hot! The people in the queue became very rough. He tried to push in but they turned him back. The visitors towered above him but he could not make out their faces. They pushed him! They pushed him and he fell on the pebbles.

He fell! What a noise! He heard the mighty breakers crashing across the sand towards him.

'Watch out!' he heard, 'that one will suck you out!'

He dug his fingers into the wet sand and clung on for dear life. The waves burst upon him and lifted him up so that he became weightless. He could not see. All he could hear was the rumbling noise and the rush of the water which was all over and all through him.

'Help Daddy! Help me! Help me, I'll drown!' Oh, how he hurt! How hot he was! The sea was hot!

"I'm so hot! So hot!" John ripped at his collar and pulled off his tie opening his shirt as far as he could. He tried to undo his boots but somehow he could not reach them for they were trapped under his bicycle.

Bicycle? His coat had to come off. Yes that was it! So hot! So hot! But he could not sit upon the sand. Sand? This was not sand, it was road! He was too dizzy to sit up.

Eyes closed now, John let the earth beneath him spin him

round faster and faster while he grew heavier and heavier. He dared not open his eyes as he felt his whole world tilting, as he felt his island tipping him into the sea.

"John! John! Oh poor John! What has happened to you?" shouted Franz as he almost threw down his bicycle, rushing to help his friend lying in the centre of the road.

"Who is it?" yelled John still not daring to open his eyes.

"It is, I, Franz, your friend," came the reply.

"Oh Franz, help me please. I feel terrible."

Franz knelt down by John and picked up his bicycle.

"There!" he said, as he placed his hand on John's shoulder. "Sit up, you silly fellow. There's nothing wrong with you. You're just a little drunk, that's all."

"Drunk!" shouted John in anger. "I'm not bloody drunk. I'm perfectly sober!"

He sat there in the middle of the lane, knees drawn up to his chin, head down and he started to shiver and shake.

"Not drunk?" asked Franz in exasperation. "What are you then? You're a stupid drunken Englishman."

John was in no mood to be spoken to harshly or to be jested with. As he sat there looking so comical, and yet so doleful, he began to cry. He did not know why he was crying. It could not have been the pain in his grazed knee or the bump on his head for he never cried when he hurt himself. He was not a baby. It could not have been his damaged trousers for he was used to his mother complaining about such things even though she always managed to put them right somehow. It could not be his bicycle lying there for it was sure to be alright, it was a sturdy machine. The bike looked fine but he did so wish it would stop swaying around.

The tears channelled down his cheeks as he let out a long low howl of misery which was broken unevenly by his sobs.

"Come, come, John, it is all right. You are just a little drunk. Here, let me help you. Germany to the rescue." He chuckled as he helped John to his feet.

Once up and almost balanced, John turned on Franz and in his drunken temper swung his arm at him. He missed as Franz stepped aside, laughing.

"I'm not drunk, I tell you. I don't drink!"

"Oh ho!" taunted Franz. "You're not drunk, eh? And you don't drink! I see! Have you forgotten the cider?"

"Shut up!"

"No, you shut up! If you're not drunk, then walk in a straight line for me," teased Franz.

"No!"

"Why not? Because you can't?"

"Shut up. I hate you!" shouted John as he swung out at Franz again, almost losing his balance.

Franz caught him.

"Come, my friend. Do not get angry. It will pass."

John was still shivering. He sagged against Franz. Franz looked at his friend's face and noticed how pallid it was.

"John, you look ill. Do you want to be sick?"

John felt very sick but could not bear to contemplate the physical function of it.

"No," he said. "I feel sick but don't want to be."

"If you feel sick, then be sick. Get it over with."

"No! Please."

"Yes, I will make you sick. Then you will feel better."

"No! No!"

"Yes, John, let me put my fingers in your throat."

John could not protest. He knew if he spoke the vomit would break through his defences. He closed his eyes, gritting his teeth, as he turned his head from Franz. The bile welled into his throat.

As Franz's fingers trespassed against the gritted portcullis John shook his head in protest. His very action, and attention to the intrusive fingers helped dispel the vileness in his throat.

"Oh, yes, John is being very silly. Franz know how to make him sick. Listen to Mummy," coaxed Franz in mock derision.

"John. Would you like cider? John, can you hear me, are you listening? What about a lovely big piece of that apple cake? Or how about some Christmas cake full of juicy raisins?"

While speaking, Franz watched his friend. His knuckles were squeezed so tightly they were white, drained of blood. His teeth were clenched, ivory set in yellow skin while his tight-closed eyelids, quivering, were beige against the sallow complexion. As Franz watched, mesmerized by the changing colour of this pathetic creature, he just retrieved himself in time to avoid the gush of filth which burst from a mouth so suddenly changed from a firm rat-trap to a large perfectly rounded and thin letter 'O'. The brown and yellow torrent burst outward in an arc which splashed up from the stones.

Gush followed gush as the vile-smelling fluid splattered, seeming to fill the air, in all directions, with its spray. The noises of John's misery were painful to listen to as he involuntarily retched and yet more of the semi-digested mixture flooded out. As he crouched there, bent over almost double in the centre of the lane while Franz kept grip of his shoulders, he felt relieved that he had at last allowed the nausea to leave his body. Each spasm was now out of his control and John resigned himself to it, letting it take its course.

Once he attained the state where he was retching, but giving vent to no more matter, he began to feel considerably better and became aware of a number of other discomforts which, until then, had been eclipsed. He was now able to be disgusted by the smell of his vomit without actually being made ill again. This was by contrast with Franz, who was feeling decidedly unwell as he inhaled the odours of the fruits of his friend's excesses. His other most pressing discomforts were the obnoxious taste in his mouth and the sensation of parts of his vomit being lodged firmly in the passages at the back of his throat. It felt as though he had disgorged a branch, a twig of which had invaded his respiratory passages at the time of mass exodus when both nose and mouth had been used as escape routes.

"Have you got a handkerchief, John?" asked Franz, the concern in his voice not completely masking his amusement.

"I don't know," was the reply. This was rather silly for his mother always insisted that he went out with a clean handkerchief even when he did not have a cold. "Why?" he asked.

"Why? Because we must clean you up, my friend," came Franz's good-natured answer.

"Haven't you got one?" asked John rather sulkily, feeling the proposed effort to search his own pockets would be too much.

"Me? A handkerchief?" asked Franz laughing. "What do you think we are, a lot of Frenchmans or something? We are members of the valiant German army. We don't need hand-kerchiefs!"

"Oh, here you are, I've found one," said John, not in the mood to be baited.

He passed the clean white pad to Franz who snatched at it, running to his bicycle.

"Stay there John. Don't go away, I won't be long," he called, as he mounted his steed and 'cycled back down the lane. John did not protest. He did not seem to have any contention left in him.

In less than three minutes Franz had returned. He dropped his bicycle next to his friend and held out the package he carried carefully. It was the handkerchief now soaking wet.

"Here," he announced, "I remember we pass a little watering place for horsen so I have your handkerchief wet for you to have a washing."

John offered no resistance as his friend deftly wiped his face and hands then attended to the soiled areas of his clothes.

"There!" he declared at last. "You now look and smell a little better so maybe you can cheer up again and we can on our way go to do the Führer's work!"

The jovial Franz might at least antagonise his friend into argument. Anything would be better than the civilian's present self-sympathetic silence. John seemed oblivious to the incitement.

"Seven," he mouthed, as Franz followed the direction of his gaze.

"Seven?" He was staring at the licence number on Franz's bike. Why had he been so blind up till now? Franz had Dad's bike, and it had taken him till now to realise it!

Franz, too, understood what John was saying, as he watched his friend's look of puzzlement gradually change to one of naked anger.

"John, John, its the bicycle isn't it?" he started falteringly. "John, I have been meaning to tell you all morning . . ."

Everything fitted into place now.

Yes, of course. This was Dad's bike! Now he recognised it. How he must have been blind earlier not to recognise his own father's machine! How blinded by his pleasure, at the prospect of spending a day with his friend, that he had not been aware of all the strange happenings which had brought these circumstances to pass!

"What the hell are you doing with my father's bike?" he demanded.

"John, I try to explain to you ..." started Franz in frustration that his friend was becoming very agitated and had obviously closed his mind to any explanations Franz might proffer.

"Eh? Why have you got it, eh?"

Franz, who had been trying for some minutes to form the words that would effect a conciliatory explanation decided there was nothing for it but to explain the matter in a brief and factual way and then to sit back and await the storm of recriminations. He could not see why there had to be such recriminations. However, he was sensitive to John's intensifying mood. He felt it was unjust that he should have to become defensive over what was, after all, a purely business transaction. Besides, why should he not be able to accept a kindness from the father of a friend?

"I have hire this bicycle from a man in a bicycle shop in St. Peter Port. Quite by chance that man, it appears, could be your father," explained Franz, relieved to have got out the words, but himself somewhat shocked by their aloofness and chill.

"A man in a bicycle shop!" yelled John. "Could be your father? What do you mean, could be my father? You know bloody well he's my father, eh?"

"Well you know ..." started Franz in a mixture of aloofness and embarrassment.

John cut across him, regardless of what he was saying, for he was in a mood of outraged rhetoric.

"You leave my father alone, you! You damn well keep away from him, do you understand? He's my father, not yours!"

"Why John, why are you like this?"

"You just keep away from him, that's all! He's in enough trouble as it is, without having to have Germans creeping round him for favours ..."

"Favours?" interrupted Franz. "How is it a favour? He doesn't even know me? I pay for this bike ..."

John, blinded with rage, persevered regardless of logic

and argument. It was as though, in his anger, he were unaware of the other's presence. His argument was more with himself than with another.

"Leave him alone! He's my father, he's not yours!" In his temper he was back at home, John the only child, John the spoilt boy, John the lonely bored and thwarted little boy, John the angry irrational bad-tempered little boy stamping his foot on the kitchen floor, the tears rolling down his cheeks as he angrily pushed his mother aside. The pull at his father's trouser legs as he tried to drag him away from his mother. And both his parents looking down at him and laughing from a great height. No, Dad would not be taking him to the pictures today, he was going for a walk with his mother!

"Listen, John!" shouted Franz, getting angry. "What is the matter with you? Why should not your father have anythings to do with me?"

John, still outraged, replied, "Because he's mine, he's not for you or anyone! You're a German! You're the enemy. You go in bad company. Go and find your own father!"

Franz's face, usually pale, went a deathly, ashen white. As he stood there breathing deeply like one who has just violently exercised, clenching his fists, staring at the angry rude little boy in front of him, he thought of the insult through which he was living. Not only was this Britisher insulting his nation, his Fatherland, and trying to, not without success, make Franz feel the inferior lost soul that he was, now he was trying to destroy him by heaping misery on his head.

"My father? Find my own father!" he gasped. "Do you know what you say? Do you?" He did not wait for a reply. "My dear father died fighting for his country and you know it! I tell you the other day! And now you mock and insult me. I tell you I will not have it!"

He stepped towards John, the white rage giving his face a mask like appearance. Jerkily, like a robot, he pushed John's shoulder so that he was taken by surprise and spun to stand at right angles to his assailant.

John, still fully concerned with his own thoughts and anger, had not been cognizant of Franz's anger or his exclamations. The surprise of the assault caused him to freeze momentarily, mouth agape.

"What was that for, German?" he uttered, the last word German loaded with sneering derision.

"That was for my father! And this is for my mother!" He pushed John again so that, losing balance he ran three steps back before he could gain control of his involuntary momentum.

"You what?" asked John in amazement, still unaware what this was all about. In a primitive need for self preservation he forgot the reason for this antagonism but he knew only that he was under attack. He retaliated with a full fist blow to Franz's face, although his punch failed to target. Franz had been well trained in the Hitler Youth.

Franz's instincts took control as he grabbed the outstretched arm, casually deflecting it, at the same time, turning and bending so John, in the full force of his forward movement, passed over him and dropped on to the lane like a bag of flour.

Before John realised it, Franz was on top of him raining punches down towards his face. he could not think why, nor could he tell what was happening. All he knew was that here was a German with a look of madness in his eyes, a German whom he had considered to be a friend. As Franz looked down and first one blow hit a lip, causing its prettiness to be disfigured with blood-coloured saliva oozing from those ivory teeth, and another which grazed an eye, then yet another causing an ear to look stinging red, he wondered why he was hating this enemy so, this enemy who was his friend.

The adrenalin flowed and tempers took over where before words had taunted into action. John, although less skilled in the arts of self-defence and surprise attack, was the heavier and stronger of the two. Before long he was straddling Franz, in the manner of a playground victor, smacking his cheeks and demanding a submission. All that was missing was the sudden gathering of spectators, spurring him on while booing the vanquished. No fickle crowd here, no pushing swaying wall of bodies, no one to hold the coats of the feuding factions, none to slap him on the back with congratulations, no friends to drop the defeated leaving him snivelling, as the transient mob moved from fight to fight, thriving on misery as though it were the food of growing up.

The only being in John's consciousness was an anxious-looking, pale-faced soldier who refused to submit. He did not have the heart to hurt him, he was beginning to lose his anger and, with it, his cause.

"Submit, Franz, and I'll let you go."

"No!" cried Franz in defiance. "How can I, a German, submit to you?"

It was difficult for John to think of an answer to this question, especially now his temper was subsiding.

Franz slightly rekindled the dwindling embers by exclaiming, partly in fun. "Anyway, John, you are a German, you love Germany. Look, you even wear the uniform!" He indicated John's armband, unable to resist a slight smile which escaped from his pursed lips.

"Why, you little bugger!" shouted John, by now acting anger rather than feeling the emotion. "I'll make you eat your words, mon vieux!"

He jogged up and down on Franz's abdomen, just sufficient for him to call out giggling,

"Oh, stop that, you're being stupid!"

"Stupid is it?" asked John, now grinning broadly, "I'll give you stupid."

He began to give his enemy the typewriter treatment, rapidly poking his fingers at his chest so that he dissolved into fits of laughter at the ticklish sensation.

"Stop! Stop!" screeched Franz, as he writhed in torment, while his laughter howled up into John's face.

John too, laughing, asked once more, "Submit?" followed by, in a stern manner, "Why stupid, eh? Explain yourself boy."

"I tell you why you're stupid," laughed Franz, "you English men say stupid things!"

"What do you mean?" asked John, both puzzled and intrigued.

"Well, you say things like you'll make me eat my words. How can I eat words? You see, you're stupid!" taunted Franz.

John accepted the taunt in the good-natured way that it was intended. He was not prepared to leave it there, however.

"Oh we'll soon see about that!" he exclaimed, as he ripped off his messenger armband. "See this here? See these words on this band? They're German, eh? Right then, you're bloody going to eat them!"

"No!" yelled Franz, realisation dawning on him, as the armband was forced up against his lips.

While this fun was taking place, in celebration of their transformation from enemies to friends once more, they were not aware of the sound of tyres, or the switching off of the almost silent engine, nor the click shut of the car door. They were also unaware of the studiously quiet footsteps behind them.

Franz's face took on the incarnation of an exclamation mark as he mouthed, barely whispering the word,

"John!"

John felt the cold hard shock between his shoulder-blades, while his friend's face reflected the sudden invasion of fear which he felt flooding his mind.

The pressure at his back had to be a revolver, this thought reinforced by the staccato German order to get up.

John stood, and, somewhat comically, raised his shaking hands, his body rigidly still, back to his assailant. He watched the dishevelled Franz struggle to his feet also, automatically clicking his heels to accompany his salute and greeting:

"Heil Hitler!"

His formality was not reciprocated by the clipped Germanic tongue.

"He is telling you to turn round," said Franz.

John felt the pressure relieved between his shoulder-blades and turning slowly found himself staring into the face of a young member of the Feldpolizei. Slowly he started lowering his aching arms. Again came the snapped order, as this smart little man almost spat out the words whilst staring directly into John's eyes. The revolver pointed at his face.

"Put your hands on your head," said Franz, very slowly and expressionlessly.

John complied.

Question followed question as the two youths stood there, shaking and fearful. Many of the questions were asked of Franz, but some were relayed to John via him.

"He wants to know why you attack me," explained Franz.

"Tell him I wasn't attacking you, we were just playing a game," suggested John.

"No, John, he must not know we are friends. What can we say?"

Franz was interrupted by the reiterated demand for an answer.

John was inspired,

"Tell him we work together, that you're from the Feld-kommandantur," he said.

Franz tried this suggestion. It seemed to convince the feldpolizist for he came back with a further question.

"He want to know your name and where you live."

A sudden irrational panic invaded John's mind. He did not know why, but he did not wish this Gestapo man to know either his name or his residence. Without thinking, he said the first name which came to mind:

"Gaudion, Paul Gaudion."

Franz looked puzzled but had to relay the information. This was followed by a reminder for his address.

As John replied,

"La Porte, St. Jacques." The feldpolizist was scrutinising him, his fixed smile almost a sneer.

"No," mouthed Franz to John, "no, you fool," the last words coming out as a whisper.

The policeman turned to Franz, realising he was trying to communicate with John, and gave a further instruction.

As Franz had feared, he asked for John to produce his identity card. Franz gulped as tremulously he instructed his friend further.

The enormity of his error dawned upon John, as he produced his card. The man lowered his revolver and snatching the card, opened it reading out loud in precise clear tones:

"Collins, John, Twelve Rue Marguerite (New Street). Danke!" He returned the card, seemingly unabashed and turned his questioning German upon Franz once more.

"He wants to know why you give your address as St. Jacques," he explained, "when in fact, you live in Rue Marguerite."

"Ah!" faltered John, hesitating as the questioning gaze of the Gestapo man focussed upon his eyes. "Let him think you asked me wrong and that I thought he wanted to know where I work."

Yes that was quick thinking, that would do nicely. The

German would probably forget the matter of the wrong name. What could he say if he were asked though?

Franz concentrated on this explanation, the man appearing to be quite satisfied as he smiled nodding to Franz, transmitting his obvious approval.

Suddenly he turned to face John, his expression a scowl of black rage. John was taken utterly by surprise as the revolver was thrust against his temple. He had little time to think what was happening.

In slow, yet perfectly clear and deliberate English, the Gestapo man asked:

"So you are a friend of Germans and you do not wish me to know where you live? This is most interesting!"

*　　*　　*

"Herr Tropp for you, Major Müller," announced Lieutenant Hansel curtly, as he showed the Civilian Administrator in to Pieter Müller's office.

"Ah, Herr Tropp," greeted Major Müller casually, as he raised himself from his chair, undecided whether he should be polite or not.

The meeting was destined to be uncomfortable for Major Müller. He had felt at a disadvantage, defensive, ever since Herr Tropp had asked for or more likely demanded, this meeting. The Gestapo Major would not normally have felt intimidated by a mere civilian but this one, he sensed, was dangerous. Hadn't he got friends in high places? The fellow was too much in the know. Why, he even knew that Franz was a party member. Why should the Feldkommandantur bother itself with Gestapo business?

Of course, Herr Tropp, as a good upstanding Aryan, had every right to be concerned. Pieter was also. Hadn't he done all the right things for his nephew? His education, places at the great Nuremburg rallies, good connections? Wasn't he now well placed, with his excellent command of English, and here in Guernsey, for great advancement in the imminent Nazification of the rest of Britain?

But to see for himself that the weakling was a coward, and worse still, to have this pointed out to him by Tropp, was almost unendurable.

189

"Well, Herr Tropp, please don't think me ungrateful for all the interest you're showing in my nephew, but I'd hate you to think I was pampering the lad. He is a grown man you know? He is fifteen."

"Yes indeed," replied Herr Tropp, "old enough to be dying for his country in Russia, don't you think?"

Herr Tropp, all the time his kindly facial expression belying the veiled threats of his admonition, went on to imply that Pieter Müller's guidance and influence had been apparently lacking, for the lad was little more than a coward. There were yet more serious deficiencies in his character.

Oh yes, the civilian knew all there was to know about the Müller family, even to the fact that the Major before him looked on Franz as a son, owing to his own deficiency to sire any of the superior gender.

"It probably was not your fault anyway," he patronised. "It was most likely the fault of your wife, some women just cannot do their duty in this regard, no matter how hard their husbands try."

Herr Tropp would not settle until his dignity had been revenged. His authority had been thwarted by that wilful Messenger and the German coward. Like a good German father, who has been disobeyed, defied even, by a recalcitrant child, all his emotions were to punish and crush the offender.

"You see, Major, your nephew is easily led!"

He explained the already known liaison between the two youths and implied that Uncle Pieter had to put a stop to it.

"Herr Tropp," said Major Müller, cold with annoyance and embarrassment, "I have already severely reprimanded Franz for his action. He will not do it again, I assure you."

"Assure me, do you?" repeated the Administrator with more than a hint of sarcasm. "Well, tell me, Major, how much do your assurances amount to?" He catalogued the whole list of his Messenger's misdemeanours, which so rankled with him, including the visit to the hospital and Franz's loitering outside the Feldkommandantur office.

"Tell me what a good German name of Müller has in common with a peasant named Collins?"

At the surname, alarm bells rang in Pieter Müller's head.

"With whom? Who did you say he was arguing with?"

Sebastian Tropp had unintentionally let slip one of his

principal cards, but he was delighted to see that it had not been entirely wasted. Major Müller's reaction confirmed that.

"Yes," he said casually, "Collins. John Collins, the Guernsey messenger for the Feldkommandantur."

The Administrator could not restrain his joy, his permanent smile becoming larger than usual, as he watched Major Müller, his brain activity racing, translating his misgivings into the expression on his face.

"Did you say Collins?" stammered the Major. "Where does he live?"

"Oh, come now, Major," said Herr Tropp, half mockingly, half patronisingly. "You do not expect me to divulge Feldkommandantur information to the Feldpolizei do you? You would not like it if I were to start doing your job for you, would you?"

His twinkling steady gaze was annoying Pieter Müller. Pieter was mustering his thoughts. It could be a coincidence, Collins? Yes, it could be just that. He needed time to think. He wished to close this interview.

As though the Administrator had completely penetrated Pieter's mind, and raided his most secret thoughts, he announced quite casually;

"Well I must leave you Major, you must have quite a lot to do. I am sure you will adequately deal with your nephew."

As he walked towards the door, and as Major Müller absentmindedly followed, in order to see his guest out, Herr Tropp turned to say,

"I won't tell you where Collins lives, we must leave something for the Feldpolizei to do, yes? But his father's name might interest you. It is Laurence Collins. Good morning, Major Müller. Heil Hitler!"

He was gone.

* * *

John, his back to the noises on which he was concentrating, scrutinised Franz who, in turn, was standing rigid, watching the departure of the feldpolizist.

Franz too was shaking, as the man crunched his boots to the car, and the wait for the departing purr of the engine seemed endless.

John dare not turn as he stood there, rigid, miserable, as the warm wetness seeped down his thighs.

With the departure of the car, Franz unfroze with relief and was laughing while crying at the same time.

"I thought he'd killed me! I thought he'd killed me!" yelled John in his unpent anguish.

"I too!" cried Franz.

It was bizarre to hear Franz's laughter, as he shouted this, while tears channelled down his cheeks and his whole body racked with sobs and laughter. It was the laughter of misery, of hysteria.

"When he pulled that trigger I died!" screamed John, his voice getting to a high pitch in an attempt to override Franz's noise.

"Shut up, Franz! Shut up, will you? Listen. Stop laughing! Stop it! Stop it, I say!" He slapped Franz across the face hard so that the white print could be observed before it was invaded by foreign pink, as suddenly as he had started.

Strangely, the action of anger had soothed John's troubled consciousness and now his concern was more for Franz immediate than himself just past. John was sorry for the assault on his friend and would have apologised for it, except that it appeared Franz had been unabashed.

"Whew!" sighed Franz. "You were lucky there. I think you have it!"

"I know," quavered John. "Tell me what it was all about."

"Well, you know," replied Franz, "he understood English all the time. He hear all your lies then you are really in trouble."

"Yes, I know. What do you think's going to happen now?"

"I don't know, John," replied Franz, his face a picture of absolute misery. "He took your identity card so that can mean only one thing, can't it?"

"What can it mean?" demanded John, again that cold irrational fear gripping at his stomach. "Go on, tell me what? He's taken my card, so what does it mean? You're German, tell me!"

Franz replied with the only answer he could. He replied with the answer which John logically anticipated but which, nonetheless, he feared,

"You will have to go to the Feldpolizei to get it back. Oh John!"

"Yes, I know," groaned John, "but what will happen to me there?"

"I don't know. Maybe nothing. I just don't know."

"I know you don't know, but what do you think?"

"I think they'll interrogate you."

"Interrogate me! Why?" shouted John. "Why should they interrogate me, eh? What have I done?"

"Don't shout at me! It's not my fault!"

"Well, it's not mine either! Why would they interrogate me? What have I done, eh?"

"I don't know. You keep ask these questions," replied Franz. "Why don't you think about me? You might get interrogated, but what will to me happen?"

"What do you mean, what will happen to you? You've done nothing wrong, have you?"

"I don't know John. Maybe there'll be a lot of trouble for me."

"Why?"

"Well, for a start, we were fighting in the road. You could be sent to prison for hitting a German, John."

"I know," breathed John dejectedly, "but we weren't fighting."

"We were, it started as a fight."

"Yes you know that, and I know that, but he wasn't there, eh?"

"That's true," agreed Franz, "but that makes it even worse for us!"

"Why?"

"Because, can't you see, if we weren't fighting then why were you on top of me in the road?"

John could not prevent a smile, at the ludicrous picture this question conjured, and was about to reply when Franz cut across his train of thought;

"And don't say it is because we are friends and are play a game," he said, he too smiling at the ridiculous way the concept sounded, when translated into words.

"Why not, we are friends. I'm not ashamed to say it," declared John.

193

"Nor I," affirmed Franz, "but they would not see it like that. I'm not allowed to mix with you Guernsey people."

John knew this was true. Despite his private feelings that this attitude of the German authorities was contradictory and unjust, he was learning to accept this from his Teutonic masters.

"It might be all right," considered Franz, shrugging in cold comfort, adding, with regard for John's anxious expression, "anyway, friend, this war will soon be over, and we'll all be friends working together."

"I hope so," replied John, but extreme doubt was implicit in his voice.

*   *   *

"Enter!" shouted Major Müller as Lieutenant Hansel jerked his way through the door, stepping aside to permit the entry of the sentry post Corporal.

"Heil," grunted Pieter Müller casually, to which Hansel jerked like a string controlled puppet and the Corporal became the ultimate in smartness.

"Hansel, kindly see this idiot out. I have far more important business than to waste time on fools right now," ordered the Major.

"Sir?" enquired Hansel politely. "You did ask to see this man in person, Sir. He is the one who. . . ." Hansel was interrupted by an anxious and irritable Major Müller,

"Don't tell me what I said. I know damned well who he is. Just make him wait outside!"

Like a clockwork soldier the Corporal stood there until activated by the officer then, as though he had been completely oblivious to the previous conversation, in which his behaviour and to which his eventual dressing down, played and were to play a part, he turned smartly, clicked his heels and obediently placed himself outside the door marked, 'Major P. Müller'.

"Right Hansel, sit down," ordered the Major. "We have some further developments on this morning's conversation. Before I go any further, I wish to remind you of your oath of obedience and that, as your superior, you owe me your strict loyalty and confidence in all this. Do you understand?"

"Yes, Major," answered Hansel, feeling mystified and

understanding nothing. "You have my strict loyalty and confidence always."

"Good," said Major Müller. "Remember Hansel, I write reports on you. When I am pleased with a man his promotion is accelerated, when I am displeased . . ." he stopped himself with a dry laugh. The implied threat was wasted on the Lieutenant.

"Hansel, this Collins person, what is his first name?"

"Laurence, Sir, I believe known to his friends as Larry."

"So!" stormed Major Müller, his first fears being realised. "So! The dirty dog!"

Hansel was then berated for having not been aware that, under his very nose, he had observed a spy and a saboteur, but had not so much as applied to have him arrested. Hansel almost noticed the unfairness of the criticism, but was distracted by the new titles accorded to the Collins criminal. Surely he was being investigated for black market infringements, not these other things? And what was this about a whole family of perverts?

Oh yes, Major Pieter Müller's anger made the whole conspiracy come clear to him now. It was perfectly obvious that the ambitious Hansel had been working behind his senior's back. How else would that Tropp be so much in the know? More informed in fact than the Feldpolizei themselves, whose job it was.

Hansel was the recipient of a furious tirade, fired by the Major's frustration. To make matters worse, the Lieutenant was now wasting his valuable time by bringing a mere Corporal to his office for disciplining! Hansel fully deserved the push administered by his angry officer.

The same Corporal, on hearing his title bandied about, assumed that he had been summoned and knocked to enter.

Major Müller quickly assumed his earlier controlled stance.

Hansel's revolver slipped back into the holster unobserved as, while keeping his back to the Corporal, he quickly straightened his dishevelled uniform.

"Ah yes, Corporal, come in!" boomed Major Müller as though he had nothing else in mind except seeing that person. "Lieutenant, is this the man you spoke of, the one who is very lax in his duties where priests are concerned?"

"It is, Major."

All three men stood grouped near the door.

"Tell me, man, did you, on the night of 9th July, detain a certain priest for being out after curfew?"

"Yes, Sir."

"What was his name?"

"Peters, Sir, Reverend Peters."

"So!" mouthed Major Müller, with a wry smile. "You have a good memory, you remembered the priest's name!"

"No, Sir"

"What?"

"I did not remember his name Sir."

Hansel coughed politely,

"I reminded him of the Minister's name, Major. He had not remembered the name but picked up the man from the list that I issued. . ."

"Why didn't he remember the name?" snapped Major Müller irritably. "Surely you're not an idiot! You are a corporal. Is it beyond the wit of a Corporal to remember a name?"

"No, Sir."

"Hansel, sit there!" ordered the Major, indicating a chair, while he moved towards his desk. "You, stand there. Stand easy."

"I take it, Hansel, you have given this fellow a good lecture and have already decided on his punishment?"

"Yes, Sir, I have."

"Good, then let us not waste any more of the Reich's time on a fool of a Corporal who cannot even remember a name," decreed Müller, sneering at the figure in front of him.

"Permission to speak, Sir?" asked the Corporal.

"Indeed not," interjected Hansel, jumping to his feet.

"What it it?" demanded Pieter Müller, enjoying the opportunity to gainsay his Lieutenant.

"Sir, I do remember names, Sir," blurted the Corporal, almost apologetically.

'This is all I need,' thought Pieter, 'a daft Corporal who fails in his duty and then, to cap it all, pleads for leniency!'

"Go on, man, explain yourself," said Müller slowly, the menace in his voice, barely disguised.

"If you please Sir, Major Müller Sir, is your first name Pieter?"

"What? How dare you!" shouted Hansel affronted at the impertinence of his Corporal, showing him up like this in front of the Major.

"Wait," countered Müller, quite intrigued by this apparent irrelevance. "Please go on, Corporal, explain yourself."

The Corporal's eyes darted towards Hansel's, meeting a black stare, portending future trouble. He returned his stare back to Major Müller, whose face was receptive with impatience. He had to proceed now, there was no alternative.

"Sir, on your door, it says 'Major P. Müller'."

"Yes, go on, go on."

"Well, Sir, that reminded me, Sir," stuttered the Corporal.

"Reminded you what, man?" asked Müller in exasperation as he looked Hansel's way. The Lieutenant averted his gaze.

"Your name, Sir, is it Pieter?"

"It so happens, yes. Now explain yourself!"

"Well, Sir, you see, I do remember names, Sir. You see, on the night I searched the Minister Peters, I found something a little strange but thought nothing more of it until I came to your office this morning and saw your name on the door, Sir. . ."

"Go on! Go on! What was it you found?"

"At the time I thought it strange for a native to have a letter addressed to one with a German name but I. . ."

Pieter Müller cut across excitedly.

"A letter? What letter? What did it say?"

Hansel too looked up brightly. He was annoyed that the Corporal had mentioned none of this earlier but he was, nonetheless, interested.

"It was a letter addressed to 'Pieter Müller' Sir."

*   *   *

Chapter Twelve

"Mum, I'll be back in a minute, please don't worry, just get your hat and coat on," beseeched Gerda. "We're going out. Just get ready, I'll be back. I'll be back."

"Where are you going?" asked old Frances anxiously. She didn't know Gerda was going out. What was this all about?

"No mum, we're going out, you and I. Get ready . . . . please." Her voice was intense. Frances would not argue. Her questions would wait.

*　　*　　*

John, even if his injuries would have permitted, was now excluded from the drama to attempt to save his life. All was set, the whole scene of pure white awash with bright light and served in surgical green. The sister was there, her nurses washed and ready. The anaesthetist had his battery of machines with their animate graphs and dials, all active and performing. The Orthopaedic Surgeon and his assistants played a secondary role and were quiet, unobtrusive as they moved and set the broken limbs. A nurse attended the mechanics of the transfusions and drips under the ever watchful, ever anxious, eyes of the sister.

*　　*　　*

It was almost mid-day by the time the two friends arrived at their first military post.

Despite their earlier adventures of feasting and drinking, with the attendant discomfort of inebriation and sickness, for John, and the shock with the feldpolizist which had left a nagging fear in the back of both their minds, the day was too good to be spoiled.

This day was one of Guernsey's best summer gifts. It was a day on which the sun shone brilliantly and continuously out of a cloudless blue sky. Each lad could feel its heat penetrating deep beneath his skin. A few hours of this would be recorded on both complexions as a reminder of this gift. John had not lost his tan from last year, despite his enforced exile from the sea this summer, but Franz could definitely benefit from the addition of healthy colour.

Even though the sun's warmth was an agreeable sensation, so they both undid buttons and tunics and loosened whatever could be loosened, removing what could be conveniently removed, and rolling up those parts of their clothing which would permit it, they were in no way discomforted for, as with all perfect hot days in the Island, the air was refreshingly cool and that slightest trace of breeze, coming off the sea, soothed and balmed them.

Their passage through the quiet lanes had been a delightful trip, alternating shade and sun as they passed hedges, banks, trees and bushes, each acting as nature's parasols to the lush green grass and pretty weeds beneath, the homes of myriad moving and sounding creatures.

The last slope up, as they approached Pleinmont, was so steep that they dismounted and wheeled their bicycles. The hedges now were of gorse resplendent in its yellow glory. The scent of the plant was heady and overpowering.

Ahead was the green headland with its yellow patches and, here and there brown streaks of sun-dried bracken. Apart from the insects, and the faint sound of far distant shouts, there was almost a dearth of sound.

The top of the lane afforded an enthralling view. With the sight came the other sounds, which until then, had been muted by their own chatter.

Franz fell silent as he absorbed the sight. John too, though not so unused to such a prospect, was overcome with the sheer joy of it and of enjoying his friend's delight. It was as though John had, in this moment, given Franz a gift and was now self-indulgently taking pleasure from his delight.

Ahead, on the green and purple headland, there were no buildings in sight. Pleinmont was set against a clear blue sky. To its right the tree-sheltered cliffs slipped down gently, like the skirts of a gracious lady, becoming the coastal plain of the south west of the Island. A plain, for the first part quite narrow, squeezed in between the parent hills of the high parishes and the white rock-scarred sands of Rocquaine and Portelet bays, widened out in low undulations becoming more apparent the further north they looked.

Franz's first impressions were of a sea, shimmering like molten silver, as the high sun reflected from the inshore shallow waters. There was also sunshine reflecting from clusters of miniature greenhouses, nestling with little houses and bungalows far away near the coastal ribbons of a road.

As he scanned the scene he saw between the sun's mirror, miles of deep blue sea leading to a distinct horizon. This feature was broken at one point by Lihou Island, squat, like a large depressed hat. As his eyes got used to the shimmering silver of the sea he observed great dark patches beneath the water's surface, patches where rocks and seaweed had their homes. Franz saw the mighty west-coast granite reefs which had so protected the community from invasion in Napoleon's times. He saw the headland fortresses which had been built to keep at bay that historic foe. Fortresses which were now being adapted by his own people; concrete on granite, looking like crudely-made sandcastles with childlike indentations from which the modern machines of war would operate. They were all too far away to be real and, like toys, posed no threat or menace to their day.

Even the groups of Todt workers from which the shouted commands of the O.T. officers drifted, as they slaved over the Führer's Atlantic Wall, looked unreal. How could there be anything sinister or unpleasant about this scene? Apart from the voices, lifted up to him on the hill from which he viewed the world in the manner of Christ offered all he saw if he would but worship Satan, he heard the noises of engines, cranes and lorries. From far out at sea came booming of heavy artillery.

"Do you hear those guns, John? They're German guns firing at enemy ships, yes?"

"Maybe," replied John with a shrug. "Maybe they're British guns firing at German ships? Who knows?"

"No I think they are German guns," insisted Franz, "for they are very powerful sounding and Germany now has control of the Channel and the oceans."

"Oh yes, sure," sneered John sarcastically. "And where did you get that idea from?"

"From the newspapers of course," was Franz's reply, as he looked at John in bewilderment, wondering if his friend was seriously doubting his statement, or if he was just leading up to one of his strange jokes.

"Hmph!" said John but he did not wish to argue. Why spoil a good day over something so trivial? Besides, his thoughts were wandering back to peace-time again, to days such as this. Had he not used to hear the rumblings of guns far out at sea, even in those almost forgotten times before the invasion? Had he not asked his father what they were? He had asked lots of people but no one had really seemed to know the answer. Some people used to say it was the French navy exercising in the Channel but none had ever seen the ships and no one really knew. He had always chosen to think it was not man-made but rather some form of natural phenomenon such as distant thunderstorms, or earthquakes on the sea bed.

Across the lane ahead of them was a barrier, behind which stood two sentries. To the right of the barrier, almost completely buried, was one of the newly built concrete bunkers covered in chicken wire, camouflaged to look like rocks and grass.

John consulted his route plan comparing it with the direction sign.

"Yes, this is it, Franz, mon vieux. This is our first call, to the Pleinmont gun emplacements. Our first one is a woman, would you believe, name of Frieda?"

"Pardon me," asked Franz. "Who is this Frieda?"

"It is a gun emplacement, you idiot. It is where I have to take this first letter, see?" explained John, smiling, as he laboriously spelled out the obvious to his slow-witted companion.

"Oh yes, I see," acknowledged Franz. "I waiting here while you hand it over."

"You're what?" asked John in surprise. "Wait here while I hand it over?

"Yes," repeated Franz, "take it to those sentries, while I here wait, then you can come back and we can continue with our ride."

"Oh no, my son!" said John, somewhat exasperated. "I'm not just handing this in to the sentry. We have to go on past that post. I've six deliveries to make at Pleinmont alone. You must come with me, Franz."

"No, that is not possible John, I can't, don't you see?. . . ."

"Yes I see!" cut in John, "I see very well. You don't want to be seen with me. Is that it, eh? You don't want your Jerry friends to see you with me, eh?"

John was feeling hurt. Hell, he had ridden all of six miles with his German friend, regardless of all the Guernsey people who might have observed him, and now, here was Franz ashamed to be seen with him! It was not as if he were an ordinary Guernsey person either. He was on official German business and with a German armband.

"No!" said Franz. "No, John, you have got it wrong. I am not afraid to be seen with you. If this were the reason I would not have coming this far would I?"

"What's your reason then, eh?" asked John, his voice full of doubting suspicion.

Franz was intransigent, even though John was unconvinced.

Eventually and painfully laboriously, as though addressing a small child, Franz explained that even he was not permitted to enter a coastal military zone without papers.

"See, Englishman, you are more a German than I!"

John conceded grudgingly.

"No, you go, John, please. I wait here and look at this lovely beaches where we swim next year when Germany has won this war."

As John moved off, he made one last attempt.

"Don't you think you could bluff your way in?"

"Bluff? What is this bluff?" asked Franz in an irritated tone.

"Forget it," replied John. "And not so much of this 'when Germany has won the war,' business, eh?"

"What?" asked Franz, but John had gone.

John encounted difficulty at the sentry post for the German did not speak English. John found himself trying to explain his business by a series of gesticulations.

The man seemed unconvinced, as he demanded his papers. Any moment too he would ask for his identity card and that lack would just add to John's problems.

202

John had to call Franz as interpreter. Despite their earlier discussion, it was now vital.

Franz was quickly at John's side. There was little chance for explanation but John managed to urge:

"Be quick about it before he asks for my card!"

"What do you mean?" asked Franz, confused, as the sentry chose that very moment to demand it.

There was a rapid exchange between the two Germans, the older man looking very puzzled by it all. John so wished he could understand what was passing between the two especially now that Franz's answers had become so subdued and the sentry was raising his voice.

Eventually the puzzled man called his partner. He briefly explained the matter to him. Before John realised what was happening both men were convulsed by fits of laughter, rocking around where they stood and slapping each other as they became weak and helpless with their own hilarity. Franz too began to laugh, a little hesitantly at first, but soon joined in, giving full flood to his mirth. Even John, who could not conceive the reason for this all, was infected by the atmosphere and first made a smile and then a chuckle. Who said Germans did not have a sense of fun?

The first sentry put an end to the frivolity, speaking to Franz, who, in turn, addressed his friend.

"Come, John, it is all right. We are both to go on together. Quick!"

"But," protested John, "what about your papers? You have no permission."

"Be quiet!" hissed Franz. "Just do what you're told! Let's go."

"What was that all about?" asked John, once they were out of hearing.

"Oh, I explain how we have a fight and the feldpolizist take away your identity card."

"Well what was so funny about that?" asked John feeling a little annoyed that he had obviously been the butt of some joke at his expense.

"Nothing really," answered Franz, unable to restrain another laugh. "It was just the way they said it and added to it like a story."

"How do you mean?" asked John still fearing that, in some way, his friend was ridiculing him.

"Oh do not keep on, John! If you wish to know all these things why don't you learn German?"

John felt suitably corrected. In fact, he had contemplated learning German but had decided that to go to the evening classes provided for that purpose would antagonise his parents too much. Instead he had resorted to the lessons printed in the newspapers but had frequently felt frustrated as the phrases seemed to bear no relationship to his every day communication needs. Last night for example had been a lesson in how to punish one's daughter for taking a half share of the cake.

> 'Why is she to be punished?'
> 'Because she is greedy.'
> 'Why is she greedy?'
> 'Because she took half the cake.'
> 'Why should she not take half the cake when
> there are two of you?'
> 'Because she is smaller than I.'

"So why did they let you through without papers, eh?" asked John.

"Oh they just say it is all right so long as we are quick."

"I see," said John. "That's good then, eh?"

"Yes that's good, eh?" replied Franz mimicking his friend, for which he was rewarded with a hard push almost causing him to lose his balance.

They raced on up the lane shouting friendly abuse at each other.

"Right," said John, as they came to the end of the lane, "this here is the start of the cliffs. I've been here before with Dad. Now I think we'd better leave our bikes and walk." He took out his plan and they both studied it carefully.

Having left the bicycles in a clearing in the centre of a large patch of gorse, they followed the path leading to the cliffs. This was a frequently used route, for the rock and earth had been much disturbed by track vehicles, with here and there the imprints of jackboots.

Once on the cliffs, they were again delighted by spectacular views. Three hundred feet or so below them, where Guernsey's granite bastions face the south, they could see and hear the gentle rolling swell breaking on the rocks. The air was filled with the plaintive cry of the gulls as their nostrils took in the perfumes of all the wild cliff plants.

Franz, who had rarely seen the sea during his lifetime, and then only from the flat aspect of Germany's North Sea coast, was completely spellbound and quite content just to walk in silence while John excitedly educated him in the sights before his eyes.

"Look, Franz, if you look very carefully that way, on a clear day, you can see the Roches Douvres lighthouse near France, and just a bit further on we'll see our own lighthouse, the Hanois."

They discerned what they thought to be Les Roches Douvres on the horizon.

"This is a very good place for fishing," explained John. "You see, if we went down there, there's a gulley. It's deep and really good. It's good for swimming too. Feel like a swim?"

"Yes, I do," said Franz, "but we can't go there. Look there." He pointed to a board with a skull and crossbones and the sobering word 'Minen'. Even John knew the German for mines.

"That's true," confessed John, "and look at all the barbed wire too. Hell, what do you need all that for, mines and barbed wire?"

"To keep out the wicked Commandos!"exclaimed Franz.

"Wicked Commandos?" asked John, incredulous.

"Yes, that's right, John. They are bad men. With us it is a punishment to be put in lonely places like this, to guard this island from invasion, for they come at night and murder us in cowards ways. These friends of mine I tell you of, who make trouble at that kitchen, are being punish in this way."

John stopped Franz, nudging his sleeve.

"Look." He pointed to a trench just ahead. In it were several soldiers relaxing in the sun, tunic tops hanging on their stacked rifles.

"That's all right," replied Franz. "Come on."

They walked past the men who simply smiled and waved, greeting them casually in German.

"You see," observed Franz, once they had passed, "they think you are German with your blond hair and blue eyes and your armband." John felt a momentary stirring of an old pride before his self disgust took control of his emotions once more.

They found construction areas of the concrete gun emplacements without much bother. They were giant rectangular blocks, three quarters buried in the earth, and camouflaged with wires and nets. Some of them had been tended with creeping ice plants and shrubs borrowed from natives' gardens. Some of these Germans were obviously home-loving gardeners.

At each site there were men relaxing in the sun, some lying down tanning themselves, some chatting, others playing cards. One man was playing a wind-up gramophone with stirring marching songs which seemed, on this hot day, to have lost their power to stir. Another man they observed was whistling as he sat peeling turnips and putting them into a huge cauldron, from time to time looking shiftily around as he popped a piece of the raw vegetable into his mouth.

They all looked contented enough, if a little bored. None seemed to be living in fear of his life. Each German in charge took the communications and was courteous and chatty. Franz enjoyed himself.

Between them, before they had reached their final Pleinmont emplacement, they had consumed a litre of vegetable soup, 200g black bread, two cups of real French coffee and a Russian cigarette each. They had also been shown into some of the completed bunkers where they had dutifully admired the great cannons and the machine guns.

None of the soldiers seemed in any way to resent having a native in their presence, in fact they seemed particularly pleased, especially when they knew John lived in St. Peter Port. Several waxed lyrical about the town and looked forward to the days of their next leave at the end of present duty tours, when they could take in the delights of the films, the concerts, the dances, public houses and the girls. Several of the young men asked John if he knew this girl and that girl, while one was even bringing the conversation round to John delivering a letter to his sweetheart. John was embarrassed, becoming evasive and, by a combination of his lack of

German, the young man's lack of English, and playing rather slow on the uptake, managed to avoid the assignment.

John pestered Franz to break off the animated conversation he was having with a very intense-sounding young soldier, for he feared the one to whom he had been talking might at any moment return with a hastily written letter. Franz turned to John and excitedly exclaimed:

"John, this is Rudolphe. You might remember him from that time at the Soup Kitchen, yes?"

Rudolphe looked at John and they both nodded. John was about to make some polite attempt at conversation but his efforts were proved unnecessary for Rudolphe turned from him with complete disregard, as though he did not exist, continuing to talk with Franz.

Franz was not aware of any slight on his friend but John was feeling insulted and annoyed.

"Come on, Franz, it's getting late, we've a long way to go."

"Oh just wait!" said Franz. "We've all afternoon and I don't have to be on duty till 18.00 hours."

"Yes, that's fine for you, Franz, but I can't be too late. My parents will be worried!"

Rudolphe looked at John with what was almost a sneer of contempt then, in complete disregard of his protestations, engaged Franz in conversation once more.

"Come, Franz, I'm off!" snapped John angrily. "You can catch me up if you like!"

Franz shrugged his shoulders presenting both his theatrically upturned palms to Rudolphe as if to say, 'Sorry about this, but you can see what I have to put up with'.

Rudolphe muttered something and disappeared.

'Thank goodness!' thought John.

"Right Franz, let's go, eh?"

"All right, John, Rudolphe has just gone to get permission to walk with us, to our bicycles."

"What for?" asked John, not attempting to hide his annoyance.

"Well, you see, he is being punished for what happens at the Soup Kitchen. That is why he is out here. . ."

"And?" interjected John rudely.

Franz, not cognizant of any rudeness continued:

"He is been separate from his best friend who is now at another cliff place we are to visit. He want us to. . ."

"Oh no!" declared John, realising they were about to be asked to deliver a message. He had not just got out of one message delivery to get another.

"What do you mean, 'oh no'? Why not? What is wrong with that? It won't put us out of our way. Look, here he is. Quick, John, get out your list so Rudolphe can tell you where Helmut is stationed."

John felt controlled by circumstances rather than being in control. He suspected to comply with this request was the easiest way.

"Very well," he sighed, as he took out his list and map together with the route plan.

Rudolphe actually smiled at John, as Franz gave him the good news. Without waiting to be asked he eagerly snatched John's papers and scrutinised them. Without reference to John he took a pencil from his tunic pocket and marked, with a circle, one of the military zone emplacements at Jerbourg, at the other end of the south coast cliffs. John was annoyed but the matter was outside his control. He nodded. Using Franz as an interpreter, Rudolphe explained where they were at present. John knew where they were. This German must think him stupid or something! Notwithstanding he marked their present position with yet another circle. John tried to snatch the map but Rudolphe pulled away, then, to emphasize the point that they were at Pleinmont, and had to make their way several miles to Jerbourg, marked the intervening coast route with a hastily dotted line.

John could contain himself no longer and grabbed back his sheaf of papers. Rudolphe grinned to see the annoyance he had caused.

"Don't be cross," said Franz in a slightly mocking tone. "He has not ruined your precious map. Besides," he added in a more conciliatory vein, "Rudolphe will come to our bicycles and show us a short way to the next place." He turned to the German to confirm this. Rudolphe confirmed with much nodding.

They made their way back to the bicycles, John feeling

completely isolated, the third making a crowd, while the others continued their private German talk.

At the gorse bushes they retrieved their bikes.

Rudolphe pointed to the next headland, to where a huge sandcastle, a concrete monstrosity, was springing up, an inverted cone whose layers of gun slits appeared stark like rows of smiling black teeth facing out to sea. The whole had the appearance of a fantastic schoolboy drawing of war.

Franz interpreted, "We can go along that road there instead of leaving the Military zone. Quick John, give him your map. This will save a lot of time!"

John did not resist. Rudolphe marked the lane and then, still addressing Franz, began marking symbols.

"He say he knows this lane," explained Franz. "Whatever we do, we must not leave it. Those there are mines." Rudolphe marked some patches with the letters M.

"And those are overhead wires with bombs attached to deter parachutists." Rudolphe drew a series of little poles with crisscrossed wires looking rather like a field of cultivated hops.

By now Rudolphe was getting quite carried away and on the cliff sides was making what, upon enquiry, John learned to be roll bombs, trenches and barbed wire. This was all clearly irrelevant and Franz retrieved John's papers.

As they parted, Rudolphe shook Franz's hand warmly. He turned to John who rather self-consciously held out his hand, in the manner of the continentals, only to have his gesture spurned as Rudolphe simply nodded his head.

*　　　*　　　*

The International Red Cross Office was particularly busy today. This always happened after a *Press* printing of letters received from dear ones in England, the recipients having agreed to share their news with others. The twenty-five words permitted were always a delight to read.

Such a printing of letters, with genuine names and addresses, proved that the benevolent German authorities really did adhere to International Conventions and did allow the post through and as such they were delighted to permit valuable newsprint space to be used in this way.

In an island population, depleted by half its numbers, and almost completely devoid of children, owing to the hurried evacuation of the previous year, apart from little ones since born, but who had not yet had chance to stamp their personality on the depressed community, what better than to read;

> 'Mr. and Mrs.Babbé of Rue des Fleures
> have heard from their son:
>> Baby son Jeffrey born 15th June,
>> both well. Now live Southampton.
>> John at school. Saw Betty.
>> Arthur getting married. Please
>> write. God bless. Love Philip!'
>
> 'Mrs Hamon of Mare de Carteret, has heard
> from her daughter who is teaching the
> children of the Câtel:
>> Very well. All children happy.
>> Lots going country homes summer
>> holidays. Guernsey Society
>> started. Saw Richard Payne.
>> Miss you. Love to all. Pray
>> Peace, Valerie.'

Another reason for the continuous flow of people, on this special day, was the list in the previous night's *Press* saying which letters were waiting for collection.

The Red Cross official, sitting at the table, was selling official letter forms at a shilling each. On these forms the sender would write his precious twenty five words on one side and the address in England on the other. Most would take their forms home with them to precis carefully all they wished to say and to censor that which they dared not mention rather than have the official blue German pencil do it for them with all the attendant delay that would involve.

Father Peters was one of this excited crowd. Last night he had read that a letter awaited him. He could barely contain himself, as the babbling queue moved slowly forward. Who would the letter be from? Would it be from his wife and the boys? Was it from his brother, now in the army? Could it be from his mother? Was it good news? Was it bad? What if it were a mistake, if there were no letter for him after all?

What if the letter had been lost? All these questions were racing in his mind when at last he reached the table.

"Ah Father Peters," greeted the Red Cross official. "Yes, we've got a letter for you. I was going to drop this in to you on the way home." The man was one of his parishioners but Father Peters had hardly noticed him. He took the type-written sheet with trembling hand. It was six months since he had received any news. So excited was he that he had to be reminded to produce his identity card, a mere formality but nonetheless necessary, as a number had to be placed on the official receipt form.

Once in possession of the sheet, he found himself unable to turn it over to read the contents. He took it outside and stood in the hot sun along with all the other individuals.

In his turmoil it seemed to him that he stood in a forest of separated people like trees, or privately existing crucifixions, all alone in their joys and in their sorrows. It seemed an age before he indulged in his own communication, an age in which he felt he took in the sufferings and sadness of those around him. He was aware of rustling of the sheets, the coughs and shuffles, the sighs and sobs as the letters were read and re-read. He saw the tearful smiles, he saw the depressed bodies and the bent dejected shoulders and saw here dull sad eyes in expressionless faces, and there, eyes shining with tears of intermingled sadness and joy.

He could not read his letter here. He folded the precious sheet, raised his cassock and slipped it into his trouser pocket. He would take it with him and read it in private while he humbly knelt on the hard wooden floor in the church.

*   *   *

John and Franz had no difficulty in following the route marked for them by Rudolphe. The course of the lane was quite obvious and, despite its scars from the military track vehicles, was, on the whole, quite well-surfaced, so they were able to ride most of the time.

When they arrived at the newly-constructed gun tower John was rather overawed by its size and monstrous ugliness. Although it was a hot summer day the sea breezes sweeping up the cliffs seemed to be attracted to this devilish icon so that it had about it an aura of chill. Both friends were silent as they approached. The whole building was in silence apart from the eerie whistling of wind. Silence, even though showing from the sweeping gun slits were several still figures they took to be the keepers of this place.

Everything in John's consciousness seemed to be of concrete. There was the tall tower slightly cone-shaped with a flat top, sides marked in parallel lines where the shuttering planks had been. The whole tower stood on a concrete apron where not a blade of grass was to be seen. The concrete apron was also occupied by concrete bunkers with concrete flights of steps leading down to concrete entrances backed by concrete passages. Around the perimeter of the concrete apron was a concrete wall with concrete gate posts.

At the concrete gateway sat concrete soldiers with concrete machine guns. The concrete guns were directed at them as a concrete officer shouted with concrete coldness, "Halt!"

These soldiers were neither relaxed nor friendly. All were cold, all were stiff and tense. There was an atmosphere of suspicion, as though all were afraid to appear anything less than concrete.

A stream of cold concrete German words tumbled from the officer's lips. Franz's German reply, although incomprehensible to John was the first human sound he heard in this whole complex.

John passed his papers and waited for a concrete demanding of his identity card. The order did not come. The officer in charge simply passed back the papers and pointed to John's message bag.

"Oh yes," said John with an apologetic nervous smile, as he fumbled with his envelopes to find the correct one. The officer's face had a set impatient expression as he posed, like a statue, in disbelief at the inefficiency of the youth. When, eventually, the correct envelope was produced, he snatched it from John with not a word.

John was cross with himself. He did not usually get so disorganised as this and realised that events earlier in the day had lulled him into a false sense of security. He was embarrassed at looking stupid in front of this inscrutable German.

"Come on, Franz," said John. "Let's go."

They moved away from the silent place. As they turned their backs on the evil conglomeration, so it faded from their minds so that they felt the warmth of the sun once more and noticed the green of the grass and bushes, hearing the sound of the gulls and the land birds again.

"Which way now, John?" asked Franz, as they came upon an unmarked junction in the deserted lane.

"I'm not sure," was John's reply. "I think it must be this way, for Icart is that way, on past the airport. But you can't always go by the way Guernsey lanes lead."

"Why? What do you mean?" asked Franz, not really interested, but making conversation for the sake of it, to animate his friend from the pervading depression of their recent call.

"Oh, it's just that the lanes are so tiny and twist so much, you could set off like this then after just a few yards, find yourself going in completely the wrong direction."

Franz chuckled at this idea. "Then we should take a compass with us wherever we go," he suggested. "Yes," agreed John, "or we might get lost for ever!"

"When I am in the Hitler Youth we are teach how to find our way without a compass, by using the sun and signs of nature."

"Oh yes," interrupted John, "it was the same in the Scouts. The sun rises in the east and sets in the west and always casts its shadow north at mid-day . . ."

"Oh well, that's good, John, so if we get lost all we have to do is to wait till mid-day."

They both laughed at this. Really they laughed much too heartily and far too long for such a minor witticism but they had both recaptured their earlier innocent enjoyment of this glorious summer's day.

"You know what?" asked John rhetorically, "you almost made a sarcastic joke then, my friend. You're learning. We'll make a Guernseyman of you yet!"

Franz did not comprehend John's meaning but he sensed his friend was pleased with him, whatever it was he had unwittingly said.

"There's another way, too, you can look at the ivy growing up a tree, like that one there." He pointed to a stunted rowan growing bent in the direction of the prevailing wind.

From where they were they could see the ivy.

"Well, if you examine the ivy growing on trees it always grows on the north side."

"Oh, that is very interesting!" exclaimed Franz with enthusiasm. "Let us see where the ivy is on that one."

They laid down their bicycles and eagerly made their way to the tree trunk.

Once there, like two little boys upon first discovering the harrowing truth about Father Christmas, they stood momentarily with their mouths agape in disbelief, as they observed the trunk entirely convered with ivy on all of its four cardinal sides. The incongruity of this struck them both at once as they reverted into one of the laughing spasms until their breaths came in rasping gasps and the tears rolled down their cheeks.

When they finally settled themselves once more, John produced his map and together they studied their way.

"We had better get out of this military zone," said John, "for we don't need to go to these headlands here and we don't want to have to go right down into the Petit Bôt valley. Besides, I don't like wandering round in these deserted places. It gives me the creeps!"

"What is this 'creeps' please?"

John tried to explain but had to give up.

"Anyway," he continued, "I don't like it here. There could be mines or booby traps or anything, or they might even think we're spies."

This last statement was said casually, almost in jest but, by the look on Franz's face, it appeared it had been received in anything but fun.

"What's the matter, Franz? Are you O.K.?"

Franz's face had gone very pale, and he bit his lower lip so that the teeth marks turned it pale pink and puple. His eyes flashed fear.

"Oh, it's nothing!" rejoined Franz. "Let's get away from here as fast as we can!"

"O.K., O.K.," agreed John, "but what's wrong? Why the hurry all of a sudden?"

"I said it's nothing! God in heaven! Always questions, questions!"

As Franz picked up his bicycle and pointed it towards the

lane he did not see its polished green frame or its shiny wheels or the green grass, the bushes or the twisty rough lane separating the tiny rustic fields. He saw instead men, their hands and feet trussed like chickens, hanging by the neck from piano wire suspended from meat hooks in a concrete wall. He saw their bulging screaming eyes, their protruding tongues, their wide open but silently screaming mouths. He watched their bodies twitching and dancing with their terrible death throes as their faces became first red and then changed imperceptably to blue.

Franz no longer heard the distant rhythm of the waves soothing the rocks and pebbles far below at the foot of the cliffs, he did not hear the birds or the gulls or even the concerned voice of his friend. All he heard was the rasping and gasping of the dying victims, with the explosions of their flatulations, as they lost control of their bowels. All the while, background music of this educational film rose to a crescendo with words in Gothic black superimposed across the screen.

'This is how Germany treats traitors.
This is the fate of spies!

*   *   *

There was a very confident, almost jaunty, knock on the door.

"Enter," demand Major Müller as Hansel appeared to squeeze his way into the room.

He was all smiles, things were obviously going well.

"You've done it?" asked the Major.

"Yes, sir, he's sweating in the interview room. He doesn't know what's hit him yet," replied Hansel with glee.

"Hit him!" raged Major Müller. "You haven't marked the man, have you, you fool?"

"Oh no, Sir," said Hansel, shocked, "it was only a figure of speech, Sir. No, he has come to no harm."

"Does he know why you've brought him in?"

"No, of course not, Sir. I thought the whole idea was to let him worry for a few hours before we started."

"Quite so, quite so," came the Major's ungracious reply.

"And what about the search?" he enquired.

"All under control, Sir," confirmed Hansel beaming. "My men are doing his house over right now . . ."

"Vicarage!" interrupted Major Müller. "The man's a Vicar. He lives in a Vicarage. God, you're ignorant!"

Hansel looked hurt.

"To me, Sir, he is nothing special. He is an ordinary man, an enemy of the Reich, so he lives in a house." He noticed the anger flaming in Pieter Müller's eyes and decided he was going too far. If he were not careful the Major would be going off on his old tack again about not having personal vendettas against men of the cloth. He detested this continual implied criticism from the Major therefore decided on a placatory course changing the subject slightly.

"We've found the typewriter Sir and, with your permission, would like to compare it with your letter Sir."

"My letter?" asked Müller, completely taken aback. "What do you mean, man, 'my letter'?"

"The letter you received, Sir, the anonymous letter, the one found on Peters' person, addressed to you. We can compare the typing with that on his typewriter . . ."

"Yes, yes, I understand that Hansel! I'm not stupid, you know."

"Well, Sir, may we have the letter please?" Hansel was beginning to sound exasperated. Damn it, hadn't the Major hit the roof when he had heard Peters was carrying a letter addressed to him? Hadn't he ordered that the cleric be immediately brought in for interrogation and his home searched? Why the devil did he react so? There must surely have been a letter? Major Müller must have learned something very important to have reacted so, especially as he was usually such a priest lover. And that was another thing; if this minister was involved in subversion, as Hansel was convinced by now he was, why was his senior officer keeping vital information from him, especially as he was in charge of all subversive matters? Hansel did not like it one little bit. He felt very much inclined to let the matter slip out when next he was in conversation with Colonel Brandt.

The Major was in a quandry. He wanted to be sure, in his own mind, that it was the priest who had written him the anonymous letter about Franz, but he did not wish his Lieutenant to know about his nephew's involvement with anything that smacked of subversion. The worm would take great delight in spreading scandal about him and his family, putting Pieter in a very delicate position, especially as Herr Tropp was already implying sinister association between Franz and the enemy. No, he had to make this discovery for himself and then crack the priest, in such a way, that Franz could not possibly be implicated. He had to conduct this without Hansel. It called for some very careful handling. Besides, it was to be tennis with Lilly Brown this afternoon.

"No, you can't have the letter, damn you! I'm much too busy to search for it now," deliberated Major Pieter Müller, as he opened his filing cabinet to retrieve his tennis racquet. "Just go back to the vicarage and type out a sheet, to show all the machine's characters, and leave it on my desk."

"Yes, Sir," said Hansel accepting defeat with good grace. "When shall we interrogate Peters?"

"When I'm ready Hansel, when I'm ready!" Then as an afterthought, "Don't you worry yourself about him, Hansel. Leave him to me personally."

"But, Sir . . ."

"No 'buts' about it, man, you're working much too hard as it is. You concentrate on all your other enquiries and leave this one to me, all right?"

Hansel had to agree.

"Oh, and Hansel, my dear fellow," started Major Müller hesitantly, as if he found difficulty, embarrassment even, in acting this friendly role, "please don't think I'm not grateful for all you're doing. You really are doing a fine job."

Hansel was surprised but the old habit, so deeply instilled, of accepting without question any information received from a superior, quickly took over and he shone forth the pleasure he felt at this rare praise, praise all the more gratefully received when it came so seldom.

"Thank you, Sir. I do my best."

"Yes, I know, dear fellow," replied Müller whilst thinking. 'If that's his best, God help us if he ever under performs!'

"Anyway," continued Müller, "please don't take too much notice if, at times, I seem a little irritable. It is just that I, like you Hansel, wish to do my best for the Fatherland and the Führer . . ."

"I . . .," Hansel tried to interrupt but Pieter was not to

217

be stemmed in full flow. It was difficult enough to start propounding these false sentiments but now he had started he intended to see it through expeditiously, as one who wishes to swallow quickly the bitter medicine in order to be able to move on to the rewarding sweet.

"I am going to give you a lot more help from now on Hansel. I really do feel we must work far more closely together. Don't you agree?"

Hansel had no option but to agree.

"When do you plan to have the fisherman along for his second session?" asked the Major, knowing full well it was planned for tomorrow evening.

"You mean de la Haye, Sir? He's being collected tomorrow evening."

"Hmm," grunted the Major pensively, as though wondering if that were wise. "I don't like to interfere Hansel. You really are doing a good job, but I'd like to suggest you bring the fellow along earlier, let's say tomorrow morning."

"Why, Sir? Surely if he's expecting us to collect him in the evening it's better that way for he'll have the whole day to anticipate and dread our next session?"

"Yes, normally you'd be right Hansel," agreed the Major condescendingly, "but do remember this is no ordinary peasant, he's a tough one. I don't really think the whole day waiting will make much difference to him."

Hansel realised it would be pointless to object for, although the Major was going through the motions of consultation, he had already made up his mind. As he was not going to have the final say in the organisation of his own affairs, it was better thus to at least have the Major being nice to him, as at present, albeit perhaps not for long.

"Very well, Sir. What do you have in mind?"

"Bring him in early tomorrow morning. Bring him to my office. I'll deal with him personally, in private."

"To your office Sir?" asked Hansel in amazement. "Surely the interrogation room would be more appropriate Sir, if you know what I mean?"

Major Müller knew exactly what he meant.

"You mean your little toys Hansel, and your bully boys? Oh no, man, your methods are much too crude. I'll get him to talk without one drop of blood being spilled, or one tooth loosened, you'll see." He looked at the Lieutenant's bewildered face adding, "You see, Hansel, I'm a true policeman at heart, not just an overgrown bully, in love with power."

Hansel neither understood this last remark nor knew whether it was intended as a compliment or an insult. He just gaped until he was dismissed with a final order.

"Oh Hansel, have a Foot Patrol standing by in the morning too."

"Yes, Sir. May I ask two questions please?"

"Ask."

"The minister, Sir, what shall I do with him?"

"Nothing Hansel, precisely nothing. Leave him where he is. In a cell presumably? I'll see to him when I return from this afternoon's meeting. What else?"

"Collins, Sir. Permission to bring him in?"

"No!"

"No, Sir?"

"That's what I said man! Just leave him for the time. De la Haye will implicate him, you'll see!"

Hansel left.

*   *   *

John and Franz finished their ride to the road block where they were to leave the Military Zone, with hardly a word passing between them.

John tried to make conversation but it takes two people and all he could get from Franz was,

"I'm all right, I tell you!" and "For God's sake, John, leave me alone!"

Despite his protestations of being in good health, Franz looked anything but well. His face had grown whiter than usual so that the modest painting of pink, occasioned by the day's earlier excursions into the Guernsey summer sunshine, yet to be tanned by the ever-present salt-laden breeze, was now lost in the ghostly white of his cemetery mists.

'Perhaps,' thought John, 'his earlier excesses have caught up with him, like they did with me?' but his enquiries on that assumption had met with a firm denial.

John wondered if he had offended his friend for he well

knew they both found that very easy to do to each other. But no, he did not appear to be sulking. It was more as though he were frightened. He was staring straight ahead, his eyes having that watering almost fiery quality as they expressed naked fear. Franz clutched his handlebars so tightly that his knuckles became almost translucent in their whiteness. John thought he observed his friend shuddering, from time to time, with teeth chattering.

At the Military Post, Franz made no move to offer himself as interpreter, as previously, so John went up to the duty sentry, producing his Feldkommandantur pass.

The sentry took John's paper and, to his surprise addressed him in English, "So you are living here in this island and for us working, yes?" His tone was more one of conversation than of interrogation.

"That's right," said John, giving vent to a nervous flicker of a smile of relief, "I was born and brought up here."

"That is good, very good," said the soldier, with a polite smile, as he handed back the pass. "Why do you work for us?"

John was surprised by the question.

"Why do I work for the Germans?"

"Yes that is what I ask." Again the polite, almost friendly smile. "We are your enemy. Why then, do you wish to help us, your enemy?"

His tone encouraged John to bravado, the sort that he had been always able to get away with when, as a child, he had deliberately bated the older men of his acquaintance. They always referred to him as 'being cheeky' but he knew that they enjoyed it, everyone loves a youngster with a bit of friendly cheek, a bit of personality.

"I don't want to help you," was his reply. "I am British. Your lot forced me to work for you."

"Ah, I see," acknowledged the sentry in mock realisation. "You hate all of us, we are all bad, yes?"

John did not answer, there was no need. Besides, if he had answered in the same vein as his earlier chatter, he would have had to declare that he hated all Germans and that he believed they were all bad. That would not have been quite true. Even in jest, he was not prepared to denounce his friend.

"Who is he?" demanded the sentry, indicating Franz who had remained well back from this conversation.

"He is accompanying me on my journey," answered John, quickly staying the word 'friend' remembering his earlier conversation with Franz, just after the feldpolizist had questioned them.

The sentry snapped a question at Franz. Franz simply nodded and looked at the ground.

"He is not well," observed the sentry, "he should not be today working."

"He's not," said John, "he just came for the ride. He was fine earlier." As these last few words came out, John realised what he had divulged and the sentry was conscious that he felt discomforted.

"So, you Britisher, you have a friend to just ride with you? So we are not all bad in your eyes? You like some Germans." He gave John a hearty push, laughing. "That is good, very good!"

Franz watching, almost smiled at this reassuring sight. His smile quickly vanished however, when he was included into the conversation. He received the German demand and immediately vomited where he stood.

"Franz!" exclaimed John, as he went to his friend's aid. "What is it?" and addressing the sentry,

"What did you say?"

The soldier looked concerned, as he nonchalantly tried to disguise this sentiment with a shrug of his shoulders.

"I ask him for his papers."

"Oh," said John, equally nonchalantly. "He hasn't got any, the other sentry post let us in at Pleinmont. They said it was all right."

"Oh?" queried the sentry, his voice suddenly losing its warmth, as his mind was invaded by shadowy doubt and suspicion. "This is a very serious thing. This I have to check!"

Franz looked at his friend. His eyes were dull and his teeth were chattering with fear.

"Don't worry," said John, "its OK. He's just going to check up that what I said was true, then we'll be out of here."

"Yes, but don't you see," whined Franz, "that's another

misdemeanour we'll have recorded against us . . .?" He did
not continue.

*   *   *

Father Peters sat crouched on a hard straight chair, the
only furniture in the tiny room, which served him as a cell.

Contrary to Hansel's protestations, his arrest had been un-
necessarily rough and his whole abdomen still ached and
kept cramping from the stomach blow he had received,
when he had been so unexpectedly dragged from his church.
As far as Hansel was concerned, what he had told Major
Müller was the truth, for this man of the cloth, in his
pretentious cassock and clerical collar, had not been harmed.
To Hansel harm was any injury inflicted that could be
observed, whereas a few punches, well concealed, were hardly
likely to come to the Major's attention. Besides, what this
mouthpiece against the Reich had so far experienced was, in
fact nothing. Nothing by comparison with what he would
get later if Hansel had his way.

The only light coming into the room was through a tiny
peephole set high in the wooden door and through the gap
under the door, seeping across the bare boards like a fast-
rising tide across flat sands. This light itself was weak, as it
in turn filtered from an almost windowless corridor. There
was no door handle, not that Father Peters had even contemplated looking for a way out.

After having spent some while in this semi darkness, the
priest had realised that the room was not windowless, as he
had at first supposed, but that the small paned sash window
had been painted over with black paint on the outside. He
knew it was the outside for some while ago he had tried to
open it to get some air, only to find it securely nailed with
rather flimsy iron bars set into the frame. It was then that
he had scratched at the glass making his discovery.

Well, whatever paint had been used had not stood up to
the weathering too well for here and there were tiny pin
pricks of white hot light setting rays through the heavy
dusty air like miniature searchlights.

Father Peters had been kneeling in the Lady Chapel
when the church door had been roughly opened. His attention

had been broken and his first reaction had been to go to the far end of the church to discover who was desecrating the House of God with such an unruly and disrespectful entry, but his heart and mind quickly returned to focus on his communication with the Lord and the letter in his hands.

The vicar's hands, so usually firm in the manner of prayer, had shaken with emotion as he had read and re-read the Red Cross letter from his dear ones. His face, usually so stern and kind with the proxied love of God for his flock, had been softened and moistened by his tears as his lips had quivered with emotion.

    'Darling,
       I miss you . . .'

"Oh God, oh my Father how I miss her. Tell her, I pray you, how I miss her. Oh my sweetheart . . ."

    'Boys well . . .'

"Dear boys, how Daddy misses you. Oh sweet Jesus protect them. How they must miss me. All the lovely times we have had together as a family. Dear Jesus, if it be your will, let this war come quickly to a finish. Thy will be done. Who is looking after my dear ones now? . . ."

    'Mother well . . .'

"Oh mother, you are home in England, the country you so pined for, now torn by war and ravaged by the engines of death. Holy Mary, Mother of God, bless my mother and keep her safe for us . . ."

    'Praying for end to war . . .'

"My sweetheart, I pray for it all the time, that this iniquity may end and that we may be united. Oh my Lord, tell her I love her, tell her I pray continuously for her and for the return of peace. But I know, sweet Jesus, I know she prays. I know we pray together each night. Thy will be done on earth as it is in heaven . . ."

    'Together again . . .'

"Will that ever be? It's been more than a year now. The longest year of my life. When I have looked ahead, the days and weeks have stretched endlessly, like an eternity of hell, but when I look back, they seem to have passed and a whole year has slipped by, almost without notice."

"Dear Lord, let it not be long before we are united once more in peace. How I long to walk on the cliffs with my darling and the children. Oh to feel the autumn gales buffeting us. Oh to walk in the Pine Forest next Christmas and pick the early primroses which are fooled and brought on by the pre-winter mildness. Perhaps next winter we will have some snow so that we can look at Herm across the water swathed in white like a beautiful reclining calf on the bright grey water? If it be thy will, Oh my Father, we will watch next spring burgeon into life, a fresh new life symbolic of freedom and peace."

'Quite safe here . . .'

"Thank you God. Protect them from the bombs and the danger and the perils of invasion . . ."

'You?'

"Yes my sweetheart, I am safe, but what is safety without my family? Father, should I have evacuated to England with my family? Was I right to send them away? Was I right to stay to tend my flock? Thy will be done but, oh my God, help me to accept thy will and to know that I have done the right thing. I should have gone. My family is more to me than my flock. No, I'm sorry Lord, help me in my moment of doubt . . ."

'Church here Anglo Catholic . . .'

"That is good news. Now I know when you worship and when I worship we are together in our ceremonies and joy in serving our heavenly King . . ."

'Love, Irene.'

He had folded and unfolded his letter as he had wept and prayed and been close to his family and his Lord and master, in whose hands he had placed their destiny that long long age ago.

He had re-read the letter and had taken Irene into his arms caressing her bare shoulders. He had run his arms down her naked sides pressing himself against her nakedness while she had tenderly and willingly submitted to the gentle but insistent pressure of his love and desire. She had thrown back her head so that her golden hair had cascaded across her shoulders like liquid metal. She had fluttered her blue eyes, closed in ecstasy, and had opened her mouth to receive his. Her breath had exhaled in desire.

"Thomas, Thomas . . ."

"You are Peters, minister of this place?"

Thomas Peters' dream had broken, as Irene had returned once more to twenty-five typed words.

"Up!" yelled Hansel as the realisation of reality had come upon the priest. "Get up! You are under arrest!" As he had yelled at the kneeling cleric he had grabbed his shoulder roughly pulling him to his feet. The letter had dropped to the floor and it had been, in his attempt to save it, that he had been dealt the body blow which was now causing him so much discomfort. The letter had been rudely snatched from the retrieving hand, scanned with a derisory expression then crumpled into a ball in front of the priest's eyes and thrown towards the altar. Father Peters did not much mind, as he heard the muffled pathetic bounces of paper on tile, for every word of the despatch was now indelibly etched onto his mind.

Chapter Thirteen

Her neighbour came straight away. She drove Gerda up to fetch Frances. Gerda had briefly told her friend as much as she knew. Her friend's silence was more comfort than any words could have been.

They sat there outside the house, John's house, her house, Frances' house, their home. She was the captive of urgent panic yet still she could not move to fetch the old lady and thereby face up to the trauma within herself. She did not know how to tell the impossible to John's mother.

*   *   *

As the two friends made the final part of their journey to the south eastern peninsula known as Jerbourg, Franz began to brighten. John was delighted to observe this change in him, for he had almost given up hope of his ever getting back to normal.

Since leaving the sentry post where their papers had been demanded, they had cycled several miles, along past the airport, and backwards and forwards to several headland gun emplacements in the military zone. Each time they had approached the zone, Franz had visibly paled and had adamantly refused to go anywhere near the barrier. Instead he had lingered, feigning illness, and had lain in the grassy banks while John had expedited his business.

John had realised his friend was frightened and that it had been something to do with the demand for his non-existant pass, but hell, it wasn't the end of the world, was it? If anyone had to worry it was he for he had to go to the Gestapo to collect his identity card, hadn't he? He had tried bringing the conversation round, along those lines, but almost to no avail.

"Come on, Franz," he had urged, "snap out of it, mate."

"What do you mean, 'snap out'?" had been Franz's reply.

"You know, you're in a bad mood. What's the matter?"

"Nothing!"

"Oh sure!" John had cajoled sarcastically. "Come on, now, I know what it's all about. You're worried aren't you?"

"Worried? I'm not worried!"

"Yes you are. You got worried when that sentry asked for your papers, didn't you?"

Franz had avoided John's gaze.

"All right, so I'm worried, but let us forget about it please!"

"Why?" had been John's stubborn reply. "Why not talk about it? If something is worrying you it's better to talk about it. A problem shared is a problem halved and all that. . ."

"I don't know what you're talking about," Franz had complained. "Sometimes John, you say very stupid things!"

John had been annoyed at this and had let his friend know his displeasure, in no uncertain terms.

"Look Franz!" he had shouted, "You're afraid you'll get into trouble for coming out of the military zone without a pass, but you won't, don't you see? If there had been any trouble they'd have kept us there, they wouldn't have let us go scot free. You heard the sentry. He simply 'phoned the other post and confirmed that he'd let you in without a pass, eh?"

Franz had agreed but had remained miserable.

"Anyway, what did he say?" John had asked.

Franz had shrugged his shoulders,

"He say it is all right but we should have gone out the way we'd come in. If we'd done that there would have been no trouble."

"But there is no trouble!" John had insisted.

"Oh yes there is, you'll see!"

"Why? Why do you say that, Franz? What trouble can there possibly be?"

"I don't know, but there will be!"

"Come on then, tell me", John had pressed. "You just can't throw out a statement like that and not finish saying what you mean. . ."

"Very well, then, if you must know, they'll probably take me away for questions," Franz had replied.

"Why?" John had asked. "And how?"

"Because, don't you understand, I was in there without a pass and they'll say I am a spy. And you!"

"Oh don't be so damned stupid!" John had exclaimed in anger.

"All right then, you'll see!" Franz had countered, equally annoyed. "They'll come for me one night, you'll see. That's how they work. That is how the S.S. work. They come for people in the night!"

John had become bored with the conversation.

"Don't keep on, Franz! We don't want to go on about the stupid S.S. again."

He had thought of that vile leering Hüffmeier with a shudder, as he spoke. "They're not interested in you. Besides, there's always your uncle. Anyway, we weren't spying, so don't carry on so."

"We may not have been spying but they could say we were and we could not prove that we were not!" This had brought the whole conversation round to differences between British and German justice, with the burden of proof being on the accused in the German system, but on the prosecution in the British system. John had made the astute observation that, as he was a civilian, he would be subject to civil law and, as he was only carrying out an authorised assignment, he had nothing to fear. If the authorities were unable to prosecute him for a non-existent crime they would find it very difficult to make trouble for Franz. Franz had been cheered by this.

As they cycled down the Jerbourg road to the point where they could observe the pale blue sea, hazy now with afternoon mists towards its horizon, their conversation changed to a deep philosophical argument on the merits and de-merits of the political systems of the belligerant powers.

Out of an unspoken gratitude to a return of normal friendly relations, between the two of them, each began to seek for good things to say about the other.

John, forgetting all the evil attributes of the Führer, Herr Hitler, bestowed upon him by his father's table-time conversations, began to enquire after the saviour of Germany. He began to remember all the good things he had read about this man in the Guernsey newspapers.

"You know, Franz, I think Germany is very fortunate

228

to have such a leader as Herr Hitler. He seems so intelligent and so powerful. Have you ever been to any of those rallies I have seen at the pictures?"

"Oh yes," enthused Franz. "I go to Berlin with the Hitler Youth. It is the most wonderful time of my life."

He began to sing the *Horst Wessel* song. John knew the tune, for it had often stirred him as the happy singing Ayrian troops had passed him, but he did not know the words. Franz, like all good Hitler Youth was able to rouse himself with enthusiasm when discussing such fundamental articles of the faith. A sparkle, which might have been mistaken for religious fervour, entered his eyes as he churned out the words teaching his convert, line by line, explaining the meaning. Soon both boys were singing at the tops of their voices.

Franz, infected by the joy he had created in John, found his old pride in the Fatherland. Forgotten now were the men in their death throes, hanging by their bruised and stretched blue necks. Forgotten were the groaning and writhing young Jews whom he had watched his friends kicking on the foot-paths during their many patriotic sorties, while he had still been learning the benefits to the whole of the free world of the glorious Fascist Reich. Forgotten also were his fears of the S.S. hammering on his door during the dead of night, to drag him away for being a coward and for spying for the evil democracies of the west.

Germany was all-powerful, Germany was all good, Germany was superior in all things and could not make mistakes for had his Fatherland not the most glorious man who had ever lived, for its leader? Therefore, Germany could not possibly make a mistake and accuse him of spying. He had only to tell them the truth of the way he felt, with unquestioning loyalty for authority, and they would believe him for they were all-seeing and all-knowing.

And here too was John, his enemy, who was also his friend. Even the vanquished nations of the misguided world recognised the Führer and his creation for what he was. John would, with his family and his countrymen, join him in the *Horst Wessel* and help to build a free Europe and then a free world. Yes, he was really proud to be German and proud to have his convert endorsing his vision.

Franz suddenly pulled on both brakes, coming to a violent halt which almost caused John to collide with him.

"Hey wait a minute Franz! What's going on? You nearly had us off!" exclaimed John, as he stopped, placing both feet on the road, turning back his head towards his friend. "What are you doing?"

Franz was smiling. It was a serene smile. His eyes glinted, as they shone out the glory of the Fatherland.

"Come here John," he whispered in a harsh rasping voice, charged with emotion.

John was puzzled as he removed himself from his bike and pushed it slowly towards Franz, standing against a huge flowering veronica bush.

"What's up, Franz? What do you want?" he enquired nervously and querulously.

Franz was not aware of John's hesitation, nor his puzzled look. All he saw was one of the unenlightened, one of the uneducated and ignorant enemy, victim of the degeneration of the democratic world, who had come to see the error of his ways and who was now prepared to accept the Führer as his own.

Franz grabbed John's wrist with fervour. John at first pulled away looking round about him with embarrassment. There was no one in sight and Franz did not seem aware that he was causing his convert any discomfort.

"John, what we were singing was the *Horst Wessel* song. We are singing of the glory of my Fatherland, yes?"

"Yes," replied John hesitantly, a little unsure of what Franz was saying.

"And we are talk of our glorious Führer, the man who will lead us all to victory and freedom, yes?"

"Yes we were talking about Herr Hitler," replied John cautiously and non-commitally.

"Well then," announced Franz, "listen to me, my friend, listen!"

He dropped his bicycle against the veronica and, standing to stiff attention, gave the smartest and most meaningful salute he had ever made.

"Heil Hitler!" he shouted, continuing with the fervour of a religious fanatic, unaware of the ludicrousness of his action.

"Heil Hitler! Heil Hitler! Heil Hitler!"

John was extremely uncomfortable. He did not like seeing his friend possessed like this. This was not the Franz who, for the past nine days, had been his brother. This was someone who looked like Franz but had not a mind of his own. It was Franz sharing the collective mind of the most enthusiastic Nazified members of the Hitlarian Youth. He now remembered the British newsreel films from before the Occupation and how the young Germans had been shown as being mindless machines, controlled by others.

"Stop, you German bugger!" he shouted.

Franz stopped dead with the puzzled look of one awakened from sleep walking. His face was pale again, his eyes stretched wide. His mouth hung open,

"Eh? What? What did you say, John?"

John was conscious that his friend had come out of some sort of trance. He wished to forget the past few minutes but realised that, if he summarily dismissed the scene he had just painfully witnessed, Franz would only insist on knowing what was the matter and would quite possibly start all over again. No, he could not bear the thought of a repeat performance!

"Franz, my friend, I think you're not quite yourself. . ."

"Not myself? What is this 'not myself'?" enquired Franz, not knowing whether John was insulting him or just making one of his incomprehensible British statements.

"I mean, you're probably not well, Franz. You know, you've been in the sun." He watched Franz's face pinch up and darken, as he received the words. Words which had left John with kindness, but had been translated into hurt. "Oh blimey, Franz, don't look at me like that. I'm not meaning to be rude. All I'm trying to say is that you're not behaving like you usually do . . ."

Franz interrupted.

"So you say I am in the sun!" he shouted, stamping his feet. "You say I am funny in the head, yes?"

"No," replied John stressing his answer with an embarrassed laugh. "No, Franz, all I'm saying is that you were behaving . . ." He paused. He was not quite sure how to continue. He feared that whatever he now said would be misconstrued.

231

"Go on!" ordered Franz irritably. "Go on, John. Finish what you are say. Tell me I'm mad! That is it, isn't it?"

"No," replied John, a mixture of embarrassment and exasperation. "Can't we just leave the subject, Franz?"

"No we cannot! I'll tell you John. You think you know me, don't you? Well you're wrong, you do not! How long have we been friends?"

He did not wait for a reply to this semi-rhetorical question.

"Just a few days. And how old am I? I am fifteen! I am a man. You think because, when you first met me, I was not well, and I was frightened, after my terrible experience in the harbour, that I am not a good German, yes? You think that I am a coward and a bad German, yes? You would like me to be on your side! I know. Well I am not a coward! I am a good German! I am not a little boy any more. I am fifteen. I am a man I tell you . . ." These last few words faded off as a vacant expression invaded his enlarged eyes and loosely open mouth.

John's mind flashed back to their first meeting, in that small room, at the Feldkommandantur office. He felt he was witnessing a re-enactment of this disturbed friend's nightmare. He did not know what to say or what to do which might comfort Franz. All he could do was to offer his hand to betoken the friendship they had. The vacant eyes did not seem aware of this hand for there was no response and John was forced reluctantly to withdraw it.

When the head has no way of dealing with inconclusive circumstances, then the heart has to take over. John stepped forward placing both hands on Franz's forlorn shoulders. Franz flinched but did not move away, his shoulders simply sagged all the more. John's experience of such things, apart from schoolboy talk and overheard snatches of adult conversation, thought to have been well shielded from the ears of the immature, was nil. However, he felt he knew his friend's illness was not physical, but was in his mind. All he could say, as he looked into the sad eyes, eyes that had witnessed such horror and such terror, eyes of a boy like himself, yet forced into seeing a man's world, was,

"Sorry, I'm sorry, Franz."

Franz turned his back on his best friend. John could not hear them, or see them, but he knew that they were there, tears of anguish, tears of bitter salt, tears of relief and cleansing, running their way down his dear enemy's face.

Words were not needed. He momentarily stood behind his friend's turned form then, slowly and deliberately, made to return to his bicycle.

"Wait!" choked out Franz, his voice loaded with emotion, his throat aching with his inward sobs. "Wait, John. Please don't go."

He paused. John stopped where he was. The comment needed no reply.

"John, I am a coward . . ."

"No . . ."

"Yes, I tell you, I run away, I am a failure . . ."

"You're not a failure, Franz," interrupted John. "Do you think I'd be your friend if you were no good, eh?"

"I don't know. I just don't know any more." The words rasped out slowly and painfully. "I am happy just a while ago. You know, when we are both singing together? I am a good German then, yes? I am a good German when I am singing the *Horst Wessel*, yes? No one could tell then that I am a coward. Then I salute the Führer . . ." He turned pausing. His eyes were ringed red. He looked his friend directly in the face and then, slowly and deliberately he mouthed these words, almost hissed. There was loathing in his voice, a loathing John knew not whether intended for him or for their author.

"You think I am mad, don't you? Because I saluted my Führer, you think I am mad! You say I have been in the sun!"

John was not sure if Franz was making a statement or if he expected a reply. He assumed the latter for Franz remained staring at him. Awkwardly he started to frame his reply.

"It's not that Franz, well not that exactly. It's just that you seemed so . . ., well so different. If you want to know really, it made you seem like, you know when you were shouting his name like you did, like a, like an enemy . . ."

Franz looked shocked.

"Yes, that's it Franz, you were no longer my friend, you became my enemy . . ."

Franz interrupted,

"But you are joining in with the songs praising the German nation."

"Yes."

"Well then," he paused, "that makes you like me. That makes you a German, John."

"No."

"Why do you say 'no'?"

"Because . . ." John felt inconclusive and yet he knew they had to clear the air. "I did it for you, Franz, not for Germany. Look Franz, you are good, you are my brother, my friend, but your people are our enemies. Your people and our people fight and kill each other. Your aeroplanes drop bombs on innocent people and kill them."

"But, like you saying, John, we are brothers. You must be on my side, for when we have won this war we can both be on the winning side."

"No."

"Why?" Franz was troubled. "Why do you not join us now? You said how wonderful you thought our Führer was, didn't you?"

"Yes, I said it," admitted John, in embarrassment.

"Well then . . .?"

"No! No, I tell you!"

"But John, we both know our two countries will soon make peace and unite together to destroy the Bolsheviks, so why wait?"

"Because I can't! How can I say 'Heil Hitler'? It would make me a traitor."

"Oh ho!" laughed Franz. "This is stupid! You would not be a traitor! Why don't you listen? I say we will both soon be on the same side so how can that make you a traitor?"

"Oh, shut up, Franz, please! It's you who's being stupid. What would my father and mother say, and my aunt and uncle, if they heard I'd said it?"

"But they don't have to hear you, just me."

"No! Never, never!"

"But you already have!" shouted Franz in triumph.

"Eh?"

There was silence. Franz seemed to have regained his earlier cheerful poise. John was relieved. He hoped this heralded a return to less serious discussions, and a complete change of subject.

"You already have," said Franz, chuckling.

"Have what?"

"You say 'Heil Hitler' just now John."

"I bloody didn't!"

"You did, I hear you. You say, 'How could I say Heil Hitler?' "

"That's not saying it," declared John.

"Yes it is, you definitely said the words."

"Yes, I said the words," replied John, "but without meaning them . . ."

"Oh, I see," chortled Franz, "if you say something without meaning it, then you have not really said it. Is that what you mean?"

"Yes," said John, stubborness extricating him from the logic of his friend's argument.

"No, John, you are wrong!"

"I'm not, I tell you!" exclaimed John with sudden inspiration. This discussion was going to be interesting, stimulating even. "Look, Franz. What would you say if someone said something under torture?"

"Pardon me?" Franz screwed up his face, puzzled.

"Well let's say your side captured one of our men and tortured him to make him . . ."

"We wouldn't!"

"Wouldn't what?" demanded John, in exasperation at having his train of thought broken.

"We wouldn't torture a prisoner of war. There is an international law . . ."

It was John's turn to interrupt,

"I said 'suppose' you fool!"

"No I won't!"

"Oh I give up," groaned John. Franz was laughing. He too had learned how to tease.

"Go on, John, just suppose."

John was annoyed but could not remain so. Franz's pleasure had infected him.

"All right, but no more rude interruptions, OK?"

"OK."

"Well, suppose this prisoner . . ."

"Which prisoner?" Franz quickly stepped out of the way of John's abortive punch.

"This prisoner has been tortured and made to say Heil . . ." He stopped, correcting himself, realising the *faux pas*. "This prisoner has been made to say 'Hitler is good' . . ."

"Oh, so now you say 'Hitler is good' . . . This is a good joke, John!"

That was enough. Before Franz realised it he was lying on his back under the large veronica bush. John was on top of him. Both were laughing. It was cool and very private there in their pale green and purple dungeon.

"OK," said John, "you won't listen to me so I will give you a lesson. I will put words into action." He poked Franz in the ribs evoking a screamed laugh from one who was ticklish.

"Now keep still and listen or you'll get some more," ordered John.

Franz, in defiant mood, wriggled and struggled but only managed to get more securely clamped by John's knees. John firmly seated himself across the prostrate abdomen.

"I warned you," said John, with laughter, as he administered more pokes. "There, let's say that is the torture and you're the one being tortured, O.K.?"

"No!" screeched Franz. "No, stop it! Stop it!"

"All right then, listen. You're my prisoner, eh?"
Franz's dilatory reply was hastened by a further dose of medicine.

"Yes, yes I'm your prisoner!"

"Right then, if I torture you, I can make you say things yes?"

"Maybe," conceded Franz with a mock sneer, although his eyes told John he was really enjoying the game.

"Let's put you to the test then, eh?"

"No John, no. Stop it! Stop it!" implored Franz, as his agony began.

"Right then, say after me, 'God Save the King'."

Horror flashed across Franz's face.

"No John! No! I can't say that. No, no please . . ." His voice trailed off into screams of hysterical laughter.

"Say it, say it, I tell you," insisted John.

"No I won't!"

More writhing laughter.

"Stop, stop! All right I say it. I say it!" John stopped the torment and Franz sagged weak with exhaustion.

The treatment having stopped, Franz regained his self assuredness and sought to bargain himself out of the difficulty.

"Yes, John, I see what you mean. I understand. I take it all back in. I understand, you do not mean it when you say 'Heil Hitler'. So can we go now please?"

"Not until you have said 'God Save the King'."

"Oh no, John, please. No!" His last word burst out of him with extreme force, as the treatment recommenced.

The outcome of their philosophical debate was inconclusive owing to the screech of brakes outside their chamber, quickly followed by the impatient sounding of a motor horn.

"Our bikes!" gasped John, suddenly realising they had casually dropped them in the lane.

"We are blocking the road," said Franz. "We must move them."

"No," ordered John. "They'll move them. We can't go out, they'll wonder what is going on."

They listened. Both were rather frightened, John at what might happen to the bicycles and Franz at what would happen if they were discovered. Both were very still.

The motor horn stopped and the engine was switched off. They heard car doors open and slam shut then the sound of angry German voices.

"What if it's the Feldpolizei again?" asked Franz, anxiously clutching at John's sleeve.

"Sssh! Listen," whispered John.

The voices got louder as they heard two pairs of boots stamping towards them.

The bikes were picked up. John strained his ears to hear what was happening to them. He was filled with anxiety now, that they would be damaged or stolen. What troubles he would face if he had to return home minus his, or his father's only means of transport with little or no hope of obtaining another.

He flinched as one of the bicycles was roughly thrown against this same bush in which they were hiding. And the other one? In his effort to hear more John held out his palm above the already rigid and silent Franz, as though warning him to remain that way. Footsteps outside, the sound of a bicycle being wheeled. Oh no! He went to move but was in turn restrained by his prisoner. Then he heard raucous laughs from outside in the sunshine, as footsteps subsided but the sound of the bicycle's free wheel mechanism continued, barely audible. The sound picture formed quickly and what happened was all over in a matter of seconds. That Jerry oaf had taken a bicycle, held it in an upright position and, pointing it down the lane, had dispatched it on its way with a mighty heave. John could see all this through his ears, as he strained, waiting for the crash.

The crash came like the clatter of a train passing over a level crossing. To John's heightened senses it was exaggerated and loud, as he imagined the bent frame, broken forks, scratched paintwork, buckled wheel and twisted pedals while the ringing of the bell signified the vehicle's pain and anguish. This was too much! He had to get out there!

Franz, knowing his friend's thoughts, and anticipating his action, held him back with both hands at the same time shaking his head and mouthing, "No."

This whole scene took place in the briefness of a moment while, as background, they heard further calls one to the other outside, the slamming of a car door as one of the occupants returned to it, and a rustling just outside their hiding place as the second man lingered.

They did not have long to wait to discover the reason for the malingering. Suddenly, and quite unexpectedly, their privacy was invaded. Where Franz lay, face up towards the leaves, from which John peered towards him, came an intrusion in the form of a jet of fluid, steaming and splattering as its force made way through the foliage and its outer edges were bounced from springy frond to springy frond, reducing it in part to a fine spray.

Franz was aghast as the stream of urine narrowly missed him and the splashing besmattered his pale face.

The sight and realisation together with the look of shock and absolute disgust on his friend's face caused John to convulse with laughter, albeit silent.

As the gush died away, and the last waft of smelly steam dispersed into the atmosphere, John had reached the stage of curious sounding nasal snorts as he tried to suppress the irrepressible laughter which racked his body. Even Franz was infected. Despite their fear of discovery, their bodies could not contain their exploding mirth as the footsteps receded.

As their laughter took control of the youths so did the car outside vibrate into life with the effect that their jubilation went undetected.

Despite the horrible mental images formed from the sounds of steel against stone, John could find no damage to his bicycle, as, with trepidation, he picked it up from where it had been pushed down the lane. His father's bike too, was unharmed.

Their next stop had to be to find a stream somewhere so that Franz could wash his face.

They both ached from excessive laughing.

*   *   *

Larry was finishing the washing up. Frances had gone for a lie down, not that she often did in the afternoon. She was not ill, she was not even upset. It was not from an over indulgence of food. Perhaps she felt relaxed. Maybe, unexpectedly, she was pleased that John had not returned home for his dinner, for this was one of the rare occasions when she could have her husband to herself, other than during the sleep time.

Why was she not feeling anxious? Surely she should have worried when John had not arrived home for his Thursday half day off work? Should she not be worrying in case he had got himself into trouble with the Germans? Should she not be imagining that he might have been sent out on one of those delivery trips and maybe got lost or had a burst tyre, or been detained or have strayed on to a mine field even? He had not even 'phoned to say why he was late. That was not like him. Nor was it like Frances not to worry. In fact, she felt so free from tension and worry that she was almost worried by the sensation.

No, all Frances could think of now, as she lay on the cool eiderdown in just her slip, and as the gentle breeze outside their bedroom window just flitted the net curtains sufficiently to make a change in the quality of the light, was that Larry, her sweet manly Larry would soon be with her in the cool privacy of their Thursday afternoon bed.

Frances, owed it to him, for was it not he who had soothed her in her agitation? Had he not explained to her that he had lent his bicyle to John's German friend? Had he not guessed that the two of them were probably enjoying the summer's day together riding, laughing and chatting?

It was good to see Larry more relaxed than he had been for many days. It was exciting to know that he was coming to her. He had not slept well lately and had been an unbearable fidget in bed, with his tossings and turnings, his troubled shouts and getting up and pacing round the room. She was fed up with it, and with his drinking of late. After all, it was she, not he, who had the job of carrying down the full jerry each morning. It never used to be like this.

If only Larry had been able to confide in her more and to tell her what was happening but he would not. He kept it all to himself, as though he were frightened to involve her. He seemed lately to be in fear of the Germans as well as indulging his usual hatred.

Larry had changed so much since the start of the Occupation. He was never frightened or agitated, or irritable and full of hatred before the Germans came. Before the invasion, he would never have gone to bed and turned away from her, feigning tiredness or exhaustion, to lie there for hours on end just staring wide-eyed at the wall.

How could he be as he was these past few weeks? How could he neglect her so, when she so needed him and the security his strength and manliness gave her? Was he taking some horrible revenge for the times when she had been too tired or had one of her headaches? But no, he was not like that, not Larry. Larry was all good, Larry never sulked or looked for revenge. Larry always accepted with patience and dignity. Then why, when her need had been as a hollow hunger in these past weeks, with all her fears and insecurities, had he spurned her? Why had he left her unfulfilled and in desperate want?

As she thought about it, the long restless nights, the flinch and regrouping of her loved one as she had tried to bring him back into her world with her gentle caresses and bodily warmth, she bit her lip beginning to tense up as though, subconsciously waiting for another humiliating rejection.

But no, today would be different. Over the dinner table Larry had let his knife and fork rest, uninterested in his food. He had taken her hands in his and had looked into her eyes, as he used to when first they were married. This time was going to be one of those Thursday afternoons from more than a decade ago, she knew it. His voice had barely whispered as his lips had hardly moved, but his words had been reiterated by the soft yet intense desire in his blue eyes, as he had said;

"Go love, let's have a Thursday afternoon. I'll be in once I've done these dishes."

He had paused, then with slow heavy words, charged with passion,

"I want you!"

And so she lay there, her peace of the present having obliterated her other miseries so that now she could not even begin to think how she could have been unhappy. For Frances there would be no more anxiously watching the clock as the hands approached curfew. No more waiting for the bang of the front door in the night, or for the call up the stairs of old Gaudion announcing the arrival of the Germans. No more waiting for news from the prison. No more fear that John was collaborating. Larry had taken all that away from her. Today he was hers, his mind no longer belonged to his fears. Today he was hers and today belonged to them.

Chapter Fourteen

During the scrub up the doctor, who had tended John from the nightmare tangle 'till the present time, had chance to impart his knowledge, and diagnosis so far, to the Consultant Surgeon.

"So, you're pretty certain we'll find some extreme haemorrhages in there, are you?" asked the Consultant.

"Absolutely," the Doctor replied, elaborating. "He was crushed right up against the steering wheel, there is extensive bruising of the abdomen and all the usual swellings associated with abdominal disturbance."

"Hmmph!" the Consultant mused. "Seems as though we'll be late home for supper!" He smiled.

The doctor knew the Consultant would not have been so flippant if he had witnessed what he had done, nor would he have talked of supper. Perhaps the doctor was not experienced enough of such disasters. Maybe he too would be like the Consultant one day and laugh off, as routine, the devastation of a human frame. He did not have time to reflect or recriminate against the senior more.

"What else?"

"Pardon?" The question had come as a surprise.

"Any complications?"

"Yes, Sir."

"Well, elaborate please, Doctor. I don't wish to have to stop for Question Time during the operation."

The Doctor elucidated the deepening shock and the fracture to the pelvis.

It was the Consultant's turn to be grave.

"So it has to be a very quick job, wouldn't you say?"

"Yes, Sir, in view of the shock, I would say very quick."

"I agree with you, Doctor. If what you say is found to be the case then the quicker we have him sewn up the better."

The Consultant nodded as he spoke as though agreeing with himself.

"It will mean then, won't it Sir," continued the Doctor, "that the Orthopaedic Surgeon will not have much time with the pelvis, if at all?"

"What? Are you suggesting it is left alone?" the Consultant raised his eyebrows at the enormity of his own hypothesis. "Send him back to Intensive Care with a passport to a wheelchair?"

"That's a decision only you can take once we're in there, Sir," was the Doctor's tactful reply.

"You're right, of course, though Doctor." He smiled above his mask. "Besides, we can't have Orthoes getting in the way can we?"

*   *   *

His rebirth into the Hitler Youth and his near baptism, together with the earlier singing of the *Horst Wessel,* the salutations of the Führer, their deep philosphical arguments on the hypothesis of the Geneva Convention, and their shared fear and relief, had made Franz Müller feel like a new man. In fact he felt like a man now for the first time in all his fifteen years.

With this new feeling of confidence, his fears of being thought a traitor behind him, he was persuaded, no he suggested even, to accompany John on his final call into the military zone.

And so the two approached the showpiece of Hitler's Atlantic Wall at Jerbourg, Guernsey's south-eastern peninsula of steep three hundred foot high cliffs. So steep are the cliffs, and so high at this point of the Island, and so isolated, that Jerbourg itself seems almost like a microcosmic mountain island fortress affording views of all the other islands in the Bailiwick with, on clear days, views of Jersey and the coast of France.

John remembered Jerbourg well. His mind was flooded with nostalgia as he approached the rise up towards Doyle Monument, a tall tower up which one could climb, on the internal spiral staircase, to reach the viewing balcony which was always cold and breezy, even on the hottest summer's day. So strong were his memories that he saw the monument still although it had long since been reduced to a heap of granite blocks and rubble, making way for the firing of mighty war cannons.

John did not see the huge blue granite blocks held together in batches by the bleached white mortar. Instead he fancied the three hundred steps down to Petit Port Bay. He could see clearly, in his mind's eye, the triangle of hard silver white sand, like a tiny wedge of plaster wall, held in position on two sides by rugged brown cliffs topped with grass, gorse, bracken and a huge variety of wild flowers. The sea nibbled at its third edge, now with gentle ripples of clear cool water, then as suddenly with mighty breakers churning and turning all who stood in their way or ran screaming with delight in their path.

This tiny wedge, after the steep three hundred step descent, always became a vast expanse of firm clean sand. John imagined the view which was now just around the corner from him. Oh, to just take his friend and run and jump down the steps. Oh, to run on to the deserted beach and to throw off his clothes on the dry pebbles at the foot of the steps and run down the hard cool sand and into those crystal clear breakers, like miniature waterfalls with the roar of mighty lions. Just to taste the salt and to feel the gentle scouring of the fine packed damp sand on his feet and legs. How he longed to run on that sand, using his big toe as chalk on the clean board. He wanted to write words in huge great letters at least ten feet across so that on climbing back to the cliff tops and the hot, wild flower perfumed air, they could regard his work now telescoped to barely legible size.

What would he write? What had he put in years gone by? No more silly messages such as, 'Intermediate for Ever', now. No he would not waste the clean sand on such trivia. Much better to put, 'God Save the King', or, 'Long Live Churchill'. Maybe not though, for then Franz would put, 'Heil Hitler'. John would not have his peaceful, beautiful Petit Port defiled in such a way! On the other hand, Franz would not realise how tiny the words would become from the top. Maybe he should let him go ahead with his tiny two foot big 'Heil Hitler' which could then be dwarfed by his own mighty British proclamation. Perhaps that would be unfair?

Maybe he could persuade Franz to do his writing close to the rising tide and then say:

"Don't look back until you reach the top, then you'll have a lovely surprise." Wouldn't that be fun, on reaching the top of the steps, to observe Franz's surprise when he realised his Germanic gestures had succumbed to nature's whims?

Maybe he should draw a mighty Union Jack? He started making one in his imagination. Should the wide white band be at the top near the pole or at the other end? Or was the wide white on the side? Possibly it was the red? As John thought about it, he realised that his concept of free Britain's flag was becoming hazy. His days of scouting, when such lessons were instilled, seemed long ago now, from another world. Wouldn't it be wonderful to see the Union Jack flying once more? Well, it did not matter really, with his drawing, for there would be no colour other than the silver grey of the sand. From a distance no one would be able to tell which bands were wide and which were narrow. Besides, it would only be Germans looking. Very likely the Germans would know more than he, on the correct way up to draw the British flag. What a sobering thought!

John supposed Franz would have to draw his swastika flag. What if they combine the two? What if he were to draw the Union Jack then Franz could flatten out the centre and draw a swastika in a circle? Yes that would look good! That would be a way of cementing their friendship. No one could object, they would, after all, just be stating a precursor of what was soon to be.

Then there would be arguments over that. Franz would probably say the swastika should be the main flag with a tiny Union Jack in the centre, but that would look ridiculous. These Germans had some really stupid ideas!

"Come on, John. Look where you are going please! You nearly have me in the hedge then!"

"Sorry," apologized John, as he was rudely drawn back into reality.

Franz laughed. John forgot Petit Port. It was good to see his friend happy and relaxed once more. He too laughed. He could not really say why he felt this way, but he suddenly felt happy and free, a feeling he had not experienced since the Occupation had begun.

"Look Franz, over there, see?" Franz followed the direction in which John's finger pointed.

"Oh yes," he said, "that is indeed a beautiful sight." He looked out over a scene of infinite, and to him, foreign beauty. To John it was still familiar despite his enforced exile of the past year.

He looked at the fields of lush grass, steeply sloping away from him down into the little valley filled with thick vegetation, almost tropical in its profusion. Here and there were patches of bright yellow gorse. Up and beyond the nearest little valley, which sloped its way steeply down to the coast, were more fields, and in the distance more seaward-bound indentations. The further north he looked the coastline took a turn to eastwards so that he could not only observe the tree and shrub-topped bastions of cliffs but could see also the granite plinths upon which they rested on the sea. The sea that was so still and calm that it was like a mirror, here and there frosted and scarred by trickling currents of cool water moving their way towards the horizon. A horizon which was itself indistinct and mellowed by heat haze.

The nearer islands of Herm, Jethou and Sark floated and shimmered on this heat haze, their greens and granites of massive cliffs dwarfed by distance, appearing as blacks and purples.

Almost as far away as the islands was that part of Guernsey which was recognisable to Franz. The harbour of St. Peter Port, with its long breakwaters reaching out to clutch at the ancient island defence of Castle Cornet. Even from this mellowing distance of several miles, he could clearly pick out the cranes and observe their miniature movements. He could see the smoke billowing from the ships at berth in the harbour.

Franz shuddered when he looked at the lighthouse, remembering the carnage he had witnessed there. He was not going to have his dream broken by such thoughts, so quickly, moving his eyes, he transported himself three miles or so further north to that part of Guernsey which is almost flat and often battles with the high tides for possession of its territory. He was dazzled by reflections of the sun upon the acres of glasshouses. No, he did not like this flat view as much, so after quick excursions across the inviting green hills of Delancey and the Vale, set in these molten glass lowlands, he returned to his first love, the awe-inspiring cliffs of St. Martin and the Parish of St. Peter Port.

How strange on this perfect and hot summer's day that Franz, a member of the mighty German army of occupation and liberation could sit in perfect peace and view a scene of unimaginable tranquillity. Looking out over the cliff tops, with the fields and woods, paths and occasional houses nestled secretly away, and the skyline shaped by yet more roofs and trees, who would have thought there was a war taking place and that in this tiny plot of beauty‐lived, side by side, a conquering race and a vanquished people? How could a place be so peaceful and so beautiful during a time of war? And how could men consider themselves enemies of each other when they stood in such a place?

"All right then, Franz, stop gawping at the view, will you. There's plenty more yet," cajoled John.

Franz, hardly aware of John's presence, had to be spoken to again.

"Come on, you stupid German," said John, with a broad grin, which belied his words. Franz's dream was broken. He quickly returned from his happy days in Herm with Corporal Schmidt, missed the trauma of the airforce raid completely, his spirit speeding like mercury, across the water, across the beautiful land, to reunite with his person once more.

"Oh yes, of course," he replied hesitantly. "I am just dreaming and . . ."

"I know you were," interrupted John, "and I'd like to know what it was but we haven't got time now, old son. Whatever it was must have been good though, eh? For you look very happy."

Franz smiled up at his friend as he reluctantly made to move.

"Yes," he agreed, "it was a very good dream, very good!"

"Right then, are you ready?"

"Ready?"

"Yes. Are you coming with me round Jerbourg to deliver the last of these despatches?" John indicated his message bag which now sagged with its near emptiness. "Or perhaps you'd rather stay here. That is, you might want to stay here rather than go through another sentry post?" He looked at

Franz with kind concern thinking the German would probably accept that option. At the same time, he suppressed his anticipated disappointment at not being able to share his most beautiful and favourite part of his island.

"No indeed, I will accompany you!" asserted Franz. "Come now, John, I am no more a coward, remember? All is well now, you will see." He stood stiffly to attention, proclaiming his new-found confidence and basking in his rediscovered faith that Germany was just, right was on the Führer's side and therefore he had no fear of being misunderstood.

"Very well then, if you're sure."

"Of course I'm sure," said Franz, scowling at his friend. "Besides I have this letter to deliver to Helmut. You wouldn't wish to do that, would you, John?"

John did not reply although his reflection of Franz's temporarily clouded visage briefly showed his thoughts.

"OK then, let's go, eh?"

"Yes, let's go, eh?" mimicked Franz mocking John's accent.

They picked up their bicycles and wheeled them to the sentry post which straddled the road.

A sentry stepped out from his concrete bunker. The bunker itself, although the usual plank marked, coarse concrete, looked somewhat different in that its occupant was obviously a gardener or, like John, detested the crude concrete intrusions. Apart from the camouflaged netting of the top, attempts had been made to turf its sides and induce ice plants to grow, besides a variety of mosses and ferns. The sentry observed John's surprise and grinned broadly with pride, at the same time letting out a stream of German.

Franz, using his mother tongue, informed the man that John was not German. With that the fellow switched to English.

Both Franz and John were taken on a tour of the bunker and they were told they must visit the one at the top of Petit Port steps, for not only had the Aryans planted most impressive gardens there, with a pond and irrigation channels, but they had also painted windows and doors on the fortress, making it look like a rustic cottage.

So friendly was this German that they found it difficult to get away without causing offence.

Fortunately, he knew of Helmut and gave them verbal

directions marking their other ports of call on John's already heavily pencilled plan.

Finally, John felt he had to be rude and break away. He referred to the deliveries he had yet to make and offered his pass, ready to explain the presence of his friend. This was not necessary, however, for when he produced his papers, the man dismissed them jovially telling him they were not needed. The man was so delighted to have their company, along with their interest and compliments of his work, that he wished he could have accompanied them. In fact that wish gave him an idea. Before they realised what was happening, he was on the roof of his hanging garden calling raucously across the gorse bushes where hid the ruins of Doyle Monument. His shouting attracted the attention of a group of soldiers who had obviously been working out of sight.

First one torso, then another, then another appeared above the vegetation, as the thin figures rose up to discover what all the shouting was about. Franz and John looked at each other in amusement grinning, for the men behind the bushes, having stripped to the waist, in order to sunbathe while playing cards, at first appeared to be sun reddened naked, until the one addressed eventually stepped out to disclose the discomfort of a hotly clad lower half.

Franz gasped, looking at John, as the man uttered some vile German swearing, albeit good naturedly. He was relieved that his friend had not understood.

"What's going on, Franz?" asked John.

"He's," said Franz, indicating the sentry, "called on his fellow guard to relieve him so he can accompany us," replied Franz.

"That's good," said John. "We'll get it all finished quicker then."

"Yes," agreed Franz, "but the other one doesn't wish to leave his game of cards."

"Well it looks as if he has," countered John, pointing to the figure, who was reluctantly approaching them.

"Yes," agreed Franz. "Our friend here has reminded him that there should be two of them in the post anyway and that he's had his half hour already."

"What's that mean, 'half hour'?" asked John puzzled.

"I think they take turns to have a rest," replied Franz.

"Are you saying there should be two on duty but they break the rules?" asked John, surprised at this unexpected lack of discipline.

"Yes, that is right, Englishman," interposed the sentry. "We like this holiday island. When it is quiet we too become tourists." He laughed.

John asked, "What do you mean, 'when it's quiet'?"

"Well, like now," replied the man. "Our officers have just in their car gone and they've left him in charge." He pointed to the N.C.O. "And he's easy, he does what he's told!"

"But what if there were a raid?" asked John puzzled at this apparent lack of concern. "What if the R.A.F. came, or the Commandos?"

The man pulled a face and looked grave, cutting the conversation short.

"You ask too many questions!" Franz pulled at John's coat and John shut up.

*   *   *

Anne de la Haye dare not let her distress communicate itself to Keith. She felt rotten, absolutely terrible. She could quite easily have slumped down at the table and sobbed her heart out. She could have just as easily left Keith and run off to her mother.

As she bit her lower lip, to keep back the floods of self-pity, she kept telling herself she must be strong for it was now that her man needed her. It was now, when he was weak, that she must be strong. She did not like the role she was being forced to play, the role of strong partner. She did not enjoy having to make the decisions and do the man's part of organising their lives but what else could she do? If she cracked now, as Keith was doing, what would be left for them? What would happen to them? It was not just 'them' meaning Keith and Anne but 'them' which included their unborn, and until quite recently, so much longed for, first child.

Anne had to be resolute. Oh, but it was hard. Easy last night when her husband returned just before curfew, staggering with Breton cider and sobbing like a little child.

Oh yes, it was easy then to comfort him and cradle his poor bruised face, gently rocking her little boy backwards and forwards until he fell asleep where he knelt at her feet. Easy then as in the flickering homemade oil lamp, she viewed his battered visage, already healing from his recent pleasantries with the Gestapo Social Services. Oh yes, much easier last night than today. Last night she had been able to think his face would heal. Yes, his face would heal and the bruises would go. His drunkenness had been just a temporary thing too.

Last night Anne knew he would be all right. Her baby had struggled inside her confirming her faith that her dear Keith would soon be his usual self. No more drunken nights for him, no more scrounging drinks from friends and acquaintances. No more borrowing from her own mother without prospect of repaying. The begging and pleading he had gone through to get those few marks! But he'd had to have them, his need for drink had been so great, in his efforts to anaesthetize his fear. Marks that would have been better spent on food. She had not reminded him, but this week had been their first week, since the beginning of the Occupation, that she had not had sufficient money to be able to use all their ration coupons, for that had never before been any problem, even for the lowest paid. Her gnawing hunger, and her recent retching on a stomach empty for two days, were of secondary importance to her at present, for now Keith's fear was slowly but surely transmitting itself to her and she was becoming clutched in its cold cruel grip.

Yes, last night had been miserable but had been bearable, whereas this afternoon was miserable and becoming unbearable. Last night she had her dreams, she had her man, they had the comfort of their bed but tonight there would be nothing, for tonight was to be their last night together and then tomorrow . . . ! She could not take much more. Tonight their last night, but what comfort is there from taking the last of anything, for in so doing, it is gone before it is taken? There always has to be promise of more in order to enjoy the present. When there is no such hope the present has been taken away before it has begun.

What would they do to her Keith tomorrow? What else

would they do to him? What had they done so far? They had taken his livelihood, they had taken his food, had temporarily removed his good looks and had borrowed his pride. All these things could come back. So what else had they done with her man? They had taken his manhood. Yes that was it, they had stolen his manhood! What was he now, lying there on the floor, groaning and snivelling? This was not the man she had married. This was not her strong, handsome, invincible fisherman. This was some poor wretch with no spirit in him, a weak broken coward of a man. They had stolen her man's manhood! And what would they do to him tomorrow? How else would they turn the screw and still further inflict destruction on their lives and their marriage?

No longer could she hold back the tears. No longer did she care. She looked down at her god lying face down on the cold floor. Everything came at once, sobs, hunger cramp and fear, as the tears of self pity and misery trickled down her cheeks distorting her vision. With the distortions cutting Keith into several globular shimmering pieces while lying there oblivious, her self pity suddenly turned into consuming anger, accompanied by hate.

As she screeched she was no longer in charge of her senses;

"Get up! Get up, bugger you! You lazy drunken heap of waste! Get up, I say!" She pushed him with her foot so that he moved like a water-filled pouch gently settling back into his previous position, oblivious to everything except his own unconsciousness.

"I told you to get up!" Her voice raised itself, almost to a scream, as she gave him a mighty kick in the ribs so that he groaned and, as though summoning up a secret source of strength, speedily rolled over to be on his back, his mutilated face towards her. He let out a mighty sigh and was still again.

After a momentary pause, while she contemplated Keith, the realisation of what she had just done came upon her and she collapsed into a dishevelled, sobbing heap on top of him, weeping and gently caressing his head as she tenderly kissed his poor swollen lips and unshaven cheeks.

*   *   *

Their newly-acquired guide looked at John's map and studied his list. John had three more calls to make on the peninsula, then both he and Franz would be free to return home.

In some ways John resented the fact that the man was going to show them where to go, for he prided himself that he knew this part of the Island better than anyone else and looked forward to boasting this knowledge to his friend. On the other hand, however, the man was serving a useful purpose for, although John knew all the paths, tracks and shortcuts, he did not have knowledge of the new fortresses and, even if he had known where they were sited, did not know their names. Besides, the fellow was pleasant company and would help expedite the delivery of the message to Helmut.

Their first call was to be at some gun emplacements on the very southernmost cliffs, overlooking a group of huge grassed peaks and rocky islets with the appearance of a miniature Himalayan range, sinking into the seas towards Jersey. This formation was known as Les Tas de Pois d'Amont on maps but to most Islanders somewhat aptly and affectionately called the Pea Stacks.

John was excited when he knew of this particular call for it would take them along paths affording exquisite views of that other seaward projection known as Icart. Even as he heard their destination he was transported on the wings of time and nostalgia to many summer days of the past as, quickly in his mind's eye, he trespassed the whole distance, taking in the fragrance of the wild flowers, grasses and gorse, while regarding the shimmering, slightly heaving mass of blue water far below, stretching to the heat-hazed and darkened cliffs in the west and the white-hot horizon of the south.

He heard the crashing of the breakers on Petit Port beach far below, with the delighted shouts of the pale but happy English visitors, kept out of sight by the convex curve of the unspoilt slopes, before they plunged steeply and rockily to the sand and boulders below.

Now he had reached the outcrop of white marble which split the granite cliffs from head to toe. What a sight here for Franz. Did not those people look tiny, like little toys?

Now he was on the headland, overlooking Cannon Rock.

How cool the green, bracken skirted, cliffs looked. How inviting to lie there cool in the lushness with the sun curtained by gently moving fronds above.

He now looked towards Moulin Huet and Saints Bay where he could just make out the tiny spots and white splashes of bathers and the little boats moored at Saints harbour.

'Look, Franz,' he wanted to say, 'see there, that rock there, over there, look? See what shape it reminds you of. Yes, go on tell me. Yes, an animal. No Franz, two animals. Look and think. Give up? That's the Dog and Lion Rock. Now can you see it? We'll see a hotel called the Dog and Lion in a minute. And do you see that rock there in the shadows? What does it remind you of? That's the Cradle Rock, see? In the middle of the bay there, there's the Seven Sisters. At high tide they almost disappear so that all the sisters stand apart.'

Suddenly he was overlooking the Pea Stacks and it was May. The cliffs were bathed in blue and pink of the bluebells and campions and here and there were bushes of white hawthorn with patches of what John knew as 'stinking onions' and 'cuckoo spit'.

'No, Franz, don't pick those. Your hands will stink. Yes stink, you know, smell. Because they're called stinking onions. Well that's what I call them. I know it's an ugly name for a pretty flower but I didn't give them the smell! We'll call them wild garlic if you prefer, I think that's the proper name.'

Looking out to sea he observed the smooth zig-zag scars of currents, as they cut the silver paper, with the little fishing boats lazily plying their trade. Everywhere was the sound of gulls, amplified by the concave cliffs and caves out of sight below.

Next, in his mind, he was inland once more, walking along a tiny dirt track of a lane bordered by hedges of wild brambles. Yes, he could hear the hollow ping pong of the tennis courts.

'We'll go in here, Franz. This is the Dog and Lion Hotel. My aunt works here, she'll be doing afternoon teas now. We'll have a pot of tea, tea for two with bread and butter followed by lovely fresh slices of her cherry cake. We can sit out under the veranda, with all the other visitors, and admire the lawns and trellis roses.'

Suddenly he was on the east coast looking down the steep crumbly cliffs towards the lonely little unmanned lighthouse appearing like a little square bungalow on the cold brown granite headland of St. Martin's point. How cold the deep clear water of Telegraph Bay always looked. How he feared to get too near the edge of the track, as it edged past the steep grassy slopes disappearing over the precipice to show the top of Benoist Isle far below, white topped with moaning gulls.

'Listen, Franz, I'll throw this stone. Listen to hear how long it takes before it hits the rocks below.'

Far out to sea was Sark, now looking black, its steep cliffs dwarfed by the distance. And behind Sark, on the horizon, was a thin golden line as the setting sun lit up the coast of northern France, giving it the appearance of a fluorescent tube.

'Oh Franz it's going to rain, I can see France so clearly.'

"We go this way now," said the sentry, not realising he was talking to one who was not really there at all. John, un-hearing and unheeding, continued down the path he took by instinct, as his dream continued.

"John!" yelled Franz. "John, we go this way, you are losing!" Both Franz and the older German stood grinning at each other as John extricated himself from his trance, looking at them with an expression which asked: 'What did you say?'

"We go this way," repeated the German, indicating a gap leading into a long field.

John, realising that the German intended taking them by a very short, and very logical, most direct inland route, but nevertheless dull and uninteresting by comparison with his recent fantasies, let it be known that he did not concur with that idea.

"Oh no! No, we'll go this way. It's not much longer and it's so much nicer. Besides . . ." He had been going to say that the farmer would never countenance trespassers on his fields but, with his complete reinstatement into the present, he realised the comment would be irrelevant.

"Come, John," urged Franz. "Let's get it over. We wish to get this job finished, do we not?"

The German sentry was amused by this trivial argument between the two.

"No," insisted John, "come my way, please. There's such a lot more to see."

"See?" questioned the sentry puzzled. "What do you mean 'see'?"

"The view," explained John, in exasperation, "you know, the cliffs and the beaches and the little paths. Please." He almost pleaded this last word, as if he were a little boy again begging and persuading his father to buy him just one more ice-cream or just one more bottle of pop.

"No!" The soldier was adamant.

'No, you've had enough for one day. You'll be sick.'

"But why?"

"Do not ask why. There are reasons but they are not for your ears."

'Don't keep asking when you've been told no. Why can't you take no for an answer?' Frances was backing Larry, but she knew in her heart, John would win and Larry would give in to him.

"Come, John, do what you're told," said Franz, getting embarrassed by his friend's behaviour.

"Oh, very well," said the pouting little face, "but tell me why we can't go my way?"

'Tell me why you won't buy me another. You've got some money, I know you have!'

"John, you can't ask these questions!" insisted Franz in his annoyance.

"That is so," interrupted the sentry. "There are things there that you must not see and which are very dangerous. You ask too many questions!"

John accepted defeat, turning to join them, following dejectedly as they entered Farmer Crocker's forbidden field.

'And don't drag your feet', snapped his mother, 'you'll wear all the crepe off your new sandals.'

The field was very long. John could not recall seeing one that size before. Then he realised, this was not just one small Guernsey field but several which had the dividing earth banks bulldozed away to form one large one. Perhaps they were making an aerodrome or a new road? What a strange idea, an aerodrome at Jerbourg! It would be like landing on Alderney's tiny cliff top runway!

Although John knew the peninsula really well, it was from the aspect of any islander exploring the public cliff paths and lanes. He did not really know the centre with its small enclosed fields and patches of heath for, in his upbringing, he had been taught not to trespass on to others' lands. True, when he was small his mother and aunt had sometimes taken him into the fields adjacent to the public paths, to pick the wild primroses and daffodils, which grew in abundance in the grass banks, or to pick sloes in the autumn to make Christmas time sloe gin, but they had never strayed too far for he had had instilled into him a feeling of guilt at such misdemeanours. Therefore today was a new experience for him.

When they reached what must have been the very centre of Jerbourg it was new for him to be able to see both the Icart headland on one side and the islands of Herm, Sark and Jethou on the other. He had never been in a position to see both simultaneously before. Likewise, he was able to see the Jerbourg Hotel, with the little cluster of houses round the old barracks, at the same time as the Dog and Lion Hotel. How strange it seemed to him that both hotels were really very close to each other and yet he always thought of them as being far apart owing to the devious coastal track one usually took to get from place to place.

Yes, John was really quite glad they had come this inland route. It was as though a whole new world of discovery was opening to him.

What a lot of underground bunkers were being constructed here. Whole rows of half-buried concrete constructions with flights of steps going down to huge thick iron doors like those on ships. There were no windows into these buildings, only ugly grids like drain covers, and little peepholes near the doors. Out of the tops which were earth and grass covered, and from a distance might appear to be just hillocks, were ugly metals pipes looking rather like chimney cowls.

Besides the bunkers there were networks of trenches, leading off in all directions, and gun emplacements in which sat soldiers and machine guns. And all this was covered with cobwebs of net and foliage.

John was fascinated and heard himself asking questions of the friendly soldier who was accompanying them. As he heard his own words spilling out, he realised he would earn a rebuff for his curiosity but it was as though he had no control of the matter. He watched Franz scowl as the questions poured out.

"What are those?" he asked, indicating what appeared to be iron crosses, set in concrete, scattered across a field near the rows of bunkers. To his surprise the soldier did not reprimand him but simply explained:

"They're anti-tank traps, not that any British tanks could get up the cliffs or even past our guns," he said with a laugh.

"Mmm!" commented John pensively.

"What if they dropped them in by parachute though?" interjected Franz, intrigued by the thought.

"Don't be daft," said John, "they'd be shot down before they reached the ground."

"Not if it was night time!" exclaimed Franz feeling annoyed to be criticised so.

"Ah, but for the night, we have searchlights, see over there. And there, see?" The sentry pointed to where there were obviously batches of lights. Franz could not see them but, not wishing to appear foolish, said he could. John, possibly more naïve, said he could not make them out, to which the man was delighted at the effectiveness of their camouflage.

"Anyway," said John, "I know another method you use to stop things coming in by parachute."

"Oh, and what is that?" asked the soldier raising his eyebrows in mock curiosity.

"You have poles with wires and bombs attached so that, if anything touches a wire when landing, the bomb goes off and, hey presto!"

"How you know all this?" asked the man, scratching his head in amazement.

"Oh, we Guernsey people know everything," replied John, with bravado.

"That is not true," countered Franz, glad of the opportunity to get back at his friend. "We were told that only today. He is not as clever as he is pretending!"

They all three laughed and the soldier did not question them further.

They had just reached a rather squat, square-looking concrete edifice, which had been coated with black paint or bitumen, alongside which a gravelled track passed, when their companion suddenly stopped.

"Quick!" he ordered. "Come this way quick, quick!"

The soldier bundled John and Franz down the steps, at the side of the black bunker, with such haste that they almost fell.

"What . . .?" exclaimed John only to be silenced by the horny hand clamped across his mouth. The soldier seemed quite desperate to keep them quiet. Franz was red faced with excitement, although he also trembled with shock.

John's surprised eyes darted at Franz but Franz was not looking his way.

They had just avoided detection by the drivers of that same car which had been inconvenienced by their bicycles. The two officers had returned early.

Their companion had to excuse himself and make his way quickly back to his post.

John had mixed feelings when the older German left, for, despite the earlier battle of wills, he had proved good company. However, John now had no-one to prevent his taking the route he had originally intended to take Franz.

"This is the way John, this is the way he directed us," said Franz.

"I know, but I think it would be better to go over here," insisted John.

"No, no, John, we can't go that way. You hear him he say we must keeping to these tracks. Besides, he say that these tracks would lead us quickly to our destinations." He paused looking rather agitated. They had certainly had quite an adventure today and he had really got to know his new friend well and did not want to spoil everything now by arguing.

"Oh, come on, Franz," protested John. "Look, I know this part of Guernsey better than anyone. We won't get lost if that's what you're afraid of!"

"No, it's not that John, it's just that . . ."

John impatiently cut him off in full sentence.

"Come on, Franz, you want to see something really beautiful don't you?" he asked, thinking of the cliff paths that would lead them round Jerbourg's south-western tip to suddenly spy the Pea Stacks in all their beautiful glory.

"Yes, I do, John, but he saying . . ."

"He said! He said! That's all you can think of!" complained John. "Listen, he thought he knew best, he thought he would take us across the centre of Jerbourg to save us time but I tell you, my way is not much further and what's five minutes more, eh? We won't get lost, I promise."

"I mustn't be late," said Franz hesitantly, beginning to waver. "I have to be back for patrol at 18.00."

"That's OK. It can't be much more than four now," replied John, cheerfully. "Come on, I'll race you!"

John set off at a run, across the field, heading towards the west side of Jerbourg, towards the thin blue grey streak of horizon showing above the distant cliff tops. He ran towards the headland of Icart, separated from them by the vast inviting bay which contained all his childhood, beach and bathing memories of Saints and Moulin Huet and Petit Port. His back now was turned upon the distant cluster of houses and hotel around the Jerbourg barracks and the small islands floating on the eastern horizon. His back was also turned upon the rows of hilly bunkers, and newly made cinder tracks, as he bounded across the lush green fields towards the paths he knew so well.

Franz, seeing his friend moving away with such speed, soon began to forget his protestations in his effort to catch him.

"Wait for me, Englishman. Wait!"

John, having clambered through hedges and banks, eventually reached a familiar track, stopping to regain his breath. Franz quickly joined him, the two making a duet of their panting and rasping.

"O.K.?" asked John. Franz nodded still unable to speak, his face red and soaked by perspiration.

"How about a lovely cool swim down there?" asked John, pointing into the bay, with a gleeful chuckle.

"No!" gasped Franz with horror.

"No? Why not? Can't you swim?"

"Yes I swim a little but . . ."

" 'Fraid to get undressed, is it? You're going to say you haven't any bathers, eh?"

"No, it's not . . ."

John was not listening.

"You could use your underpants you know."

"I know." They both laughed.

"We could dry in the sun."

"Yes but . . ."

"Oh, don't get worried Franz, it's only a joke. I know, we haven't got time. Besides I'm not stupid. I know it's against the law to go bathing. Bloody stupid law if you ask me, eh? Bloody stupid German law, eh?"

He waited for Franz to rise to this, in offence but forestalled it by hitting him a friendly blow in the chest, then rushing off up the lane to avoid retaliation.

"You wait John! You wait 'till I get you . . ."

John stopped,

"I'm hot, couldn't half do with a drink. And you Franz?"

"Yes, indeed. I think I'll have a glass of beer, please."

"O.K. I'll just settle for a milk-shake myself, with ice-cream of course."

"Mmm that sounds good, John. Would you like some jelly and custard too?"

"Stop it," cried John, laughing. "You're making my mouth water."

"I'm what? What you say?"

"I said, you're making my mouth water, it's an expression, just a saying, you know?"

"Oh," said Franz, his momentarily serious face giving way to a faint smile, "that is good then, yes?"

"Is it? Why?"

"Because, if your mouth is watering, then you won't need a drink, yes?" He laughed at his own wit.

"Oh no!" groaned John with exaggerated laughter. "I do believe little Franz has made another joke! Very good Franz, you're learning. We'll make a Guernseyman of you yet!"

"Come, Franz, this path takes us along by the Dog and Lion hotel. I want to show you."

"Why?" asked Franz.

"Why? Why not?" replied John. "It's on our way anyway. I want you to see it. It's where my aunt used to work before this bloody war started."

As they walked along, at times side by side, while at times forced to go into single file because of the encroaching brambles, the hot afternoon sun scorching their sweat soaked faces, John told Franz of the hotel he was soon to see. Oh yes, he would love its bungalow form with rose covered verandahs, looking out on to veronica bordered lawns and large tennis courts. And the roses, everywhere roses and rockeries. Already they could see the chimney pots.

They should not have come. It had been silly of John to expect this place, of happy childhood memories, to have been unchanged by the despoilations of war.

Franz who had, from John's conversation, conjured up an idyllic vision of the building with its gardens, too was shocked. Yes, Franz was shocked, for his imaginings had been spoilt. But for his friend, it was part of his real past that had been desecrated.

Franz looked first at the sight before his eyes and then quickly turned away to face John. John had taken one look at the hotel then, mouth open with disbelieving shock, had turned away pale and shaken.

Where once had stood the long verandahed bungalow building, now stood a trail of separate rooms, the gaps filled by collapsed corrugated roofing and broken asbestos walls. Doors were broken from frames, glass was missing from windows. The remaining roofing had been painted with dark green and brown camouflage. Some of the walls, which had always looked freshly painted in mock Tudor markings, were now daubed grey and green, while in those places, still sheltered by verandah, the original paint had faded and peeled through the neglect of two hot summers and one winter.

Uncle George's roses had all grown wild, the lawns looked like rough pasture. His trellises had all been broken down. Even the fences of the tennis courts, and the stones of the rockeries, had been removed. There were no more squarely boxed veronica hedges but just huge rounded green and purple, wild growing, shrubs. The usually busy place was silent, the silence of death!

Franz did not need to ask what the matter was, he knew. He realised and understood what John was feeling in his suffering, as surely as if he were looking upon the desecration of his own village in Germany. There was no need, indeed no time for explanations. He moved swiftly and skilfully to save his friend from further misery.

"Come, John, forget about it. This is war. Let us go. Quick! Show me these lovely cliff paths of yours and these stacks of peas. They will not be spoilt."

Even in his state of unhappiness and shock, John could not prevent a smile at Franz's mistaken title for the Pea Stacks.

"That's better, my friend. That's right, you smile and be happy again. We will build your lovely hotel again once this stupid war is finished."

John nodded silently brushing away a trespassing tear, with the back of his hand, while his laughter shone through and his thoughts changed from unhappiness to security in his trustworthy and thoughtful companion.

Without looking further at the desecrated memory, they turned towards the gorse and hawthorn bushes through which their way led.

On rounding the next corner they were confronted by a barricade of rolled barbed wire. It stretched across their path from hedge to hedge. It would have been impossible to cross.

Both looked at the other and shrugged.

"Hell!" gasped John. "What the hell do the silly buggers want to do that for?"

The question was rhetorical but Franz attempted an explanation which came across more as an apology.

"I'm sorry, John, but this is a war. Maybe . . ."

"Oh don't keep on, Franz!" snapped John. "Now we're in trouble. If we can't go that way it means we've got to go all the way down that lane and find the cliff path which leads from Telegraph Bay. Come on, it's a long way!" John did not further the conversation but retraced his steps as he stamped ahead with the speed of one in temper. Franz followed close on his heel, looking pale and anxious.

Back past the semi-ruined, deserted hotel they went and rushed off down the cart track which would eventually lead them to the steep cliffs of the east coast linking up with the small path leading to the Pea Stacks.

"Oh no!" groaned John, the sentiment echoed by an equally distraught German exclamation. "What the devil is going on?" He looked at Franz finding his own anxious expression reflected there. They both examined yet another barbed wire barricade which was thwarting their progress.

"What will we do John?" asked Franz almost frantic now. "Where do we go now?"

"I don't know. Wait a minute. I've got to have time to think."

"But we can't wait," whined Franz. "We have no time. It must be getting late and for Patrol I will be late. I have to get back, John . . ."

"Oh shut up, can't you!" shouted John. "It's not my fault, is it?"

"It is! It is!" shouted Franz, petulantly stamping his feet. John thought he was about to burst into tears. "If we had gone the way we were supposed to this would not have happened."

"Shut up, Franz for heaven's sake can't you? We can't go right back all that way now and that's for sure."

"Yes, let us go back, John," begged Franz anxiously, almost pleadingly. "I cannot be late. Let us go back so I can return and you can go on alone."

"What, you want to leave me now? No Sir! No, Franz. You stay with me, O.K.? Don't go off now, please. Look, I'm sorry I lost my temper just now. Please stay."

Franz could not refuse such a cry from the heart.

John had an inspiration,

"Listen, Franz, we can't go back all that way but if we go through this hedge here and across the field we should be able to get to the Pea Stacks that way. There are a few gorse bushes at the other side of the field but that's better than barbed wire eh?"

"I don't know John," replied Franz hesitantly. "What if there is more barbed wire at the other side of the field?"

John thought.

"I tell you what Franz, let's give it a try, eh? If there's barbed wire in the way then we'll come back and I'll let you go on to Town and I'll continue alone, all right?"

Franz reluctantly agreed.

*   *   *

Frances looked so peaceful as she lay there. Larry so loved her naked body.

The gentle breeze lifting the net curtains came in from the cauldron summer's afternoon outside. Despite the heat, the breeze was cool as it filtered in. The air in the room was cool as though taking its freshness from the silken eiderdown on which Larry's goddess lay.

He looked at his love as she lay there all tension and anxiety now washed from her face, its whiteness enlivened by the gentle flush on her cheeks and contrasted by the shiny black of her crimped curls.

He wanted to be with her all over again. He wanted to kiss her all over and to slip into eternity once more.

Larry pulled on his trousers, declining to use his shirt. He decided that an occasion such as this warranted a cup of tea, after which his angel, refreshed and tranquil would call him again with that same urgency that he was willing to fulfil. This all of course, if John had not returned by then.

What was the time? Nearly half past four! How strange, no John when today should be his half day off!

The muted ring of the breeze driven chimes from the Town Church clock, confirmed the half hour, as Larry gently turned the door handle.

It was strange that Frances was not in a nervous or agitated state over their son's absence. Doubly strange for her, for she always saw trouble where there was none. Larry took it as an extreme compliment to his prowess, that his reincarnation of their bygone 'honeymoon' Thursday afternoons, had relieved her of all other thoughts.

*   *   *

The hedge of hawthorn through which the two passed, to get from the lane to the field, had proved no problem and they were soon racing across the high grass of the rough unused pasture.

The other side of the field was bordered by a low broken

down granite wall beyond which the land began to slope towards the cliffs. Over the top of the bramble, gorse and hawthorn clumps they could already see the tops of the Pea Stacks with the myriad circling gulls, their plaintive cries echoing, amplified by the empty pebbled beaches and rocky amphitheatres hidden from sight below.

They picked their way carefully through the obstacles, holding back a springy thorned branch here and a lethally armoured bramble tendril there. Stepping into dried bracken here and pushing quickly past gorse, to avoid its spitefulness there.

Each step took them closer to the cliff edge, each step nearer revealing more of the blue green shaded and sun bright beauty of the Pea Stacks.

They had reached the point which must be half way into this band of heath, separating fields from grassy cliff slopes and narrow paths, when John decided to consult his map. At a slight clearing, which led off in two directions, he had to decide which natural path to take. He sat down on the tight springy carpet of shiny cliff grass while Franz squatted beside him.

"I thought you know this part well?" said Franz questioning John's referring to his map.

"Ah, but I do!" was John's haughty reply. "But that was before the war, eh? I wouldn't know where the enemy forts are though, eh?"

Franz shrugged as John continued his studies, muttering to himself.

While this was taking place Franz's attention was taken by a persistent buzzing from behind a nearby bush. Wishing to relieve himself anyway, he indulged his curiosity and moved towards the noise.

"John! Quick here!" he called, breaking John's concentration by his urgent tone. John scrambled to his feet and quickly stood beside his friend.

"What do you think, John?" asked Franz.

Before their eyes was the carcass of a fairly large animal in an advanced state of decomposition. It had been disembowelled, the haze of flies around it seeming to direct the awful stench towards them. The corpse's insides were a seething mass of white maggots.

"Ugh!" exclaimed John, covering his nose while he stared transfixed at the vile sight. "That was once a goat. See Franz, you can tell by its hoofs and horns!"

"Yes," agreed Franz, "but what do you think killed it?"

"No idea," said John. "Goats have always been kept on these cliffs for as long as I can remember. I've never heard of one dying here though."

"Perhaps . . ." Franz stopped himself, the thought was too horrible to contemplate.

"Go on," urged John, "perhaps what?"

Franz knew that his dreadful thought must indeed be true. He could not bear the realisation alone. It had to be shared with John. He clutched John's arm.

"Don't move!" he ordered in a raucous whisper.

"Eh? What?" asked John attempting to shake himself from his friend's grip.

"Be still, you fool!" insisted Franz, more forceful now than John had ever known him. "Look, John, don't you see, that animal was killed by a mine!"

"Eh?" John became silent and very still as Franz excitedly explained his thesis.

"We are in a minefield, John. Look, see?" He pointed to the decomposing creature in front of them. It lay in a small crater the size of an upturned dustbin lid, tiny ripples of disturbed gravel and stones radiating from it.

John did not argue. They just looked at each other in horror.

"But that's bloody stupid," said John at last. "Where does the minefield start, eh?"

"I don't know," said Franz. "It can't be far or we are stepping on one by now."

"Hell!" gasped John, with a shudder. "What shall we do?"

"We can't move," replied Franz forcefully, the words sounding almost like an order.

"Well we can't stay here!" exclaimed John in exasperation. "Should we go back the way we came? If, you say the minefield has just started, then all we've go to do is go back."

"But has it just started?" queried Franz. "What if it started where we climbed over that wall into these bushes?"

"Phew!" John let out a long breath of dismayed disbelief. "That can't be possible Franz, surely we'd have stepped on one if we'd come all that way?"

Franz interrupted, pleased to be able to show his superior knowledge in such military matters.

"Not so, John, in minefields, the devices are scattered in an irregular way. Sometimes they are far apart but sometimes there might be several next to each other. It is done like that to deter the enemy so that they never know and will not dare to enter a field."

It was John's turn to interrupt.

"What do you mean 'they will not dare to enter?' How do they know they're in a minefield in the first place?"

"Because . . .," began Franz in exasperation at his friend's incredible ignorance of such things, "because there are notices put up to say 'mines'."

"Oh that's bloody silly!" said John. "What's the point of putting in a minefield if you then go and tell the invaders it's there? How are you going to kill them off, if you warn them of the danger first?"

"Don't you know anything?" shouted Franz. He was about to explain the logic but it was John's turn to express anger.

"I tell you what I do know," he said. "I didn't see any of your damned warning signs!"

"That's true," agreed Franz slowly, with a puzzled look.

From where the pair stood they could see the field they had left minutes before. It looked an awfully long way if their steps had to be retraced. Besides, if it were mined the whole way, there was no guarantee that their return journey would be as fortunate. Looking the other way the distance to the edge of the scrub seemed just as far.

It was, as Franz looked in that seaward direction, that he suddenly made his discovery.

"Ah! That's the answer John." He pointed.

"Eh? What you on about?"

"There look, see those posts? Those are the warnings of the edge of the minefield."

John looked and believed, whistling slowly through his teeth. There, at the seaward side of the scrub, was a single strand of barbed wire linking metal sign posts. It was a hell of a way!

"That's it, then," said John. "We either take our chances and go back, or we risk it forward, or we just stay here." He shrugged his shoulders in despair.

Franz too despaired, his face becoming lined and white as though he had aged with all the cares in the world.

"That's why we didn't see signs of warning when we left the field," he said. "We wouldn't expect the enemy to come from inland."

John nodded assent.

They each turned to the other and with one voice asked,

"What shall we do?"

The irony of their identical, futile questions eased the tension slightly and they both laughed nervously.

John had an idea.

"What if we start shouting, surely someone will hear us?"

Franz agreed hesitantly suggesting.

"We get into a lot of trouble."

"I'd rather get into trouble than end up like that." John indicated the goat. Franz nodded agreement.

"Well, who's going to start?" asked John impatiently.

"You," urged Franz, "please."

John very self consciously, and rather half heartedly called out,

"Hello. Anybody there?" A few seconds later he heard his own words echoed from the Pea Stacks and rocks below. This caused Franz some amusement so that he became anxious for his turn.

Between them they took turns at shouting. With practice they became less self conscious and their voices became more urgent and louder.

Chapter Fifteen

"Gerda, love, you can't face telling Frances, can you, dear?
I understand." The words of her friend, as she leaned across
and took Gerda's hand in hers, words which put the distress
into some form of perspective, seemed kindness and concern
itself. It allowed Gerda's flood gates to open and she cried
as though she had never cried before, while her friend gently
rocked her in her arms.

This therapy completed, Frances was fetched, already
waiting in the hall, hat and coat on.

*   *   *

The Consultant Surgeon eyed his staff, he surveyed his
theatre and looked down at the bare flesh already swabbed
with spirit and framed in towelling.

He was so used to his trade that he hardly realised he was
dealing with a fellow human, except when he looked towards
the head which must surely belong to the flesh upon which
he was soon to operate. His eyes caught those of the
anaesthetist, alert above his mask. With his eyes asked;

'All right?' The Anaesthetist nodded his assent.

A quick word with his orthopaedic colleague to inform
him of their projected concerns. His colleague accepted
mutely, as the day accepts the inevitability of the night to
follow.

*   *   *

When the door rattled then was roughly pushed open so
that it swung freely, its knob hitting the wall, the diffused
light fell on Father Peters' startled face.

The priest had fallen asleep huddled on the bare floor of
his dark cell room. He had fallen asleep out of misery and
boredom and his stomach ached from the blow which had
earlier been administered.

Father Peters looked up anxiously and puzzled, blinking
into the square, golden light reflected face of the soldier who
impassively looked down on him as though a giant troll

from bygone Mother's stories. The priest had no idea what time it was. Could is possibly be still the day in which he'd been arrested, or was it now the next morning? Friday, was it? How long had he slept? He felt stiff and cold. Yes, it must be Friday. He must have slept for at least twelve hours. Hours broken by feverish delirium and debilitating abdominal pain.

"What do you want?" asked the priest. The answer was a quick inclination of the soldier's chin as he stepped back, inpatiently clicking his heels. Father Peters took it that he was being invited to accompany him.

The brightness of the daylight caused the priest a biliousness, as his visual consciousness was assaulted by brilliant flashing catherine wheels, shrinking as they entered his mind, always followed by more and more, faster and brighter and reducing as they converged.

Father Peters needed to be sick, as his vain attempts to lift the sash window signified to his captor. Realising the impending disaster to his charge, the German quickly grabbed his arm and half pulling, partly pushing, forced Father Peters the few steps to a tiny room in which was found a lavatory and wash basin.

Having relieved and refreshed himself, and thankful at feeling so much better, the priest put himself at the soldier's disposal once more.

By a sequence of directional nods and, not over rough pushes, Father Peters was made to lead the way to Major Müller's office.

The soldier's curt knock on the door was answered by a muffled order to enter. The priest stepped inside Pieter Müller's office while his guard uttered a few stiff words then left.

Major Müller sat at his desk, ostensibly studying papers and so lost in his task that he did not notice Father Peters. The priest was left standing but strangely he did not feel too uncomfortable at this lack of courtesy for it was the behaviour he would have expected from the engineers of National Socialism, currently liberating Europe.

Pieter had recently returned from the tennis club and was inwardly delighted that he had beaten Lilly Brown, the club champion. Although he did not wish to appear at all hurried or anxious to expedite his business with the priest, he had, in fact, made it his very first assignment upon returning. So keen was he, in fact, that he had left the club early and upon returning to the office had, so far, postponed his afternoon tea.

The casual way which he flicked through his papers then eventually laid them aside, removing his glasses and looking up into Father Peters' face, hid well the heart thumping in his breast with the knowledge that now he was about to embark upon one of the most delicate interviews in the whole of his Gestapo career. He had to handle the priest in such a way that he would be too frightened to implicate young Franz in any scandal, but at the same time, ensuring he did not antagonize the fellow. Pieter knew from experience that these men of the cloth had the ability to dig their heels in over matters of principle, damn them!

The Major knew nothing about Father Peters, other than the distorted description which came from Lieutenant Hansel. This meant he would have to use all his skills and really analyse the man through general conversation and interview techniques. He would need to know just how far he could push him. It would not be easy.

Pieter far preferred to play tennis and, when he was not playing tennis, to ponder on playing tennis. He was quite content, in the normal course of events, to delegate his work to fanatics such as Hansel then only to take over the culmination of investigations, together with the accrued credit, once the hard work had been completed.

Today was different, however. He could not entrust the task to his subordinate any more than he could bring the successful results to the attention of his superior, Colonel Brandt, for no one but he and the priest was to know what would pass between them, within these four walls. Today it was not just the security of the Reich which was at stake, but the future of the Müller line!

"So, you must be the Reverend Peters," boomed Major Müller, full of casual, false confidence. "I know a lot about you and am pleased that at last we meet."

He stood, looking almost about to proffer a hand, but, thinking better of it, awkwardly half bowed and casually sat down again.

"Please to sit down," he ordered sternly but kindly.

Father Peters, rather surprised by this unexpected show of cordiality, but nevertheless still on his guard, almost smiled and then took the chair indicated.

Pieter Müller felt decidedly nervous. This would not do. It was he who was in charge of the interrogation, not the priest. Why then was he so ill at ease while the cleric looked so serene and relaxed?

"Well, Minister, tell me, have you always lived in this island?" he asked, looking up with a casual, forced smile.

"No." The single syllable issued without trace of anger or insolence.

"I see. Well then, tell me, where did you live before being in this beautiful place?"

"Live?" asked Father Peters in a dream-like tone. "Are you ordering me to tell you? Is there not some international law which prevents you asking such things?" His face remained impassive. Pieter was not sure whether the man was being deliberately awkward or whether this was just dry British pedantry.

"Oh, come now, Minister, I am just talking to you as a friend. Surely . . .?"

He was interrupted and lost his train of thought as the priest cleared his throat.

"Excuse me Mr Müller, I assume that is your name, it is on your door, but I would hardly think 'friend' is a particularly apt term, not after the way I have been treated today. Besides I don't really see . . ."

Major Müller interrupted, "Treated today? What do you mean, 'the way you have been treated today'?" He banged his desk forgetting the delicate position he was in. "What do you expect, eh? You are helping the Feldpolizei in their investigations. Do you expect an hotel?"

Father Peters too rose to this. "I don't expect anything Mr Müller. For a start I don't know why I have been brought here. You're quite right, I don't expect hotel treatment, especially from Germans," he paused, "but I do not expect to be harassed and arrested without any reasons given. Nor do I expect to be punched, then locked up in a cell!"

273

"You what?" Major Müller was aghast. "Punched? What is this punched?"

"Oh, come now, Mr Müller, surely you know the behaviour of your own men? Surely you know their methods? You're not telling me you didn't know how I was handled are you?"

"My dear Minister, believe me, I did not know you had been mistreated. Believe me, I will investigate this thoroughly."

"Don't bother, Mr Müller, just let me go from here, that will do."

"That is not possible, I am afraid. You are my guest, you see, and we must spend some time together doing the work of the Reich. By the way, minister, I am a Major. Kindly refer to me as such."

"Very well, Major. Would you then kindly refer to me as Reverend and not Minister?"

"Indeed yes, I will call you Father if it pleases you."

They both smiled at this shared humour. Father Peters smiled for he knew the Major had been irritated at being referred to as 'Mr.' and because he realised the Major knew he preferred to be known as 'Father', but had deliberately tried to provoke him. Major Müller smiled to think that he had allowed himself to be deliberately annoyed by such a trivial matter and that he had made a fool of himself by commenting about it. He was also amused to think both he and the priest had been playing the same game.

"I think we understand each other," said Major Müller.

"I do believe you're right," replied Father Peters, despite himself beginning to like traits he observed in the lethargic middle-aged Nazi in front of him. "You asked how long I have been here in the Island, well you see I came here . . ."

"Yes, yes. Quite so," interrupted the Major. "Forgive me Father but, before you continue, would you perhaps care for a cup of tea?" His eyes sparkled as he made the invitation. How could the priest refuse such a Christian act of kindness?

"Yes, Major, I think that would be very good. Thank you."

The tea was ordered and both men settled down to niceties and small talk.

By the time the silver tray bearing a silver teapot, real

tea, milk, chunks of fresh black bread and margarine was brought, Father Peters had already smoked his way half way through a cigar and was busily making amusing exchanges with his host.

With tea poured out and the fresh bread and fat inviting attention, Major Müller, still very much the actor, judged the moment right to steer events. Almost casually he asked:

"Tell me, Father, do you know someone in your parish by the name of de la Haye, Keith de la Haye?"

As it happened Father Peters did not know the person, at least not by name. He was mystified by the question, momentarily taking his guard.

"No, I don't know anyone of that name. Who is he? Should I know him?"

"Oh, I thought you would know him. He lives in the town."

"Where?"

"In the town. He is a fisherman. You know a fisherman, yes?"

"No, as a matter of fact I don't believe I know any fishermen in my congregation."

"How strange," said the Major, "I just thought you might know him. Actually he lives quite close to one of your flock, Laurence Collins."

Father Peters almost choked on a mouthful of tea, having to lower the bone china cup into its soiled bone china saucer.

"I see, you know Laurence Collins then?" commented the Major, with obvious delight. Well, that was the quick unexpected thrust. Now to turn the blade before his opponent had time to regroup his thoughts.

"Father, you are implicated in a black market ring with Collins and de la Haye. You are guilty of crimes against your own people, and against the Reich!" He watched with pleasure as the priest visibly paled, his mouth falling open, while he struggled for words.

One more twist and he would have him where he wanted. One more turn and he would be ready for mercy and glad of terms. Pieter was sure now that he had made a correct assessment. He would take him to the edge of the precipice of dilemma, hold him there for a few seconds, staring down on to the jagged rocks of disaster, then rescue him, pulling him back with the hand of honourable compromise.

"Father Peters, you are involved in subversion. You are working against the Germans. You may be misguided, yes, but you are nevertheless guilty. We can have you destroyed for this!"

This was it, the shock followed by the devastating consequences. Now the priest would be ready to crack. Any moment now he would be squirming and asking first what he, the Major, meant and then what he could do to be spared. Major Müller knew the type, he knew the signs.

Both men waited, staring at each other. Müller's eyes blazed with induced anger, Peters still looked amazed. Not a word came from the priest.

"Well?" boomed the Major, jumping to his feet. "What do you say to that?"

"I say it is a lot of nonsense!" ejaculated Father Peters, as he too jumped to his feet, not with induced anger but with very real and confused anger.

Pieter Müller was taken aback by this denial.

"You fool priest, you fool!" This time his anger was real. "Don't deny it, you fool. We know you're involved. We've had your 'phone tapped. We know you spoke to Laurence Collins about the occupation forces eight days ago. Think back to the Wednesday before last, to a 'phone call you made, deny it if you dare!" He stepped towards Father Peters, who involuntarily stepped back. Pieter Müller looked like an overbearing school teacher about to shake the recalcitrant if he did not quickly own up to his misdemeanour.

"Well, speak man! You know you're in this ring of black market and subversion, I know you're in it, the Guernsey police know and half my officers know. You cannot deny it!"

Silence.

"De la Haye, the cheap little fisherman! You're in with him are you not? He does your stealing from the occupation forces for you, and Collins is your organizer, yes?"

Again silence.

"And what is your part in all this? That's what I mean to find out!"

"I don't know what you're taking about," replied Father Peters. "This is all a lot of nonsense!"

"It is not!" shouted Müller. "You are involved right up to your neck!"

"Prove it."

Incensed, Major Müller let vent to his feelings. "Prove it? We do not need proof, we are the forces of victory! I know you are involved, that is all the proof I need to have you convicted and punished!"

He snatched up the letter from his desk.

"See priest? This letter here, it came from you. It was seen in your possession eight days ago and was typed by you on your typewriter, yes?"

Father Peters was pale. He opened his lips to speak but could think of nothing constructive to say.

"Oh yes, Father," said Müller sneeringly, "I forget, you British like proof. Well let me tell you, we have it! The keys on your typewriter correspond with the type on this letter." He beamed with delight as he continued, "We will even find your finger prints, will we not?"

"Will we?" Father Peters shrugged indifferently, then, added, almost as an afterthought, "Tell me Major, what made you think I wrote that letter in the first place?"

"Because of your involvement with Collins."

"So what has he got to do with Franz Müller?" asked the priest.

"Ah you admit it, then!" shouted Pieter Müller.

"I admit nothing, Major, this talk is just between the two of us. Look, I'm not sutpid. You've got the typewriter, I take it, and you can prove I wrote the letter, so what? What does that prove about subversion and black market?"

"I ask the questions, Peters," snarled the Major, playing for time. He looked at the letter. "You asked who Franz Müller is. I have no idea. Tell me who he is."

Father Peters smiled. He was enjoying his antagonist's discomfort.

"Come now, Major, you know who he is. I know who he is. We both know, don't we?"

Major Müller squirmed. He was definitely losing control of the interview.

"Major Müller, we are talking of the same person are we not, Franz Müller, your nephew?"

The Major nodded and made to speak but Father Peters cut across.

"Good. Well we've established that at least. Maybe now you will have me arrested for trying to help someone who is dear to you? Perhaps you will send me to a concentration camp for helping to save Franz's life?"

"It's not like that at all," interrupted Major Müller feeling rather stupid and ineffective. "My nephew has nothing to do with it. It is your black market business and subversion that concern me."

"I tell you, Major Müller, I know nothing of what you speak! True, I have tried to help Franz, but this other business is all nonsense!"

"It is not," insisted the Major. "You have been implicated. On Wednesday evening last week you spoke with Collins on the telephone. You discussed Germans."

Father Peters could now see the link. It must have been the evening when John 'phoned him to ask his advice about Franz and the getting of a letter to his uncle. Yes, that was it. It all fitted in. It was that evening he was stopped and searched. So that sentry did notice the letter after all. Phew! That was why de Bourgonnière said they had his name on lists. Yes, this all explained a lot. All he had to do was to explain that he had been speaking to John Collins and not his father and the trouble would be cleared up. But should he implicate John in this way? What was all this talk of black market and subversion though? Was John's father involved in such things?

"What are you thinking, Father?"

I'm thinking how all this is a storm in a tea cup."

"What do you mean?"

"I mean, Major," began the priest wearily, "that I am a priest, a man whose job it is to help people in trouble. And what happens when I do? What happens, for instance, when I try to help your nephew? I am brought here, ill treated, kept against my will and accused of all sorts of nonsense I've never heard of."

"Oh yes, you are being very clever, Father. You have thought this out very carefully. You are bluffing. You hope to ease my suspicions, but I am not so easily fooled. Tell me what you know about Collins and de la Haye or you too will appear in court."

"Appear in court? Good! You do that, Major. I'll quite happily tell your court how I have been treated. You may not have much respect for my position, to you I am just a prisoner, a member of a vanquished nation, but just you remember this; Britain fights on and the free world watches. There are many in your country who still have a high regard for the church. There are many who would be greatly disturbed if the news got abroad that I was being victimised for carrying out an act of mercy."

"But this has nothing to do with the charge," blurted Major Müller in exasperation. "Franz has nothing to do with it!"

"So you say," retorted Father Peters, "but you're just using the incident to get me to implicate two people I do not know."

"No. No. No!" stormed the Major, rising to his feet and thumping his desk, not so much in anger, but more as an act of despair. "I am not using Franz in that way! I do not want you to mention the incident with him. I want him left out of it!"

"I see," said Father Peters slowly. "Yes, I begin to see very well indeed. You seem frightened by Franz's involvement with this alleged misdemeanour, is that it?" He sensed his power over the Gestapo Major.

"Leave Franz out of it and you'll be safe," he proposed hurriedly, as though afraid the words would change their mind and not issue.

"Are you threatening me, Major? Let me tell you I don't respond to threats!"

"I am not threatening you, Father Peters, I am giving you facts. A choice, if you like."

"A choice? Go on, surprise me," replied Father Peters, almost sarcastically.

"Very well; my nephew is not to be mentioned by you at any time during any enquiries that take place. In return for this, when Collins is arrested and convicted I will do my best to keep your name out of it. . ."

"You're asking me to become involved in a deal which

will lead to the arrest and imprisonment of one of my own countrymen?" uttered Father Peters, incredulous and in anger.

"Let me finish. . ."

"No, let me finish Major. . ."

"Silence!"

There was silence.

"Go on, Major," hissed the priest controlling his seething hatred, "what is your other choice?"

"Collins is arrested, my nephew is arrested, you suffer the same fate, as does Collins' son, the one who has been illegally befriending my nephew and involving him in all this corruption."

"Some choice!"

Both men eyed each other. The priest was dejected and angry for he was dealing with a fool, or was the man just incredibly subtly clever? The Major was beginning to regain his confidence. Had he at last regained the upper hand in the interview? Had the priest realised he had lost and that his choice was in fact no choice? Was this why he now looked so broken, so dejected? It had been a good idea of his to bring the younger Collins into the argument.

Any doubts of professionalism, or betrayal of confidence, that Father Peters might have had up until then, about involving John Collins, were now swept aside by Major Müller's latest statement.

"You're a fool, Major! Don't you see? This is all a nonsense."

The Major was taken aback by the statement but could only listen as Father Peters continued hurriedly.

"Look, Major, the damned 'phone call you were on about wasn't between Mr. Collins and me, it was a 'phone call from young John Collins asking my help to get a message to you. Can't you see? There was nothing about black market or subversion! Do you understand that?"

The realisation dawned on Pieter Müller, as he nodded his head gravely.

The silence seemed interminable. At last the Major spoke.

"It seems I was wrong, Father," he said apologetically. "I was wrong all the time. I see now, you only wished to help Franz. What can I say?" He paused embarrassed.

Father Peters was not the sort of person to take enjoyment out of a fellow creature's discomfort.

"There's nothing to be said, Major," he replied, light-heartedly, as he rose to his feet. "That's the end of it."

"I wish that were so, truly I do," said Major Müller, raising his hands in the manner of one almost in despair.

"Pardon me?" asked the priest, incredulous and puzzled.

"I said I'm sorry Father, it's not quite as simple as that. May I suggest another cup of tea? This is going to take a long time. We have a lot of serious talking to do."

*   *   *

"Why doesn't someone come?" gasped John hoarsely. Both he and Franz had been calling for help for a very long time. It must have been an hour at least. Both were tired and thirsty. Franz's voice had almost gone now, partly through exhaustive calling and partly through anxiety that the time must be fast approaching for his 18.00 hour Patrol.

Between them they tried to estimate the time, by working back through all their adventures so far that day, but their varied estimates, tempered first by an urge not to face up to reality, then by the despair of the defeatist, were in no way as accurate as all the natural signs which led them to the irrefutable conclusion that they were in dire trouble.

With the rapidly lowering sun, and the already perceptibly lengthening shadows, the change in quality of the light, the darkening of the east-facing Icart cliffs, the gilding of the distant thick piled carpet which was Jersey, the already stiffening refreshing evening onshore breeze, came their fears and recriminations.

"It's all your fault, John," whined Franz. "There'll be such trouble now!"

"Oh, shut up will you, Franz! You think it's bad! Think what it's like for me. You're OK, you're a German. They won't hurt you. I'm the one who's in trouble, not you."

Franz uttered a derisory laugh, "It just shows how much you know!"

John was not prepared to enter that circuitous discussion of logic again, but departed into his own self-sorry state.

"What will my parents think, eh? They'll be worried to death by now. What shall we do?"

"You're lucky to have parents!" exclaimed Franz. "At least they can help protect you when you get taken in."

"What do you mean, 'protect me when I get taken in'?"

"You know," explained Franz, "when the Gestapo take you in after all this. They can't just do away with you if they know you have got family who know where you are . . ."

"Do away with me?" exclaimed John, clutching at Franz's arm with fear. "You don't mean they'd . . .?" The thought was too horrible for him to complete the sentence. Franz looked at his friend's frightened face and forgot his own misery.

"Oh, John, I'm sorry!" he said, as he hugged him to reassure him. "I shouldn't have said that. Oh, I'm sorry John. Of course you'll be all right."

John felt temporarily reassured. It was strange how the strength of human contact had the power to remove the deepest fears and put them into perspective. Even in this place, surrounded by instruments of carnage, he was able to feel at peace while he was with his friend.

In an attempt to repay Franz's solicitations, John replied, "You too will be all right, Franz. Not only are you German but also, you have your uncle to help you out of trouble."

Franz began to shake.

"That's the trouble, John," he said. "You see, he told me last week that if I ever get into trouble again he will disown me. What will I do?"

It was John's turn to act as comforter. He placed a reassuring arm across Franz's shoulder,

"It won't be that bad,". he counselled. "He won't disown you, you'll see. Parents and people like that, like your uncle, always say things like that but they don't really mean them, eh?"

Franz, not at all convinced by this, but trying to sound so, said, "I hope you're right."

"Of course I'm right," replied John giving Franz's shoulder a squeeze. "Come on, let's call some more, before it gets dark. I don't fancy a night out on the cliffs."

"Nor me," added Franz with a shudder, as he moved to stand up. "I think it would give me these creeps."

"Creeps is not the word, mate," added John, in mock fear, having temporarily forgotten his own worries whilst comforting his friend. He anticipated the tales he was about to tell.

"I could tell you some really creepy ghost stories about these cliffs and the ruined Jerbourg castle. My uncle used to tell me some wonderful tales."

"Oh no!" exclaimed Franz in playful horror, which really requested the opposite. "No, John you must not."

John rose to his feet and they both eyed each other's expression with amusement.

Their momentary oblivion, from the cares of war, was shattered rudely. From out of sight round the eastern corner of the cliff edge path came an even louder, even more intense clanking, rattling noise of an engine. It sounded rather like a distant steam engine without the hiss of steam.

"Ah!" started Franz. "At last . . .!" he did not finish his sentence but, in his excitement, began to rush forward towards the sound.

"Stop!" yelled John. "Stop, Franz, you bloody idiot!" then screaming, "For God's sake, stop!"

Franz, his right foot frozen in mid air, like some grotesque statue of one turned from life to stone, with the changing of the wind, realised what he was doing.

"Oh John! Oh John! The mines! The mines! I forget! I forget! I'm sorry! I'm sorry!" he repeated in a contrite murmur, as he returned to his friend's side.

"Don't worry about it," said John, as he dismissed Franz's apology with urgent irritation. "Just shout as loud as you can when, whatever it is that's making the noise, comes round the corner. Give it all you've got and wave your arms!"

As he spoke, a miniature one-man tank came into view round the corner of the path.

*   *   *

Morten looked at his watch and swore out loud. Two of the 18.00 hour Patrol turned their heads slightly and grinned at each other. This earned them each an earful of abuse so that

283

their faces took on the more usual, non-committal, leaden expression of 18.00 hour Patrollers.

It was now 18.05 and no Franz Müller, damn him! Well, as much as he liked the lad he couldn't cover up for him like this, especially not over matters of discipline. Morten would soon become a laughing stock with the other men if he did. Heaven knows it was bad enough now with all the rumours he had to keep suppressed. He couldn't go on forever using his friendship with S.S. Hüffmeier to intimidate subordinates into silence. Besides, the boy deserved to be punished for this. It was a flagrant abuse of privilege. He had got off lightly as it was. Hadn't he got off his confined to house status thanks to Morten? It hadn't been easy to convince Weiss that the boy was truly contrite and now a fully conformist Town House man.

So how did the youth repay these efforts? By taking advantage and missing out during his first week of duty at the new time, damn him!

It was no good, two minutes more and he would have to set procedures in motion. Pity though, for he really liked the boy. He really did seem promising. However, there were other fish in the sea, and probably more willing and co-operative. Still a great shame, though!

Maybe Weiss would take a more lenient line than usual, but Morten doubted it really? Weiss did not owe him any favours. If anything he owed the Captain a favour for dealing so lightly with Franz yesterday morning. Had not Morten, more or less, given his word that Franz could be trusted? Hell, this was an embarrassment!

'Franz Müller really deserves it if he gets punished, yet I don't want it to be too bad,' thought Morten. 'I don't want to lose him just yet, not after all my hard work on Tuesday evening. No, that would not be fair!'

*　　　*　　　*

Frances was the first to wake. She lay face down, her nakedness cool against the eiderdown. Her back was delightfully cool, almost chilly as the now strengthening breeze lifted the net curtains and tantalized her bare flesh. As she lay there, still bemused with the sleep of love's aftermath, she felt she was a young girl once more. All she was conscious of was her own fulfilled body and her sense of contentment.

As the seconds passed, her initial selfish awareness widened, seeming to take in all the surrounding stimulants simultaneously. She lay on the top of the bedclothes. The sun was fast sinking towards the prison roof, soon to invade her privacy. Larry lay naked beside her. The evening breeze was beginning. Something was wrong! What was it? Frances knew she should be worrying about something but, as one when untimely wakened, not knowing when it is or where they are, could not clutch her fear from the atmosphere.

The Town Church began to chime.

'What time is it?' she thought. The bedroom clock had stopped. The Town Church chimed the first quarter and Larry slept on his watch. 'Quarter past,' she thought, 'Quarter past. Quarter past what?'

Was it quarter past five, quarter past six or quarter past what? Her fears and worries came home to roost.

"Larry! Larry love, wake up! Wake up!" She frantically shook her tranquil love into life.

"Eh? What is it? What's up?"

Larry quickly collected his dispersed thoughts, weighed up the situation and sat on the edge of the bed.

Gone now was Frances' tranquillity. He looked at her and observed the recent girlishness transformed into her more usual wizen anxiety, as her lined face and fearful eyes willed him to look at his watch.

"Quarter past six," he said, shrugging his shoulders. "No John yet?" he asked rhetorically knowing the answer from Frances' wringing hands, and deep fearful eyes, before he had even asked.

"I've just woken," she began. "I heard the clock and didn't know if it was quarter past five or quarter past six. Oh, what can have happened to the boy, Larry?"

Larry sought to reassure her. He patted her wrist and gently pecked her nose but, in her agitation, she stiffened and pulled away. Larry's temporary annoyance at this was muted by his own misgivings. He stood up quickly, slipping on his crumpled clothes, in so doing, flipping over one of the empty tea cups on the tray by the bed. Frances started at the noise and rapidly busied herself with her dressing.

285

"He might be home already," suggested Larry in an attempt to be cheerful.

"Oh, don't be so stupid!" she said, on the point of tears. "Have you ever known him to go about the place quietly? Besides, he'd have looked in on us, wouldn't he? He'd have come to tell us why he was so late."

"I hope not . . ." started Larry, thinking to make capital out of the humour of the suggestion, but deciding that it might not be appropriate at the moment.

Frances, having completed her hurried dressing, rushed past Larry and, with no regard for his half naked form, clutched at the bedroom door wrenching it open, to stand on the cold linoleum of the landing.

"John! John! Are you there, love?"

*   *   *

"It's no good, Morten, I will have to report your little friend," snarled Captain Weiss, on his face a sneer which could either be construed as contempt for the weak Patrol Leader standing before him, or disgust at the ill discipline of the young soldier who had not reported for 18.00 Patrol.

Morten shuffled his feet in his discomfort. He could not let it go without some attempt at explanation, without some effort to save Franz from the full disciplinary might of an antagonized disciplinary procedure. He owed it to himself to say something. He owed it to young Franz even, for was he not potentially in the lad's future debt, if all went well?

All could have gone well! Now the young fool had spoilt it through his lack of control! Why, oh why had he let Morten down in this way? Morten, who intended him nothing but kindness? Well, almost.

What could he say that might help matters? What if he made things worse? Here he stood, Morten the Patrol Leader, in front of his Captain. Both cognizant of the other's weaknesses but the difference being that one was in charge and the other not, and both knew it.

Many times Morten had faced his superior in this way and many times Weiss had accompanied his admonitions with a cover up for the weakness which had been the cause of the impasse. Would he do it again? Would he save Franz? Morten doubted it!

Only yesterday Weiss had needed a great deal of persuasion to permit Franz to be removed from confined-to-house status. That had not been given lightly. It had been impressed upon Morten that the boy had already been overindulgently treated and the Patrol Leader had been reminded that it was at his request, he had not been banished to the remote cliffs along with the others of the Soup Kitchen incident. Also, that in return he had promised to take the lad under his wing and be responsible for his good behaviour and complete cooperation with the house personnel. By cooperation Morten thought he knew what Weiss had expected, and by personnel he imagined that Weiss had meant himself, the Captain. Morten had undertaken the task of training, gleefully.

"Captain Weiss, Sir," attempted the Patrol Leader, "Would it not be possible . . ."

"No Morten. No! Damn you," interrupted Weiss, "I am sick and tired of covering up for you in this way! No, I will not bend the rules to save your boy. He's had a chance and what has he done with it, eh? How has he repaid my leniency? Answer me that."

"But, Sir, he is only a young lad. Could he not . . ."

"Precisely, Morten, there you have it! Only a young lad. Quite honestly man, you ought to have more control over yourself in these matters."

"What matters?" asked Morten in shocked innocence.

"Oh, come now, Morten! You know very well what I am talking about. Everyone knows. You, S.S. Hüffmeier, the young flowers of Germany. At times I find you quite sickening." Weiss grimaced, Morten looked away. He wanted to say 'You hypocrite!' but he knew nothing would be served by it. He had gone through this routine so many times before. No, he had to choke back the words. After all, Weiss was in charge, not he. Morten had no rights. When it was all considered he was completely in Weiss' hands for, once outside the regulations, as he frequently was, he was also outside their protection. True, he could give Weiss' own supposed indiscretions away but what satisfaction would there be in dragging Weiss down if he too was destroyed in the process? No, far better to remain philosophical about it all and look for a new boy, one a little more predictable, more amenable.

"It's no good, Morten. The boy is no good. He will have to be reported A.W.L."

The Patrol Leader did not argue but just stared blankly ahead.

Weiss, mistaking his erstwhile companion's reaction as one of shocked despair, sought to justify his position.

"We have to set an example, Morten. He's had his chances. Come man, shape up a bit! There will be others. Besides, from the little I saw of him at the Relaxation, it would all have turned out to have been rather a wasted effort, eh? Jules didn't have a lot to say for him and that's unusual for Jules!" He forced himself into an impression of a hearty guffaw. "We all know Jules, anything under eighteen and in trousers . . ."

Morten nodded slowly. Weiss did not need to go on in this way. He knew how to accept the inevitable, he knew how to drop people for expediency.

"What will you do then, Captain?"

"I'll have to telephone the Military Police."

"And what will happen then?"

"Quite honestly, I have no idea. I've not had to deal with such circumstances before," replied the Captain.

*   *   *

Larry knew it would all be a waste of time but nevertheless he went, to try to placate Frances, who was almost frantic with worry. It was now well past six o'clock.

First of all Frances had pleaded with Larry to contact the Police. "Phone!" she had said. Well, the Police would be Larry's last resort. As Bert had said, it would be unwise for the authorities to have any cause to link the two Collins' names. Of course, should the visit to the Feldkommandantur at St. Jacques be futile, then Larry would sacrifice himself for the sake of his son. But even then he would try first through the good offices of Constable Bert Bisson.

As Larry made his breathless way to La Porte, his mind was full of awful imagery. John lay at the bottom of a cliff, his bones broken, as the roar of the rising waves, which were soon to put him out of this world, drowned his screams and cries for help. His son was caught in barbed wire, suspended helplessly over a sheer drop. The lad had misunderstood an instruction and was now under arrest, held incommunicado, awaiting interrogation. What if it were worse? Suppose they had shot him first then challenged him? Was he in hospital? Would they treat his injuries? Was the boy beyond saving?

As he anticipated, the civilian office was closed. Only a solitary sentry stood there, eyeing him suspiciously.

He should not have attempted to trespass through the gate, there was no point. Larry now realised his foolishness as he tried to explain his mission to the four young Teutons who surrounded him.

"Why for, you here?" he was asked, as his identity was checked.

"My business is with the Feldkommandantur," was Larry's surly answer.

"Is closed," was the steely reply.

The coolness of his questioners was not warmed by his own offensive tone. He tried to explain he was looking for his son, only to be told Germans alone worked there.

When Larry contradicted this, one of the group muttered in the incomprehensible master tongue. It seemed that the 'English boy' was known after all.

Larry sensed he was being made the butt of some joke, as a slight mirth passed through his captors, then he gradually became enlightened.

"Yes, we know your son. He works for the Feldkommandantur. He likes his work, yes?" The question was rendered rhetorical as the Aryan continued, "He is friendly with one of our young soldiers. They are good friends." He smiled.

The Germans were intransigent. No, they would not contact the Administrator. They saw no reason to enquire of the Gestapo.

"Go to your own Police. If your son is injured or dead our Police will tell your people eventually. If he has his German friend with him, they might work a little quicker. Go to your own Police!"

Should he go straight to the station, he wondered? If he did, what could he say? They were all bastards anyway, well, most of them. What if he went straight to the Gestapo, what would they do? If John were in any trouble, wouldn't that make it worse for him? And what was that they were saying about his German friend? Franz he supposed. What were they implying? Were they saying the friendship was peculiar? Or were they just saying it was odd because two enemies were friends? There was nothing wrong with John! Was there? Were they saying he was funny? No, not Larry's son! Larry's son was not queer! No, that was just typical Jerry talk. To them, anyone, not German, was a bit queer. They just had no idea.

But, as Larry rushed back to Frances, he had time to recall the conversation he'd had with John about the German lad and his involvement with those older men.

No, he would not think about it! Here he was worrying his insides out when probably by now the lad was back home with his mother. With his mother! What was it they said of only sons with doting mothers?

*   *   *

John asked Franz what was happening and why the gathered soldiers were doing nothing to effect their rescue. Franz explained they were waiting for plans of the minefield to be fetched from Intelligence Headquarters.

"Intelligence Headquarters!" exclaimed John. "Hell, we're in for it then! They'll all bloody well know, the Feldkommandantur, the Gestapo, the lot!"

"What did you expect?" asked Franz, with just a hint of sarcasm, but too weary to pursue the newly acquired British art. "Did you imagine we get away with it, then? John, for us my friend, this war is finish!"

"Eh?"

"Perhaps it is better we blow up on the mines now," suggested Franz, his voice leaden with seriousness, "for if we are rescue we two are finish anyway."

John knew the dreadful purport of Franz's message but it was too awful to be heard spoken out loud.

"Don't be ridiculous!" exclaimed the civilian, but he knew the sound of his words carried no conviction.

It was true, they both knew it, like the one day insects, they had gone through the friendship stages of pupation and chrysalisation and had just had their one glorious day of summer. Their adventure this day, with all the memories etched for them, as they would continue their separate fates, until, short or long, they would each reach their individual extremis, now had to be paid for with their misery. The two friends would have to become enemies once more. Perhaps exploded· enemies with scattered limbs? Possibly captured and punished enemies? But one thing was for sure and very, very clear; their fates would be fates of shame. Shame was to end their friendship, disgrace their war.

"No, you're right, Franz," conceded John. "We're for the chop, mate, that's for sure," but he was by now so weakened by misery and anxiety for it to hold any more real terror for him.

"Anyway, let us think ourselves lucky," Franz added, "for their other plan was even worse!" He shuddered at the prospect. "Well, I heard them talking of two plans really. . ."

"And?" John interrupted.

Not noticing his friend's ill manners, Franz continued.

"The first plan is to make us lie flat then they are going to fire their rifles, from where they stand, to hit the ground, every metre or so, so that we can step safely where the bullets have land."

John gave a low whistle at that idea.

"I don't like that idea one little bit," he said. "What made them change their minds?"

"They do not want to waste their ammunition," replied Franz.

At that, John was almost amused, and a faint flicker of a smile just slightly lit his pursed lips, to Franz's annoyance, as he felt he was being disbelieved.

"If you think that is funny you should have heard their other plan," he said.

"Oh?" queried John, sounding quite defensive. "Go on."

"They wanting me to lie down and you to walk to them."

"Why?" asked John, aghast at the thought. "Why?"

"Because then, if there were any mines you step on them and I am safe."

291

"But why me?" John shouted. "Why not you?"

"Because, they say you are not a German," came Franz's reply, "therefore it not matters if you are killed, so long as I am safe, for I am a German."

"Hell!" said John, shaking at the prospect. "They really considered doing that?" His fear beginning to form itself into anger.

"Don't be cross with me," Franz begged. "It was not my idea."

"O.K. O.K., I know," John replied. "What stopped them?"

"They are afraid they might get injured in the explosion. Besides they did not wish to get into trouble for wasting a land mine."

Once the plans had been brought from Intelligence Headquarters the two were quickly and rather ruthlessly directed to safety. A squat little officer shouted orders to Franz, his very tone being such that they obeyed his instructions without question, although not without much doubt and fear in their own minds. Their sweating and shaking bodies agonized at every step which brushed them through bracken and gorse, brambles and springy tufts of grass. By the time they had reached the outstretched hands, which cruelly grasped them like vices, they had died as many steps and turns as they had planned. Subconsciously they felt they should have been treated as heroes for having braved such an ordeal. Therefore the harsh treatment now meted out to them, in contrast to their expectations, seemed doubly cruel. The hands forced behind his aching and tired back, to John, seemed like the dislocation of his limbs. The handcuffs placed behind Franz, to him felt like barbed wire. The vicious shouting, to both their aching heads was like the pummelling of one racked with biliousness. The vigorous shaking endured by Franz was like a bouncing from rock to rock as he fell down the cliffs. The staring of the hard cold eyes, divested of all pity and human sympathy, seemed, to the self-pitying John, like a mighty condemnation for some heinous offence. And, as foretaste to interrogation, the slap across the already sunburned face, to Franz, seemed like a scalding with iced water.

Franz was led along the path first, to the accompaniment of raucous shouting, with much pushing and jostling, by the

292

soldiers to whom his chains were attached. John was brought along behind, less harshly, he felt. His own stumbling, occasioned through mental and physical exhaustion, together with hunger and extreme thirst, was not uppermost in his mind, for he was very concerned at the treatment Franz was receiving. Franz seemed to be bearing the brunt of it all.

At the bunker's entrance, in which John was detained, Franz was led away into a nearby trench, out of sight, while John was stood still against the concrete wall. Franz tried to turn his head back to look at his friend, as he disappeared from sight, but his movements were roughly checked.

All John was left with, as he leaned against the hot concrete, exuding its earlier summer sun's indulgence, was Franz's cries of pain and pleas for mercy, accompanied by the dull thuds of fists against flesh, and the rasping, half laughed, demands of his captors.

Their separate fates had begun. The end had announced itself.

*   *   *

"England man come!"

"Me? Yes what do you want?" he asked almost gleefully. He enquired in the excited manner he had used only recently when, being told by the tremulous Miss Le Huray that the awful fate of working for the Germans awaited him, he had joyfully demanded, "When do I start?"

"England man, come! We go to Feldpolizei now! Quick, quick!"

John shuddered and paled as he was pushed before the man into the now fast-fading and softening summer evening light. The heat still exuded from the concrete jungle of paths and walls, while the smells of the wild flowers and gorse, trapped in the still and warm summer air, pervaded everything, filling his nostrils and mind with pleasantries.

His emotion was soon contrasted by the rough handling and shouting he received from the two other soldiers, who attached themselves one to each side of him, as he was jostled quickly up steps and along the dry dusty path.

"What's the idea?" he demanded.

293

Both captors stopped momentarily. Who was this pig to speak to them in such a tone?

They muttered, then both closed in from either side closing in on him hard and fast so that he was crushed between their hefty shoulders. John gasped, as all the air was forced from his lungs and he collapsed on to the path, his throat scooping helplessly for breath, while his cold eyed, silent captors simply watched his convulsions unmoved.

* * *

"Up Englander lover!" yelled the Corporal to the wretch who lay exhausted and bruised before him. "Now we take you to learn what the Führer thinks of traitors and spies!"

Franz heard the voice, it was in his, the master tongue, but it was not part of him. It was for Franz Müller, but Franz Müller was now no more.

* * *

It no longer mattered what happened to either friend, for their war was now ended. A war which, for a few days, they had defied and refused to acknowledge, now held them in its vice. The mines had not destroyed them for they still lived but only long enough to endure the slighted war's revenge.

Yes, both friends lived a little longer, perhaps to suffer a little more to purge their blasphemy, but never again together. Now each would pay his individual price.

Mum and Dad could not save John now. No, not even Uncle Bert with all his Police connections. Probably that man too, just as the recidivist's parents and all their contacts, would be dragged into the infernoK?

Mum had been right when she had said John would be the death of them all. Histrionic words but oh so prophetic and with such application to all their lives.

Franz's Gestapo Major uncle would no longer be able to save his weakling of a nephew, this failed German youth, the like of which were so despised by the Führer. Even if he wished to withdraw his threat, to disown Franz Müller, now it was too late. Nothing could save the lad.

So, for Franz Müller, not yet sixteen years old, it was to be the ignominy of retribution and correction by the S.S. he had so feared since the day he had first met his enemy friend.

Herr Tropp would expedite both their fates. The civilian administrator for the German Reich would see that his hurt pride was revenged tenfold and more. Nothing would prevent it, for such a purging of perversity was right, and right was the kindly-faced gentlemen's to bestow.

Both enemies had stepped on that wartime mine, invented by warriors. Both had walked on to the devastating implement planted to destroy enemy friends. Both were now as surely dead as if their mine had been just the indiscriminate mechanical destroyer. The only difference was that their separate deaths would be slower and by more gradual degrees. Their lonely deaths would be by the slow withdrawal of life and hope and good memories, as death and bitterness would creep in to take their place. It would be a slow process which would suck from them all that had been of true value in their friendship.

Both would gradually learn to hate that they had ever been friends. Each alone, with no chance of unsullied memories of the other's goodness, or of the enjoyed and shared times, would bitterly regret that they had ever met.

The words Traitors, Treason, Collaborator, and Quisling were to be their decorations for anti-war services. These rewards were to scar their souls as both, utterly alone, would come to rue the day they had ever been so completely selfish and thoughtless as to try to ignore the tide of hate and war. Such friends can only deserve the fate of enemies.